The New Woman

LISA EL HAFI

Print ISBN: 978-1-09834-847-2

eBook ISBN: 978-1-09834-848-9

FLORA

THE COLUMBUS EXPOSITION, CHICAGO, MAY 1893

Standing among the crowd at the Chicago Exposition between Lizzie Pinchot and Bea Johnson, Flora could hardly contain her excitement. She was impatient and wished that President Cleveland would wind up his speech. She came to the fair with so many expectations, to not only satisfy her curiosity about the amusements and display of oddities from around the globe—an Algerian village brought over in its entirety from Africa, natives from other exotic countries, as well as representatives from European countries—but also see the new technological wonders that would change the world, most importantly the electrical lighting that illuminated the entire exposition.

As the president pronounced the Chicago Columbian Exposition officially open, an explosion of light enveloped the buildings, and the spectators. Rows of small luminescent lights illuminated magnificent white buildings, constructed in a variety of architectural styles, varying from large square Neoclassical structures to some that looked almost Oriental with large domes. Dazzled, Flora could hardly wait to begin her visit. She had already consulted The Time Saver, but she now took a moment to circle the exhibits that interested her.

Lizzie interrupted her planning. "Put down that book for a minute, Flora. I want you to come and see Little Egypt with us. Apparently, she dances practically *au naturel*, at least that's what my brother told me. He saw her at a bachelor party at Sherry's."

Bea pursed her lips and glared at Lizzie. "What an idea! Do you want Ned to find out that Flora went to see Little Egypt? It's not as if we were little nobodies from Albany or Rochester. She knows who we are and she will not hesitate to tell all of New York that we came to her show." Lizzie rolled her eyes. Everyone in their set knew that Bea was one of the most proficient and vicious gossips in New York.

At the mention of Ned's name, Flora's thoughts drifted to the man she was promised to marry in six weeks—Ned Dodd, attorney-at-law, who represented J.P. Morgan in his most important legal matters as they related to his business. Although still a junior partner, Morgan trusted Dodd with his most delicate cases. Flora admired her fiancé and had somehow convinced herself that admiration was a manifestation of love. She would often compare him with her former suitors. She had had many beaux, after all she was twenty-one, attractive, and came from the crème de la crème of New York Society.

But Ned from the beginning treated her differently than the other men, allowing her a certain autonomy, which she greatly appreciated. She never considered herself one of Gibson's "New Women," but she realized that the old Victorian mores were no longer fashionable among the younger women in New York. Ned, she felt, would prove to be a pliable and forward-thinking husband, not to mention a wealthy one. Yet she felt something was lacking in their physical relationship.

Of course, things had not progressed beyond some stolen kisses and caresses. What troubled her was the fact that she didn't want more and felt nothing when he touched her. She hoped that those feelings would come to her on their wedding night. She told herself that this must be the normal course of marital relations and put it out of her mind. Suddenly Bea's shrill voice interrupted her musings.

"Oh, just stop your bickering girls," said Flora as she gathered her skirt and tried to maneuver her way through the crowd. "I have to fly. You go to Algeria. I have loftier interests. I want to see the future."

"What a bore," said Bea. "How disappointing! The Ferris wheel ride is not ready yet.

They say it won't run until sometime in the summer."

"I am devastated for you," Flora smiled. "I will see you both at the Grand Courtyard at nine o'clock." She disappeared into the crowd. Her time was limited and she had no time to waste on mere curiosities. The Krupp's Pavilion received a three-star rating by *The Time-Saver*, but when she entered the great hall and saw the huge guns, Flora experienced a wave of anxiety and distress. Why would anyone create such weapons and against whom would they use them? She closed her eyes and imagined the terror and carnage that such enormous guns might cause. To her knowledge, the world was enjoying unprecedented peace and prosperity and she could not imagine why the Germans thought it necessary to experiment with the giant cannons and deadly machine guns. With visions of horrific explosions and men rendered limbless and mad, she rushed out of the building into the brightly illuminated avenues of the fair. The white light calmed her nerves and lifted her spirits; its purity washing away her despair. As she walked along the embankment, electric launches floated by and she decided to board the next available boat. She ate a quick supper at the Transportation Building and considered which exhibit to see next, realizing that only two hours remained before she had to meet the girls at the Grand Courtyard.

She approached the Electricity Building with great curiosity, entering the exhibit called "Theatoirum." Edison's latest invention was on display. Its odd name "Kinetoscope" did little to describe its function, which was to show short clips of moving pictures. Her friend Anne Morgan, daughter of J.P. Morgan, often spoke highly of Edison who had installed electricity in their Fifth Avenue mansion. Morgan had funded many of Edison's inventions, but he invested most heavily in Edison's D.C. electricity plants. Apparently, Morgan and Edison did not succeed in obtaining the contract to electrify the Columbian Exposition. A man named Nikola Tesla with the backing of George Westinghouse electrified the fair.

That name lingered in her thoughts as she entered a large theater that was filled to capacity. She pushed her way closer toward the stage in order to get a better view of the scene that enthralled the crowd. At first, she thought that she had stumbled onto some kind of magic act. But slowly, the mysterious man explained the science behind the bolts of lightning that he held in his hand. He had dark hair and almost iridescent blue eyes. He spoke with a seductive foreign accent. Slowly the voice, the eyes, and the man drew her in, seducing her and filling her with wonder. As he explained that this form of energy would transform the world and bring light to cities and towns, she felt a shift in her own world. Her face grew hot and she experienced a tingling that spread from her extremities through her entire body. The scientist touched a large globe, which was full of what seemed to be lightning.

"Ladies and gentlemen," he said. "I assure you that this form of electricity is perfectly safe. It is my hope that in the future you may perhaps illuminate your homes and stores with Alternating Current. My name is Nikola Tesla, and I welcome any questions or comments that you may have."

A few of the spectators asked questions. Others made rude comments.

"He's no Edison." Sneered a rotund man with a Midwestern accent."

For some reason the comment annoyed Flora. She felt that she wanted to defend Mr. Tesla, even though she had never met him. Suddenly she experienced a pressing desire to speak to him and as the audience left the theater, she approached the stage.

"Good evening Mr. Tesla," she said, trying her hardest not to blush. "I was very impressed with your demonstration. Although I am not a scientist by any stretch of the imagination, I do enjoy learning about the latest inventions. I can't say that I understand how you managed this display of electricity or how it works, but I am truly interested in learning more about it."

Tesla took her hand and helped her up onto the stage. A feeling resembling a slight electric shock, flowed from his hand to hers. He began to explain about the theory of Alternating Current electricity and its advantages. He then went on to list the possibilities he saw for the betterment of mankind. Most of what he said went over her head, and Flora had to make a concerted effort to understand his speech because of his thick accent and odd way of forming his sentences.

"My dear lady, I hope that I do not bore with my inventions. I cannot help but to go on and on when anyone expresses interest. But it is unusual for a beautiful lady to want to learn about electricity."

She reddened, ashamed to admit even to herself that she really was not interested in the physics of electricity, but rather in him. Looking at her watch, she realized that it was after nine and Lizzie and Bea must be wondering where she had gotten to.

"Mr. Tesla, I must fly. My friends are waiting for me at the Grand Courtyard.

However, do you think that we could continue our conversation tomorrow? I happen to have a free evening and I would like to hear more about your inventions and your business ventures with Mr. Morgan."

The combination of his sensuous smile and piercing blue eyes excited her. She could see that he had difficulty speaking to women, and he seemed to struggle to gather his thoughts.

"Indeed, dear Miss, I would enjoy meeting with you tomorrow evening. Shall we have dinner? I know a charming German restaurant here at the fair and perhaps after we might return to my study so I may show you some of my plans for future inventions."

The next evening, at the Palmer House Hotel as she exited the modern elevator, one of the first in Chicago, Flora came face to face with Mrs. Walter Palmer. The wife of the wealthy hotelier was truly in her element. She had invited the elite of Chicago Society and the well-heeled travelers from New York Society to a brilliant reception organized for the Spanish Infanta Eululie. But the guests complained about the overcrowding and the heat and no one could seem to make out which of the guests was the Infanta or if she was in fact present at the affair. Flora tried to slip out unnoticed, but Lizzie caught her sleeve and asked her where exactly she thought she was going.

"Lizzie, I have an engagement and I cannot explain. And you will be my dearest friend if you do not ask any questions." She said.

Caught off guard, Lizzie was speechless for a moment, and then she whispered as discretely as possible. "I will not way a word, but what can I possibly tell Bea. You know that she can't be trusted. What do you want me to tell her?"

Trying her best to slip away without speaking to Bea, Flora quickly said. "I know. Tell her that I am having dinner with one of Ned's cousins who lives in Chicago. She doesn't know his family, so it won't be a problem. And Lizzie, please don't ever ask me where I really went tonight."

The very mention of Ned's name and the fact that she used his family as a cover for her rendezvous caused her to flush with shame. She admitted to herself that she should be ashamed of her feelings of desire for Nikola, but digging deep into her soul, she found no evidence of it. It confused her that she should feel that she was doing nothing wrong in satisfying her need to be with this man, this stranger. Even as she dressed for the evening, she considered the inevitability of her determination of acting on her desire for the man who she had come to think of as the magician. For there was no logic in what she planned to do. As she dressed earlier she chose an improbable gown, a sheer Worth creation layered over a fitted silk lining. For the first time since she was fourteen, she neglected to wear a corset. She contemplated this decision as she made her way to the Exposition, and it quickly came to her that she was to take on the role of the seductress. She was not entirely confident that Nikola desired her for she sensed timidity in his manner. With Ned she had allowed little liberty when they were alone. Once when he had begun to caress her neck, she abruptly brushed away his hand. Even after their engagement, she would not permit anything beyond a lingering kiss. Perhaps if she had allowed him to go further, she might have uncovered the same passion and longing that she was feeling for Nikola. She knew that she loved Ned for who he was and for the life that he would give her. But she had never experienced the fire and the craving that consumed her as she walked into the restaurant and saw him waiting for her.

The restaurant, as he had described, was an elegant resort that catered to a tonier class of customers. Even so she would not have been comfortable entering without an escort. He gently took her arm and escorted her to a table that was tucked away in a discreet corner. They ordered steak tenderloin and pomme de terre Dauphinoise and a dusky red wine. She ate little, but drank more than she was accustomed to, which helped her overcome her usual reserve.

"Mr. Tesla, I do not quite understand how your system of electricity differs from Mr. Edison's. The lights shine as brightly in Anne Morgan's house as they do in this restaurant. Is there a great difference in the cost?"

"Please do call me Nikola. May I be presuming to call you Flora?"

"By all means Nikola." She said smiling.

"It is quite complicated to explain. But my system, after many experiments, has proven to be safer. Mr. Morgan, who finances Edison's system, went to many great lengths to try show the contrary. Edison went so far as to invent an electric chair that works on my alternating current system. Unfortunately, it did not work, and the condemned man suffered many horrors. It was not a quick and painless death."

"You mean to say that his goal was to show that your system can be dangerous and deadly?" Flora had known of Mr. Morgan's ruthlessness in business, but this was beyond the limits of human decency.

"Yes, that was his goal. Unfortunately, he proved the reality to be quite the opposite." Tesla said with a hint of irritation.

They had finished their coffee, and Tesla suggested a stroll along the lake before returning to his office in the Electricity Building. As they walked slowly, Flora admired the enormous white buildings awash in the artificial moonlight. She felt a sense of wonder when she glanced at the man walking by her side, and she could not resist the urge to take his hand. She detected a slight reaction. He started to withdraw his hand, but then grasped hers even tighter. A few minutes later, they entered the Electricity Building and made their way to his private study. It was a small room cluttered with books and various strange mechanisms. A strange smell emanated from the equipment and permeated the study. Nikola invited her to relax onto a threadbare sofa that she guessed served as his bed.

Suddenly uncertain about where things were heading, she began to talk nervously.

"Did you bring all this equipment with you from New York?" she asked.

"Why yes, I did." He sat down next to her on the sofa. "I must have every precaution in my demonstrations. Although my system is very safe, I do not trust anyone to touch the equipment. There are many who would like to discredit my work."

Nikola moved closer to her and tentatively held her face in his elegant hands.

Then his exotic steel blue eyes took her in. She felt heat emanating first from her face, and then from her entire body. When he kissed her, she responded with more passion than she ever imagined she could feel toward a man and she even went as far as to place his hands on her décolleté. His response to this was immediate. He kissed her again, this time opening his mouth and coaxing her to open hers. Never having kissed Ned in this manner, she was at first surprised, but then aroused, her body responding in way she had never expected.

"Nikola, help me undo my gown. There is a clasp. That's it." She said.

"Are you sure my dear? Do you really want me to…?"

"Yes, I am quite sure. Please, I am afraid if we don't do this now, I will regret it for the rest of my life. Please Nikola."

He undressed as quickly as he could and helped her slide off her gown. She stretched out on the sofa and held out her arms to him. She had not realized how tall he was until he reclined alongside of her. His thin and angular body excited her. He was strong and tender as he caressed her thighs and her breasts. He wanted to take his time, but she could not contain her desire and lifted her body to his.

He moaned in a deep voice, saying something in his native language that she did not understand. At first her eyes were closed as she braced for the pain that she knew came the first time one made love. The pain came briefly, but was followed by exquisite pleasure. He moved in her and she responded at first with sighs and finally with loud moans. She could not believe that these sounds were coming from her. He responded to her moans with more ardent movements and finally called out her name as they both reached climax.

They lay on the sofa, each unwilling to move and break the spell of what had just transpired. A mix of emotions overcame her as she wished she could remain in his arms for the rest of the night, but feared what might come if she they were discovered. She could never tell a soul what she had done and she knew that she must never see Nikola Tesla again.

BERNADINE

GALVESTON, 1897

Martha Jones did her best to hurry the servants along, but the sticky July heat rendered the two Russian girls lethargic. She regretted hiring them, considering their broken and heavily accented English made communication problematic. But she had wanted to help out Rabbi Cohen, a highly respected member of the Galveston community. As the leader of the island's Jewish residents, his responsibilities went beyond the traditional role of a religious leader and scholar. He took on the role of an employment agent and legal advisor for his people. He also mixed with the gentiles in Galveston, performing works of charity for the less fortunate as well as attending the parties of the wealthy families, including the Kempners who attended his temple.

Martha admired the Kempners for their charitable nature and modern ideas on issues such as the education of their daughters and their willingness to mix with people of all backgrounds. Martha and Lucius Jones belonged to the growing class in Galveston known as nouveaux riches. It didn't hurt to entertain families like the Kempners and the Sealys. The guest list for the party that evening included both families, although the Sealys, devout Baptists, most likely would decline because Martha had chosen to serve alcohol.

It could not be avoided. The dinner party in honor of the Arthur Van Wies family needed to meet the standard of a New York soiree and that included serving the best wines and spirits that Galveston offered. The Van Wies family including Arthur's wife, Agnes, his daughter, Clara, and son, Theo, had made the trip south for two purposes—a business proposition and a surreptitious scheme to arrange an advantageous marriage between the wealthy Jones' daughter, Bernadine, and the dashing Theo.

"Reva, please be careful with that vase." Martha said trying not to show her annoyance as the young girl tripped over her own feet. "Take it into the kitchen and ask the housekeeper to make an arrangement with the lilies that were delivered. Oh, and please bring the calling cards from the foyer table to me at once."

Martha shuffled the cards, checking for any last-minute cancellations. She did so want to show their New York guests the best of Galveston Society. Galveston, although small and provincial compared to New York, could claim a certain cachet old-world charm mixed with a cosmopolitan population. With its booming cotton trade and busy port, the population had expanded and the construction of exquisite homes along Broadway kept the builders and artisans busy. New Orleans had lost its luster after the C ivil War, and Houston had yet to cast off its image as a backwater town.

To Martha, her lovely home reflected the wealth and sophistication of Galveston and all it had to offer. She hailed from an old, respectable Galvestonian family that had fallen on hard times when her father died and left them penniless. When she met Lucius, he had not yet made his fortune in the cotton trade, but she admired his tenacity and his honesty. And although she considered herself fortunate in her fate, she had greater aspirations for her beautiful daughter, Bernadine.

Lucius pushed his way into the room, perspiring and breathless. He seemed out of sorts.

"What's wrong, dear?" She asked.

"I don't like all this fussing over a few Yankees," he replied. "Don't you think I didn't make inquiries? They ain't so well-off as they make out."

Lucius didn't suffer fools easily, and Arthur Van Wies presented himself as a wealthy man from the top tier of New York Society. Despite Martha's enthusiasm for the possible match, her husband had grave doubts about the financial status of the Van Wies family and he didn't care much for their haughty airs.

"But Lucius," said Martha "his son seems quite taken with Bernadine."

If only they could get through the evening with grace and see what might develop between the two young people. If marriage was not in the cards, at the very least her daughter might mix with people from outside their small circle in Galveston. However, she hoped that if the evening went smoothly and things progressed, that her daughter might get to take a trip to New York in the near future.

At that instant Bernadine came through the front door arm in arm with Hattie Kempner, followed by the ever-present Albert Lasker, a Jewish lad two years her junior. The three often spent their afternoons walking The Strand or volunteering in the poorer quarters of Galveston. No one could miss the fact that Albert had a hopeless crush on Bernadine.

Martha glanced at Hattie's face, taking in her features. Yes, one could call her attractive, even pretty. But standing next to her daughter, her beauty faded. Bernadine's beauty seemed to emerge from some unknown ancestral fount. Her dark hair and tanned skin hinted at some Spanish blood, which would not be unusual considering the many Mediterranean peoples who had passed though Galveston. Contrasting with her dark, exotic beauty, her daughter had inherited Martha's sky-blue eyes with the same ring around the iris that made them even more striking. Her other features were classic—high cheekbones and forehead and full lips. But the one incongruous aspect to her classic beauty was a nose that turned up slightly at its tip. It was the one component of her physical beauty that hinted at an independent and defiant nature.

Albert Lasker walked over to greet Martha. She admired his openness, easy manner, and quick wit. The young man, having yet to cast off the traits of adolescence, possessed a self-confidence that put him at ease among any society, whether it be the wealthy set of the Broadway mansions or the Negro dockworkers. Had it not been for his youth, and, of course, his Jewish race, he might have made a fine match for her daughter.

"Hello Albert." She said. "I hope that you will be coming back for the party tonight."

"Of course, Mrs. Jones. I wouldn't miss it." He said smiling brightly. "We were on The Strand, and the girls insisted that I buy some decent gloves to wear."

"I hope they didn't make you spend too much." She said.

"Not too much." He answered. "I hear that you are entertaining some of New York's crème de la crème tonight."

"Yes, they are a very old and distinguished family. Theo is quite dashing and Bernadine has been spending a great deal of time with him."

Martha could see the boy's face darken. She felt bad for him, but after all, he had no claim on Bernadine. Her future would be bright, and it would not be in Galveston, if Martha had anything to say about it.

Earlier that day Albert had seen Theo leaving the brothel that backed up to the Artillery Men's Social club. If Martha had any inkling what Theo Van Wies had been up to that afternoon, her enthusiasm for a match might weaken. Arthur Van Wies and his son painted a portrait of affluence and sophistication, offering a life of luxury and glamour to an aspiring mother and a naïve girl.

The evening turned warm, but a breeze off the bay provided a small measure of relief. Fans, placed high on the ceilings of every room, circulated the air. Martha had placed fragrant bouquets of lilies and jasmine throughout the room to add a touch of the exotic. The first guests began to arrive. Lucius had insisted on inviting all of his business associates from Houston, as well as his close friends from his hometown in East Texas. She had tried to dissuade him, but he remained adamant, grousing that if she insists that he spend so extravagantly, it may as well be of some business advantage.

Martha graciously welcomed a group of dowdy women from Beaumont who were entering the hall with their boisterous husbands. The business associates were more subdued and they greeted her politely. She made an effort to make them feel welcome, all the while urging her husband to lead the men into the billiard room and keep the drinking to a minimum.

The Kempners arrived with Rabbi Cohen and his wife, a Spanish Jew with olive skin and almond eyes. She had stopped over in Galveston on her way to South America where her family had arranged an advantageous marriage. But she fell in love with the attractive rabbi, and they married within a month of their first meeting.

Hattie Kempner entered on the arm of Albert Lasker. She looked lovely in a cream-colored gown, embroidered with gilt and beads on a gauze netting. The dress, cut in the latest style evoking a wasp effect, emphasized her waist and bust, yet retained a modicum of modesty with its high collar. Martha worried that what she had chosen for Bernadine might pale in comparison, but she knew that her daughter's athletic and graceful figure would allow her to show off any dress to its utmost advantage.

Albert keenly scanned the room, examining the crowd and noticing the disparity of the guests, their apparel, their manner, and their speech. He greatly admired Lucius Jones, a self-made man, who kowtowed to no one. Proud of his origins and his friends, he made no attempt to hide or alter his Texas drawl. As he wandered into the billiard room, he heard the booming voice of Lucius.

"He's all hat and no cattle. I wouldn't give him a damn nickel."

To which a stout man in a gaudy and unflattering suit replied. "But y'all gonna let him take your sweet daughter up to New York City."

"My daughter can make up her own mind." Lucius thundered. "If she's set her mind on this man, I'm not going to stand in the way of her happiness, though I don't trust the New York dandy any further than I can throw him."

Albert walked back into the large salon and among the all too familiar faces he noticed two women—one an elegant woman of a certain age and the other a stylish girl in her early twenties with her hair done up in a "Gibson Girl" topknot. Both women distinguished themselves from the Galveston women by their choice of gowns and accouterments. The younger woman wore a gold-colored dinner dress made of silk, cut low and worn off the shoulder. Albert stood quite close to the duo, pretending to listen to a young man touting the future of the city of Houston. But he fixed his attention on the words of the two ladies who stood nearby and spoke freely, never suspecting that he was listening. After all, he was only an awkward teenager of no importance.

"Mama, do you think it was all right to eat the shrimp? Is it the season?" asked the younger of the two.

"Clara my sweet, there is not a season for shrimp," said her mother. You are thinking of oysters. I don't expect the Joneses to serve oysters. First of all, it is not the season. But even if it were, I don't know if they are available in Texas. Remember we are in Galveston, not New Orleans. Thank goodness that we return home in a few days."

Albert identified the mother and sister of Theo Van Wies. Clara had the same dark hair and velvet brown eyes, whereas Theo had a well-shaped sensual mouth, Clara's lips were somewhat a pout, giving her expression a truculent aspect.

"Mama, you are too severe. The terrine appears excellent, as does the fish entrée.

As for the Texan men, I find them charming. When they speak, well, it's almost like singing. And they are very gallant. In some ways they are superior to men from the North, who rush around, thinking of nothing but making money, and yet never take the time to enjoy the finer things in life. They could learn a thing or two from these gentlemen. I have not met one who spends the day passing out their cards, trying to drum up business. Furthermore, I'm quite sure that they don't spend their free time and their money on prostitutes and drink."

"Don't be naïve, my pet," Mrs. Van Wies said, with an insolent smile. Her mother glanced at her son, who glided on the dance floor with Bernadine. "Your father told me where your brother was today and believe me there was no shortage of clientele, and on the very day he plans to propose to that lovely, innocent girl. Let us hope that things proceed as planned. If she will not have him, you may have to marry one of your charming, rich Texans. Then you would be obliged to live in this town and the charm would soon wear off."

"Don't worry, Mama. She is besotted. I have seen the ways she looks at him. But you must talk to Papa and have him lay down the law, at least until they are back in New York and married. Theo should stay out of the brothels and above all he must avoid his other vice."

Agnes flushed and whispered to her daughter. "Hush, Clara. Don't speak of it. He gave me his word that he is no longer indulging."

Mrs. Van Wies turned and quickly regained her composure. "Here they come. Don't they make a handsome couple?"

"Bernadine dances like a dream. She led the Star Quadrille as if she has been practicing for years," said Theo, slightly out of breath.

"Theo, we have cotillions in Galveston that I have attended since I was a child," Bernadine said, smiling sweetly.

"Of course, my dear. And what delightful friends you have, particularly the Kempners. I hardly knew what to say when Hattie told me that she attends college. I can't say that I approve of young girls receiving a college education, I mean to what end? Travel is the thing. A European tour opens the heart and mind, does it not Clara?"

Bernadine glanced at Hattie who was deep in conversation with Albert. Although Hattie never boasted or took on superior airs because she attended college, Bernadine had seen the changes in her friend. One could not help but to remark a new confidence and composure that her friend attained since beginning her studies at Sophie Newcomb College in New Orleans. Hattie and Albert would speak of places and things of which she had no knowledge. She could not help but feel regret and even a pang of envy that she lacked the requisite knowledge to explore the topics that her friends discussed: history, arts and also significant political events taking place in the state and the country.

She briefly looked at Theo and told herself that if he cared for her as he had proclaimed, then perhaps he did not desire an educated wife. Perhaps he desired to influence her and to mold her into a proper New York Society wife. All she knew was that from the moment she had laid eyes on his handsome face and looked into his deep, brown eyes, she knew that she must win his love.

Interrupting her reveries, she turned to Clara Van Wies.

"How fortunate you are, Clara. So, you have toured the continent? How wonderful. Did you spend a great deal of time in Italy? Lord, how I dream of visiting Florence."

Clara glanced at her mother and gave a supercilious look to Bernadine.

"Well, honestly, I can't say that I have ever been south of the Cote D'Azur. Mama and I spend a great deal of time in Paris when we are abroad. Of course, there is the obligatory visit to the Louvre. I do not claim to be well acquainted with the arts. There are so many diverting things to fill up one's day in Paris. But most of our time is spent at the establishment of Monsieur Worth. Well on our last trip I was bouncing between the Meurice and Chez Worth like an Indian rubber ball. To be honest, the food is so sublime in Paris that they had to make alteration after alteration to my gowns."

Theo placed his hand delicately on Bernadine's waist, almost to emphasize the contrast between his sister's figure and the lithe, athletic build of the woman he was courting.

"Mother, would you and Clara excuse us? Bernadine has promised to show me one of the watercolors hanging in the conservatory."

"Certainly, Theo," Agnes replied, smiling slyly at her son. "I am sure we can allow you two a moment alone. But please take care not to monopolize Bernadine's attention. I am certain that she has promised to dance with many of her guests. After all she has obligations as one of the hostesses of this lovely party."

Theo bent down and whispered, almost hissing in his mother's ear, his dark eyes narrowing, almost menacing.

"Mother, if you don't let me do this now, she may realize that I am not as I dissemble to be. Let me get this over with!"

Agnes Van Wies embraced her son and smiled warmly at Bernadine. "Bernadine my dear, I will go speak with your lovely mother. I feel that I have just begun to know her.

Bernadine and Theo walked arm in arm into the conservatory, a small, cozy room furnished with luxurious overstuffed settees, couches, and chairs, covered with exotic silks. The hunter green walls and curtains gave the room a certain formality. Bernadine loved this room. Well-appointed with many objects and paintings that she had lived with since she was a child, some might think it too Victorian and hopelessly out of fashion.

And she did notice the slightest look of derision on Theo's face as he took in the room.

But he quickly recovered his composure and smiled sweetly as he led her to the settee. The half-open slats of the shutters allowed the golden light of the setting sun to filter into the dim room. This light fell directly onto a decorative standing screen, which faced the couple. The screen stood about five feet high and bore the image of a large peacock created with enamel paint, the total effect producing a glowing impression. Hues of indigo and turquoise blues mixed with rich emerald green evoked sensations of tropical and sultry landscapes.

As Theo took her hand and caressed it, he looked into her eyes and began to speak in a soft, husky voice. Bernadine had dreamed of this moment since she met the stunningly handsome man a week ago. Yet she wondered why he glanced at himself in a mirror while smiling with a strange air of satisfaction.

"Bernadine, I cannot tell you how much I have enjoyed myself and how welcome you have made me feel. Your parents and all of your friends are charming."

Blushing Bernadine replied, "We Galvestonians are reputed for our hospitality."

Theo grasped her hands tightly and began to speak urgently and passionately.

"Dearest, you are lovely. Your beauty is almost disconcerting. I can tell you that I have met a great variety of girls from the best families in New York, Philadelphia, even as far south as Baltimore. In all frankness, if they are pretty, they lack wit. If they have wit, well, they are far from beautiful. But you have everything that a man could desire. If you will have me, I promise you will have everything that your heart desires."

Overwhelmed, Bernadine felt a stirring in her body as she took in his handsome, chiseled face and his lean, strong body. She leaned into his arms and allowed him to kiss her, first lightly but increasingly more passionately and she responded in kind. He kissed her neck, her arms and finally he took her hand.

"So, it's agreed," he whispered in her ear. "You will be Mrs. Theo Van Wies?"

At that very instant, the angle of the sun filtering through the shutters shifted and fell directly onto the eye of the peacock, transforming it. Its narrow eye seemed to be menacing her, no, warning her. She looked into the intense brown eyes of Theo and then into the fearsome eye of the peacock, yellow with streaks of black. Her mind reeled as it tried to fathom the message emanating from the eye, a message of caution or forewarning as if to presage some dark future cataclysm. Trying to brush away the feeling and telling herself that it was absurd, she could not be sure if she imagined it or not, but she thought she heard the words: *"No, this is not for you."*

Theo roused her from her dark thoughts with a passionate kiss, and all of her fears seemed to melt in the heat of their passion. Moments later the couple stood in the parlor, surrounded by family and friends, who offered congratulations and good wishes. They drank champagne and made lofty speeches about married life and children to come.

Arthur Van Wies looked visibly relieved, as did his wife and daughter. Things had worked out after all.

Martha Jones hugged her daughter and her husband shook the hand of his future son-in-law, which he found cold and limp. He tried to be happy for his daughter, but he had an awful feeling in the pit of his stomach.

Albert Lasker approached Bernadine, gently shaking her hand and wished her a lifetime of happiness. As he turned and kissed Hattie on the cheek, he said, "I must go."

FLORA

JANUARY 1894, NEW YORK

Flora's labor had come too early and Ned was frantic. She had awakened in the middle of the night with strong pains and he had sent for the doctor, who arrived within the hour. Two months' premature labor could mean a death sentence for either mother or child or both. However, miraculously both Flora and her little girl came through fine.

Dr. Ross, an obstetrician whose patients included almost all the ladies on Madison and Fifth Avenues, gave Flora a queer smile.

"You must be quite relived, my dear lady. On my way here, I considered transferring you to a maternity hospital, even though I knew you would object. But it seems that things were not as dire as I first imagined."

Weak and pale, Flora did not answer. What could she say? He knew that he had just delivered a full-term child and he had attended the Dodd's wedding seven months ago. She was grateful that whatever professional oaths he had taken prohibited any discussion of the discrepancy of the dates. But she worried about Ned. He was no fool.

Not being a suspicious man, he opted to believe the doctor's explanation about mistaken counting of cycles and babies that thrived in the womb. He did not want to doubt his wife, but for the first time in their marriage, he began to imagine the worst.

Did she love him? Did she have a lover before their marriage? After all, he was not exactly in her social set. True, professionally, he could match any man born to wealth and privilege. But he belonged to the category of men one called nouveau riche, even though he worked as legal counsel for J.P. Morgan. Then again, he thought, why should she have married him if not for love? Yes, he decided, she did love him. And more importantly she seemed to respect him. In honor of their love, Ned decided never to question Flora on her past or on the early arrival of their child.

The child, they named Mae after Flora's mother who had died only two months ago. She resembled neither her father nor her mother, with her dark hair and olive-toned skin. Ned knew that he descended from a Jewish line on his mother's family and naturally assumed this explained his daughter's coloring. None of this mattered because the child enchanted him with her sparkling blue eyes and her sweet smile and he fell in love with her instantly.

A precocious child, at the age of eighteen months, she spoke in coherent sentences. She adored books and demanded that either Flora or her nurse read two or three books before she would go to sleep. The family engaged a French governess, so by the age of two and a half, Mae spoke two languages fluently, with an impressive vocabulary.

Meanwhile, Flora lived the life of a wealthy New York woman. She was on the threshold of the new century, but still living in the old. Her family had always been on the list of Mrs. Astor's "four hundred," so the Dodds attended the balls and the dinners of the Vanderbilts, Stuyvesants, and Belmonts. She shopped at Lord and Taylor's.

She even left her husband and young daughter to travel to Paris to be fitted for gowns at the House of Worth. New York was changing, but Flora decided to "not change with the times." Above all, she craved security in a happy home. She had risked everything for one passionate night in Chicago and she was fortunate in her choice of husband. He had never questioned her fidelity. In return, she supported him in his professional life by introducing him to the wealthiest and most powerful families in New York. She left the past in the past, knowing that she could depend on her friend Lizzie's discretion about her adventure in Chicago.

Although they had never spoken of it, she was sure that Lizzie guessed the nature of what had transpired that evening when she did not remain for the Potter's party at the hotel. She could trust Lizzie, but when it came to Bea, she was not so sure.

DORE

ELLIS ISLAND, MARCH 1896

Dore Abramowitz held tight to her young mother, the two pressed together among hundreds of exhausted and excited immigrants on the lower deck of the steerage section of the ship. In the distance, she saw the grand lady, holding a torch to light their path to a promising future, a path that gave them freedom to make a better life. Dore's blue eyes widened as they passed the statue and she wondered if all the promises her parents had made about a life of peace and riches would be kept. Only ten years old, she felt a deep sadness to leave her home in Russia. She had friends and had the good fortune to attend school, an unusual privilege for a Jewish girl. He father made a good living as a tailor and had his own shop. The tailor of choice for the well-off Jewish population of their town, he also dressed some of the middle-class gentiles, who could not afford to travel to Moscow or Paris for the latest creations. Poverty did not make Isaac Abramowitz leave Russia. His dream of making it big in America convinced him to sell their belongings and purchase the passage for his little family. Aside from his dream, there was the growing nightmare of the Tsar's violent pogroms against the Jews in Russia. He did not need to be a genius to know what was coming, and he wanted no part of it.

He had married Rebekah the year after Dore's mother died giving birth to a stillborn son. So, she was the only mother that Dore ever knew. Because Rebekah's marriage to Isaac had been arranged against her will, she lavished all her love on the child and encouraged her innate intelligence. She insisted that Isaac allow the girl to attend school so that she might make something of her life.

Now waiting to disembark the ship and board the barge that would ferry them to Ellis Island, Dore trembled with fear. Her father had made sure that they wore clean and well-tailored clothes for the arrival at the great hall, where they were to undergo inspection and interrogation. He had told her the stories brought back from would-be immigrants who had been sent back on seemingly baseless pretexts. She was devastated when he refused to bring her grandmother because he claimed that she might hurt their own chances of making past the scrutiny of the immigration officials. She made a silent oath that she would never forgive him for leaving the elderly and defenseless woman behind.

Rushing onto the crowded barge, they struggled to carry their heavy luggage.

The scene was chaotic, but Dore tried to appear calm for the sake of Rebekah whose face had turned ashen with fear. A half-hour later they stepped onto Ellis Island, onto American soil. Rebekah's face regained its lovely color, and Dore let out a sigh of relief.

As they trudged on toward a large brick building, men in dark uniforms separated the arriving passengers into groups of thirty, consisting of an assortment of humanity: men, women, and children; Slavs,

Italians, and Irish. A dissonant cacophony of languages and laments rose over the crowd.

As they entered an immense hall, she could hear some of the officials shouting instructions in Russian. Dore realized that she hadn't eaten since the previous day as her stomach began to rumble. She held tight to her parents, afraid of being lost in the throng of people shoving to get to the front of the line. At that moment the guards began to separate the men from the women and children. Her father obediently joined the other men who walked toward another large hall. Rebekah let out a small cry and Dore grabbed her hand, looking into her eyes as if to beg her to remain calm.

When she and her mother reached the head of the line, an unpleasant woman, who wore the uniform of a nurse scowled at them. Her icy hands unbuttoned Rebekah's and Dore's collars. Presently a man in a white coat approached her, palpated her neck, looked into her ears and ran his hands up and down her spine. Although her heart raced with terror, Dore worried about Rebekah, knowing her to be timid and fearful of being touched by strangers.

The next part of the examination horrified her. The doctor took out a threatening looking instrument, using it to grab her eyelid, pulling it up in order to examine her eyes.

This excruciating and unsettling procedure, she later learned, examined the passengers for signs of Trachoma. If the examination proved positive, the immigrant received passage on the next outgoing vessel without exception. Dore noticed the doctor and nurse scrutinizing the faces of the passengers, searching for something in their expressions and reactions. It occurred to her that they might be looking for signs of mental derangement.

She often saw men and women mumbling to themselves on the streets of her town. Perhaps Americans didn't allow those unfortunate souls to live in their country. Well, she thought, it might be a good thing. Her family left Russia to escape a form of insanity, the madness of a government and its people, who persecuted the Jews, who had lived among them for centuries.

After the examination, a woman marked some of the other women's coats with a piece of chalk. These unfortunate ones would not be allowed into the country. Although relieved that she received no mark, she could not help feeling bad for those who did. She smiled when she noticed a woman, who examined her chalk marking and discretely turned her coat inside out and proceeded to the exit. Perhaps, she thought, the woman was extremely clever or maybe she had been forewarned. She caught her eye as they filed out, and they exchanged smiles.

Hoping that they would be able to finally leave the great hall, Dore felt a tightening in her chest when she saw hundreds of people waiting in line or sitting on benches. She realized that they had yet another trial to face before they would feel the breeze of American freedom on their faces.

They found Isaac standing in line, and Rebekah broke into tears of relief to see that he passed the medical examination and had not been turned back. After an agonizing and tedious wait of five hours, the Abramowitz family arrived at the front of the line. There they faced an exhausted-looking man with bulging eyes, who spoke with his assistant in English. His subordinate then spoke to them in Russian. Without even looking at them, he blurted out a series of questions, hardly waiting for a response.

"Do you have a job lined up? Do you have relatives meeting you?"

Isaac had been warned about the first question regarding a job. He had been told that it was wise to answer "No." The officials knew that there was plenty of employment for men pouring into New York. Low-paying jobs awaited unskilled men, women, and even children. But these low-paid bureaucrats didn't want to hear that an immigrant might be taking a high-paying job from an American born and bred.

"Can you write?" asked the translator.

Isaac tried to hold back his anger and contempt. "Of course, I can write. Even my wife and daughter can write. We are educated people, not peasants."

"Did someone in your country force you to leave?" asked the official with a slight smirk.

"Yes, the Tsar," Isaac responded, suppressing a laugh.

BERNADINE AND FLORA

NEW YORK, JANUARY 1898

Bernadine perused Mr. Moses *King's Handbook of New York City* as she rode in the coach with Clara. They made their way up Fifth Avenue past the graceful and massive homes of Mrs. Astor, passing along the way, Mrs. Vanderbilt's Chateau. Mr. King wrote extensively about these two families claiming that each could claim a fortune of more than one hundred million dollars. His book also listed families of lesser fortunes ranging from two to twelve million. She had spent the past two months under the more modest roof of the Van Wies family on a less-fashionable, but still respectable, block off of Madison.

Her fiancé and his family thought it advisable that she spend a substantial amount of time in New York to acclimate herself, as well as to affect a sort of transformation, mostly involving her manner and speech. She received elocution lessons four times a week from a stern and somewhat bitter woman, whose reduced family fortune required her to find employment. Along with the goal of erasing any trace of Bernadine's Texas drawl, her tutor had the responsibility of enlightening her student regarding suitable comportment in various social settings. Recently the lessons had become burdensome and frustrating. Yesterday she had spent twenty minutes working on vowels without much progress. Her teacher finally abandoned the phonetics lesson and handed Mr. King's handbook to Bernadine.

"Well, my dear, I think perhaps we shall dedicate the rest of our lesson to the hierarchy of New York Society. You need to know not only how to speak correctly but also what society you should cultivate."

Today Clara had suggested that they call on Flora Dodd. Her mother, Mae Courtland, who recently passed away, was a distant cousin to Agnes Van Wies. Calling on a family member of considerable standing in society would be an opportune way to allow Bernadine to test the waters. Clara chatted away as they rode the long distance uptown to the Dodd's new residence in The Dakota.

"Apparently many of the younger set have abandoned the brownstone for the French flat. I'm not sure I would be comfortable having people living above me and on either side. But I have heard that the apartments are spacious and elegant."

Bernadine did not respond. The beauty of Mr. Olmstead's design of Central Park captured all her attention. The gardens and the great expansive of greenery soothed her nerves. She admired the meandering pathways and the effect of dappled light shining through the leafy trees.

"Bernadine, are you listening to me?" Clara carped. "I want you to try to make an impression on Flora. The Courtlands are old money and they go way back to the Dutch, just as we do."

Bernadine nodded absentmindedly. She had heard it a hundred times since she arrived in New York. The old-moneyed Dutch mattered much more than the nouveaux riche. Her marriage to Theo will connect her to the long line of people who mattered and therefore she must do her best to fit in. The constant harping on her future obligations as Mrs. Theo Van Wies began to irritate her.

Had it not been for Theo, she would have taken a train to Houston weeks ago. His caresses the evening of the party in Galveston presaged the passion of their courtship and engagement. His sensual nature became more and more apparent. On certain occasions, she feared that he had gone too far and she thought that she ought to have put a stop to their lovemaking. But her own desire got the best of her and she found herself with her blouse and corset undone and his hands caressing her breasts.

She wondered that he did not worry that someone might surprise them in the parlor, but it did not seem to worry him. Aside from the physical nature of their love, her fiancé surprised her with his worldliness. He knew about all the latest books, plays, and political intrigues. They would talk for hours, or rather, he would talk and she would listen and marvel. So, she tolerated her vapid future sister-in-law and forged ahead with her self-transformation, knowing that she would soon be home in his arms.

Their coach came to a stop under a large arch that covered the porte cochere of The Dakota. High gables and deep roofs adorned the building along with an abundance of balconies and balustrades, the overall effect evoking Northern Renaissance architecture.

As they entered a large courtyard, Bernadine glanced up and was surprised to see the figure of a Dakota Indian. Clara laughed and said sarcastically that the inhabitants believed that the Indian watched over them. Bernadine smiled. If the truth be told, she liked the idea, but not wanting to risk the ridicule of Clara, she said nothing.

They ascended to the sixth floor in an exquisite Art Nouveau elevator. The butler guided them down a corridor that accessed all the rooms of the apartment and they entered an elegant parlor, tastefully decorated with modern furniture. Bernadine noticed the beautiful floor inlaid with mahogany and cherry woods.

Upon entering the room, Bernadine saw a lovely woman, who appeared to be in her mid-twenties. In her lap sat a child of approximately three years of age, an exotic little girl with a mass of black curls and startling blue eyes. The tenderness between mother and daughter reminded Bernadine of her family and friends in Galveston, which contrasted greatly with the coldness and distance that existed between the members of the Van Wies family, with, of course, the exception of Theo.

Flora Dodd stood to greet them, kissing Clara lightly on the cheek and taking her hand. A nurse came in and as the child left the room, she murmured a sweet *au revoir* in perfect French.

"Welcome to New York, Bernadine. I hope that you are enjoying your stay.

Clara tells me that you are to be married in March."

Clara smiled and interjected. "Yes, we are not going to make it a big affair.

We will bring up her family, of course, just the parents. We have ordered the dress and trousseau. Worth couldn't quite meet our time frame. What a shame."

"Well my dear," said Flora turning to Bernadine, "you must feel like you are in a dream. From what Agnes has told me, things are proceeding so quickly. It must seem like a whirlwind."

Bernadine blushed slightly, unsure of herself. She gave only a cursory answer so that she could master her vocabulary and accent, trying to hide her slight Texas drawl.

"Everybody has been kind and attentive. They have introduced me to some lovely ladies, who all promise to attend the wedding."

"Yes," said Clara interrupting, "we went to see Alva Vanderbilt. Oh, I mean Alva Belmont. She was telling us all about the Bradley-Martins and the costume ball that they are holding next month. Imagine choosing seventeenth-century royalty as a theme. I expect that we will see some extravagant jewels. By the way, are you going Flora dear?"

"Yes, we received the invitation last week," said Flora. "Ned is adamant that we should not attend. He is not at ease at the elaborate affairs, especially in costume. But as many of his clients will be attending, as well as Mr. Morgan, we have very little choice."

Struck by Flora's comment, Bernadine had naturally assumed that Mrs. Ned Dodd would be as excited about the ball as Clara and Agnes, who exhibited great relief when the invitation came in the mail a few days ago. The family had once been counted among Caroline Astor's all-important 400. But in the past year they had not been invited to one ball or even a dinner at the Astor home. It would have been a blow to be excluded from a party given by someone so obviously nouveau riche as Cornelia Bradley-Martin.

"What costume have you chosen?" asked Clara.

"Ned is dressing as Cromwell, and I am to be Anne Boleyn."

Clara seemed puzzled. "Why, Flora, I would expect that he would dress as Henry VIII. Who is this Cromwell?"

"Clara, he was a chancellor to King Henry," said Bernadine. "It was he who helped send Anne Boleyn to the chopping block."

"You are well-informed, Bernadine. It seems that the Texas schools cannot be faulted on their education of women," said Clara, with a sarcastic tone.

"It's true that Cromwell advised the king on matters of the state and the royal marriage," Flora confirmed. "But Ned decided to dress as Cromwell because he was known to be a brilliant lawyer and I am guessing that my husband wants to remind Mr. Morgan that he is fortunate to have him on his legal staff."

Clara sat on the sofa next to Bernadine affecting a carefree air, while smoothing her skirt and pulling at some lace on her sleeve.

"Of course, Flora, we are not intending to dress as royalty. Frankly, I feel no need to impress the Bradley-Martins. I don't care if they do have a castle in Scotland. The fact is that her father was a wood merchant from Albany, who somehow managed to accumulate a fortune."

Bernadine blushed and turned away, trying to hide her embarrassment. The remark offended her deeply. After all, Clara knew that Lucius Jones made his fortune as a cotton merchant. She took it as a deliberate affront. The irony of the situation infuriated her. She insulted the very man whose fortune offered financial relief to her own family. Her father had sent an advance on her allowance, which covered the expenses for not only her costume for the ball but also those of Theo and Clara. The majority of the Van Wies family jewels had long ago been sold off to pay the expenses of maintaining the appropriate lifestyle of members of wealthy New York upper crust.

Flora discreetly watched Bernadine and felt her discomfort. She had immediately admired the young woman for her beauty and innate intelligence. She felt sorry for her having to defer to the demands of the Van Wies family and she wondered what she saw in Theo. Yes, he was handsome, but she knew his character to be somewhat questionable. But the poor girl must be blinded by love and, most likely, totally ignorant as to the reputation of her fiancé. In any case, she thought, it was not her place to disillusion her. She decided, instead, to take Bernadine under her wing and guide her through the labyrinth of New York's social hierarchy. The young woman needed some polishing and guidance, and Flora decided that she would take on the task.

Turning to her guest, she inquired about the details of the upcoming wedding and honeymoon. Bernadine's face transformed, with a beaming smile and glistening eyes, as she informed Flora that Alva Belmont had offered her home as a venue for the ceremony and reception.

"How marvelous," Flora exclaimed. Alva was a dear friend of my mother. Her daughter Consuelo and I were inseparable when we were young. I will be glad to coordinate things with her, if you like."

"That is so kind of you," said Bernadine. "I would be most grateful for any help. My parents won't be coming up until the week of the wedding, so I am afraid my mother will not be able to help with the arrangements."

"Are you sailing for Europe right after the ceremony?" Flora inquired.

"Oh, we are not going to Europe. My father has arranged for us to honeymoon in New Orleans. The weather there in March is quite mild and I hope that many of my friends will make the trip over from Galveston to wish us well."

"Well, I imagine that you will have a wonderful time. I have been to New Orleans, although I was quite young. It is an enchanting city."

The two women stood to take their leave, and Flora embraced Bernadine warmly.

"I will contact Alva immediately to see what I can do to help with the arrangements." Said Flora. "Perhaps we can have tea next week?"

As Bernadine rode away from The Dakota, she felt that she had made a new friend, who she could meet on her own terms.

BERNADINE

NEW YORK, MARCH 1898

The bride and the groom departed the Belmont mansion before the other guests.

Because she had no female friends, aside from Flora Dodd who was married, Bernadine threw the bouquet to a cluster of silly young women who stretched out their arms and leaped in all directions in order to catch it. After a short carriage ride, Bernadine and her new husband arrived at the Waldorf Hotel.

Bernadine took her small case into the bathroom to change into her nightgown.

As she left bedroom, she turned and her regard fell upon the fireplace. A chill ran down her spine when she looked upon the fire screen, fashioned out of brass and painted metal, it contained the figure of a peacock. Her mind reeled, and flashes of the image of the peacock on the screen in her home in Galveston appeared like a tableau in her mind. A wave of anxiety washed over her body, sending a tingling sensation from her shoulders to the tips of her fingers. In the bathroom she stared at her reflection in the mirror and mechanically removed her dress and removed the pins from her hair. She had looked forward to this night ever since Theo had asked for her hand, but now she was riddled with apprehension. Why did the peacock reappear tonight of all nights? Why did she suddenly doubt her decision to marry a man that she had known for only a few months?

Her physical attraction to Theo overwhelmed her and she realized now that she had not approached this marriage rationally. As she brushed out her long, dark hair, she tried to quiet her fears. She told herself, it was only a silly peacock.

Theo was standing next to the bed when she walked into the large, luxurious bedroom. He grasped both her hands at first gently then his grip tightened, pulling her closer; his dark eyes were staring at her breasts, burning with a passion that seemed almost menacing. Suddenly, he pushed her violently onto the bed, tearing at her nightgown with such force that he tore the delicate lace and exposed her arms and breasts. He then proceeded to grab hold of her breasts, not caressing, as he had done in the past.

Now he was clutching and squeezing until she cried out in pain. His breathing became irregular and he began to moan loudly, his voice becoming harsh. Suddenly, he shoved her back towards the bedpost, her arms hitting the hard wood sent waves of pain from her hands to her shoulders. This man, the man whom she adored, transformed before her eyes into a brute. Confused and terrified, Bernadine asked herself what had happened to the tenderness that had tempered his passion these past few months. Having just turned seventeen, she had never experienced the act of lovemaking, but she knew that sex should not involve brutality and pain. Theo began to bite her shoulders and breasts, and her cries of pain only increased his passion, causing him to bite harder. She begged him to be gentle, telling him that she had never been handled this way before. Suddenly, to her horror, he slapped her and then clutched at her hair, pulling her head back and began squeezing her neck. His breath grew quicker, and his voice became harsh.

"Take these rags off," he said as lifted her gown and tore off her undergarments. Frozen with fear, she instinctively pressed her legs together, which only increased his anger. He took hold of her legs and with great force separated them and thrust himself inside.

"Cooperate, you whore" were his last words before he began his fierce movements. Tearing at her with his manhood, with his hands, and with his teeth.

She screamed one last time, and he emitted a loud, guttural moan, followed by a stream of obscenities, words that she had never heard before and with this his body went limp. At that instant, Bernadine's gaze fell once again upon the peacock on the fire screen, recalling the menacing eye of the peacock in her home in Galveston warning her, *"This is not for you."*

Theo brusquely stood up and walked into the bathroom. She watched his beautiful naked body as he walked away, wondering how a man of such breeding and culture could be such a brute. How could he leave his new bride bleeding and in agony and walk away so calmly with no sign of regret?

When he came out of the bathroom, he was wearing a silk robe, having combed back his dark hair with aromatic oil. His features took on a sardonic aspect. She cried softly, covering herself with the lovely lace bedclothes, which were now stained with blood. Theo leaned against the mantel of the fireplace and lit a cigar. His dark eyes, now devoid of the tenderness and sensuality ever present during their courtship, made her shudder. He remained perfectly still for several minutes, occasionally glancing at himself in the large mirror over the mantel, and finally walking over the large bed, he gripped her arm with such violence that her trembling body slid from the bed onto the floor. He then crouched down beside her and grabbed her face. His elegant, immaculately manicured hands with long, fine fingers brutally clutched her cheek and she felt the ring, which she had placed on his finger hours before, cutting into her skin. For several minutes he made no movement, offered no explanation for his bizarre behavior, and she realized that he must be mad.

Finally, he abruptly rose and pulled her to her feet, led her to a chair and pushed her down with such force that she almost lost consciousness. She struggled to regain her composure, while Theo remained eerily calm. Instinctively holding back tears, she regained control of herself at last. The realization hit her that she no longer knew the man standing in front of her; perhaps she never had.

Theo began to speak in a low derisive tone. "Bernadine, you now see me as I truly am. It has been difficult to dissimulate, but it was necessary for the sake of my family."

"Theo, I have no idea what you are talking about. What has come over you?"

"Now it is too late for questions. You are to sit and listen to what I have to say."

Walking over to a large leather chair, he began to speak in a more moderate tone, calmly and deliberately as if speaking to a young child.

"I know that my treatment of you tonight must have been a great shock. I cannot apologize, for this is who I am. It is not in my nature to treat a lover with tenderness. To be frank, I find no satisfaction in sex without violence."

"No, Theo, that can't be true. You have shown be both passion and tenderness in the past few months. You have shown me love…."

"All an act," he interrupted. "Since we never actually made love, I was quite capable of deceiving you. It's not that I have anything against you, Bernadine. You are a beautiful, young woman and you will make a fine wife. But, how shall I put it? I prefer a rougher trade, both in women and in men."

"Men! Are you telling me that you sleep with men?" She said incredulously.

"Yes, men, and whores, whoever is game for the kind of treatment that you just experienced. This is what I want and what I need."

Her face reddened and finally her fear turned to anger.

"Well, I will not submit to this. You are mad if you think that I will!"

He sneered. "Of course, I know that you won't put up with my behavior. I never expected you to. But you really need not worry, for I will never touch you again and I don't expect you to share my bed."

"Then why did you marry me?" she asked.

"You can't be that naïve, Bernadine. You must know why: your father's money and your allowance and inheritance. You know about my family's financial troubles. It was no secret."

She tried her best to quell her tears, not wanting to give him the satisfaction of seeing her distress.

"Yes, I know that you need my father's money. But I thought that you loved me, and I was more than happy to share it with you."

"Bernadine, I never loved you. I don't think that I have ever loved anyone."

As the reality of the Theo's deception sunk in, her mind raced, and she tried to make sense of it. Could she have really been so naïve? She berated herself for her haste in agreeing to the marriage and for being seduced by Theo's looks and seductive manner.

Then her thoughts shifted. Yes, she had been stupid. Her father had tried to talk her out of the marriage, but she wouldn't hear of it. But all that didn't matter. What mattered was the fact that she had married a monster and now she had to find a way out.

Grasping the arm of her chair, she tried to pull herself up and meet his eyes with a look of defiance. Then with great effort she got to her feet and walked to the fireplace, holding onto the mantel for support.

"Am I to understand that you expect me to go along with this farce? You want me to remain in this marriage because it is convenient for you and your family, to the detriment of my own happiness?"

He responded with a tone of surprise. "Why, of course. We wish it, and so it will be."

Her anger and shame finally rose to the surface and she found her courage.

"I refuse! I will not live a lie. I'll speak to my father, and we will have this abomination of a marriage annulled."

"You will? That will be awkward and inconvenient for everyone. Our family enjoys a fine reputation in this city, and I have made a great effort to be discrete about my sexual predilections. It is true that our family's fortune is depleted because of father's unwise investments, but we are still universally admired by New York Society. Many families are in the same situation and many young men marry into money to infuse new money into their bank accounts."

Bernadine responded with a bitter edge to her voice. "I will not stay in this marriage to pay for your sister's clothes and your father's club and fine cigars. My father has worked hard to earn his fortune and I won't let you flit it away."

Theo's face reddened with anger and disdain. "Your father is a bumpkin with no class. We thought he would be very malleable when it came to this marriage. I must say we were disappointed when he seemed to raise objections. But now it's too late. If you try to annul this marriage, it will create a scandal for your family. People will say that you are lying or simply that you are mad."

"No, they won't. And anyway, I don't care."

"Really? Do you want to tell your father that his sweet daughter fell in love with a monster? Need I point out what that would do to his regard for you?"

"He will understand. I'll simply tell him that I made a mistake," she said, opening her robe. "And when he sees what you have done to me, he will beat you senseless and call his lawyer!"

Theo's face underwent a transformation. For a brief moment his arrogant smile disappeared, replaced by a hint of apprehension. She felt a momentary sense of victory, but it was short-lived.

Taking her hand, he said with false tenderness, "We will not be seeing your father, or anyone for that matter. I wanted to surprise you, and I asked your parents to keep the secret. We are sailing for Europe this afternoon, and I have arranged for an extended honeymoon. We shall be on the continent for five months. It is, after all, the season in Paris."

"I'm not going to Europe with you. I'll go see my father as soon as I can dress."

"I am afraid that you are too late. I told your parents that we were taking the ship today, so they decided to leave for Galveston directly after the wedding. If I am correct, their train left about two hours ago."

"You have thought of everything, haven't you? But do you really want a wife who fears you and shrinks from your very touch?" She said, realizing that she would never have the courage to face her father with the truth anyway.

"I promise you, Bernadine, that I will never touch you again."

To her amazement, he approached her and gently took her hand.

"You will enjoy a full life with all the privileges due to a Van Wies and all the material comforts that a lady of your station in society should expect. And I will continue my life as before, ever so discreetly and you will tolerate this, for you have no choice. I'll allow you great latitude in your choice of friends, be they gentlemen or ladies, but do not presume to go too far as too as to embarrass me or my family."

Bernadine's anger and her courage subsided, and she was filled with dread, which gave way to acquiescence. Trapped in a fraudulent marriage, she knew that she now must find a way to navigate through the sadness and despair that lay before her.

DORE

NEW YORK, JANUARY 1898

Dore's father, Isaac Abramowitz, had carved out a place for himself in the clothing business within a year of the family's arrival in New York. He had established several sweatshops in their neighborhood on Essex Street. Dore could sense Papa's frustration and disappointment at having lost his prestige as a skilled tailor. He no longer had the clientele of middle-class professionals and wealthy Jews that he had enjoyed in Russia. And though he no longer feared the threat of the Tsar's pogroms, he lamented the decline in the family's fortunes and the misery of their living conditions. They still lived in the same tenement building that they moved into upon their arrival. No money remained to put toward a nicer apartment; every penny went into Papa's business undertakings. Both her parents worked from six in the morning until eight at night. Mama worked at home because her father didn't want her mixing with the *hoi polloi* that worked in the sweatshops that he ran. His job as a middleman, better known as a sweater to those in the trade, involved establishing contacts in the garment business and then doling out the work to families that lived in the tenements in their East

Side neighborhood. He rented the sewing machines to the families, oversaw the work, paid the poor souls a pittance for each garment they assembled, and then collected them for his contacts in the factories and wholesale business. In this new life in America, he made only two concessions to Rebekah and Dore—he allowed his wife to care for the four-year old daughter of their neighbor and permitted Dore to attend school instead of working to help support the family.

Their neighbor, Rachel Serfati, a widow, who had lost her husband in an accident just before the birth of her daughter, Leah, often bragged of her descent from Sephardic Jews from Spain. It pleased her to distinguish herself from the Eastern European Jews, whom she considered to be her inferiors. Her daughter had the same dark eyes and abundant dark curls as she. She asked Rebekah to help care for the girl when she was away at work during the week.

Rachel had found work in the home of a wealthy Jewish banker, who lived on the West Side, north of Seventieth where many of the well-established Jews whose fathers and grandfathers had made their fortunes in finance and speculation were settling.

She worked as a lady's maid in the home of one of the sons of the famous Seligman family. Normally, Jewish women abhorred going into service, but she had to support her daughter and the money was better than working in a sweatshop. Her good looks and polite manner had helped her procure the position, as the lady of the house preferred a Jewish maid to the usual choice of an Irish girl.

So, Rebekah cared for little Leah during the week, and she slept with the Abramowitz family in their small apartment, sharing a mattress on the floor with Dore.

Dore attended a public school that drew its students from the neighborhood, an enclave of Eastern European Jews, as well as from surrounding areas populated by Slavs, Italians, and the few Irish families that remained. The Irish kids did not like to mix with the Jews. They mocked the new arrivals, who spoke to each other in Yiddish. Dore made a point to speak only English, even when addressed in Yiddish by one of her friends. This proved to be of great benefit to her progress in English and she spoke without accent, almost like a native New Yorker. She had even avoided picking up the accents that one heard when Italian and Irish children spoke English and was careful to avoid the local slang that the other students used. Her teachers were impressed and often pointed her out as an example to be imitated by her classmates.

Second-generation Jewish students also spoke flawless English and most claimed that they could not speak Yiddish, although Dore didn't believe them. They ridiculed the "Greenhorn" Jewish immigrants, as well as the Italians and the Slavs. A girl named Sarah, who preferred to be called Sally, led a group of ten boys and girls, who relished taunting students who did not possess the adequate language skills or the courage to defend themselves. One day Dore had enough.

"Schmul, Schmul, the dunce of the school," Sally taunted a skinny boy who had just started school the day before. He smiled at her because he did not understand her insults. Sally's cohorts, David and Frieda, joined in the tormenting of Schmul.

"What, they didn't feed you enough on the trip over?" David ran over and tried to tug on his payot, the long sidelocks worn by greenhorns.

Dore grabbed David by the arm.

"Ay!" he screamed turning to her red-faced and in visible pain. "What do you think you're doing? That hurt, you little idiot."

Dore drew close to his face. "You are a simp. Does it make you feel like a big man to pick on a skinny boy who can't defend himself? Go pick a fight with Giovanni over there. What? Not so brave, are we?"

David stood there gaping at her. "And who do you think you are?" She said turning to Sally. "Just because your grandparents came over before my family or Schmul's doesn't make you any better or smarter than us. I know my grades are better than yours."

"Oh, you just be quiet, Dore. My grades are just fine, and at least I don't live in a tenement in the Lower East Side."

"I don't see you being driven home to the Upper West Side in any fancy carriage." Dore shot back.

Sally's face whitened, and she pressed her lips tightly together. Dore knew that she had hit a sore point. Sally's father had just lost a lot of money in a failed business scheme and now, what with the bribes he paid out and the money he invested, things were dire. Sally had bragged and bragged how she would no longer be attending public school because she was to enroll at an exclusive private school uptown.

"Dore, who are you to criticize anyone?" said Sally. "I happen to know that your father is a sweater. Everyone knows what that means. He is practically a slave driver, making everyone, including children, work so that he can make a profit. I do feel sorry for your neighbors, the women and children, working for him day and night down on Hester Street."

Dore kept her peace for she could not deny the truth about her father. Looking Sally directly in the eye she said, "Well, we are not responsible for our fathers' sins. I heard that they give scholarships at some of the progressive schools. Maybe you can apply for one. I'm thinking about it myself after I finish the year here."

In fact, she had no plans to pursue her studies after eighth grade, for she knew her parents considered her to be sufficiently educated for a girl. She would finish the year and graduate. At thirteen, it was legal for children to seek employment. She would not miss the cold, crowded classroom, where sixty children crammed into each room, sitting on uncomfortable chairs at long tables. She marveled that any learning actually took place. But she would miss learning, discovering the history and literature of her new home. And she could not help but to think it unfair that the majority of the Jewish boys in her class intended to go on to high school and then to the university.

Suddenly her attention was drawn back to Sally, who was mocking her.

"Really Dore, I don't believe you for a minute. Your kind always ends up working in a factory, or maybe if you're lucky as salesgirl in a store. I will look you up if I am on Broadway looking for some gloves."

Dore could feel her face blush with shame and anger, for she knew that Sally was probably right. She might work in a store, or perhaps in an office. After all, she could read and write. If only somehow, she could afford stenography and typing lessons, she could find a job in a business office or maybe even an advertising firm. She tried not to become swept up in her dreams. How she hated Sally for reminding her who she was and what the future had in store for a poor girl from the Lower East Side!

BERNADINE

PARIS, APRIL 1898

Theo and Bernadine Van Weis planned to spend a month in London after a rather rough crossing of the Atlantic; the turbulent waves rocked the ship and the wind made it difficult to stay on the promenade deck. So, she was relieved when they debarked in London with the intention of spending at least three weeks in town and perhaps a week in the country. But Theo grew bored and restless after the first week. He had seen his London tailor and been fitted for ten new suits and two coats. And as he planned to buy his shirts in Paris, he decided that they should leave for Paris. Bernadine protested that she had wanted to visit the British Museum and that one needs at least two to three days to really take in all its wonders. But Theo would not relent.

So, a week later they stopped at the Ritz, the newest and most fashionable hotel in Paris. If not for the waiters' inability to communicate in English properly, a person might imagine himself sitting in the lobby of the Waldorf Astoria. The very same crowd of New York's crème de la crème, the Jay Goulds, the Belmonts along with Alva's daughter, Consuelo, now the Duchess of Marlborough, and other familiar faces were fixtures in the lobby and dining rooms. Theo, in his element, darted from table to table, greeting family friends and former business associates of his father. It surprised Bernadine that he made very little effort to include her in the social whirl, aside from parading her occasionally at teatime so that the doyennes might admire his taste in choosing his new bride.

During her first week she made the obligatory trip to Chez Worth to order her new wardrobe. Theo accompanied her to each appointment and chose the dresses, gowns, and capes, even the feathers that would be attached to the newest style of hat. He did not interfere with her choice in undergarments. Yet he insisted on handling the most garish black lace corsets and garters that were on display.

Given the choice, she opted for less-constricting corsets and discreet garters.

Worth had eliminated the large leg-of mutton sleeves, still worn by the women in America, as well as the V-shaped bodice. Instead he proposed a straight-fronted corset, which altered a woman's figure, giving it the shape of an S. The total effect accentuated the bosom. The skirts lacked embellishment of any kind, which contrasted with the highly ornamented bodices. They ordered ten day-dresses, mostly made of silk or muslin, and six gowns, mostly lace and silk. The day-dresses had high necks and a preponderance of ruffles. Several of the gowns had a daring décolleté. She had noticed that even though Theo had no carnal desire toward her, it excited him to see other men respond to her sensually. She found it disturbing that he found other men's desire for her exciting. She wondered if he did it for some perverse need to see sexual desire in a man's eyes or perhaps it was just one more way for him to degrade her.

After her first week in Paris, going to fittings at Worth and lunching at Maxim's with women who lived on Madison Avenue, she decided to spend a few days visiting art museums and galleries. She asked the concierge at the Ritz for suggestions regarding galleries that she could visit. He advised her to start at the Louvre to get a feel for classical art.

She walked into a gallery filled with the works of Rubens, stopped and turned, not knowing where to look first. The artist's rendering of flesh surprised her; the pink and white full-bodied women and the sensuality affected her emotionally and physically.

Later she would visit other galleries where some modern painters were exhibiting their work. She saw works by Claude Monet, Édouard Manet, as well as a name that was unfamiliar to her, Camille Pissarro. This new art, this movement called Impressionism, showed the world in a new light that dazzled her. It opened up a new perspective on nature and the world in general.

Upon her return to the hotel, she was greeted by the delightful surprise of the sight of Flora Dodd seated in the lobby with Lizzie Pendergast. Little Mae, approximately four years of age, skipped through the lobby, examining the light fixtures and touching the plants. Bernadine marveled at the precocious child and it pleased her that Flora made no effort to discipline her or rein her in.

Bernadine practically ran through the lobby, abandoning all decorum, she hugged Flora and then Lizzie. Although both ladies were happy to see her, she noticed their expressions of surprise.

"We missed you in London, Bernadine," said Lizzie. We hoped to surprise you and Theo."

"What happened?" asked Flora. "You left so suddenly. We had a wonderful tour of the Lake Country planned and we wanted the two of you to come along."

"Well, it all fell through anyway" said Lizzie with a hint of sarcasm and disappointment in her voice.

"Are you blaming me, Lizzie?" Flora shot back. "Ned was called back on urgent business. When Mr. Morgan telegrams, he runs. But look how things turned out. Here we are in Paris with the bonus of running into Bernadine. Now, you will have a chance to get to know her and you will understand why I am so glad to count her among my friends."

Lizzie smiled and looked thoughtful. "Are you forgetting that she is on her honeymoon? I am quite sure that she and Theo would prefer spending time alone, without the distraction of two women who want to flit around and see the sights of Paris."

"Not at all" interrupted Bernadine. "My days are my own. Theo has been to Paris many times and has no interest in museums and riding the *bateaux mouches* down The Seine. I have just spent the day entirely on my own visiting the Louvre and some marvelous galleries."

At that moment, Mae walked over and embraced Bernadine, sweetly whispering in her ear. "I am your best friend and I want to tell you something. Do you see that man over there? Well, he explained to me how the elevators work, with cables and electricity.

And he also told me how they use a system, I think he called it *pneumatic*, to send messages throughout the hotel. And guess what? He said that next year they will be putting telephones in every hotel room!"

She gave the little girl a hug and then turned to Flora. "Mae never ceases to astonish me. I don't know how she could communicate with the elevator operator. My communication with him has been limited to the number of my floor. How she was able to attain all this information from him is mystifying."

"I do not mean to boast," said Flora. "But my daughter is fluent in French. Her governess is from the South of France, the town of Toulouse, I believe. A friend of mine, who was raised in France, told me that Mae speaks with a distinct regional accent. Frankly, I wouldn't know the difference," she said laughing.

"It's remarkable," said Lizzie. What were you telling me about German the other day?"

"Well again, it will sound like I am bragging," said Flora. "There is a gentleman who lives on our floor at The Dakota who is from Germany. He is some kind of doctor.

Anyway, Mae has taken a liking to him and his wife. She often pops into their apartment. I mean really, I have no idea what they talk about. Well, she now has learned quite a bit of German vocabulary and a few phrases."

Lizzie pulled Mae up onto her lap. "Well, my little wunderkind, shall we do something fun and frivolous tomorrow? Ladies, I have heard the most wonderful things about the department stores in Paris, or as they are called, *Les Grands Magasins.*"

"I don't know," Bernadine sighed. "I spent several days at the House of Worth ordering my wardrobe, and I don't think Theo has budgeted for more clothes."

"But, Bernadine, one does not necessarily go to the department stores to buy," said Lizzie. "It is so diverting just to visit the spectacle, or so I am told. First of all, they are conveniently located on Baron Haussman's grands avenues, so that one may handily visit both in one trip. I suggest that we start at *Les Galeries Lafayette* in the morning, have luncheon there, and spend the afternoon in *Au Printemps*."

Flora stood up and smoothed her skirt and held out her hand to the little girl.

"Mae, give Auntie Lizzie and Auntie Bernadine a kiss. We need to go and get you settled with Mademoiselle . You are having dinner with her in our room, for Mama is invited out to dine tonight with a very famous gentleman."

In fact, Flora had managed to obtain an invitation to a dinner given in honor of Camille Pissarro and his wife Julie, who had been his mother's maid. They lived outside Paris in Louveciennes but were spending a few days at the home of a wealthy Jewish family, Monsieur and Madame Bloch. Alva's daughter, Consuelo, knew the Blochs quite well and had arranged the dinner invitation for Flora and Lizzie. But the presence of the great artist and his wife was an unexpected pleasure. Madame Bloch had written in her invitation that she had invited the eminent writer, Emile Zola, to attend the dinner, but unfortunately, he was otherwise engaged.

Flora approached Bernadine, taking her arm a leading her discretely to quiet corner of the lobby.

"I don't know if your husband can spare you tonight, but if he can, would you come with me? Lizzie is going to the opera with some friends, so I planned to go on my own, but I would prefer to not be the only American. Could you possibly ask Theo if he would mind?"

Bernadine hesitated, momentarily, thrilled at the prospect of actually meeting Pissarro. She had heard Theo discussing Zola's connection to The Dreyfus Affair over drinks at the hotel. She noted the condescension in her husband's tone when he referred to the object of the scandal as a dirty little Jew. She cringed at Theo's blatant display of anti-Semitism and hoped that people seated close to them in the bar hadn't heard his remark. She decided that she would tell him that she would be dining with friends of Consuelo and that she would be accompanying Flora Dodd, but she would not mention Pissarro. He did not need to know the details.

Taking Flora's hand, she walked with her to the elevator. "I will ask Theo, but I am quite sure he won't mind. I would be delighted to accompany you. I never expected to have the opportunity to discover French domestic life, not to mention the incredible luck to meet such a talented artist, especially since I have spent the afternoon looking at his work.

"Meet me in the lobby at eight o'clock," said Flora. "The invitation is for nine.

The French dine late."

"Bernadine, embarrassed by her lack of sophistication, asked coyly, "Flora, how shall I dress? Most of my evening dresses are terribly, shall I say, risqué. Theo insisted on the most shocking display of décolleté."

Flora smiled and lowered her voice to a whisper. "We are talking about the French. They are not like Americans when it comes to modesty. However, given the age and social position of our hosts, I would limit the display of your flesh, beautiful as it is. Try to find whatever you have that is the most modest."

Bernadine was relieved to find their suite empty. As was often the case, Theo had gone out without telling her or even leaving a note. So, she took her time to dress for the evening, knowing that he would most likely be out until the early hours of the morning.

With any luck, she could avoid any discussion of the invitation to the Blochs.

Their coach stopped at an impressive home called *La Maison Biron.* It was situated on the fashionable Rue de Varenne adjacent to a park. The house was built in the eighteenth century, as were many of the homes in the neighborhood.

As their coach pulled up to the lovely home, Bernadine commented on the size of the home.

"Alva Belmont and the Astors insist of building copies of European homes. But they are twice or three times the size."

"Yes," said Flora. "I believe that all the style and elegance are lost in the translation. Of course, I would never say as much to Mrs. Astor."

They entered the home through a luminous foyer with magnificent marble floors and elegant chandeliers. At the doorway to the grand salon, an elegant woman of "a certain age" approached. Tall and elegant, she had black hair with a shock of gray that framed her slender face. Bernadine silently admired her gorgeous gown of mint-green silk and gauze.

She held out her hand to Flora and then kissed her on both cheeks, as was the custom in French Society.

"I am Juliet Bloch. I am so glad that you were able to come tonight," she said in lightly accented English. "And this must be Madame Van Wies. Welcome, my dear."

She turned to a distinguished man whom Bernadine assumed was Monsieur Bloch. "*Mais, qu'elle est charmante.*"

"Ladies, may I introduce my husband, Pierre?" she said.

Monsieur Bloch bowed to the two American guests, smiling sheepishly. A tall, thin man with a large nose and a magnificent, curled mustache, he presented the perfect portrait of a French gentleman of high society.

"It is my *plaisir*. I am sorry that my English is not so good. It is my wife who speaks the English in this house as she did her studies in a London school for young ladies. So, I will just say welcome to our home."

Juliet interrupted as she led Bernadine and Flora across the room toward an elderly couple.

"*Monsieur et Madame Pissarro, je vous presente Madames Dodd et Van Wies des Etats Unis.*"

Camille Pissarro laughed amiably. "Juliet, there is no need to translate this evening. Have you forgotten that I was raised and educated in St. Thomas? I speak English and even Danish." He bowed his head ever so slightly and smiled at Bernadine and Flora. "It is nice to meet such lovely ladies who hail from my side of the Atlantic."

"It is wonderful to meet you Monsieur," said Flora. "I have seen quite a few of your paintings at our Metropolitan Museum. My friend, Bernadine, has recently become quite an admirer."

Slightly embarrassed, Bernadine blushed and felt suddenly tongue-tied. The elderly artist flustered her, with his piercing brown eyes and his bushy, long, white beard.

"Yes, Monsieur, I must admit that until today I was not familiar with your work.

But I spent the afternoon at several galleries, and they were full of your paintings. I am drawn to your landscapes."

"Thank you, my dear," he said almost sadly. "Unfortunately, because I suffer from a malady of the eyes, I am reduced to painting all my outdoor scenes from hotel windows. This is the price of old age."

Worrying that her guest might fall into a state of melancholy, Juliet announced that dinner was served.

"Bernadine, would you sit next to Monsieur Pissarro and Flora, you next to Pierre?

Our dinner will be intimate. As you know, we were expecting Monsieur and Madame Zola," she said addressing the guests. "But he has been called away on an important matter."

"It is a shame that he couldn't be here," said Pissarro. "I wanted to see how he was progressing with this Dreyfus Affair. You know, it is a matter that is close to my heart, as I am Jew, even though I am not religious by any stretch of the imagination."

A team of footmen efficiently served a lovely salad of delicate endives, accompanied by a poached salmon with a mousseline sauce, followed by squab farci with a mixture of herbs and chestnuts. A dry white wine accompanied the first course and a full-bodied Bourgogne complimented the entrée or *le plat*, as the French called it.

Over dessert, which consisted of assorted sorbets and plates of pastel-colored confections called macarons, the conversation turned to the topic of Emile Zola's work "*J'accuse.*"

From what Bernadine understood, Monsieur Bloch had great misgivings about the effect Zola's stand was having on French society's views on its Jewish citizenry. Of course, he thought it an outrage that the army officials had imprisoned Alfred Dreyfus for a crime he did not commit.

"The trial and imprisonment," Bloch hesitated, searching for his words, "can only be seen as a clear display of anti-Semitism. But now the judgment is in, and Zola is stirring the pot. I ask you, who will be the ones to suffer? After all Zola is not a Jew."

Juliet's color rose as she tried to temper her speech. "Pierre, we can no longer cower and fade into the background. There is no going back from this. Emile has been very courageous, and we need to be grateful to him for standing up for us. And as far as who will suffer, have you not heard the government's threat to exile him?"

Flora ventured a thought. "We have many influential Jewish families in New York, Madame. They are quite successful, and we mix more and more. To be honest, our husbands do not admit them to their clubs, but we ladies often meet for luncheon either at restaurants or in their homes."

Pissarro interjected, "In St. Thomas, we have our own community, our synagogue, and our traditions. But as I am from wealthy family, I cannot claim to have suffered in my youth because of my religion. The Danish, who made up the greatest part of the population of the island, welcomed us in all aspects of daily life, including into their schools. But here in France, it is another matter." Looking at his wife, he added, "Even Julie's family has disowned her, and she has not spoken to them in twenty years."

After dinner, the guests drank their cognac in a small parlor and the conversation turned to the latest novels, theater, and exhibitions. Pissarro spoke of an artist named Toulouse-Lautrec, a strange little man from a town in the Pyrenees. Of aristocratic birth, he unfortunately suffered great physical deformities, which affected his ability to walk.

"He spends all his time in the Moulin Rouge," said Pissarro. I do not deny his talent, but I cannot approve of his obsession with Louise Webber, the creator of the outrageous dance they perform up there on Montmartre. The cancan they call it. He actually paints posters of women dancing this obscenity. It is a shame to see a man waste his talent on such absurdities."

Monsieur Bloch's suddenly became more animated, his interest piqued.

"Have you heard that Lautrec invented a new cocktail? It's called *tremlement de terre* or as you say in English, *Earthquake.* Apparently, it's a mixture of half absinth and half cognac."

Bernadine timidly interrupted, "I must say that this is the first time that I have tasted cognac and I adore it. But I am unfamiliar with absinthe. Is it a sweet drink?"

Juliet interrupted her husband who was about to answer. "*Oh, ma chere!* This spirit is a curse. Avoid it at all costs. One becomes dependent on it and cannot go a day without imbibing. It is known to be toxic, if consumed in great quantity."

"Thank you for the warning, Madame," said Bernadine. I do not drink very much as a habit, but I will certainly pay attention to what is in my glass in the future. I will pass on your advice to my husband, as he seems to enjoy the diversions of Montmartre."

Flora discreetly glanced a warning to Bernadine. She did not like the way the conversation was turning. "Bernadine, it is getting late. Madame Bloch would you be so kind as to have the butler call for our carriage?"

After thanking their hostess for the lovely evening, the two women climbed into their carriage. Once inside, Flora took the opportunity to caution her friend not to be so forthcoming about her private life with Theo in society, French or American.

"I am sorry," answered Bernadine, her face hot with embarrassment. "It just slipped out," she said sighing sadly. "Flora, I think that

Theo may have already fallen into the abyss. He spends almost every night at the Moulin Rouge or one of the other theaters. He rarely comes home until early in the morning."

Flora took her hand. "I am sorry to hear it. I truly thought that when he married you, Theo had given up on his old vices. Perhaps when you return home he will reform.

The delights of Parisian nightlife are often a great temptation to American men."

Bernadine returned to the Ritz to find that Theo had not come back, and she did not see him when she awoke at nine. She quickly dressed, for she had promised Lizzie and Flora that she would visit *Les Grands Magasins* with them.

When she entered the lobby, her spirits were immediately lifted when she saw Mae. They had not told her that they intended to have the child come along to the department stores. Flora insisted that Mae needed to leave her books behind and spend some time with the ladies.

They entered *Les Galeries Lafayette* through the main entrance. Impressive plate windows beamed, displaying the store's latest fashions for men and women, as well as cashmere throws, with a few articles of furniture mixed in for effect. The store's interior, constructed in the style of Art Nouveau, had elegantly etched glass ceilings and enormous electric light fixtures; decorative glass cases displayed sparkling costume jewelry, elbow-length kid gloves, and fans embellished with ostrich feathers.

Passing by life-like mannequins sporting the latest Parisian fashion, Flora commented. "Lizzie, look at the cut of that dress. I love the tiered skirts."

Inspecting the dress, Lizzie frowned. "I don't like the form it gives to the body at all. It will bend us into an S-shape, not to mention the bodice, which gives no definition to the breasts."

Flora shook her head. "But I do love the look of the waistline. We would have to buy some straight front corsets. They are so uncomfortable."

"Of course, Bernadine could carry it off without the corset. Don't we wish that we had her small waist?" said Lizzie.

"You forget Lizzie, Bernadine hasn't had any children yet."

Bernadine blushed and smiled. "I have no immediate plans to have children."

Lizzie and Flora couldn't help but laugh. "Plan or no plan, things happen," said Flora.

A saleswoman came over with a model wearing one of the new S-shaped dresses.

"*Mesdames,*" she said in heavily accented English, "this is what we call the monobosom. Parisian women are mad for this style, though I dare say that it will take at least a year for it to catch on in America."

Lizzie said, "Well, Mademoiselle, we are from New York City, and I dare say that we have no lack of chic ladies, who know their fashion and style. I am not sure this dress will ever please American women, or men for that matter."

Mae giggled. "You tell her, Aunt Lizzie." And then the little girl turned to the saleswoman and spoke to her defiantly. "*Oui, Mademoiselle, nous sommes bien avance en pas mal de domains en Amerique, surtout les science!*"

"What did she say, Flora?" asked Lizzie.

Flora laughed and took Mae's hand to lead her away. "I am not quite sure. But I know that it was rude, and I am sure she said something about science."

Bernadine bent down and hugged Mae. "Well, I just adore her and from the little French that I have studied, I understood that she spoke in defense of her country. Bravo, Mae!"

The ladies returned to the Ritz around five, in time for tea. Bernadine excused herself and went to her room. She opened the door with great trepidation, not knowing in what state she would find Theo, or indeed if he would be there.

She found him sprawled out on the sofa, his face ashen and slack-jawed, his eyes half-closed. Not sure if he were sleeping or just in a stupor and afraid to disturb him, she quietly walked into her bedroom. She freshened up in the bathroom and when she walked back into the bedroom, he was leaning on the doorframe with a belligerent look on his face.

"Theo, I was frantic when I returned last night, and you were nowhere to be seen."

His expression appeared frozen somewhere between exhaustion and contempt, as he stumbled into her bedroom, knocking over a small chair; losing his balance, he collapsed onto the bed.

Bernadine's worry turned to annoyance.

"Oh, do pull yourself together. I don't care what you do during your nightly debauchery, but you said yourself that you have a reputation to maintain, for yourself and for your family. Are you forgetting that it is the season here in Paris? All of New York Society is here, including my friends, who are beginning to ask why we are never together in the evenings."

"I'm not worried about Flora." he said. "She is family, even though she hardly acknowledges the tie anymore. But she is not the type to gossip anyway."

"True," she said. "But Lizzie Pendergast is constantly with Flora, and I'm not so sure about her. She has also noticed your nightly absences. Furthermore, Flora did make a comment on our way home last night from dinner with the Blochs"

Theo suddenly pulled himself up out of the bed, his speech slurred.

"Who? With whom did you dine last night?"

"I left you a note when I couldn't find you. I dined with the Blochs. Camille Pissarro, the artist, was there with his wife. You know his paintings are sure to increase in value, so you might consider …."

"I did not see your note," he said glowering at her, as he grabbed her wrist. "If I had, I would not have allowed you to dine with those people. The Van Wies family does not dine with Jews in public or in their homes, even if the homes are in chic neighborhoods. How dare you take such liberty?"

Bewildered by this harsh rebuke, Bernadine remained speechless, trying to grasp the reason for his anger. Theo had never expressed his hatred of Jews before their marriage. Had he not met the Kempners and Rabbi Cohen the very night that he had asked for her hand? Although she had noticed that the family had no close associations with Jews, she had never appreciated the degree of animus they felt toward them. Of course, Theo's parents were dreadful snobs, but she had always thought that their disdain was based on class and money, not religion.

Her rage helped her overcome her fear, and she would not allow Theo to intimidate her any further.

"I will dare, and you will have no say in the society that I keep. The Blochs are fine people of good breeding and education. They are friends of Monsieur Zola, a brilliant writer, willing to suffer for his beliefs and ready to risk his very freedom. Again, I remind you of our agreement. I have kept up my end of the bargain. I cannot say the same of you. I know that you have been spending your evenings in Montmartre and I am not ignorant of what passes for entertainment in the cabarets and brothels. Do as you wish, but do not assume to dictate to me whom I may dine with and what society I may seek out!"

Theo made no response. Staring into his unfocused eyes and daring to lean in closer, she smelled his foul breath.

"What is the matter with you?" she said. "I have seen you drunk before, but this is absurd."

He pulled out a small flask and poured its contents into a glass of water, producing a white liquid.

"Try some of this, my dear. It will calm you down and transport you into a dream. It tastes like licorice. Try it," he said clutching her chin and bringing the glass to her lips.

"Take it away!" she shouted, "I know what it is. If you want to abuse your body, go ahead. But I will not touch that poison."

A few hours later, Theo had gathered his wits and dressed for dinner in the hotel dining room. He was pleasant to Flora and Lizzie and even made an effort to be kind to Mae. Bernadine had stood up to him and it seemed to have had an effect. But she had decided that they must take the next available boat back to New York.

After dinner she spoke to him calmly, convincing him of the necessity to go home. The one thing that she could depend on was his fear of showing his true nature to people in their set. Being the season in Paris, his activities would not go unnoticed much longer.

When she informed Flora of their departure, her friend protested and begged her to stay. Mae cried and would not be consoled.

"I promise to see you at least once a week when you come back to New York," she told Mae.

"That is a promise that I will hold you to," said Flora.

Although she loved Paris, Bernadine was happy to return to New York, where she would set up her bedroom on the opposite side of the house from Theo's room. She hoped that once they were home, he would not have easy access to absinthe, and might live a more honorable life under the scrutiny of family and society.

BERNADINE AND FLORA

SEPTEMBER 1900, HOUSTON, TEXAS

Rabbi Cohen's telegram arrived at teatime.

SEPTEMBER 8, 1900—8 O'CLOCK P.M.

Houston, Texas

Hurricane struck this morning. Mother and Father killed. Please make your way to Houston soon as possible.

My deepest condolences.

Rabbi Henry Cohen

Bernadine dropped her teacup, as her consciousness slipped away, everything went dark. Clara rubbed her hands and called to the servants to bring smelling salts. Agnes took the telegram from her hands and read it, feeling genuine pity for her daughter-in-law. But for an instant a calculating expression flashed across her face. Clara was administering the smelling salts and Bernadine opened her eyes slowly. A chill went through her body and she began to shiver. Agnes called for a shawl and some more hot water for tea. She told the butler to call Theo and Arthur at the Metropolitan club and tell them to come home immediately. Maids dashed up and down the stairs, as the driver came in to announce that he had brought the carriage around and would pick up the men at the club.

Bernadine had not fully recovered from her shock when her husband and father-in-law walked in the door. Theo made a great show of holding her hand and consoling her, calling her darling. Instead of soothing her, his pretense angered her. Gradually, her head cleared, and she realized that she needed to make arrangements to travel to Houston. She dried her eyes with her handkerchief and gathered her wits as best she could.

"Arthur," she began slowly, fighting back tears. "I will take the first available train to Houston. Would you mind inquiring which line is the most direct?"

"Of course, my dear," said her father-in-law. "Shall I send a telegram to your family's minister for the arrangements?"

Confused, Bernadine looked at Arthur oddly. "Minister? No, Arthur, Rabbi Cohen will make the arrangements. Didn't you see his telegram?"

Arthur tried to hide his disdain, but it was evident to her all the same. She tried to maintain her composure, but grief suddenly overcame her. The thought of the task that lay ahead left her dazed and incapable of taking the first step in planning the trip. She needed support and compassion. But the two people whom she had always turned to were gone, and Theo and his parents offered neither warmth nor comfort. Her thoughts turned to Flora, who had become her friend and confidant these past months.

She could not think of anyone better equipped to help her through the challenges that she would face when she returned to Texas.

She telephoned Flora, who agreed to accompany her to Texas. When she told that maid that she would need only a small valise and that she need not bother to pack for Mr. Van Wies, she observed her mother-in-law's worried expression. Bernadine understood that the family put great stock in Bernadine's infatuation with their son, and they were depending on him to deal with her kindly, especially now.

"Dear, am I to understand that you don't wish Theo to go with you to Houston?" asked Agnes.

Bernadine did not answer but looked at her blankly.

"I do think that you should reconsider," said Clara, putting her arm around her waist. "I think he is helping father with the arrangements. I will go get him for I am certain that he will want to be with you. You will need a man to help you iron out all the legal matters."

Bernadine shook her head, fighting to maintain her composure. Clara's mention of legal matters alarmed her, and she felt her face grow warm.

"Thank you, but our family lawyer, Kenneth Simpson, has always handled my father's legal affairs and he will continue to do so."

"But you should not be alone," said Agnes. "The trip will be wearisome and difficult, not to mention the panic and confusion you will encounter upon your arrival in Texas."

"But I will not be alone" she said. "Flora Dodd will accompany me. "I feel the need for female companionship. Of course, I would never presume to impose on either of you," she said looking at both women.

She could not miss a concerned look that passed between the two and she guessed that they did not appreciate her display of independence. But she refused to let them influence her decision.

Bernadine and Flora reached their destination after a grueling six-day journey. They had to change trains in Baltimore and had a layover of five hours in Mobile. The station had no ladies lounge, and the waiting room, packed with passengers headed to Houston, was visibly full of dread and grief about family and friends who had perished in the hurricane.

When they arrived in Union Station in Houston, the scene was ghastly. Residents were fleeing the island of Galveston in droves and thousands of wretched people, entire families wandered aimlessly. Charitable institutions had set up booths to provide what aid they could, but it all seemed futile. She and Flora pushed against the fleeing crowds headed into the station and onto the platforms. Finally, they reached the great hall and Bernadine let out a shout of joy when she saw Albert Lasker. She could not fail to recognize him, even though his body had filled out and he wore a stylish beard. He approached her and shook her hand in a somewhat formal manner. She brushed it aside and embraced him; losing all her composure, she began to sob. For the first time since she had heard the news of her parents' death, she allowed herself to feel the full extent of her grief as she sought comfort in the arms of her childhood friend.

"I'm so sorry, Bernadine," he said kindly. "You know how I felt about your parents. They were like family to me. I don't know if they wrote you, but my mother died last year, and we have had no news of my father since the storm."

"Yes, my mother wrote me about your mother's death. I sent a letter. Didn't you receive it?"

"No. I have been living in Chicago, working in advertising for the past two years."

"Oh, I see," she said. "Don't give up hope for your father. He might be in the hospital, possibly in shock."

"That's possible," said Albert. "They are still finding survivors, many of whom took refuge on rooftops and some who were in attics just above the water level."

Seeing Flora standing patiently on the side, Bernadine blushed and quickly apologized. "Oh, Albert, pardon my manners!

This is my dear friend, Flora Dodd. She has been as kind and welcoming as any sister. I could not have borne the trip without her strength and comfort."

Flora took Albert's hand. "Albert, I am sorry that we have to meet on such an occasion, but I am pleased to meet such a steadfast friend to my dear Bernadine."

Once in the coach on the way to the hotel, Bernadine noticed that Houston had sustained substantial damage. Streets had flooded, trees felled by the winds still littered road.

"It was almost impossible to find a hotel room in Houston," said Albert. "Since all Galvestonian of means have filled the rooms. Rabbi Cohen asked the Kempners if they would intervene on your behalf."

Albert helped the ladies down from the coach and approached the reception desk.

"Mr. Kempner has reserved a two-bedroom suite for Mrs. Theo Van Wies. She will be sharing her accommodations with Mrs. Ned Dodd of New York. The law firm of Williams and Simpson will be covering all expenses."

"Yes sir," said the clerk.

"Oh yes," said Albert. "Please arrange for a carriage to be brought around tomorrow morning at nine o'clock to take the ladies to the law firm. May I also remind you that Mrs. Van Wies is mourning her parents, who were lost in the storm?"

An hour later Bernadine, Albert, and Flora met with Rabbi Cohen in a discreet corner of the lobby. Flora had initially declined to join the group out of consideration for her friend's privacy, but Bernadine had insisted that she be there.

Rabbi Cohen spoke softly, easing into the details of the tragedy. "The day of the hurricane there were two trains that were scheduled to arrive in Galveston, one from Houston and another from Beaumont. Your parents were on the train from Beaumont."

"I suppose he went to see friends," said Bernadine sadly.

"Actually, it was strictly a business trip," said the rabbi. "I know it was unusual for your mother to accompany him, but her presence was required for the signing of some important papers. I understand that you will learn more about the details of this transaction during your visit with the lawyers tomorrow."

"Indeed," said Bernadine. "Mr. Simpson sent a letter explaining that he would be discussing my trust and my father's investments. And of course, there is the reading of the will."

The rabbi nodded thoughtfully and continued. "As I was saying, your parents were on the train from Beaumont, which, as you probably remember, stops at the Bolivar Peninsula. The storm was at its height and the tracks were already covered with several inches of water. Still the passengers were hopeful when they saw the ferry in the distance. However, the captain had no choice but to turn back. The waves were strong, and they risked overturning the vessel. I spoke with the captain and he is guilt-ridden about leaving the passengers behind. But he had his own passengers' safety to think of.

There were so many heart-rending incidents during the storm—children torn from their father's arms, families clinging to rooftops washed out to sea, and diners in a restaurant crushed to death when a printing press on the floor above crashed through the ceiling."

Rabbi Cohen's voice trailed off. "I'm sorry. You have no need to hear all this. You have your own grief."

Bernadine's heart ached for her fellow Galvestonians. She had always admired the rabbi's dedication to all the people of the island and she now she wished that she could do something to ease his suffering.

He went on to tell her about the exact circumstances of Lucius and Martha Jones' death. The two carriages stranded on the tracks, as the water began to rise, contained ninety-five souls. As the water began to rush into the cars, ten people decided to brave the rising water and make for the lighthouse on the peninsula. They joined fifty other people who had already taken refuge there, all crammed in and hardly able to move.

These ten survived.

"I had occasion to interview a gentleman, an old acquaintance of your father, who was one of the ten left," said Rabbi Cohen. "He related as best he could the last minutes he spent with your mother and father."

His voice shaking, the rabbi told Bernadine about these last minutes and how her mother had comforted a young girl of twelve, who was traveling alone. When your father had decided with another gentleman to make for the lighthouse, he begged his wife to leave with him. But the young girl was frozen with fear and would not leave her seat.

"Your mother, loving and kind woman that she was, would not abandon the girl." He said.

It did not surprise Bernadine that her father would not rather die than leave his Martha behind.

"Have they recovered their bodies?" she whispered.

"No," he said. "They may have been washed out to sea or cremated, as were many who washed up on the beach."

Bernadine's face became pale and she almost lost consciousness. But Flora grabbed her hand and she recovered. This image of her parents stranded on the train with the water rising would haunt her for the rest of her life. She could feel the panic that her mother must have experienced at the end, the terror of fighting for her last breath. Suddenly, she began to sob irrepressibly.

Albert, who had remained silent, finally spoke. "I am sorry Bernadine. I wish I could do something to help, anything. But …." The young man, usually so eloquent, was suddenly speechless.

"Thank you, Albert." Said Bernadine. "Having you with me is a comfort. I thank you for that."

As her shock subsided, it was replaced with a sensation of emptiness and black despair. Why hadn't she perished with her parents? After all, what did she have to live for? She would have gladly given up her life, sad farce that it was, if only her parents might have lived.

Suddenly Rabbi Cohen roused her from her dark reveries, telling her that the Kempners sent their condolences.

"There is to be a memorial in two days on the island," he said.

"I'm not sure that I will be able to attend," she said. In fact, she had already decided that she would never return to Galveston as long as she lived. She would later learn that many Galvestonians had reached the same decision. The majority moved to Houston and some to New Orleans. The storm would alter the state of Texas forever. Galveston would no longer be the bustling port and center of trade that it had been for over a hundred years. Houston's star was rising.

The next morning, they entered the law offices of Williams and Simpson, located in a new seven-story office building on Lamar Street. An attractive receptionist escorted them into a spacious office. Kenneth Simpson rose and embraced Bernadine, gently guiding her to a comfortable leather chair. He regarded Flora quizzically, asking her to make herself comfortable in another chair.

"Mr. Simpson, this is Flora Dodd. She is my closest friend and confidante, so you have no need to censor yourself. Once you inform me regarding my financial and legal circumstances, I will need a friend in New York to help me, how shall I put it, to help me navigate the treachery of the Van Wies family."

A puzzled expression crossed the attorney's face. Most likely he had expected Theo or Arthur Van Wies to accompany Bernadine to the reading of the will.

However, he did not to bring up the matter.

Bernadine appreciated his silence on the absence of her husband and his family, but she did feel that he should know the truth about their financial circumstances.

"I do feel that you should be aware," she said, "that my husband's family has had many setbacks in business. Their money is inherited, and to be quite frank, their fortune has dwindled considerably in recent years. I believe they anticipate that my inheritance will provide them with some relief in that regard."

Mr. Simpson cleared his throat, and his face reddened. "Well, that's the rub my dear. There is indeed a large inheritance, what with the cotton trading business and some considerable real estate that your father purchased in Houston over the past two years. Your parents were returning from a business trip to New Orleans the day the hurricane hit. I had drawn up papers for the sale of his cotton trading company to his largest competitor in Louisiana. Martha needed to accompany him to complete the sale, as she was part-owner. It is extremely fortunate that the sale was strictly on a cash basis. A cashier's check was deposited into your father's bank account over week ago. I have all the papers right here, if you would like to see."

Bernadine read through the legal documents, and Mr. Simpson pointed to the figures. She gripped the papers, her eyes widening. "Is this indeed the correct amount, Mr. Simpson?"

"It is," he said with some pride. "Your father was a very successful man. I knew him since he moved from Beaumont and I was his lawyer from the day he started his company, which, as you can see, he sold it for a million dollars. In addition, you will notice that he acquired a substantial amount of real estate here in Houston, including property along Lamar Street as well as several lots in an up and coming residential area called The Houston Heights. I would estimate the total value of the real estate to be approximately two-hundred thousand dollars."

Flora smiled at her friend, who looked at her with relief. Through the darkness of her grief, Bernadine saw a flicker of hope. Now she would have the money to leave Theo and begin a new life as a wealthy, independent woman.

"Now, Bernadine," said the lawyer. "This is your father's will, which he made out immediately after your marriage. He stipulates that you should not receive your full inheritance until you reached a certain measure of maturity. He suspected that your husband's family was not as financially solvent as they led him to believe. Frankly, he did not want them to take advantage of your love and generosity, for he feared that they could easily burn through your fortune."

Bernadine gave an audible gasp and looked at Flora nervously.

"Therefore," Simpson continued, "he asked me to withhold the bulk of your inheritance in trust until you reach the age of twenty-seven."

Bernadine looked at him in disbelief.

"You will, of course, receive your allowance, with a slight increase each year. On your twenty-seventh birthday, you will come into the total amount, which in the ensuing years, I am confident, will have increased substantially. I am working with some very talented investment men, conservative men, who do not take risks."

Finally, she could no longer remain quiet. "Am I to understand, Mr. Simpson, that I have to wait eight years for my financial independence?"

"I am afraid that is the situation," he said. "Your father was most adamant. Your mother tried to convince him to let you come into your money next year, but he would not agree. He was most steadfast in his belief that you would profit from a few years of the experience that life has to offer. To be frank, he wants you to take the reins, so to speak. He intimated, no, he outright asserted, that he did not want the Van Wies men and their silly women spending his hard-earned money."

Bernadine blushed, "I understand completely. My father was a wise man. If only I had taken his advice when it really mattered."

Bernadine and Flora left the law firm of Simpson and Williams and returned to the hotel. They settled into a cozy corner in the tearoom, sitting in two armchairs, the sun streaming through the half-closed shutters. Flora began to speak hesitantly.

"I am sorry about the turn of events. Even though you are the only person in the Van Wies household who does not live for money, it would be nice to be independent. You might find a suitable home, perhaps a brownstone, and establish a life as a couple, whatever that may mean."

RACHEL

NEW YORK, 1902

Rachel Sefarti, confident in her exotic beauty, aimed high. She had no intention of working as a lady's maid for the rest of her life. She had, in fact, caught the eye of young David Seligman, the son of her wealthy employer. He had just finished his last year at New York University in the Bronx. He had just returned home after finishing his course in law.

Rachel had first known him as an awkward teenager, but he had turned into a striking young man, tall and dark with chiseled features. He had always been sweet on her, but he was five years her junior and she had not encouraged him. But now the age difference no longer mattered to her. At first, he would pass her in the upstairs hall and smile shyly, sometimes brushing her arm as he walked by. Little by little the smiles became bolder and his intentions became clear. One evening while his parents had gone out to dinner, David sought out Rachel in her room on the top floor of the mansion, knocking gently on the door, he softly asked her permission to enter. At first, she hesitated, calculating the consequences if they were caught, but her desire, awakened after so many years of lying dormant, compelled her to open the door. He did not waste time with words but gazed into her eyes for a brief moment before kissing her roughly with unrestrained lust. Rachel responded in kind with uninhibited caresses and moans, as physical passion overtook her body. She had led and empty, loveless life since the death of her husband, so she surrendered to her pent-up feelings and made love for the first time in years. David Seligman would help her make up for those years of loneliness, visiting her in the servants' wing whenever possible.

The lovers met only when the Seligmans were out and they had the house to themselves, a rare occurrence. However, several weeks after their love affair began, they were overjoyed to learn the Seligmans received an invitation to weeklong party in a mansion along the Hudson River. David begged off, saying he had to study for his law boards and could not be distracted by silly girls at a house party. For the entire week, the couple spent their nights in each other's arms. Confident in his love for her, Rachel expressed a physical passion that she knew David had never experienced. She experimented with carnal acts that she had never dared contemplate, even with her late husband. The other servants had been given leave and they had the house to themselves, so they felt unfettered in expressing their passion with loud moans and cries of passion. David expressed amazement for her daring and talent at bringing him to climax as much as five or six times in one evening.

He had experience with prostitutes and he thought silently that her skills surpassed those of any encounter he had had with professionals.

He could not get enough of Rachel, so much so that he abandoned all caution and went to her room on the day of his parents' return from the Hudson Valley. Mrs. Seligman had told Rachel that they would be returning on the six o'clock train and the staff was told to be back in the house no later than five. Mrs. Seligman had come down with a dreadful cold, so they took the morning train, which arrived a noon. The coach pulled up to the house a little after one o'clock. David's mother walked upstairs to her bedroom and called for Rachel to come to her room to help her undress and then unpack her bags. When she did not receive a response, she walked down the hall and opened the door that led to the stairs to the servants' quarters. Shocked by the loud moans and sounds of lovemaking, she went to find her husband. She could not believe that Rachel had taken advantage of their absence to bring some downtown swell into their home.

She called to her husband for she did not dare confront her maid and the strange man.

The reality that confronted Mr. Seligman when he opened the door turned out to be much worse than what his wife had imagined. He could hardly believe his eyes; his son in the throes of passion with the beautiful, naked servant. For almost a minute, they did not realize that they had been discovered. David looked up in horror to see his father, who threw a blanket over their naked bodies and demanded that they dress. After Mr. and Mrs. Seligman severely reprimanded their boy, and then they dismissed the maid and dispatched her to the slums of the East Side, never to return to service in any decent home.

Rebekah, who was taking advantage of the mild afternoon weather, was sitting on the stoop in front of their tenement. She had allowed nine-year-old Leah to play with some of the neighborhood children and had begun to worry because she had lost sight of her. Her wary gaze searched up and down the street looking for the girl.

Suddenly to her surprise she saw Rachel trudging down Mott Street carrying a suitcase, her face tear-stained, her eyes swollen and staring blankly, as she navigated the crowded street.

Taking Rachel's suitcase from her hand, she helped her up the stoop and the dark stairway to her apartment. Rachel hurled her suitcase across her apartment, breaking a lamp and a few ceramic keepsakes. Throwing herself on the bed, Rachel allowed herself to release her pent-up rage and despair.

Sitting down next to her on the bed, Rebekah tried to calm her by stroking her disheveled black hair. But she pushed her hand away violently.

"Leave me alone, Rebekah. You have no idea what I have been through."

"Please, let me try and help. What happened? Did Mr. Seligman abuse you in some way?"

Rachel laughed sardonically. "No. I would never allow anyone to handle me without my consent. But I am sure he wouldn't have minded. For five years I worked for these people, cleaning and serving. I catered to Mrs. Seligman's every whim. Just who does she think she is? Are they better than me? After all they are Jews like me, not Episcopalians like the Astors. I love him and he used me. Oh, David, why didn't you stand up to them? Coward!"

Rebekah understood. She had suspected the affair between Rachel and her employer's son. She could not bring herself to comfort her friend, because it was a sin.

And although it upset her to see Rachel so distraught, she could not summon up any sympathy. After all, she had not thought of Leah when she was lying in the arms of her master's son. Aside from the occasional gift of candy or toys, she never really thought of the welfare of Leah.

"What will you do now?" she asked.

Rachel stared at her suitcase. Drawing in a short breath, she slowly turned to Rebekah. "I don't know, but I will never go back into service."

"Would you like me to ask Isaac if he can find you work at the factory?"

Rachel's face reddened, and her tone was hard. "You think that I could work in a factory?"

Rebekah's eyes flashed. "And why not? Doesn't your own daughter sew on sleeves and collars? You didn't want her to go to school and now she has no choice but to work in a sweatshop."

Rachel threw back her head and stared defiantly. "Leah is going to be a beauty one day. She does not need to waste her time in school. And I will find my way. I have heard of some ways to make big money. I have always underestimated myself and I realize now that I have a lot to offer. When the time is right, I will be able to help Leah, and perhaps then she will forgive me."

She picked up her suitcase, threw open the door and exited the apartment.

Turning back one last time, she said. "I will not keep the apartment. I guess you would not mind if Leah stayed with you permanently. Take good care of her and teach her never to trust men to fulfill their promises."

DORE

NEW YORK, 1902

When Dore arrived home from her new job as a cash girl at A.T. Stewart department store, Rebekah ran to meet her on the stoop. She asked her if she had seen Leah somewhere in the neighborhood.

"Yes, I saw her outside the delicatessen, and I told her to come home for dinner. She said that she would be home shortly. You know that she needs some time to run and play after sewing all day."

Rebekah sighed. "It's just as well; I need to talk to you, and I need your advice."

She explained what had happened to Rachel and asked Dore's advice on how to break the news gently to Leah.

"I will tell her," said Dore. I am closer to her. She thinks of me as her big sister.

It's not as if Rachel has had a big presence in her life. Every decision that she made for Leah reflected her own self-interest. Making her work in a sweatshop and denying her an education so that she could bring in a pittance. If I hadn't taken the time to teach her, she wouldn't even know how to read or write."

Leah ran up to the stoop, breathless and flushed. Rebekah asked her to sit down.

"Dore wants to talk over something with you dear. I am going up to finish dinner."

"You look nice Dore. I guess they didn't work you so hard today." Said the young girl.

"Appearances can be deceiving sweetheart. It was a long day. But before we go up, I need to tell you something."

Leah's face reddened, as if she was trying to remember if she had done something wrong. "Rebekah said that I could play with my friends and I didn't go very far. We were in the alley. That's why she couldn't see me."

Dore began to braid Leah's wild mane of black hair as she tried her best to think of a way to soften the shock of the news about Rachel. "Leah, your mother came by a little while ago."

Leah jumped up and opened the door to the building, but Dore took her hand and stopped her.

"No, Leah she has already gone. She wanted me to, well, to explain why she had to go away. She said that the Seligman's weren't paying a decent salary. Recently a houseguest from Chicago, a fine and wealthy lady, had secretly offered your mother a job as head housekeeper with a generous salary. They are a prominent Jewish family in their community and are known for their kindness and generosity."

The little girl's expression transformed from one of expectation to despair.

Large tears filled her large brown eyes and ran down her cheeks.

"Do you mean that Mama has already gone and left me behind?"

"Yes darling, I am afraid so. You see the lady from Chicago wanted her to accompany her on the train. She said that she needed her immediately and if she couldn't leave today, she would find a housekeeper in Chicago."

Inconsolable, Leah threw her arms around Dore and hid her face from the neighbors and friends in the street. She did not want them to hear her sobs, because although she was hurting, she was also proud.

Dore drew her closer and whispered. "I know that this is hard, but you are not alone. You still have a home with us, always. And I am sure that your mama will work hard and save her money so that she may come back to you soon."

Leah lifted her face and looked directly into Dore's eyes. "I wish I could believe that, but I don't. I will never see her again."

Dore's heart broke for Leah for she suspected that she spoke the truth. But she said nothing as she led her new little sister up the stairs into the Abramowitz's apartment.

Later that evening while undressing, Dore managed to have some rare minutes of privacy in the apartment's sole bedroom. She looked at herself in the mirror. Wearing only a sheer undergarment, she observed that her figure had filled out. The young sixteen-year-old woman who stared back at her from the mirror possessed a tall, lissome body. Her breasts were round and full, but her hips were too narrow. Unfortunately, she did not have the popular hourglass form that inspired the latest fashions, but she knew that fashions changed almost every year. Although she sometimes struggled with her long, curly hair, she now realized that it was one of her greatest attributes, the blond curls framed her face and complemented her blue eyes and aquiline features. Yes, she reflected, men might find her beautiful. But she had other things on her mind.

She had been working at A.T. Stewarts as a cash girl since leaving school, receiving a meager wage of two dollars a week. She might earn three-fifty if she managed to pick up extra hours, which she often did. The grueling work involved standing from eight in the morning until seven in the evening, climbing ladders and fetching items for the snooty salesgirls, who ranked only one row above her in the pyramid of the department store system. Yet they outranked her and never let her forget it. Her legs and feet ached every night. Sweet Leah would rub her calves and her feet with her small hands, which were numb from sewing all day.

The money helped since her father's sweatshops had not been very profitable in the past two years. Many factories had opened up in the area around Union Square, and young women preferred to work in the new buildings with their large windows and abundance of light, which made their labor easier as they could see what they were sewing. This meant that Isaac's business, which recruited home workers, had fallen off, and Dore's small salary helped to ensure that the family could afford to eat decently at least a few times a week. Since Leah worked in a neighbor's apartment during the day, Rebekah worked a few hours in a grocery store on Hester Street. So, the family got by, but they could not afford the luxuries of new clothes, books, or even meat more than once a week.

Later that evening when Isaac returned home, he gathered the family into the small area of the apartment that served as the living room. "I have news." He said.

The family had taken to speaking English more and more. Dore had insisted, saying that they would never rise up and climb the social ladder if they continued speaking in only Yiddish. Although everyone in the stores on Hester Street spoke it, one never heard it in the department stores and restaurants along Broadway. She noticed a stern expression on Isaac's face and understood that he had something important to say.

"You know that business is not going so good. It's going nowhere. All the girls and some of the men have gone to the factories."

"Yes, Papa. I have seen the young women going to work. They seem happy to be out in the daylight," said Dore.

"So good for them," said Isaac. "This is exactly the problem. I can't go on with the sweatshops. I need to make a change. So, I have a friend and this friend is called Simon Braverman. He's no greenhorn. He's worked his way up to supervisor at the Triangle Shirtwaist Factory, the big concern off of Washington Place."

"Do you think he can get you orders for piecework from some of your shops?" asked Rebekah.

"No, that's not it." He answered in a curt tone. "He is not just a floor supervisor. He is supervisor over the floor supervisors and he has a say in new hires. And he has promised me a job. Can you imagine that I am going to be a tailor again?"

Dore meekly interrupted. "Papa they don't use tailors in the factories.

"I know that girl. I will be what they call a cutter. I am in charge of cutting out the patterns. It's a shame for a man with my talent must do this to feed his family, but it pays ten dollars a day, steady salary.

And Braverman said that in time he might be able to promote me to floor supervisor."

"Papa, how wonderful!" said Dore. "Won't it be good not to be a sweater anymore?"

Yes, wonderful," said Isaac. But it's not so easy that I just snap my fingers and Simon gives me this job. He makes me a condition."

"What condition?" asked Rebekah.

"Well, you see, it's like this. This Braverman has a son. Meyer is his name, bright boy. Now, Simon is by no means a wealthy man, and he has a large family, not to mention two brothers waiting to be brought over from the old country. So, in a funny way they need our help."

Dore said, "Papa what are you saying? Will you please come to the point?"

"Just give me a minute here!" shouted Isaac, who searched for his words. "So you understand that Meyer can't pay for his school and a place to live. Because he will be in school for a long time, he can't support his brothers and sisters, or bring his uncles over. For the next four or six years he will need help. And Simon has asked me for help, for me to get the job as a cutter at the Triangle Shirtwaist Factory."

Dore blurted out, "How on earth can you help his son go to medical school?"

Rebekah began to cry as she grasped her husband's hand. "No, we cannot do this to Dore!"

"Do what to me?" she cried.

"Simon wants that you should marry his son."

"Marry!" Dore screamed. "Papa, I am sixteen. I have a job, and an eighth-grade diploma. I am not some ignorant bride from the old country who is looking for the price of passage from a husband she has never met."

"This I know," shouted Isaac. "But I also know that I cannot go on working as a sweater and that I need to support my family. If you marry Meyer, you will have a doctor for a husband. All they ask is that you help support him during the years of his studies. I will also contribute a small part of my salary to the Braverman's household."

Rebekah had calmed herself sufficiently to interrupt her husband. "Won't we be losing money with this proposition?"

"No!" Isaac rebuked his wife. "I told you that he has promised to promote me. He also suggested that he could find a place for Dore at the Triangle in the office, since she can read and write. So, you see how this helps everyone, especially you Dore, Mrs. Meyer Braverman, a doctor's wife."

Dore had never stood up to her father, even though she no longer felt the blind respect for him that she had as a child. Overcome with anger and confusion, she could not believe his willingness to sell her future and her happiness for a job at the Triangle.

She had heard of so-called "student marriages," and she had always found the very notion absurd. She knew a girl at work who supported her husband while he attended City College. She bragged to everyone that she would be leaving her job as a salesgirl when he obtained his law degree in a month. She promised to invite all her co-workers to tea as soon as she and her new husband were settled. However, Rose, one of the waitresses in the staff dining room, had seen the girl's husband at a Saturday night dance with a younger and more beautiful girl. Dore knew that this was no big surprise. Married students often dropped their wives for younger and more attractive girls, once they had obtained their degrees.

"Papa," she said with a voice trembling with emotion. "How can you ask me to do this? I have no desire to marry, and even if I did, I would like some say in my choice of husband."

She could see her father growing impatient. She knew that he did not see her as an educated and independent woman, but as a pawn to be used for his advancement. This realization only increased her anger and determination.

"If you do not marry Meyer Braverman, I will not get the job at the Triangle, and if I don't get this job, we will starve. The day of the sweater is over. I would think that you would be happy for me to make this step up. I am ashamed of you."

"But Papa," said Dore crying quietly, "I don't even know this boy.

Rebekah held her, trying to soothe her. Finally, Dore's tears stopped.

"Papa, I will do as you wish, but I will never work in a factory. I will stay at Stewarts, and I will work hard to become a salesgirl or perhaps someday even get a better job." Trying to put on a brave face, she smiled. "Maybe this Meyer is not so hideous, and he might be kind. I think that I would make a fine doctor's wife."

Isaac put on his coat and left the apartment, probably to give the news to Simon and celebrate with some schnapps.

Rebekah checked the bedroom where Leah had been sleeping, glad that she had not witnessed the argument between Dore and her father. Assured that the girl was fast asleep, she turned to Dore. "I do not want you to make this sacrifice. You are too young, and you need time to find a man that you love. You have told me that you understand about love, and what happens between a man and a woman. You should know that it isn't always pleasant, especially if you do not love your husband."

Suddenly it occurred to Dore that Rebekah had not loved her father when they married. He was a young widower with a good job as a tailor. But had she been in love with him? After all, the marriage was arranged. Had she learned to love him over the years? They did not have any other children, and they were not overly affectionate, not in front of her. She considered her own life, stretching out in front of her, years of sharing a bed with a man she might not love or even like. She would consider all of this after she met Meyer. For the time being, she would have to do what her father demanded.

The introductions took place three weeks later at a dinner given at the Braverman's residence, located in a new apartment building on the East Side. Its spacious separate dining room provided a more convenient venue for the occasion.

Mrs. Braverman, a stout woman with bulging eyes and thick lips, opened the door. Her husband, a wiry man with an unpleasant face, stood behind her. Three young girls, ranging from approximately six to nine years of age, sat quietly in the parlor, silently staring at their father, apparently afraid to encourage his anger. A young toddler, sitting slumped in a small chair, immediately evoked pity with her thin limbs and ashen skin.

A few minutes after the introductions were made, a young man of about twenty sauntered into the room. He did not offer his hand to anyone, but simply bowed as if acknowledging their presence was sufficient. He resembled his mother, with the same bulging eyes and thick lips. He had curly hair and thick eyebrows. Not the handsome hero that Dore had read about in novels, but then she had not really expected that. She could only wish that his character did not match his appearance. But the minute he opened his mouth, all hope dissipated. He turned to her and spoke in a high-pitched, nasal voice.

"So, my father tells me that you don't want to work at the Triangle. Pity. He says he can get you as much as five dollars a day if you can take steno and type."

She was about to speak, but he cut her off.

"But then your mother said that you don't even have those skills. Still you could learn. I know some missions where the social workers give free lessons."

Dore squared her shoulders and tried to answer in a calm and polite manner,

"No, Meyer, I am not interested in working at the Triangle. I have been told by my supervisor down at the store that they are seriously considering promoting me to salesgirl in a few months. I believe the beginning salary is six dollars and after a year, there is the possibility of earning a commission on items sold."

Meyer answered dismissively. "Well, it's fine with me. I just think that my dad has some influence down at the factory, and it might help in the long run."

Dore tried to control her frustration and her tone when she responded to Meyer.

"I have no desire to work in a factory. Furthermore, I have heard dreadful things about the way girls are treated there. It's been said that they are verbally abused by their bosses and are made to work all hours. I prefer to work in a place of beauty. Besides, I am of an artistic nature. I love to draw, arrange flowers, and I know that I have a flare for the latest fashions. I do not see myself spending my days sitting in a long row of sewing machines, making the same shirtwaist over and over again.

"I will not dictate to you where you must work," said Meyer. "And if you can bring in more money, that's even better. But it is essential that you and your father contribute to our living expenses and my tuition while I study. Of course, I do require that you be a good and considerate wife."

Simon interjected. "Of course, she will be a wonderful and obedient wife. Mind you, we are not looking for grandchildren in the near future. We have a family friend who will advise you on that matter. You and Meyer will have a private room that we will fix up in the back of the house. It's big enough. I have been using it for storage, but it will do nicely.

Meyer interrupted his father. "Of course, I will need to study during the evenings, so you will be spending most of your time in the parlor. You can help Mama with the little ones. She is always so exhausted and since we will not have our own children right away, you will have the time."

Mrs. Braverman spoke up, her voice abrasive and loud, her speech still slightly accented, revealing her family's Russian origin. "The wedding will be in August before Meyer starts his medical school. I will see to the arrangements. We will not bother you with these things, Rebekah. Of course, the ceremony will take place in our schul. We have joined the Reform Temple, so the ceremony, and the dinner, will be mixed."

Dore noticed that her father's face had grown quite red and that he seemed to be restraining himself from protesting. But she knew that, considering that he did not have to pay for the wedding and the aid that Simon was providing with his new job, he had to remain silent. It must have been difficult for a man like her father, a devout Jew, who studied Torah and attended schul every Sabbath, to see his daughter's marriage celebrated with a mixed reception. If he only knew how much she had enjoyed dancing with boys, the rare times that she had had the opportunity. Rebekah said nothing, but Dore knew that she must be disappointed not to have any say in the planning of the wedding.

Dore married Meyer Braverman in August of 1902. She had just turned seventeen. The ceremony, held at Temple Emanu-El on Fifth Avenue, seemed cursory, lacking many of the traditional prayers that Isaac and Rebekah deemed essential. Simon had dared to suggest that Isaac might cut his payots and trim his beard for the occasion, but to no avail. He did accept the handsome black suit Meyer offered. Rebekah wore a stylish gown and fixed her hair in a stylish coiffure worthy of a Gibson girl. Dore's modest, but stylish, wedding gown was presented to her by her friends at A.T. Stewart's department store. She did her very best to portray the shy, happy bride. She smiled at Meyer and the rabbi when he congratulated them after the breaking of the glass. She even held Meyer's hand at the table and looked into his eyes when they danced.

Later that night after an awkward attempt at lovemaking, she hugged herself as she lay on the single bed. Cold and aching, she felt disgusted by what had just transpired. Meyer seemed to have attained some satisfaction after brutally penetrating her. He had not even kissed or caressed her. All she felt was pain and embarrassment.

Fortunately, he had turned away and told her to go to sleep on the other bed. She realized that she had entered into a true student marriage, a business arrangement. She made up her mind that she would treat it as such and that like all business arrangements, each party must profit, or the deal was off.

FLORA AND BERNADINE

NEWPORT, RHODE ISLAND, AUGUST 1902

The late afternoon sun cast long shadows on the courtyard in front of Belcourt, where Flora and Ned awaited their turn to greet Alva and Oliver Belmont. Bernadine descended from her carriage and Ned offered her his hand, escorting her to the front of the reception line. Oliver Belmont had built the "summer cottage" before he married the gregarious Alva after her divorce from Vanderbilt. She had since made what she considered to be necessary alterations to the mansion.

Mae suddenly appeared, running toward Bernadine, and then hugging her tightly.

"I haven't seen you in ages," said the young girl. Mae appeared older than eight, tall and slender, she possessed an unusual calm demeanor. No longer the impish child that Bernadine had seen in Paris, she emanated an air of intelligence. She distanced herself from the girls and boys her own age and gravitated toward any adult who was willing to engage in serious discussion.

"I can't believe how you have grown," said Bernadine. I haven't seen you in months. Where have you been keeping yourself?"

“I have been at school,” said Mae. “I am at Horace Mann. They have placed me with older children, three years ahead of my age.”

Bernadine noticed a flash of annoyance on Ned’s face at Mae’s bragging, but did not react. Dazzled by the enormous house, with its slate mansard–style roof, she greeted Alva and Oliver and asked Flora if she could accompany her on a quick tour. Built with brick and granite, the architect had placed an inordinate number of dormer windows, not exactly the fashion at Newport. Because Oliver Belmont greatly admired the Renaissance, certain conventions had been overlooked. Belmont adored horses and the livery that went along with them. The entire first floor of the home had originally been composed of carriage space and stables for prize horses. But Alva had recently converted this area into a large banquet hall. She made some concessions, allowing the grand foyer to retain its Renaissance style, and not remodeling several rooms of Gothic design, which featured huge stained-glass windows emblazoned with Belmont’s newly created coat of arms. The house boasted a grand hall on the ground floor, draped in blood-red damask, and an additional grand hall on the second floor. A grand stairway, an exact replica of the one in the Musée de Cluny, connected the two. Myriads of smaller formal parlors opened onto one another, each decorated in varying periods of French décor.

After touring the house, Bernadine and Flora hurried to one of the lawns to watch Mae take part in an archery competition, but they could not find her.

“I am afraid that Mae does not enjoy the usual activities for girls her age,” said Flora. “I must say that she is quite a good archer, but she just doesn’t enjoy competing.

Next year I wanted to enroll her in cotillion classes, but that's most likely a losing battle."

They walked back into the house, strolling from room to room, admiring the tapestries and the detailed plasterwork on the ceilings. They suddenly practically collided with Alva Belmont.

"Flora, you will be happy to know that I just received a long letter from Consuelo. She refuses to bring my grandsons for a visit," said the portly, but still attractive woman.

"I suppose she still blames me forcing her into the marriage with her Lord."

Flora smiled and glanced at Bernadine. She wanted to be sympathetic because she had grown to care for Alva in recent years. She looked on her as a wise aunt. Yet she knew, as everyone in New York Society did, that Consuelo had been utterly miserable when Alva forced her into a loveless marriage with Charles Spencer-Churchill. She had known Consuelo well since they were young girls, and her friend had shared her confidence regarding her secret engagement to Winthrop Rutherford. Her heart broke for Consuelo when Alva broke it up.

Alva's severity with Consuelo now seemed quite hypocritical. For she, herself, had divorced William Vanderbilt only months after her daughter's marriage and then had married Oliver the following year.

Flora embraced the older woman, feeling truly sorry for her. "I received a letter from her a few weeks ago," she said. "She seems happy, and is doing such good work for the tenants on Charles' estate. She says he hardly knows what to make of her. She is a great success in English Society, and is considered to be one of the greatest beauties in London."

This seemed to console Alva, and she smiled sweetly at Flora.

Flora kept to herself the balance of the letter, in which Consuelo recounted a love affair that she had entered into with Charles' cousin.

Bernadine had not yet moved to New York at the time of Consuelo's forced marriage. She had never even met her. But from what she had learned from the gossip at society teas and ladies' luncheons, she felt compassion for the young beauty in her unhappy marriage. Was she not, after all, in a similar situation? No, she must be honest with herself, she thought. No one had forced her to marry Theo. Quite the contrary, her late father had made his objections clear. She realized that she had only herself to blame.

Alva called for the housekeeper, who showed the two women to their rooms. She accompanied them to the third floor. Their rooms were located in the same wing. The Dodd's had a large, airy room, which would enjoy the beautiful morning sunlight. Down the hall, Bernadine had a smaller room since she had come on her own. Theo had made the usual feeble excuses about business meetings he could not miss. By this time, few people believed his claim to be in business. Looking out the window of her small, but pleasant room, she saw couples strolling on the lawn. Beyond that she could just glimpse the sea. The effect made her melancholy, wishing she had someone with whom to share the loveliness of the view and the peaceful moment.

The voice of the housekeeper disrupted her reverie. "Ma'am, drinks will be served in the grand hall at seven, and dinner is at eight in the dining room."

When Ned returned to the room around six, he did not try to hide his bad humor.

Mae had argued with some of the children regarding the name of a species of butterfly or insect. It had turned nasty and several of the little girls were in tears. The boys mocked her, which only served to anger her further. He was concerned about his daughter. She did not fit in with children her own age and preferred the company of adults. Her teachers had spoken of this to Flora, but she had brushed it off. But Ned had had enough.

He entered the room in a huff.

"This is the limit, Flora. I don't know what you were thinking putting Mae in that school. It's much too progressive and allows the children too much freedom. Look here, I am as modern as the next man, but I do not want to see our daughter grow up to be a social outcast."

Flora was torn. She wanted Mae to fit in and to have friends. But her daughter did not fit in due to her intellect and her curiosity. She preferred learning about chemistry to playing dress-up or gossiping with girls her age. She took great pleasure in going to the Museum of Natural Science and learning about the planets. Tea at the Palm Court held no charm for her. She had tried to introduce her to her friends' daughters, but they never called for a second visit. More and more, she wondered if Ned still doubted that she belonged to him. After all they looked nothing alike, and Mae's temperament was foreign to both parents.

She tried to reason with her husband. "Ned, there is nothing to be done. What is your solution? She is an unusual girl and would not be happy in one of those fashionable girls' schools. You see how she is with other children."

Ned became even more agitated. "Well, you are her mother," he shouted. "Your only responsibility is to see to her upbringing and education. I am much too busy in the firm to deal with her. Perhaps you can look into finding a governess and some tutors?"

"I will see if I can find a suitable tutor. Perhaps one of her teachers can recommend a few. She is quite advanced in her studies of math and science, so we will need to find someone knowledgeable."

"Well, do that. But I'm not sure a girl should waste her time studying science. Just handle it. I don't ask much of you."

Ned was usually kind and understanding and his tone of voice jolted her. Moreover, she had been looking for the right time to tell him the happy news. After years of trying, she was three months' pregnant. She knew that he would be thrilled, but now she had mixed feelings. She decided to wait to tell him. Perhaps tomorrow he would be in better spirits.

The Dodd's descended into the grandeur of Belcourt's grand hall by the long and elegant staircase. Pure silk damask and paintings by Legros and Boucher covered the walls, and in the grand hall, paneling and intricately carved oak adorned the ceilings. Electric lights blazed from imported French chandeliers that dated back hundreds of years. The Belmonts, like their wealthy neighbors, decorated their summer cottages with furniture, tapestries, doors, and entire rooms, imported from European chateaux and mansions. The glaring difference between Oliver Belmont and the rest of the Newport Society was in the location and orientation of his home. While all the other cottages of Newport shone like jewels on a necklace along Bellevue Avenue, Oliver chose to face Ledge Road. In this manner he turned his back both on the nouveaux riches that he despised and the denizens of the mansions in New York, who snubbed his wife for having divorced William Vanderbilt.

Alva and Oliver greeted their nonresident guests who had driven over from their cottages on Bellevue Avenue. Flora marveled at Alva, who had moved so seamlessly from one man to another. In less than a year, she had married a man even wealthier than her former philandering husband. She remembered seeing Alva cozying up to Oliver in his box at the Coaching Club Parade, and that was months before her divorce. Perhaps they had already started an affair. But whatever the case, she had been the first woman in such a high position in society to file for divorce. Things were changing in New York, albeit slowly.

Walking over to speak with her hosts, Flora noticed that they were in deep conversation with Elizabeth and Harry Lehr. Harry was considered to be the biggest dandy in New York. Everyone knew that he had married Elizabeth for her money, even though any man would be happy to possess a beauty like her, even if she didn't have a dime. Harry and Oliver conversed animatedly, reminiscing about the automobile parade held on the lawn of Belcourt in 1899. The event had been America's first sports car demonstration, a race that ran through a course set up with dummy traffic police and nursemaids.

"I'll never forget that roadster that Tessie Oelrich was driving," said Harry, laughing sarcastically. "Do you remember the stuffed doves she had in the back, Oliver?"

"Who could forget that?" said Oliver. "All these women who have taken to driving alarm me. Do you realize that there have been three women killed in automobile accidents this summer?"

"Isn't it horrifying?" interjected Alva. "Poor Mamie Stuvesant Fish ran over a servant three times when she was learning to drive. I expect my new bubble to be delivered any day. It's being shipped from London. I am also having a chauffeur brought over. Consuelo is sending me one of her former employees. I do hope he can learn to drive in New York."

Flora looked at Ned. “Do you think that I could learn to drive and have my own ‘bubble’ soon?” She smiled at Alva, who had coined the term ‘bubble’ to refer to automobiles.

Ned was taken aback. “I don’t think that you need worry about driving all over town. I have my car, and I am more than willing to let you have it along with Frank anytime you wish.”

“Don’t be alarmed, Ned. I was not serious. What would I need a car for? We have a perfectly lovely Victoria for my shopping, and the old Gran Daumont is much more suitable for our evenings out than your automobile. My coiffure is destroyed each time I ride in that contraption.”

Ned spoke gruffly. “Well, if you do want to use the car, you only have to ask.

Frank will run you down to Broadway anytime as long as I don’t need it.”

At that moment, everyone’s gaze shifted toward the staircase, as Bernadine descended, her head held high. She suspected that some of the guests might know the truth about Theo’s character. She did her best to seem gay and unaffected by her unhappy marriage. Above all, she would not give them the satisfaction of seeing her suffer. Even with all the beautiful women at the party, especially Elizabeth Lehr, she could feel the gaze of men on her. As she had dressed earlier, she chose the most daring gown that she had packed. Perhaps the time had come that she should meet some men, if only for some innocent diversion. And if something more serious came along, well, then she would deal with that too.

She wore a rose- colored dress, cut to show off her lissome figure. She knew her best assets, and tonight she wanted them to be noticed.

She had lost none of her youthful appearance, and because she had borne no children, her waist was as tiny as that of a girl of sixteen. She had piled her dark brown hair into the alluring Gibson style, but a few wisps escaped and touched her beautiful forehead. Her skin tanned by the hours she had spent outdoors during the summer accentuated her piercing blue eyes.

A young man of twenty-five, tall and well-built, stared at her from across the room. He had curly blond hair, a chiseled jaw and emerald green eyes. He quickly crossed the room, approached Alva and asked if he might speak with her.

"Mrs. Belmont, I would like to thank you again for including me in this evening's society. Might I ask you for an introduction to one of your beautiful young guests?"

Alva smiled. She loved the company of young men and she thought that Bernadine would enjoy the company of Eliot Havemeyer, who as far as she knew, had no serious romantic attachment at present.

"I assume that you are referring to Mrs. Theo Van Wies."

Eliot's face took on a despondent aspect on hearing the name Theo Van Wies.

Alva continued enthusiastically. "It seems that you are in luck, Eliot. Not only is she here for the entire week *sans mari*, I have seated you next to her at dinner. I do not have to tell you that planning the seating for this evening has been a monumental puzzle. First of all, there is the surplus of single men. And then there is the bother over what to do with Mrs. Ogden Goelet."

Eliot smiled congenially but paid little attention to Alva's gossip and travails.

Fascinated by the young beauty who slowly crossed the room toward them, he pretended to listen to his hostess's prattle.

"You know, I never thought that she would actually accept my invitation, knowing that Mrs. Stuyvesant Fish would attend." She continued, seemingly somehow pleased with the impending scandal. "The two had a terrible row over a Russian Duke last summer. Apparently, Mamie Stuyvesant refused to have Jimmy Cutting to her ball, and therefore, Mrs. Goelet refused to attend and bring along her houseguest, the Russian Duke. Well, this was an absolute disaster, as the Stuyvesant ball was being thrown in honor of the Duke. So naturally, I have seated Mrs. Goelet and Jimmy at the opposite end of the table from Mamie. Oh, here is Mrs. Van Wies."

"Good evening, Alva," said Bernadine trying not to stare at the handsome young man standing beside her.

"Good evening, Bernadine. May I introduce you to Eliot Havemeyer? His father has done quite a bit of business with Oliver in the past and I have known him since he was a boy. Eliot, Mrs. Theo Van Wies."

"Please call me Bernadine."

"With great pleasure," said Eliot.

"Oh, I see that Azar is about to announce that dinner is served. Eliot would you escort Bernadine?"

Presently, a tall, dark man wearing an elaborate golden costume and a fez walked into the hall to announce dinner. Bernadine turned to a stunned Eliot. "I see that you don't know Azar. He is the majordomo. Apparently, he is Egyptian. He has been with Oliver for years. Isn't he divine?"

At the table, the conversation turned around the various activities planned for the week: a tennis tournament on Wednesday and an archery competition that was to run until Friday.

"Are you entered into any of the sporting competitions, Bernadine?" asked Eliot.

"I am entered in the ladies' archery contest. I used to be quite competent as a girl. I don't like to boast, but I won the Galveston Archery Club's medal two years in a row."

Eliot smiled. "Somehow it doesn't surprise me. I am sure that you are a woman of many talents."

"Mr. Havemeyer, please do not think that I am susceptible to compliments.

"I thought we agreed that we were to call each other by our Christian names," said Eliot.

"Yes, that is true," said Bernadine. "But I expect you to be a gentleman and be completely honest with me."

Eliot smiled and apologized. "I truly regret underestimating you. It's just that most young women of your set seem to require, how shall I put it, a certain boost to their fragile egos."

Bernadine laughed. "Well, in me you have found the exception. If you tell me what you really think, we will get along much better."

"Bernadine, since my greatest desire is to know you and your deepest feelings, I will, from this point on, be completely open and honest with you. Let me begin by telling you that I have known Theo since we were boys."

She felt her face warm with shame and anger. She had hoped to make this week a respite from Theo.

"I can see that any discussion of your husband is distressing to you, and I apologize for bringing it up," said Eliot. "But as we are to be honest with one another, I feel that I should let you know that I am not ignorant of the suffering that you must endure."

"In that case, I thank you for your frankness."

"I will not elaborate too much. I can only relate what I know first-hand from my dealings with him. We were at Groton together. He was an upperclassman, a senior, and I was a freshman. Several of my classmates complained of his cruelty. Some said they had been physically abused as well as intimidated and threatened in other ways. I kept my distance and he left me alone because our families knew each other. After he graduated, I never saw him. However, he is a member of my club, The Metropolitan.

I have seen him on occasion, but I still keep my distance. Now that I think about it, it's been over a year since I have seen him there."

"How odd," said Bernadine, "for he claims to spend most of his evenings there."

Eliot looked away, regretting that he had hurt her by revealing the truth.

"There is much more that I could tell you, but it is second-hand information and I would not want to repeat any exaggerations or lies."

"I already know what he is capable of. I would rather that we put him out of our minds. I want to try to enjoy this week as much as possible."

Looking directly into her eyes, he asked her boldly, "May I serve as a diversion. I will do my best to make this week pleasurable and diverting. Shall we start with a walk in the garden after dinner?"

They walked in a small rose garden under the stars. They could hear the waves of the ocean that bounded the Belmonts' property. And even though she had cut off the discussion of Theo at the dinner table, she now felt that she needed to know what Eliot knew about her husband's behavior.

They sat on a bench in a secluded part of the garden. "Eliot, I need to know the truth about Theo. Someday it may be useful to me, that is if I am ever in a situation to leave him."

Eliot tried hard not to show his satisfaction at the possibility of her being a free woman. He did venture to take her hand. He could feel that she was tense, so he did not put his arm around her as he had planned.

"I do not want to hurt or shock you, so please stop me if I say too much."

"Eliot," she said calmly. "I doubt there is much that you can say that will come as a surprise to me. I have been married to the man for five years."

"Well, I am not sure about that," he said. "I have seen him at Sherry's with girls, who are what we call 'professionals'. They were asked to leave by the management. But in the past several years, he has been more discreet in his activities. Perhaps he has tired of the usual resorts. But more likely, he has discovered more exotic and forbidden paramours. I was told that he narrowly escaped a raid by Roosevelt's vice police on a brothel known to offer up little boys and girls. Now, I would like to say that I have been misinformed, but my source on this is infallible."

Bernadine hands tingled with shock. She began to tremble. "I knew that he was capable of such degeneracy, but it is horrible to have confirmation." She began to cry softly. "I bear some responsibility. I should have left him, exposed him. But I was afraid, and you see we have an agreement."

Eliot hesitated, trying to comprehend her meaning? "Agreement, what kind of agreement?"

"On our wedding night .... No, I cannot talk about it. Please let that remain buried in my soul forever."

Eliot said nothing, but he could imagine how Van Wies must have abused his young bride. "I will not press you, but I can imagine."

Brushing way her tears, she continued. "The next morning, I wanted to leave, but he had me trapped. He revealed his true predilections and character, saying that he didn't love me and that he had married me only for my money. I tried to leave, but he had thought of everything, including a honeymoon to Europe that lasted months. I was too ashamed to tell my father the truth and Theo knew it."

"But what is this agreement?" he insisted.

"He promised never to touch me again, if I would keep up appearances and live as his wife. Of course, we have separate bedrooms. Mine is on the other side of the house from his. I insisted that he be as discreet as possible. He said that I might live my life as a young woman of New York High Society, travelling whenever I liked, seeing whomever I liked. His only condition was that I do nothing to embarrass him or his family. Isn't life absurd?"

Eliot could not help himself. He put his arms around her and held her, kissing her forehead and stroking her hair. Then he kissed her first gently, but she responded ardently, pressing her lips hard to his. At first, he thought that he had gone too far, but she responded by parting her lips and allowing him to run his tongue over her teeth.

Suddenly she pulled away. "I think we had better get a hold of ourselves, before someone notices." She caught her breath as she fixed her hair and straightened her dress.

"I am sorry if I was out of line. Believe me, I mean no disrespect. I admire you and my feelings got the better of me. You are just so lovely, and so brave."

"Don't misunderstand me, Eliot. I don't regret what just happened. I quite enjoyed it. You may not believe it, but in a way, that was the first pure, loving kiss that I have ever experienced."

"I do believe it and I hope that it will not be the last—I mean our last kiss. Could I see you tomorrow?"

The next morning Bernadine awoke to a cool breeze coming through her open window. She felt lightness in her arms and legs, her heart raced with expectation.

She experienced a sensation of pure joy. She and Eliot planned to meet after breakfast, but first she had to withdraw her name from the archery completion in order to free up her days to be with Eliot. They had agreed to be discreet, but she did not care if gossip did reach the ears of Theo or his family. In fact, it would give her great satisfaction for the news to reach Clara that she had a young and handsome admirer. Her sister-in-law had few beaux and was thought of as being on the verge of spinsterhood. She often wondered why no men called on her. She suspected that because of Theo's reputation, men whom she found acceptable wanted nothing to do with the family.

After breakfasting in her room, Bernadine joined a group of ladies in the morning room. Flora chatted gaily with the lovely Mrs. William Leeds; whose husband belonged to the set of nouveaux riches who were buying cottages in Newport. It surprised Bernadine that they had been invited. But Alva had invited them to stay while they were looking for a cottage to buy for next summer. Bernadine was pleased to see how Alva flouted the strict social conventions that she once upheld. However, kindness was not her only motive for having the Leeds as guests. These people would soon lead the business world, and she wanted Oliver to have the most advantageous financial contacts.

Flora and Bernadine left the crowd in the morning room and walked outside.

"Bernadine you looked radiant last night. Wherever did you find that gown? I have seen nothing like it," she said.

"It's funny that you should ask. Worth is now selling patterns in New York. So, I had it made up here. I have been giving it much thought, and I have decided that I am going to start shopping in the haute couture boutique at Wanamaker's. Of course, I won't get my gowns there, but I will buy shirtwaists and other casual clothes."

"What a wonderful idea. It is a good thing to give business to American dressmakers, especially since so many are manufactured right here in New York. I may just do the same."

"Yes," said Bernadine. "We can make the rounds when the new lines come out in September."

Flora smiled slyly. "By the way, I looked all over for you last night. I saw you were seated next to Eliot Havemeyer at dinner. He is divine and he is from a fine family, big real estate agents and developers."

"Divine is the word," said Bernadine. We didn't talk much about his family or his line of business."

"I can just imagine," replied Flora. "Well, you are entitled to a little flirtation and fun. Believe me, people vacationing in Newport are too wrapped up in their own intrigues to gossip about others. There is a sort of code to let things slide. Of course, you cannot let things go too far."

Bernadine smiled, and ignored Flora's last comment. "Perhaps he can help us find a brownstone to rent. I cannot bear another year living with the Van Wies clan. If I have my own home, I can arrange things so that Theo's room is on another floor and I won't have to hear him coming in at night. I still have five more years before I come into my money and then I can buy my own brownstone."

"When the time comes, perhaps you might buy in our building," said Flora. "By the way, shouldn't you be getting ready for your archery competition?"

Bernadine looked around to see if anyone could overhear her. "I have withdrawn.

I am meeting Eliot at the Newport Yacht Club. He has invited me to spend this afternoon on his parents' yacht."

"You're going alone with him?"

"I am not sure what the plan is, "answered Bernadine. "I am to meet him in front of the club in an hour. I must fly. I have got to change. I can't imagine what I will find to wear. I did not plan on going yachting when I was packing."

Flora watched her friend, who was flushed with excitement, exiting the morning room, weaving deftly through the grouping of guests and furniture. Haunted by the memory of her own transgression in Chicago, she felt shame for her own actions, and at the same time satisfaction for her friend who had the right to some happiness and passion.

But her thoughts quickly shifted to her own future happiness with Ned. She wanted to speak to him alone, but she saw him, through the large windows of the great hall, in front of the house, surrounded by a large group of men. They all talk loudly and boisterously, admiring the collection of Oliver's cars that had been brought out and put on display on the front lawn. Ned seemed captivated by a beautiful, shining black machine and touched its doors and hood with his gloved hand. She decided that, given his high spirits, she should seize the opportunity to tell him her happy news. She walked over, kissed Ned tenderly on the cheek, and asked if she might have a word. They strolled over to the back of Belcourt.

"Are you all right, my dear?"

"I felt a need to have the cool sea breeze on my face," she said timidly. "In all honesty, I am feeling quite weak, and I had a dizzy spell this morning while I was dressing."

The distress and concern on Ned's face put Flora at ease. For she knew that no matter what, he still loved her.

"Shall I ask Alva or one of the staff to call a physician?" he asked. Flora usually enjoyed good health, and when ill, she rarely complained.

"I have already consulted a doctor. Two weeks ago, I went to see Dr. Carlson. I have wanted to tell you about it for all this time, but I couldn't find the right moment. You have been so busy at the firm and last night you were very short with me about Mae."

Ned grew pale, visibly panicked, and his mouth was drawn into a tight line.

"What did Carlson say? Did he perform any tests?"

Flora smiled and took Ned's hand. "He examined me and found that I am going to have a child."

Ned wrapped his arms around Flora and breathed a large sigh of relief and joy.

Fortunately, no one saw his reaction, for he jumped up like a little boy who had just won a prize. He kissed and hugged her.

"I never thought it would happen, not after so many disappointments. I have always wanted a brother for Mae. She will be so happy. I am so happy, my dear. How far along are you?"

Flora smiled, "I am three months along. Dr. Carlson said that means there is very little chance of losing this one. But, Ned, you know I cannot guarantee the sex of the child. We may be giving Mae a little sister. Would you be happy if that were the outcome?"

"Of course, my darling," he said. But in truth he was hoping for a son.

Flora now hoped that whatever doubts and resentment he felt toward her would subside. She hoped that he would be more flexible concerning Mae's education and more understanding of her independent nature.

Bernadine had decided to wear a simple shirtwaist with a minimum of lace, which she paired with a navy skirt that was the latest fashion. It cinched the waist, and with the aid of the new style of Swanbill corset, produced the fashionable "S" silhouette prized by the modern Gibson girl. Bernadine had bought three of these skirts, in black, brown, and navy. But she had never actually worn a shirtwaist before, since many considered it to be a lower-middle-class fashion. But today she considered it appropriate attire for yachting, and besides, she saw many young women in Newport had started wearing them.

She would wear a pair of sensible shoes with low heels and of course a hat. She had bought a wide-brimmed straw hat, adorned with white ribbons and flowers, which she now placed on her head, pinning it carefully into her beautiful, thick hair.

She looked at the clock on the dresser and quickly picked up her parasol and descended the staircase and practically ran out of the front door. The Belmonts provided carriages, which were lined up in front of the house, to spirit the guests to the beach and various clubs frequented by Newport Society. She quickly climbed into a light phaeton and directed the driver to take her to the Yacht Club.

For a moment she felt that she might lose her resolve and ask the driver to turn around, but she then she saw Eliot, strikingly handsome in a white suit with a crisp white collar. He saw her carriage draw up to the club and ran over to help her down. When he took her hand, she knew that she would have no regrets for coming. He guided her over to the docks.

"How do you feel about taking a short cruise?" he said, leading her to a small dock."

"I would love to," she said. "Do you own a yacht?"

"My parents do," he said. "I haven't quite made my mark in real estate to afford one myself. But it is a goal. I don't want to go on depending on my parents to enjoy the luxuries in life."

They walked toward a secondary dock, where a small, but solid boat awaited them. "This is the tender. It will take us out to the Silent Siren."

As they boarded the yacht, and entered a large salon, she asked Eliot why the boat was named the Silent Siren.

"My father named it in honor of my mother. You have not met her. She is a lovely woman, but she is extremely shy and reserved, a trait that many admire in her."

"I would love to meet her." She said noticing that there were no other passengers to be seen. "Will she be joining us for luncheon?"

Eliot stopped and looked at her with a cryptic expression, examining her face as if trying to gage what she was feeling. "My parents are not in Newport. They have gone to Europe for the summer. So, I must be honest. There will be no one on the boat but us, and of course the crew, the very discreet crew, who are well-paid and have been with the family for years."

"I quite understand," said Bernadine. "I suppose that you expect me to protest and make a scene. Do you want me to be indignant and tell you to go to the devil?" She could not contain herself. She began to laugh until tears came, filling her eyes.

Relieved, Eliot began laughing with relief. "Honestly, I didn't know how you would react. All I know is that from the moment that I saw you coming down the staircase at Belcourt, I have loved you. I know that must sound absurd and perhaps you think that this is a ploy that I use with women with regularity. I assure you that nothing could be further from the truth."

"I don't doubt that you believe that you love me. And I must admit that I have great affection for you. I am not sure if I can say that it is love. I have been reckless with my emotions and that is how I ended up married to Theo. But I sense that you are different and somehow I don't think that I would be here if I didn't trust you."

His look of compassion and tenderness warmed her heart and her body. She let herself relax, taking in the smell of the sea and the fine leather furnishings of the room.

Sheltered from the bright sun and the prying eyes of other New York gossips, she took off her gloves and relaxed onto a comfortable sofa.

Thompson, who was Eliot's personal valet, had served a cold lunch laid out on a table in the adjoining dining room. He entered the room briefly to announce that luncheon was served.

"Thompson has been with the family since I was a boy. He is discretion incarnate," said Eliot.

"Thank you for reassuring me. I do care about my reputation, but perhaps not for the reasons you may think. It's important to me to stay above the fray of gossip, precisely because I don't want people to think that I have been influenced or perverted by my husband. It is also, as I told you, part of our agreement. As long as I have to stay in this marriage, I want him to keep his promise to never touch me again."

He sat down beside her on the sofa, and she removed her hat. As she loosened her hairpin, her hair came loose and tumbled down around her shoulders. "Oh, that wind really had its way with my hair. I must look like a wild woman."

Eliot touched her hair. "Yes, you are wild. You are wild and beautiful, and I don't think that I am very hungry. Would you mind if we waited for our luncheon?"

He put his arm around her waist and guided her through a hallway that opened to a large suite. A beautiful sitting room, covered with blue velvet and lavender silk, lead to a bedroom. He picked her up and carried her to the bed, kissing her slowly to see how she would respond. The ardor of her response surprised and thrilled him. He set her down on the end of the bed. Throwing off the bedspread, he tore at his clothes, taking off his tie and undoing his high collar. He sat next to her and began to unbutton her blouse, taking care not to tear the lace. She laughed, excusing herself and entered a small dressing room and slowly unbuttoned her shirtwaist, and skirt. She frantically unlaced her corset and returned to the bedroom, wearing nothing but a thin chemise.

She stretched out next to him on the bed and she lightly caressed his naked chest, moving her hands over the lean muscles of his arms. He took her hands, kissed them and then moved on to her face and then her lips. She opened her mouth, welcoming his tongue and responded with hers. He paused, slowly helping her remove her delicate chemise, and his body reacted to the vision of her magnificent body. He tenderly traced her breasts with his hands and then with his mouth.

Bernadine moaned with pleasure. For a moment, remembering her night with Theo, she feared that she might feel pain when he entered her. But she felt only pleasure, sensual and liquid, sometimes slightly savage, but mostly tender. Her craving grew as he moved in her, until her body pulsed and contracted, and she could not help but cry out as she experienced orgasm for the first time. Her cries intensified Eliot's desire and as he moaned loudly as he climaxed, falling exhausted into her arms.

Exhausted, the spent the next hour dozing, only to wake and make love again.

At two in the afternoon, they dressed and went into the salon to eat the cold meats and fish that Thompson had left on the table.

"You are very fortunate in your parents' choice of servants," she joked. "I wonder, Eliot, if he is accustomed to this sort of activity?"

Eliot protested. "He certainly is not. I have had my share of lovers, but they were not women of our set. I do as most young men do. I go down to The Village, or I find a high-class professional girl. I am afraid that Thompson might disapprove of our meeting here today, but he is very loyal, especially to me."

"Tell me, Eliot," she said, suddenly turning serious. "Have you ever been in love with any of these women, I mean one of the high-class professionals or perhaps a Bohemian girl from The Village?"

He remained quiet for a moment. "Once I thought I was in love, with a beautiful Jewish girl, who had literary ambitions. But she threw me over for a poet, and an anarchist at that. But what I feel for you is different. Even though we have just met, I know what I am feeling is real."

Bernadine's mood abruptly changed. She appeared angry with herself. "I was such a fool when I thought that I was in love with Theo. But I was only sixteen, and I had no idea what I was feeling. But even then, I had doubts. What have I done to my life? I have been foolish and weak."

"Don't be so hard on yourself. You are young and you have the rest of your life. We have the rest of our lives. Leave him!"

Bernadine turned her face away. "Eliot, I wanted to leave him. But there were reasons, financial mainly, that stopped me from asking for a divorce. His family is still very powerful, and they can do much to ruin my reputation."

"But I cannot bear the idea of you living in the same house with him. It's intolerable!"

"Perhaps something might be worked out. If you could help me find an affordable apartment, I could live on my own. I could ask for a separation, not a divorce. You see a divorce would involve a scandal. First, I would have to find grounds, and that would mean publicly exposing Theo's degeneracy. I know that people guess at what his vices may be. But if I file for divorce, it would be public, so humiliating."

Eliot kissed her tenderly. "Well, I won't push you. But please tell me that we can go on seeing each other."

"Of course, we can, and we will! I count on you and Thompson for your continued discretion. We must be careful."

"Darling, I will find ways for us to meet. You do realize that I am in real estate and that I have access to many empty houses and apartments. There is no end to the possibilities."

FLORA AND BERNADINE

NEW YORK, OCTOBER 1902

Bernadine stepped down from the hansom cab delivering her to The Dakota. She had taken precautions to schedule her visit when Ned would not be at home. She could never quite get used to the cold wind that blew up the large New York avenues. Her gloves never seemed to keep her hands warm, and her cheeks flushed and her eyes watered. She had a terrible secret, once that be shared with the only person in New York who she could trust.

The maid knocked on Flora's bedroom door and announced Mrs. Van Wies. When she entered, she saw her friend had not quite finished dressing.

"I'm sorry, Bernadine," she said while taking great care to put the finishing touches to her hair. "My maid has not yet mastered the art of the new coiffeur. How I hate trying to keep up with this new fashion. I wish Mr. Gibson had never created his images of the Gibson girl, the New Woman. It seems an imposition and a waste of time to create these enormous chignons. And I absolutely refuse to use false hair. I know everyone does it, but not me. I cannot abide the idea of wearing another woman's hair."

Bernadine smiled. "I sympathize with you. Bridget, the maid that Clara and I share, has been sent to take classes with Monsieur Bernard. She is a dear and if the truth be known, cannot abide Clara. She told me that she needs to place a dozen pieces to create a proper chignon for my sister-in-law. Here, let me help you; I have learned to do my own hair. As a matter of fact, it has become a necessity."

"Necessity?" said Flora quizzically.

"Yes, it has to do with why I wanted to speak with you privately and in the strictest of confidence."

Flora turned her head away from the mirror and looked at her friend with an expression of concern. Bernadine realized that Flora seemed to suspect the nature of her predicament. Settling into a comfortable armchair, she began slowly to explain her situation. As she recounted the beginning of her affair with Eliot in Newport, she blushed with embarrassment, fearing that her friend might judge her harshly for her infidelity. But having told Flora of Theo's cruelty and the emptiness of her marriage, she felt sure that she would understand the need she had for some measure tenderness in her life.

Since Newport, we have been meeting in various homes and apartments that Eliot's firm is representing. It is quite safe, as Theo believes that I am searching for a residence for the two of us. But recently, well, I have been thinking about getting a place of my own."

Flora's face brightened. "You mean that you are finally going to leave him?"

"Well, I am gathering my courage."

Rising from her dressing table, she took her friend's hand and began speaking quietly and with a serious tone. "Are you in love with Eliot? I know his family, and I know him to be a fine young man. But are you sure about him? Bernadine, you cannot afford another mistake."

When she did not respond immediately, Flora began to worry. "He hasn't tired of you, has he? I mean, he isn't seeing someone else?"

"No, no. It's not that at all. Bernadine threw herself into her friend's arms, crying. "We love each other so much. He wants me to leave Theo. But, but …." She tried to control herself and took a deep breath.

"Well, what is stopping you? You love each other and he is not married. Divorce is not social death these days. Alva Belmont blazed a path for women who are suffering in unhappy marriages."

Bernadine had stopped crying but spoke with a quivering voice. "Oh, Flora. I'm terrified. I am almost positive that I am pregnant."

Bernadine could see the expression of shock on Flora's face. But then she saw her features soften into a look of sadness and compassion. Relieved, she instantly knew that she could trust her friend to keep her secret.

"You say that you are 'almost positive' that you are expecting. So, I assume that you have not been examined by a doctor."

"I would not know where to go. I can't go to the Van Wies' family doctor. But I have missed two of my cycles, and I am experiencing horrendous nausea in the morning."

Flora appeared dispirited, shaking her head. "Then I would say that there is little doubt that you are pregnant. I can take you to my doctor to confirm it. I have been seeing an obstetrician who works at Mount Sinai. I am sure that he would be discreet."

"I don't know what I am going to do," said Bernadine. "When Theo finds out about this, he will be livid. Do you think that there is anything I can do? You know what I mean."

Flora's eyes widened. "You mean …?"

"I have thought about it," said Bernadine. "I know there are ways, of … of … doing away with the problem. I don't know that I could actually go through with it, but do you think that your doctor could help?"

"It is quite out of the question!" Flora shot back. "He is a respectable physician with a solid reputation. I had to work hard to convince Ned to allow me to deliver in the hospital this time, instead of at home. I was only because Dr. Carlson's practice includes so many of his colleagues' wives that he agreed."

"I'm sorry, Flora. I am so confused. If you could make the appointment for me, I would be most grateful."

Flora's mind went back nine years ago to the moment that she found herself in the same situation as Bernadine and faced a similar choice. She had been devious. She had passed Mae off as Ned's child. But deception is never a good option, and she had paid dearly. Not until she became pregnant with her second child did Ned soften toward her and show her the love and affection that she had known before Mae's birth. And worst of all, she knew that even though he loved her, he no longer fully trusted her. Some things could never be regained, once lost. Having revisited her own failings, she changed her tone, comforting her friend. After all, she could not judge her.

"I will make an appointment for next week under the name of Deborah Vernon."

"Deborah Vernon?" asked Bernadine a little bewildered.

"Oh, she is a character in an obscure novel I once read. We can't very well use your real name, at least not right now. I imagine that the Van Wies are ignorant of your predicament."

"Of course! I haven't told a soul, except you. I absolutely dread telling Theo. Obviously, he will know that it's not his child since we have only shared a bed once. He has not touched me since that frightful night."

"Goodness, now I understand the gravity of your situation," said Flora. But I think you must tell him and soon. I imagine he might be more amenable to the idea of divorce."

"You might be right. On the other hand, the family is in great financial difficulty. Theo has been gambling and spending great sums of money on his other vices. Because of him and bad investments, the family fortune is quite depleted. They may delude themselves into believing that Theo is the father of this child."

Flora appeared baffled. "Are you telling me that, if his parents don't protest that he will go along with the pretense? He will let you pass off another man's child as his own?"

"I don't know how he will react," cried Bernadine with frustration. "He has never loved me, so he cannot feign a broken heart. But I know that he will be furious with me for not living up to what he calls our 'arrangement'. He had agreed that I should live my life, 'as long as I did nothing to bring shame to him or his family'. If the truth ever came out, it would certainly tarnish the Van Wies name."

Flora tried to comfort her friend. "Perhaps he will divorce you, and this could turn out to be a blessing in disguise."

"One can only hope," said Bernadine.

"However, if things are dire and you feel that you must pursue your original plan, I may have a way of helping. I have a friend who goes to many of those progressive meetings. Have you ever heard of Emma Goldman?"

Bernadine was dumbfounded. "You know Emma Goldman?"

"No, but my friend knows her. She may be able to help."

Flora hated to lie to Ned, but she did not dare tell him the truth about where she and Bernadine were going that evening. She had told Ned that she had been invited to a meeting at Anne Morgan's new woman's club, The Colony Club. She had politely turned down Anne's invitation and made plans to meet her friends Frieda Bernstein and Bernadine at Lillian Wald's settlement house.

Lillian Wald, a well-known social worker from an upper-class family, had opened the Henry Street Settlement House. It provided food and aid to needy woman and children, as well as basic medical care. Tonight, the outspoken anarchist Emma Goldman was to speak. Frieda, an attractive, young newlywed from a wealthy Jewish family, had put her name in for consideration for membership at the Colony Club on the basis of her close friendship with Anne Morgan. But Flora feared that some of her views were a bit too radical for many of the members.

One could not find a woman more controversial than Emma Goldman and tonight she planned to speak the problems of overpopulation and birth control. Emma had training as a nurse and had even practiced in a prison where she was confined. Frieda had told Flora that she knew Emma well and perhaps she would be willing to advise her friend Bernadine, who was in a difficult situation.

The Henry Street Settlement House occupied an entire city block. The ladies met on the sidewalk outside the main entrance.

"Frieda, I would like you to meet Bernadine Van Wies. She is a lovely transplant from Galveston, Texas. She is married to Theo."

Frieda did not seem to recognize the name. Obviously, she belonged to a different circle. This seemed to put Bernadine at ease. "It's a pleasure to meet you. I think my family has some distant cousins in Houston, although we have never met. I am so glad that you have come tonight. Shall we tour the facilities before the meeting?"

They visited a gymnasium and a public playground at the back of the house.

She seemed particularly proud of these amenities. "The playground provides a safe environment for the children. If you ladies have ever visited a tenement, you would see that there is no space for children to play, so you will often find them on the street. With the trolleys and horses, it is quite dangerous."

Flora had to admit to herself that she rarely frequented the Lower East Side tenements. In fact, she only glimpsed them occasionally when her driver Frank took a shortcut or lost his way on one of her shopping trips. Both she and Bernadine blushed with shame upon learning the living conditions of children in the slums.

Flora noticed a lovely young woman with a mass of blond curls approach Frieda, hugging her warmly. Frieda seemed surprised. "Dore, I had no idea that you were coming to the meeting. I did not think that you had time to volunteer for social work."

Dore smiled, "I am here to support Emma. She has been a great help to me personally, as well as to other young women. I hesitate to say more, although I assume that your friends know the topic of her speech."

"Oh, forgive me, said Frieda "please let me introduce my friend Flora Dodd. And this is her dear friend Bernadine Van Wies. Ladies, this is my friend Dore Abramowitz. She lives in the apartment building that I lived in with my parents, before I married and moved uptown."

Frieda had lived one floor up from the Braverman's before her marriage to the son of wealthy Jewish stockbroker. The two friends managed to stay in touch, mainly through Frieda's shopping visits to Wanamaker's where Dore worked.

Dore smiled amiably. She could see that Flora was pregnant, about six months. Obviously, upper class, they resembled clientele that occasionally shopped in prêt-à-porter in her store. She could not ascertain if they were here as "tourists," slumming to see how Jacob Riis's other half lived or if they decided to volunteer in some capacity at the settlement house. She doubted that they had come to listen to Emma's advice on birth control.

Bernadine turned to Dore. "It's a pleasure to meet you Miss Abramowitz. We are aware of the subject of Miss Goldman's talk tonight. It may surprise you to learn that women who live on Fifth Avenue have the same concerns as women on the Lower East Side.

Perplexed and slightly flustered, Dore approached Bernadine. She sensed that this young woman might have indeed come to seek out Emma's help and that she might be in trouble. "Mrs. Van Wies, perhaps you would like to see some more of the playground? Over in that far corner they have built some lovely swings." When they were out of earshot of the other women, Dore looked at Bernadine and could see that she appeared distraught and that she turned her head trying to hide her emotions.

"Mrs. Van Wies, do you mind if I speak to you frankly?"

"No, not at all," she said, her voice was shaky. "But why don't you call me Bernadine?"

"Of course. Bernadine, I mentioned that Emma Goldman has helped many people, including Frieda and me. You see, my full name is Dore Braverman. I am married to a medical student named Meyer Braverman. He does not love me, or I him. We have what is called a 'student marriage', arranged by our parents for mutual profit. I think it is absurd that my family left Russia, with all its archaic traditions, so that I may make a marriage like my grandparents made in the Shetl."

Bernadine looked at Dore with a perplexed expression. "I thank you for your frankness about your situation, but…."

Dore interrupted. "I am telling you my story with the hope that you might benefit from my experience. You see because my husband is a student and, well, since we don't love each other, it would not be convenient or desirable for us to have children. He is finishing his first year of medical school and hopes to be a successful doctor. I am pursuing a career of my own. We have been living with his family for several months. In the first month of our marriage, I was expected to perform my wifely duty. But since family wanted me to help support Meyer's studies, they gave me the name of a woman who could help me prevent pregnancy. That woman was Frieda. Frieda introduced me to Emma Goldman, who helps young women like me by teaching us about contraception. Fortunately, in the past two months my husband has not touched me. Frieda heard from some gossip in the building that he has taken a lover. And that suits me fine."

"Again, I appreciate your honesty and your good intentions," Bernadine said. "But in my case, you see, I am beyond help. You see I am married to a man who I despise, although I thought I loved him before we were wed. But once he revealed his true nature and brutality, I, I...." She choked on the words. "He is violent and incapable of love. He had me only once on our wedding night and we have not been together since."

Dore understood and wanted to spare Bernadine the embarrassment of the gruesome details. "So, I understand that your predicament is of a different nature."

"Yes," said Bernadine. "Recently a man has come into my life. I don't know why I'm telling you this, except that I feel that I can trust you. Well, we have been lovers for several months and now, well, I am carrying his child."

"Oh, I see. How far along in the pregnancy are you? Honestly, you are so slim that it's hard to tell."

"I am three months along. I saw Flora's doctor today, and he confirmed it. Although, I am in love with my young man, I am in a difficult and complicated situation.

I had even contemplated ending the pregnancy."

"I understand," said Dore softly. "An impossible situation. I know that there are doctors, especially if you have the means, as I'm sure you do, who will perform abortions. I have heard from Emma and Frieda of some very capable midwives. That may be a better solution because they are very discreet. In fact, their very freedom depends on discretion. Whereas physicians might let things slip and given that they have contact with people of your station in society, there is sure to be a greater risk of discovery."

"I honestly don't know if I can go through with an abortion. But I dread my husband's reaction when he discovers my infidelity. He will surely use it against me. I would like a divorce. I am fortunate in that I have my own money, but I will not have access to it for five years. So, I am not free. I have not told my young man about the baby. I need to make a decision soon."

Dore looked concerned. "Soon indeed. Three months is late in a pregnancy to undergo an abortion. It could be dangerous, under the best conditions." She hesitated, looking straight into Bernadine's eyes. "Having just met you, I would not dream of influencing your decision. Things will work out one way or the other. At least you are in a more advantageous position than most of the women that Emma helps. You have money and connections. My only advice is to be thick-skinned and ignore what people whisper behind your back. Oh, and whatever you decided about this pregnancy, come back to me, and I will show you can continue to enjoy making love with your gentleman without risk."

Talking with Dore relieved Bernadine. She thought it odd that she found it easier to talk about such things with a woman who she hardly knew and who came from a different world. She gave her a hug and promised that she would keep in touch through Frieda. Dore seemed surprised. They rejoined Frieda and Flora at the door of the settlement house.

The four women entered the main hall of building, crowded with young women in shirtwaists and elaborately adorned hats. Flora commented to Bernadine on the care that these hardworking women took in their appearance. "Look at their hats, Bernadine," she said.

Dore smiled. "You do realize that these are the girls who make and sell the clothes that middle-class ladies wear. And make no mistake about it, more and more, these young women and the middle class will set fashion trends. I know this. I plan to make it my life's work to know."

Flora and Bernadine stared at her quizzically. "How exactly are you going to manage that?" said Bernadine.

"Right now, it is just my dream, a hope for a future career in fashion. I am a salesgirl at Wanamaker's. So, if you ladies desire to help me along the road to my dream, please feel free to stop by prêt-à-porter and I will wait on you personally."

"Perhaps we shall do that," said Flora.

Emma Goldman spoke for about an hour. Bernadine found her criticism of capitalism too radical. However, Emma's discussion of women's rights and particularly free loved intrigued her. Unfortunately, the speech ended with the Goldman's promotion of anarchy to the point of violence. This Bernadine could not approve.

She noticed that Flora found the entire speech distasteful and she had seemed particularly troubled during the discussion of free love—her face was flushed and her eyes cast down. As the audience applauded, Flora said, "I must be going. It is getting late."

The women said their goodbyes, hugging each other and promising to visit Dore at Wanamaker's.

Bernadine quietly entered the front hall, taking care not to wake the family. She passed Theo's room, but could not tell if he had come in yet because of the closed door. She slipped into her bed, realizing that she needed to devise a plan soon. Her decision to marry Theo had been based on pure but misguided emotion. Now she needed to think clearly.

Could she go through with an abortion? If she were carrying Theo's child and not Eliot's, she might not agonize so much. But this baby, conceived in love and passion, had nothing to do with Theo. She felt sure of Eliot's love and she loved him. She could not kill his child. She would have this baby. Now she had to find a way to tell Theo, and the very thought of telling him terrified her.

The next morning Bernadine knocked on Theo's door. At first, she heard no response or movement and she thought that he had again spent the night out. But after knocking a second time, she heard him groaning and mumbling. She turned the knob and found the door unlocked. Not knowing what state he might be in, she hesitated.

Realizing that she had to tell him sooner rather than later, she gathered her courage and entered the room. The scene that she encountered stunned her; bedclothes strewn about the room, his suit and shirt stained with blood hung over chairs and the dresser. She gasped for air in the stuffy room and put a handkerchief over her nose to block out the odor of perspiration mixed with cheap perfume. Theo stretched across the bed, his arms dangling off the side. He stirred and opened his bloodshot eyes. His skin had become even grayer and had the texture of crepe. She noticed for the first time that his beautiful black hair had begun to thin.

Speaking with a hoarse voice, Theo expressed surprise to see his wife in his bedroom. "To what do I owe this honor? I apologize for the state of the room, but I came in quite late and, as you see, did not take time to put things in their proper place."

Bernadine vacillated between fear and disgust. Deciding that she needed to approach things from a position of strength, she opted for a display of disgust and impatience. "Theo, I need to speak with you about a serious matter, and it cannot wait. So, I would appreciate it if you could dress and meet me downstairs in about an hour. I have ordered the carriage to be brought round, as I would like to have a private discussion. I do not want to be overheard or interrupted by your parents or Clara. We will go to the park."

"Are you quite serious? You want me to go to Central Park at this ungodly hour?"

"Theo, it is now ten o'clock. Please be downstairs at eleven or I will make a scene. You know that I have lived up to your conditions and given you latitude in your behavior, but there is a limit. Furthermore, the situation which we need to consider is of the utmost importance and concerns both of us."

For the first time in years, she saw a hint of concern in his eyes. As he had descended further and further into his decadent life, he worried less and less about the opinion of his family and society. But now, he would have to confront an inconvenient reality. She could only guess at his reaction and she steeled herself for his abuse.

The carriage dropped them across the street from The Dakota at the entrance to Central Park. She instructed the driver to come back in an hour. Then she led Theo down a discreet path where she often walked Eliot when she did not want to be seen.

Theo continued to grumble and protest. "What an ungodly hour! What is so important that it couldn't wait until later in the afternoon?"

"As I told you it is a matter of some urgency and it cannot wait. I never know when I can catch you at home these days, so please stop complaining. There is a bench over there where we can sit without the risk of being disturbed."

Predicting a violent reaction and wanting to avoid the embarrassment of a public scene, she had chosen this spot. Aware of his potential for brutality, she took some comfort that they were in the park and she could cry out for help, if necessary.

They approached the bench. "Theo, I need to sit down. I am feeling quite faint…."

Suddenly, his expression changed, and he seemed to come out of his fog. He looked at her strangely and his features distorted into a sardonic smirk. "I seem to have an idea of the reason for the urgency of the conversation."

"Has my little wife gone and got herself into trouble?" He said with a sarcastic and malicious tone.

Bernadine began to cry, but quickly regained her composure. She had promised herself that she would not be intimidated. After all, by what right did he dare judge her?

"In fact, as you say, I am pregnant. I went to a doctor, and it was confirmed. Don't worry. I went under an assumed name. I was very discreet. But soon, discretion will not be an issue. I have met a man that I have been seeing for several months. To put it in the simplest terms, we love each other. I know this concept is foreign to you, but there it is. I would say that you have sufficient grounds to divorce me. I don't really care anymore what people might say. After all, divorce is not as unheard of as it once was, at least in New York Society. I am only grateful that my parents are not alive to see me in this predicament. It would have humiliated them. But they are not here. Since you have never loved me, you cannot now object to divorce. Your family will surely suspect that this is not your child." She said placing her hands protectively on her stomach.

Theo remained silent, sneering at her. She waited for him to speak, but he said nothing.

"I haven't come into my money, so things will be difficult for me," she said. "But I will get by on my allowance and the help of Eliot."

Suddenly, he came to life. He shouted, "*Eliot*, so we have a lover named *Eliot*, do we? Well, how nice. I am assuming you are about three months along. It must date back to your visit to Newport. I know what passes for sport and entertainment there, especially under Alva Belmont's roof. I hope this *Eliot* is someone of our class. You didn't give yourself to one of Oliver's automobile mechanics, did you?"

"Of course not!" Bernadine could not bear his disdain.

"Well, as long as the man is white and above average intelligence. He isn't a Jew, is he?"

"And if he were?" shouted Bernadine.

"If he were, we would tear this child from your body. Believe me, I have had to send a few women to abortionists. But as I am confident that you would not make love to a Jew, we will not have to resort to that."

"What do you mean we won't have to resort to that?" she asked, not knowing what he had in mind. "I am going to keep this baby. I don't know why you think you have any say in the matter. I want a divorce. I cannot go on living in the same home with you and your family."

Theo's voice became strangely quiet. "Are you mad? I thought that I explained our situation on our wedding night. Nothing has changed. You will continue living in my home as my wife. If you do not, I will find your *Eliot*, and I will destroy him. Don't doubt that I can. I have means at my disposal that you cannot even imagine."

She looked at him incredulously. "What are you saying? What means are you speaking of?"

"Never mind. Do not ask what I can do. You don't want to know. We are not going to lose you and your fortune now. I owe that much to my parents. Besides, my habits have become very expensive."

Bernadine felt her courage being sapped, as she understood the depths of her husband's depravity. Perhaps Theo had access to drugs or arms. She thought about the houses of prostitution that he visited. Yes, he could easily find a way to hurt the man she loved. That she would not allow.

"Listen to me," he said. "I reiterate that you will continue to be Mrs. Theo Van Wies. Now that you are having a child, we must make a better show of things. Oh, won't mother be pleased? This child will be known to all of New York as my son or daughter, and there is nothing you can do to change that. After all, we are man and wife. I said that you might lead your life and amuse yourself, but you were careless. I thought that you were smart enough to take precautions. But I do thank you for being discreet. As far as I know, there has not been a whisper of suspicion regarding infidelity on your part, so of course, everyone will assume the child is mine."

A bitter taste came into her mouth, and she hissed at him. "But really, Theo, you have not been a paragon of discretion. You are known as a philanderer."

Again, he smirked. "Well, I thank you for my reformation. Now that we are having a family, I will have a clean slate. I will play the loving husband and doting father. You remember how well I can perform.

It will be difficult to break some of my bad habits, but I do believe that I am up to the task. Now, I believe it has been about an hour, and Charles will be waiting with the carriage. Shall we go?"

A week later Bernadine sent a message to Eliot through his office. She had done so many times, as they had established the pretense that he had become her agent, helping her to find an apartment or brownstone. Not only did the ruse provide an excuse to meet, but also afforded the couple time alone in vacant apartments and houses where they could spend hours in each other's arms. In her message she asked if he could meet her in the early afternoon at a restaurant in a side street off upper Broadway. She hoped that he might arrange to show her an apartment on the West Side and that they may have one last afternoon together. A feeling of dread and deep sadness overwhelmed her as she considered the scene that would soon play out. Theo had forbidden her from seeing Eliot, threatening to have her followed in order to discover his identity. Knowing Theo's capabilities, she decided that she had no choice but to end the affair. So, she took great care in arranging their last meeting, choosing a small out-of-the-way restaurant run by Greeks, where they would not run into any of his business associates.

When Eliot walked in, his face revealed his amusement and confusion as to her choice in restaurant.

He smiled. "What are you up to, darling? You have certainly chosen a colorful place to meet."

She stood up and shook his hand, playing the part of client with her agent. "I need to speak to you about something quite serious. Oh, Eliot, do you think we could go somewhere, where we can be alone?"

Eliot smiled. "I suspected as much. I have a key to a brownstone on West End Avenue. It is a new construction, so there are no furnishings. That means no bed. But we can manage."

Bernadine tried to hold back her tears. She did not want to discuss the situation until they were alone. "That will be fine. So, there will be no janitor or manager on site?"

"No," he said. "They haven't hired any staff yet. That is why I have a key.

What is wrong, my love? We have always been careful, but you seem a little skittish today."

"We will discuss it when we get to the apartment. Is it far from here?

He took her arm, and they walked out into the street. "Actually, we can walk from here. It's a fine day for the end of October."

They climbed quickly up to the second floor and arrived at a wide, airy landing. Eliot took out the key and opened the door to a large and bright apartment. Bernadine imagined, for a brief moment, that they were entering their own home after a brisk afternoon walk. She let herself dream for a few seconds that they were newlyweds starting a life together as Mr. and Mrs. Eliot Havemeyer. But she quickly pushed the thought from her mind because she could not endure the agony of thinking about what might have been. Eliot took her through the apartment to the large, empty bedroom.

"I knew that there was carpeting when I decided to bring you here. It's not the luxury that we have become accustomed to, but I think it will do." He smiled awkwardly, grabbed her tightly and embraced her.

She tried to stop him. "Eliot, we have to talk."

"Whatever it is, it will have to wait, my love. You know how I get. It must be three weeks since we have been together. I need you now."

Bernadine could feel his urgency and his desire, and it transferred from his body to hers. She knew that this would be the last time that they would make love. Would it not be better if at least he did not know the reality of their situation? She tore at her clothes, taking off her shirtwaist and skirt. At seeing her passion, Eliot quickly undressed and kissed her as they first sat and then lay down on the floor. She could sense that he could not hold back for long, but she took his hands and placed them on her breasts and begged him to take his time.

"Please, Eliot let's take our time. I want to experience what I felt the first time we made love."

Bernadine went into the bathroom to finish dressing. When she came out she saw Eliot sitting on a window bench. As he fixed his tie, he looked exhausted, but content. He motioned to her to come sit next to him.

"We don't have a lot of time," he said. "I have an appointment with a banker in an hour. Fortunately, we are meeting in branch that is on Broadway in the sixties. I can grab a hansom cab, if there is one to be found, and be there in fifteen minutes. And though I am glad that I had the unexpected pleasure of your complete attention today, I know that you have something you want to say to me. I can only imagine one thing. You have found a way to divorce Theo. Did he finally do something illegal? God knows he crossed the into immorality long ago"

Bernadine put her hand gently to his mouth and shook her head. Tears welled up in her eyes. Her throat tightened as she began to speak. "Darling, please let me speak. The situation has become hopeless. A few days ago, I went to a doctor, and he confirmed what I have suspected for the past few weeks. I am carrying your child."

"Is everything all right? Are you feeling quite well?" An expression surprise and concern spread across Eliot's face.

"Physically, I am doing well. The doctor said that I am about three months pregnant. I am sure that the baby was conceived during our first time together in Newport. Somehow it seems fitting and significant that it should be so. I am carrying your son or daughter and after a period of torturous doubt, I have decided not to end the pregnancy."

Eliot shot up from the window bench, confused and angry. "Whatever do you mean? You wanted to abort our child? What were you thinking? Well, thank god you came to your senses."

Bernadine had never seen him so angry, his muscled tensed and his jaw clenched. "Please, calm down. I never seriously considered going through with an abortion. I love you too much, and I will love this child. However, you will have to come to terms with the reality that we are facing. There will be no divorce. I had it out with Theo, and he has made it clear that we are to continue with the life that we have been leading."

"How is that possible?" asked Eliot, not believing what he was hearing. "He knows that you are pregnant with another man's baby, and yet he is willing to stay in your marriage?"

Bernadine let out an ironic laugh. "Willing is not the word that I would use. Insistent would be more appropriate."

"I don't understand. From what I know of Theo and his family, they are extremely proud and arrogant. It is inconceivable that he would pass off another man's child as a Van Wies. He does not love you. I don't think the man is capable of love, only lust and perversion. I have kept silent long enough. I am going to have it out with him."

Bernadine tried her best to calm him. She held his face in her hands and looked into his eyes. "He doesn't know that you are the father. He has no idea as to the identity of the man that I love, and he never will."

Becoming agitated almost enraged, Eliot protested. "This is impossible. I will not let him raise my child as his own. I tell you, I will not! What hold does he have on you? You need not stay with him. I will marry you and support you."

"There are things to be considered. If I do divorce him, which is not an easy task under the best of circumstances, it will take months, even years. It will be contentious. Arthur and Agnes will surely make it known that I have had an illicit affair, which resulted in pregnancy. The taint of illegitimacy will be on our child. If I stay with him, he promised to play the role of the proud father, and of course, his family will go along with it."

This did nothing to mollify Eliot. Touching her stomach, he spoke sternly. "This is mine, a Havemeyer, not a Van Wies. How can you deny me a life with my child? More importantly, how can you raise him with a man like Theo as a father?"

"Darling I have no choice," she said trying to maintain her sang-froid. She needed to maintain her composure. If she showed any weakness, it would only serve to convince Eliot that he must fight for her, which she could not allow. For as much as she wanted a way out of her infernal life with Theo, she would not risk Eliot's safety.

She hardened her tone and calmly explained the situation. "Eliot, as of now Theo does not know that you are the father. I did let your first name slip out, but he has no idea who you are. If he does not know your identity, we are all safe. This is my decision. I bear responsibility for my unhappiness, for I insisted on marrying a man that I did not know. It's true that I was young, only sixteen when we became engaged, but that is no excuse. My father tried to talk me out of marrying into what he called a pompous Yankee family, but I would not listen. I was dazzled by Theo's good looks, and I mistook infatuation for love."

Now, difficult as it was, she resolved to protect the man she loved by ending their affair. "There is no more to discuss, Eliot. I have no choice, and neither do you. We will not see each other again. If we run into each other at a party or at the theater, we may speak casually, as acquaintances. I release you from all our bonds, our attachments of love that we have shared. Most of all, I am grateful to you for showing me that I am capable of love and passion. And I thank you for this child. For me, he will always be ours, yours and mine. The world may not know it, but we will." She stood up and ran out the door before he could respond. She ran down the stairs, blinded by tears and went out into the cool October day.

DORE

NEW YORK, NOVEMBER 1904

Dore hopped off the streetcar and walked across a busy street in East Harlem.

The Abramowitz family had moved into what was known as New Law housing or model tenements. Many of the working poor had saved up enough money to leave the Lower East Side tenements to find better living conditions much further uptown in Harlem. Most of the inhabitants in the new neighborhoods were Jews, with a few Negroes who spilled over from the adjacent streets. Perhaps the fact that many real estate developers were Jews encouraged the migration of many Jewish immigrants and first-generation families. Considerable unrest on the Lower East Side and a rent strike had been mounted in the spring, creating tensions in the old neighborhood.

Isaac and Rebekah rented an apartment with an airy light court instead of a narrow airshaft and windows in three of the five rooms. They had their own indoor toilet, which was a great luxury.

As Dore approached the corner across the street from the apartment building, she noticed Leah joking with a group of much older, tough girls. Leah had just turned thirteen, and the other girls looked to be at least sixteen years old. She strode over to the doorway where the girls had congregated and grabbed Leah's arm.

"What do you think you are doing loitering on the street like a little ruffian? You are much too young to be frequenting those sorts of working girls. I haven't spent my time teaching you to read and write so that you could waste your time with girls like that. Just look how they are dressed and those outlandish hats. And I will not have you exposed to the language that they use. What are you doing out on the street anyway?"

Leah, who was growing into a dark and exotic-looking adolescent, lowered her eyes. She seemed embarrassed. "I am sorry, Dore. I don't usually stand around with those girls. But they were being friendly, and they are so funny. You know the way they talk with the new slang. Rebekah sent me to the bakery. They are selling the day-old pastries for a penny."

"Well, go on ahead. I will see you later in the apartment."

When Rebekah answered the door, Dore took in the new decorative touches. Rebekah hanged curtains over the windows and lovely, inexpensive prints adorned the walls. She hugged her mother and settled into the only comfortable chair in the apartment.

"I saw Leah in the street talking to a group of tough girls. Have you considered allowing her to stop working and returning to school?" asked Dore

"We asked her, but she is not interested in school," Rebekah said, shrugging her shoulders. "And since you brought up the subject, Isaac insists that Leah is old enough to work at the Triangle. I argued against it, but he insists. Simon Braverman found her an apprentice position where she will be learning to work a sewing machine. In a year or two, she will make enough money to help out with our living expenses."

Dore could hardly contain herself. "How can Papa not see the advantage of allowing her to go to school? Even if she resists, he should encourage her to educate herself. Why the Braverman's daughter just started high school. If Leah could attend for a few years, she would be able to find a job as a stenographer or even a secretary. Those positions may not pay a fortune, but there is room for some advancement and the working conditions are much better than those of the factories or even the department stores."

"I agree with you, Dore. But Isaac has not had much luck in the factory. He was hoping for promotion or a raise, but Simon gives only empty promises. We need the extra money to keep up on the rent. I do not want to move back to the Lower East Side."

Dore simmered with anger. "Well, that's just fine and dandy! Why am I in this miserable student marriage, living with these arrogant people? The whole point for us was Papa's advancement at the Triangle. By now he should be a supervisor."

Rebekah flushed with shame. "It seems Mr. Braverman exaggerated his position and influence at the factory. He was able to get your father the job as a cutter because, after all, he was a fine tailor. But he has not come through with his empty promises."

"So, I have wasted almost three years of my life for nothing? I could have finished school. I have been told by many people at the store that I am bright and that I have talent. When is Papa coming home? I want to discuss something with him."

"He has gone down to his social club," said Rebekah. "He spends all his free time there." Suddenly, she began to cry. "I am sorry, Dore, so sorry. I should have stood up to Isaac and prevented your marriage. I guess I still have the soul of woman from the old country."

Dore softened. "Don't say that, Mama. I don't blame you. I wasn't really forced into marriage. That is not possible in this country. But I did think that I would be helping you and Leah. And now, what lies ahead for her? Why don't you walk me out to the streetcar?"

As they walked out of the building onto the street, Rebekah turned to Dore.

"I wasn't going to say anything, but I feel that you need to know the truth about everything that concerns Leah. While we were still living in the old neighborhood, Rachel came to see me. She made a point of coming when she knew that Leah and Isaac would not be at home. My goodness, she looked like a tart, all powder and rouge, dressed in what passes for the latest fashion. The cut of dress was outrageously daring."

Dore feigned interest. "Oh, really, how is she doing? I suppose that she is no longer in service, so where is she working?"

"Well, that's just it. She came out and told me, plain as day. She is working as a prostitute. She was brazen as could be, quite pleased with herself. Claims that she works for a very respectable house, which caters to a clientele that includes wealthy men from high society, financiers, and government. And though she said that she has not saved enough money to take care of Leah, she claimed that she is putting money aside for their future, whatever that means."

Dore was skeptical and at the same time felt pity for Rachel. "She always was proud, claiming to come from fine Sephardic line. Look how low she has fallen. I feel sorry for her, but I cannot forgive her for abandoning Leah." She looked up. "Oh, there's the streetcar. I'll come back next week if I can. Maybe I can talk some sense into Papa."

The next morning Dore was standing next to a display case with Josephine O'Neil and Ira Frankel discussing a new arrangement of scarves. Suddenly they heard screaming from the stockroom and ran to find a cash girl named Daisy, crying and pale with fear, she had backed away and cowered in the corner. Standing over her, a brash middle-aged man gripped her arm as she winced with pain.

"He grabbed me and tried to kiss me!" she cried.

Katherine Boerne, a large woman with a slight German accent approached.

"I saw the whole thing. He didn't know that I was back there, but I was. He backed her into a corner and was forcing himself on her."

Ira called over Richard Fowler, the department supervisor. "Fowler, you need to hear the girl out."

"What is the problem?" said Fowler

Daisy said, "He kissed me. But that's not all. He was trying to lift my skirt. I may be young, but I know what he was trying to do. He has no right, just because he is the floorwalker. He is disgusting! Oh, he so old, and his breath reeks...."

Ira turned to Katherine. "Please tell Mr. Fowler what you witnessed."

"Mr. Fowler, it was just as she said. Furthermore, he has tried to force himself on several girls. It is common knowledge that he has no problem abusing a pretty girl if he gets her alone. He has never had the nerve to try it on me," she said with smirk, placing her hands on her ample hips.

"Daisy continued. "Wait. That's not the end of it. He grabbed my arm and twisted it. Then he said that if I didn't meet him after work that he would report me for stealing."

Fowler remained noncommittal, not wanting to take sides in front of the other employees. But he took Charlie aside a few minutes later. "Keep your hands to yourself, Charlie, especially when there are customers in the store. I don't care what you do after work, if a girl is willing. But quit threatening the young employees. I have gotten complaints about the high turnover on your floor from upstairs. You understand?"

Charlie scowled and slunk away.

Dore turned to Josephine and said, "That cretin tried to have his way with me when I first started. But now that I am a married woman, he leaves me alone. I can honestly say that it is the only advantage that I have gotten from my marriage."

Josephine sighed. "I wouldn't know about the advantages of marriage since I am a bachelor girl, twenty-six and never even been engaged. But I know a thing or two about working around men, no disrespect intended, Mr. Frankel."

Ira Frankel smiled and made a slight bow. "No offense taken."

"The virtuous Mr. Fowler asked me to go dancing and to a bar with him a few years back," said Josephine, "and him a married man with five children."

"Is that true?" asked Ira. "He is a department supervisor. That is uncalled for."

"Uncalled for or not," said Josephine, "it happens all the time."

Ira shook his head with annoyance. "It always amazes me how men can be so self-satisfied. Once in a position of power, they proceed to ill-treat everyone who is subservient to them. But what really galls me is that they have no desire to improve themselves and to climb the ladder to find more gratifying work."

Dore looked at him with admiration. "What wise words, Mr. Frankel. However, I must inform you that men are not alone in taking this attitude. Many women are, as you say, 'self-satisfied.' Just finding a husband, any husband is as far as they can see. Then they claim their life's ambition fulfilled."

Josephine excused herself and walked away to tend to some other displays. As head window dresser she supervised all the displays on the ground floor.

Ira Frankel turned and looked at Dore with approval. "You seem to be a bright, young woman, much too bright to be stuck in sales."

"Thank you, Mr. Frankel," said Dore. "And if I may be so bold as to ask you a personal question?"

Ira nodded his head. "Of course, but if you are going to be asking a personal question, you must call me Ira."

"Well then Ira, why are you so different from other men? You never abuse your position to push yourself on salesgirls. Some of the girls joke that you must have a beautiful girlfriend who is a tyrant. But I always defend you and say that you are far too strong-willed to let anyone control you." She felt herself beginning to blush. She had no business talking to any man in such a frank manner, especially a man who worked upstairs in administration.

"I appreciate your candor and your curiosity, Dore. I will reward you with an honest answer. I have no time for distractions. And I do not wish to jeopardize my position at Wanamaker's by chasing after female employees. Frankly, I have priorities. You see I am not a self-satisfied man. I enjoy my job, but I know that I am capable of much more. I started out in sales in the men's department. I worked there for three years while going to Pratt at night, where I studied marketing and advertising. Then Wanamaker's moved me into the advertising department, where I illustrated catalogues and circulars. I have recently been promoted to account manager. When I have saved a little more money, I plan to study psychology at City College. I don't know if I will go for a degree, but I think it will help me understand the consumer's mind, which I can apply to advertising and marketing."

Dore looked at Ira with admiration, taking in his handsome features and curly dark hair. She considered him to be a good-looking man, yet she felt no physical attraction to him. "If I were a man," she said. "I would be like you. I wouldn't let anything stand in my way. But I was taken out of school at fourteen to work and married off at sixteen. I have always regretted not having finished my education."

"It's never too late. There is such a thing as night school. I know from experience that it isn't easy to work all day and then go to school. Then of course, I am not married, so I had no time constraints, I mean as you must have."

Dore shrugged; a little embarrassed, she confessed, "I have no time constraints, at least as far as my husband is concerned. My marriage was arranged, you know, a student marriage. I was trying to help my family. It was foolish, the biggest mistake of my life."

Ira seemed genuinely touched. "Student marriage, yes I have heard of that. Absurd! I am truly sorry that you find yourself in this untenable situation. But I have a feeling that you will find your way."

Josephine, having heard Ira's response, came over to offer her opinion.

"Find her way, indeed. This girl has talent. I have seen her drawings. She has great artistic capability and a flair for fashion. I suspect that given an opportunity, she will go far. I was going to ask Mr. Fowler if I might not take her on as assistant window dresser. But seeing as you outrank him, Mr. Frankel, I will ask you. She has been helping me out a bit with ideas for the Christmas display, on her own time of course. Could you speak with them upstairs?"

"Not only will I speak with them, I will present it as a fait accompli."

"Excuse me sir?" said Josephine. "What kind of plea?"

Ira laughed. "Josephine, that just means that I will tell them that Mr. Fowler and I have given her the job. Of course, there is no need to bother Fowler with the details. I will take care of it."

Overjoyed, for the first time in years, Dore felt encouragement and hope. "Mr. Frankel, I mean Ira, I don't know what to say. How can I ever thank you?"

"By working hard and making Wanamaker's windows stand out among the other department stores. Do you think that I might have a look at those drawings? Perhaps we could meet at that little café on 44th that all you ladies frequent? I think that it is a respectable establishment."

Josephine gave Dore a little nudge. "Go on, my girl. You should be proud of those drawings."

I don't mind at all, Ira. But I hope that Josephine hasn't given me too much of a buildup."

The next evening Dore met Ira in front of the small café near Wanamaker's.

"Shall we sit in that booth near the window? The light is better, and it will be quieter."

Dore had been in the little Italian café on several occasions with some of the girls from the store. A favorite gathering place, the employees often met up for dinner before going to a show or to a dance hall. She knew that Josephine had a high opinion of her artistic ability and eye for displaying fashion. But she never expected that she would intervene on her behalf with the men upstairs. And how lucky was it that Ira Frankel accepted her recommendation.

Ira ordered a beer, and she asked for tea. She wanted to have a clear head when she showed him her drawings.

"This is a recent drawing of a gown that is inspired by the latest Parisian designs. I absolutely devour the fashion magazines for inspiration. I have a friend who orders some of her clothes from Paris and makes the trip every other year to buy the latest styles."

Ira thought it strange that the young woman of little means had a friend who travelled to Paris to buy her wardrobe, but he did his best to hide his surprise.

Showing him several of her sketches, she drew his attention to certain details.

"I don't know if you can see the changes in the cut of the dresses. Perhaps men don't notice these things."

"Dore, in most cases, I would agree with you. But remember that it is my job to notice trends in fashion and in the public's taste in general. Advertisers not only predict what the public wants, in many ways they dictate the consumer's desires."

"Really, I find that very interesting. I have always thought that the way fashion is presented, whether in a magazine or in a fashion show, can change a woman's taste or predilection for certain styles or colors."

"Indeed. And it is our job to display the dress or any merchandise to its best advantage, whether in print, on a model or in a window. Now, let's have a look at these drawings."

She began to pull out one drawing after another. "Do you see the difference in the silhouette? There is a gradual softening of the line." She pulled out a French magazine and showed a drawing. "Do you see it? It is subtle, but the S curve is gradually disappearing. The European women prefer a slimmer look. And, of course, you can guess what this means for lingerie."

"You have me there, Dore. What does this mean for lingerie?"

Dore blushed, realizing that men had no understanding of all that went into creating the tiny waist and large bosom silhouette that women favored. "It means that we may expect a revolution in corsets."

"A revolution in corsets? He asked. "What exactly does that look like?"

"Well, I can't be sure," she continued. "But if the S curve is on its way out I imagine that we will have a different sort of corset, less confining. And that might mean lighter, more delicate lingerie will follow. Of course, I can't be sure. But it seems logical. It will be a gradual change that will evolve over several seasons in Paris and then eventually make its way to our shores."

"This is enlightening and quite fascinating," said Ira. "Now look here, Dore. Earlier when I was speaking to you about going to Pratt or perhaps even Parsons, I was speaking in philosophical terms. But now I am convinced that you should make a go of it. And since you are to be a window dresser, much of your work will be in the evenings after closing. In that case, you could attend class in the mornings and work late afternoons and evenings. What do you say?"

"What do I say? I say I would love to go to school. But unfortunately, I don't have the money to pay for it. I am dependent on my husband and his family for housing."

"That is unfortunate. Do you think that your husband would object?"

"My husband doesn't care what I do, as long as I bring home enough money to help him to pay for his studies. Of course, he has almost finished medical school, and he will be starting a job at Mount Sinai in July. He won't need my income."

Ira seemed encouraged. "Now perhaps he will support you in return."

She laughed bitterly. "There is no chance of that. He won't need my income, but he will still be happy to continue using it for his family."

"That doesn't seem fair. I assume that he is a second-generation Jew?"

"Oh yes, and he never lets me forget that I came through Ellis Island as a child."

"Really?" said Ira somewhat surprised. "I would never have guessed. You have no accent."

"Ira, many of us worked hard to fit in. You can't imagine how hard it was for us in school, even among other Jews. Well, I wasn't having any of it. And that meant speaking and acting like an American, not a Russian girl from the Shetl."

Ira smiled and patted her hand. "There is no shame in being an immigrant. My parents came through Castle Garden. I cannot tell you what to do. But I would find some way to make that husband of yours pay for school, fancy doctor."

On the way home Dore considered Ira's words. Make that husband of yours pay."

Friday afternoon three days later, Dore left work to meet Meyer in a quiet restaurant in Greenwich Village. Surprised and annoyed by the request, he first refused. After all, they never saw each other outside the house and barely spoke, even in the bedroom where they slept in different beds. But she insisted and threatened to come to the hospital where he was interning, so he relented.

When he entered the restaurant, she sensed his irritation and confusion. "Can we make this quick? You know that I have exams to study for."

"I am sorry to inconvenience you in any way. But seeing that I have helped you these past years, you owe me a few minutes of your valuable time."

"It's true that you helped, but I wouldn't exaggerate your contribution."

He was so arrogant that she felt sick to her stomach. Sitting across the table from him, she realized how unattractive he had become, with a receding hairline and sallow complexion. "I helped pay for your tuition, all while living with your big-headed, small-minded parents, not to mention your obnoxious brothers and sisters. And let's not forget the first few months of marriage when I let you maul me. God, what torture!" Once her anger started spilling out, she could not stop. "And I managed to avoid pregnancy. Thank God for Emma Goldman and her midwives."

Meyer being as snide as he could be said, "Spare me from Emma Goldman and her midwives. They are a bunch of butchers trying to pass themselves off as doctors."

"Hold your tongue," she snapped. "They have helped thousands of women avoid having unwanted children. Does your latest gal have help in that department? I certainly hope so."

Meyer's faced reddened, and he lost his composure. "What are you talking about?"

"Meyer," she said laughing sarcastically. "We haven't had relations in two years. Do you think that I am naïve? I heard about your girls. It is quite easy to keep informed without even leaving our building, thanks to the gossips. The talk is that you are a believer in free love outside of marriage. That is exactly what Emma Goldman promotes. So, don't be a hypocrite."

"You are being absurd," he muttered. "I have no idea what you are talking about."

"Well, I do, and so do you. Apparently, your latest is a sweet, young thing from Ohio who is in nursing school. But I venture to say that she is not so innocent anymore."

His temper flared. "Don't you disparage, Alice!"

"Oh, so it's serious, is it? And her a shiksa! What would Mama and Papa say?

I think that I shall enlighten them as to what their gifted son has been up to."

Meyer lost control, his voice rising almost to a shout. "Don't you dare!"

People turned around and began to stare. But Dore went on, not willing to hold her tongue any longer, letting out years of frustration.

"And while I have your parents' attention I would tell them about all the other women. Not only do they subscribe to the "free love" philosophy, a few are avowed anarchists. Did you go with them to their meetings in order to get them into bed? Down with capitalism, Herr Doctor."

"You will keep your mouth shut," he said nervously. "You know that the doctors at Mount Sinai are against radicalism in all forms. I can't have any of this coming out. Not now."

Speaking quietly, with a menacing tone, she went on. "So now for once I have your attention. Yes, the loyal husband and promising physician is listening to his ignorant wife. Well, that's fine. I am here to make a bargain. I have had it with you Bravermans. You think you are so superior because you got to this country fifty years before I did. Well, I left school to help my father and then we both helped you. But I am done. I will not spend another night in your house."

"Where will you go, back to your parents' house?"

"Although that is none of your business, I will tell you. I plan to find a small apartment with a lady friend. Also, I attend to go to school. I can pay for my own living expenses, but now you will pay my tuition. After all, you owe me."

He laughed until he realized that she was in earnest. "Don't be absurd. I can't pay for your school. And what do you plan to study, how to sell dresses?"

"Precisely, I intend to go to Parsons and study fashion design and merchandising.

Of course, I will go part-time and continue to work at Wanamaker's. It might interest you to know that I got a promotion. But it is not enough for my tuition, so you are not off the hook."

She could see Meyer weakening. For once she had the upper hand. "I don't know if I can swing it."

"You will have staff housing, so you will not have to pay rent. You will have to tighten your belt, no more dances and concerts with Alice."

He winced at the mention of his girlfriend's name. Dore felt sorry for her because Meyer would leave her in the end. He would never have to courage to marry a gentile. Poor Alice didn't realize that she had been in a "student marriage" without the benefit of being married.

"Look Meyer I have kept quiet because I was raised to be a well-behaved, obedient daughter, who believed that she was helping her father. But now I want my life back. I am almost nineteen, and I have wasted three years on you. Wasted, because my father has not moved up at all at the Triangle, and now he pushed Leah into working there"

"How can you blame me for any of that?" he said meekly.

"Quite simply because your father is a liar. He made promises to my family that he did not keep. Enough already!"

She sat for a moment in silence staring at this weak, unattractive man. How did she bear it? "I will come home tonight, and tomorrow, we will tell your parents that we are divorcing. If you agree to my terms, you may make me out to be the villain. You can even say that I found a sweetheart at the store. I don't care what your parents' think of me. So, I will let you save face and I will keep all your secrets."

"Well, you leave me little choice. We'll tell them tomorrow. Tonight, is Sabbath dinner."

Dore rolled her eyes. "Oh yes. We mustn't ruin the Sabbath."

A few nights later, Dore and Josephine were busy working on the window display, looking through a copy of L. Frank Baum's *Merchants Record and Show Window*, the window dressers bible.

Dore looked pensive. "Do you think we could get our hands on a Maxfield Parrish poster for the background?"

"I suppose we might," said Josephine. "But I am not sure that we could find one with a Christmas theme."

"An Art Nouveau Christmas sounds like a brilliant idea," she said, flipping through the magazine. "Hey, did you hear that Baum is publishing children's books now? He certainly is a man of many talents."

"And imagination," added Josephine.

Suddenly, they heard a timid knock on the glass of the front door. Dore scrambled to exit the display window to open the door. "Josephine, I hope you don't mind that I invited a friend, who is also a client, to see how we decorate the windows."

A lovely young woman walked into the store. Fashionably dressed, she carried herself with the elegance and confidence of a woman of upper-class society.

"Josephine O'Neil, I would like you to meet Mrs. Van Wies," said Dore.

"How do you do, Josephine? Please do call me Bernadine."

"I'm very pleased to meet you, I'm sure. It would be a pleasure to show you how we design the window displays."

"Thank you, Josephine."

Dore interrupted. "How is the little one?"

"Oh, she is just thriving. I can't believe that she will be two years old in a few months."

Dore turned to Josephine. "I met Bernadine's daughter Martha a few months ago. What a beautiful baby! She has eyes just like her mother. Look at Bernadine's sky-blue eyes with those exotic rings in the iris. But she is not dark like her mother. She has curly blond hair."

Bernadine blushed, embarrassed by the praise. But she smiled with satisfaction when she thought of Eliot's blond hair that Martha had inherited.

"Bernadine, it was Josephine who was instrumental in my promotion to assistant window dresser."

"Along with Mr. Frankel," said Josephine coyly. Then she added in earnest, "Don't listen to her, Miss. It was her talent and hard work that helped her climb the ladder.

Bernadine gave Dore a little hug. "I am so happy for you. I envy you young ladies for finding work that you enjoy. I often wish I could find some meaningful occupation. Not that I don't adore being a mother. But it would be nice to have a reason to leave the house besides shopping or going to luncheons."

"Well, maybe we can find you something in the catalogue department," Dore said laughing. "But if you are serious about finding a meaningful work, I know that they need help at the Henry Street Settlement House."

Bernadine looked surprised, but her features quickly took on a serious aspect.

"Do you really think that I could be of help?"

"Of course," said Dore. "Many wealthy ladies help out. It seems to be quite the fashionable thing to do."

"If you would come with me to inquire, I very much like to see how I might help," said Bernadine.

"With pleasure," said Dore. But since I have you both here, I would like to share my news. Josephine you will not be surprised. I hope that you will understand Bernadine. Over the weekend, I broke the news to the Bravermans. Meyer and I are divorcing. They were stunned! I must admit that I took great pleasure in their dismay. I could see my father-in-law's mind working like an adding machine, subtracting my salary from the family income and thinking of whom he could swindle next. He has no idea that I have blackmailed Meyer into paying for my school tuition. When he figures that loss in, he will be enraged, not to mention extremely worried."

Josephine couldn't hold back. "Bravo, Dore! I have been waiting for this day."

Bernadine remained speechless but seemed pleased. "It is their loss. I wish I had your courage."

"They are losing more than they realize. I imagine Simon will have one of his precious girls drop out of school to pay the bills. Henrietta is fifteen and has started high school. She isn't very bright, but she can certainly work as a stenographer at the Triangle."

"You are the smart one," said Josephine. "But where are you going to live? I can't see you living with your parents, not after having lived as a married woman."

"Actually, I was going to ask for your help in that matter. Do you think that we might get an apartment together? Two girls can live quite nicely on window dressers' salaries."

Josephine practically jumped with excitement. "How could I say no to such a proposition? I can finally move out of my parents' house. Do you realize that I have been giving them my salary envelope for years? And they think that they are generous when they hand back two dollars for me to go to a show or buy clothes. It's time to free the Irish slave! Shall we start looking next week?"

"I need to start looking tomorrow. I have been staying with my parents, and I don't want Papa to think that it will be permanent. I told my mother about the divorce, and she is going to explain things to him after I move out."

Bernadine shyly interrupted. "Would you ladies mind if I came with you? Perhaps I could learn a thing or two about what life is like outside my little circle. It would also be useful if I ever find a way to leave Theo. Who knows?"

"Of course," said Dore. "Let's meet near the park tomorrow around ten."

BERNADINE AND FLORA

MARCH 1905

Her driver dropped Bernadine off at The Dakota at ten o'clock on a breezy day in March. She ascended to the Dodd's apartment and was met by Mae, who threw her arms around her waist.

"Bernadine, it's been ages since we've seen you," cried the child. "Mommy look who has come to visit. I wish that you had told me. We are on our way out. Father is taking Wren and me to the zoo."

It had been months since she had seen Mae because she had been busy raising Martha and volunteering at the settlement house. The sweet eleven-year-old girl's large brown eyes glistened with tears of disappointment. Bernadine noticed that she appeared tall for her age, with an enchanting face, unusually shaped with extremely high cheekbones. An aura of intelligence emanated from her expression. She could not explain her deep affection for the girl. She felt a connection different from the strong maternal bond she had with her own daughter. Her love for Martha exceeded anything that she had experienced in her life, even her love for Eliot. Because many people found Mae so strange, she could not help but feel protective of her.

Ned Dodd came breezing into the parlor carrying a small boy with straight blond hair and blue eyes. He did not resemble his older sister in the least. He put the child down. “Go say hello to Bernadine, Wren. Remember what we taught you.”

The boy walked over to Bernadine and bowed, grasping a few of her long delicate fingers in his little hand and giving it a shake, he murmured, “How do you do?”

Bernadine smiled. “Very well, thank you, young man. How you have grown since we last me.”

“That’s my fine young fellow,” said Ned to his son.

Bernadine could see the love that Ned felt for his son, yet it saddened her to observe the preference for the boy overshadowed his love for Mae. She noted the expression of regret and worry on Flora’s face.

“Perhaps next time I come to visit I may bring my little Martha? She is a about your age. You could show her some of your toys.”

Ned looked around the parlor, where boxes stood in corners and all the tables and been cleared of knick-knacks and photographs. “Well, as you can see, your next visit will have to be to our new brownstone on Madison and 80th. I have made the final arrangements, and we will be moving next week. I plan to take the entire week off work. I can assure you that Mr. Morgan is none too happy, not with all that is going on this week.”

Flora said proudly, “Ned, you have been a great help to him in ironing out the legalities of buying out the coal and steel companies. He can do without you for one week.”

“I dare say he will have to try. I am not worried. He has thanked me generously with stock in the company and the profit from that has allowed us to buy our new home.”

He put on his coat. "Now I think it's about time that the children and I get started for the zoo. I'm sure that the monkeys are waiting impatiently for our arrival."

Mae ran over to Bernadine and hugged her. "I wanted to tell you about the new book that I have been reading. It's about evolution. Do you know what that is? If you have time one day, I would like to explain it to you and perhaps we could visit the Natural Science Museum."

"I would just adore that," said Bernadine as Mae walked out of the parlor and took her brother's hand. She turned to Flora. "Ned seems to be over the moon with little Lawrence. I love that you call him Wren."

Flora seemed miles away. "Oh, yes. That was Mae's idea. When he was born, she said he looked like a little bird. Bernadine, I need to speak to you frankly, as my dear friend."

"Of course, you know that you can always trust me. You do seem preoccupied, which is surprising since everything seems to be going so well for you now."

"In general things are wonderful. But I am worried about Mae, well, and her relationship with Ned. He often gets annoyed with her and makes no effort to hide his disappointment. She doesn't fit into his idea of how a young girl should comport herself. Whereas, I can see the pride he is already taking in his son, even though he is only three; it is obvious that he doesn't feel the same about Mae. I worry that she has noticed, and it must confuse her."

"Are you sure that you're not imagining his preference for Wren?" asked Bernadine.

"Not at all. He is planning Wren's life and his expectations are high. My goodness he has already contacted board members at Groton, and he has decided that Harvard would be the best fit for his son."

Bernadine tried to appear nonjudgmental. She did not want to insult Ned, but it galled her to see how he neglected Mae. "I'm sure Wren will do well, but he should take more of an interest in Mae. She is a brilliant and curious girl. What does he propose for her education?"

Flora appeared frustrated yet resigned. "She has been tutored at home for the past few years."

Bernadine bristled. "Don't talk to me about tutors. In Galveston, I was tutored at home while many of my friends went to private schools and on to college. My father didn't see the need for advanced education, and you see where that got me. If I had only gone to college, perhaps I would not have married so young. An idle mind is a curse. Mae is probably more in advanced than her tutors in some things. What she needs is a challenging school and supplemental lessons in science."

Flora stood and walked over to the window, trying to hide her emotions.

"Bernadine, I have tried to talk to Ned, but he wants his daughter to receive a traditional education. She will be turning twelve soon, and we have secured a place for her at Spence for next year. He spoke with Clara Spence, and he very much approves of her philosophy of education."

"I understand your situation. Frankly, I am not sure that I have the strength of my convictions since I allowed myself to be trapped by Theo and his family. Fortunately, Martha is too young to understand our domestic farce. So, I would not venture to tell you how to handle Ned. "

"I guess, in some ways, we share the same dilemma. Of course, I would not compare my marriage to yours and I wish I could help you find a way out."

Bernadine shook her head and sighed. "I think that we will end up talking in circles. Sometimes there is no easy solution. Let's talk about your new home. If I am correct 80th and Madison is one of New York's most fashionable neighborhoods."

Flora's face relaxed, and she smiled. "Yes, it's a fresh start in many ways. A lovely new home, where I am sure we will be happy. Ned has never been so attentive to my every wish. We have spent a fortune on the interiors and the furnishings." Looking at Bernadine with an air of contentment, she went on, "Despite our disagreement over Mae, our marriage has never been happier. Ned has never been so affectionate and passionate toward me, at least since our first weeks of marriage. It all started a few months after Wren was born, and we began sharing the same bed again."

"That is wonderful. You certainly deserve to be happy. Having success in business and the birth of a son have softened him. He does seem so much more relaxed." Bernadine lowered her gaze, and her eyes glistened.

Flora put her arm around her friend's shoulder. "Oh, I am sorry. Are things between you and Theo any better? I mean, he hasn't tried to, well, handle you again?"

"No," said Bernadine acerbically. "Nothing like that. But he has started up with his old habits. For two years, he was discreet. He didn't spend his nights out and he perfected his portrayal of the good husband and father."

"I have heard about his reformation from many a society lady at tea. You don't often hear it from men though."

"Well, I suppose men have greater access to the other world he lives in, so they are harder to fool. But he makes a show of walking with Martha and me in the park. He even suggested we start going to church. I had to laugh."

"At least he is trying to be a good father. That is one bright point," said Flora.

"Not in the least!" scoffed Bernadine. "At home he ignores Martha and he is angry if she makes too much noise and wakes him in the morning. Once I heard him tell her to shut up. I believe that she is afraid of him."

"That is awful. I would imagine that his parents would intervene. After all, Martha is their granddaughter, or so they believe."

"They have spoken to Theo and I even think that he is trying to be kinder. But it all depends on his mood and level of intoxication."

"I wish you could find a chance of happiness. I thought that you might have found some hope when you found Eliot. I wish that had worked out for you. I never understood why he didn't fight for you. But you must take heart, for in a few years you will come into your money. Then you can leave that infernal marriage and live happily with Martha. And at least you are spared the horror of sharing Theo's bed"

Bernadine smiled sardonically. "Thank God for that. But I sometimes get lonely for the touch of a man. I had no idea until I was with Eliot how much I longed for physical love."

Flora spoke firmly to her friend. "There was a time in my life when I would have suggested that you take a lover. But now I feel that would be a great error. You hold the high moral ground amongst all the Van Wies. Keep it. I would counsel you to find another outlet for your energy."

Shaking her head as if to chase away the sadness, Bernadine brightened. "Actually, in addition to raising Martha, I have found a very worthy way to spend my time. I have been volunteering at the Henry Street Settlement House. Lillian Wald is doing marvelous things to help poor women and working girls. I haven't mentioned it before because I was afraid you wouldn't approve. I have been teaching young women to read. I go in the evenings because the girls work long hours, and evenings are the only free time they have. Poor things, they are always so exhausted, but they really want to improve their prospects. Most of them work in factories, garment or bookbinding. Their only hope of advancement is to learn to read and write so that they might find jobs as salesgirls or, if they are bright enough, in an office."

Flora said enthusiastically, "I think what you are doing is very noble. I wish that I could do something worthwhile. But I would never be able to leave the house in the evenings. You mustn't neglect Martha."

"No, I would never do that. She is already in bed when I leave. And if she wakes, Mademoiselle Monique, the nanny, is there. Theo and his father are often at their club in the evenings. Of course, Agnes and Clara never miss an opportunity to make snide comments, which I ignore. But one time when I had had enough, I snapped at Clara. I told her that she should want to volunteer since she has no husband or child to occupy her time. I said that it would make her feel needed. I know that was cruel, but I truly don't feel sorry for her."

Flora rang a bell for the servants to bring tea. She stood up and walked slowly around the parlor examining pieces of furniture. "I have been trying to decide what I absolutely must keep for the new brownstone. I am disposing of the table lamps and all of the knick-knacks. They are so Victorian. We are doing up the new house in the Art Nouveau style. I have the most divine decorator. She is a friend of Anne Morgan, Elsie de Wolfe. She did the interior design of the Colony Club. Oh, I forgot to tell you. I hope you don't mind but I put your name up for membership."

All the while that Flora was prattling on, Bernadine had only one thing on her mind. The fact that Flora was going to dispose of her lamps and other furnishings that she found too Victorian. She abruptly interrupted.

"Flora, forgive me, but what are you going to do with the furniture that you no longer want?"

"Honestly, I haven't given it much thought. I was thinking of having an agent try to sell it at an estate sale. Although I don't think these things would bring in much. They are so out of date."

"Would you mind terribly letting me have whatever you don't take with you?

I know how to put these things to good use. I am sure that some of my students and their parents would be most appreciative to have them, even if they are out of date."

"Of course, Bernadine. Can you arrange the hauling and such?"

"Yes, I will take care of everything."

Having settled the question of her unwanted items, Flora changed the topic somewhat brusquely. "Do you think that you could take some time off from your volunteer work? I was planning a trip to Paris at the end of April. I'll be staying at the Ritz. I'm going over with Elizabeth Lehr. Harry is not going, so we won't have to put up with his antics. Alva said she would try to come. I won't stay long, as I don't want to be away from Ned and Wren for too long."

Bernadine noticed that she had neglected to mention Mae, and she blushed with shame for her friend.

"I'm not sure. I don't want to leave Martha. The idea of Agnes and Clara filling her little head with nonsense terrifies me, not to mention how Theo might treat her."

"Oh, please do come. I want to replenish my wardrobe. You have such good taste and I would appreciate your advice."

"Bernadine hesitated, "I don't know."

"I propose a compromise. You can bring Martha, and I will bring Wren. What an adorable pair they will make."

"What about Mae?" Bernadine asked.

"Oh Mae, she would be bored to death. All she is interested in are her books.

She will want to stay here and study. After all she will be going to Spence next term."

BERNADINE AND DORE

JUNE 1905

Wanamaker's doors had just closed for the day, a particularly busy day since a shipment of Parisian designer dresses had arrived in the morning and needed to be unpacked and put on display in the new designer salon. Dore supervised the entire process in her capacity as Executive Fashion Liaison with the Advertising Department.

Having finished her first term at Parsons, Ira Frankel convinced the men in the store administration that she would be an asset to assist with the marketing of women's fashion, both designer and the less-expensive, off-the-rack dresses. Now that Wanamaker's had decided to open a new exclusive salon, dedicated to European designer imports, Ira asked her to take on full responsibility for its launch and subsequent oversight.

Although exhausted, she waited expectantly for Bernadine, who had asked for a preview of the dresses. She walked to the downstairs employee entrance to meet her friend since no one could enter through the main doors after hours. Bernadine glided through the employee entrance with grace, as if she were walking into Sherry's or Delmonico's.

Her dress with its high waist and décolleté flattered her figure. Its lavender color complemented her blue eyes.

"Thank you for letting me have a peek at the dresses before the crowds descend on the store," said Bernadine.

Dore gave her a brief hug. "You bought that dress in Paris, didn't you?" she asked with assurance.

"You have quite the eye," said Bernadine. "I went with Flora, and we bought out the Grands Magasins. I still have a few trunks that are coming over in a week or two. Those are the custom-made dresses, a few gowns from Worth and some everyday dresses that I bought from a new young designer."

Dore led her over to the newly designed elevator with its Art Nouveau iron and brass door. "Let's go right up. We have set up the Salon on the fourth floor in a very discreet corner. I want your honest opinion. I chose all the dresses and gowns from French magazines without the advantage of a trip to Paris."

As the women entered the Salon, Dore switched on the electric lights. Dazzled by the entire effect of the illumination by sconces and several chandeliers, Bernadine remained speechless for a few seconds. Then she exclaimed, "My, it's beautiful. You have arranged it brilliantly. Honestly, it reminds me of one of the designer salons at *Au Printemps.* So, show me what you brought over."

Dore guided her slowly through the racks of dresses, although mannequins wore the most expensive gowns. "Do you really like it? I designed the layout myself. I have a friend from Parsons who helped with the painting of displays and fixtures. Anyway, look at the dresses. You see that I insisted that we show the new flowing cut here. The other departments will continue to sell the older lines with the S curve and the corsets that go with that look. But here I'm trying to show what we might be seeing in the future of ladies' fashion. I even persuaded the bosses upstairs to let me display and Empire waist gown. What do you think?" she said pointing to mannequin.

"Oh yes, it's lovely!" said Bernadine. "You have a wonderful eye for color. Deep blues and indigos are my favorites. Although I am not quite sure if that high waist will ever catch on in New York. I did see a few French women wearing that style. But it is considered a little *avant-garde.*"

"This is why I am going to Parsons. I am learning about not only design but also marketing, you know, selling. Knowing how to advertise a dress or hat will dictate what women will want to wear. Advertising, that is all I am planning to study next term."

They walked over to a grouping of chairs with a very modern low table that had been placed in a corner of the salon. "It was my idea to place these tables and chairs here. I thought that we might have live models walking around to show the dresses to their best advantage. I also thought that it is likely that some gentlemen will accompany their wives and it would be most convenient for them. The longer they stay, the more likely they are to buy."

"Dore, you must be exhausted, working here and going to school."

"I'm young and believe me, it's much better than what my life might have been working in a factory."

"It's hard for me to imagine you in that life. You are so elegant and talented. Even the way you speak has nothing to do with the girls who I work with at the settlement house."

"Are you still teaching them to read and write?" Dore asked.

"Yes, and a few of them are very bright and have made progress with their spelling and punctuation. I may even be able to find a few of them positions as stenographers."

"Perhaps you can ask Flora to use her husband's connections with his lawyer friends?"

"That is a thought," said Bernadine. "But I must admit to being a little disillusioned with many of these girls. I mean you should see what the books they are reading. Do you know about these so-called dime novels?"

"Yes, some of the girls used to read them when we were in school. Many still do."

"Well, these girls are mad for them. I picked one up and read it, utter nonsense!

I don't see how reading fantasies about poor working girls meeting and marrying Wall Street tycoons can be helpful. They are delusions. Believe me, I know what comes from marrying a delusion."

Seeing her friend's frustration, Dore tried her best to defend these working girls.

"I understand. I have seen the young women in the old neighborhood reading these books. Even Leah, my adopted sister, has taken to reading them. It annoys me when I think that I spent the little free time that I had teaching her to read, just so that she can waste her time on those silly stories. But they are poor and everyone needs to dream of a way out of a miserable life."

"Yes, we all need a dream and hope," said Bernadine sadly. "I would, however, advise the girls who may be lucky enough to obtain interviews at various firms to tone down their attire. My goodness, the way they dress is shocking. How do they afford it? It seems that every week or two they have a new shirtwaist, each one with the latest cut or style of frill. And the hats that they create! Such confections! I admit that they are creative, but sometimes, they are gaudy, with an over-abundance of artificial flowers and feathers."

"Bernadine, can't you see that they are trying to imitate what they believe ladies of the middle and upper classes are wearing?

"I suppose so," she sighed. "But with little success."

Dore smiled ironically. "You have to understand how these women live. I do. I was brought up in their environment, in the tenements. They are trying to reinvent themselves, just as I did. They have limited options, these immigrant girls. Most will work in the factories, or if they are lucky, as salesgirls. They know when they interview for a job that they are being judged by their prospective employers. The boss does not want to hire a greenhorn. He will choose the girl with the overdone hat over the girl with the scarf or shawl on her head every time. He will pick the girl with the painted face over the one who is clean-faced. These young women understand this. If they want to get the job or the beau, they have to look American."

Dore thought of herself when she first worked at A.T. Stewart as a cash girl and how the senior sales girls looked down on her. She had learned to dress as stylishly as she could on her meager salary. Gradually, as she obtained her own sense of fashion, she had been able to work her way up at Wanamaker's. She wished that she could make Bernadine understand the difficulty of the journey that she had made, and was still making to become an American New Woman.

"I have never thought about their motivations, at least not in that light," said Bernadine. "But it makes perfect sense. Dressing stylishly gives them a sense of self-worth and independence."

"And you have hit the nail on its head," said Dore. "Independence is something these girls crave. They scrimp on lunch in order to buy a new shirtwaist. Most immigrant girls give their pay envelops to their parents and are allowed only a dollar or two for themselves. What they keep goes toward a new hat or perhaps a show."

"I feel a little foolish. After working at the settlement house for well over a year, I realize that I never truly understood my students. And I have never appreciated how hard you have worked in pursuing your dreams. I admire you more than ever Dore."

Dore was silent for a moment and then answered, her voice trembling. "I think it is only fair to admit that I have no idea what it would be like to lead your life. How you ended up with a man like Theo and why your feel forced to stay with him is beyond my understanding."

"It's quite simple," said Dore. "I married a man who dazzled me. He seduced me because he was handsome and sensual. He and his family promised me the glamor and glory of being part of New York Royalty. And I, little fool that I was, believed in this dream, until wedding night when the nightmare began."

Dore was confused. "Nightmare? I know that you don't love your husband, and from what I gather he has an unsavory reputation. But are you in danger? Does he beat you?"

Bernadine felt her face redden with anger. "No Dore, he doesn't touch me anymore. He only handled me on our first night, but he was not gentle or loving. If he had he not been my husband, I would say that he savagely raped me."

Dore gasped in horror. "I had no idea! Why do you stay with him? No matter what power the Van Wies family wields, you shouldn't stay with him."

Bernadine looked away in shame. "You have told me about the injustice that women of your class endure. It is cruel, but it is not unique. There are some women, like Alva Belmont, who have fought back and seized control of their own destiny. But that is still rare. Just pick up Edith Wharton's *House of Mirth* and read about the fate of *Lily Bart.* I know that it is just a novel, but it reflects the reality of how a woman without money and connections may stumble and perish. I will not be a *Lily Bart.*"

BERNADINE AND THEO

NOVEMBER 1907

On a dull November afternoon, the Van Wies had just finished their obligatory Sunday luncheon, the only time the family gathered to share a formal, but bland meal. Agnes, the matriarch, remained in bed where for the past few months she spent entire days due to debilitating headaches and intense attacks of shaking due to her nerves.

The very picture of the Victorian woman, she had become a martyr too sensitive to face the realities of her crumbling world. For weeks, she had been taking her Laudanum religiously. But in the past few days, she had secretly increased her dose.

Mademoiselle Monique came into the dining room with Martha's coat to whisk her off for her walk in the park.

"Nanny," said Clara, delicately wiping her mouth with a napkin to remove the last crumbs of chocolate cake, "when you return, see that you keep little Martha quiet. You know that my mother needs her sleep."

It annoyed Bernadine that Clara and the rest of the family called Monique "Nanny." She always felt that it was meant as an insult.

Theo looked up and asked her to have the carriage brought around on her way out.

"Where are you going?" asked Clara. "You remember that we have a serious issue to discuss."

"I remember!" he said, almost shouting with annoyance. "I promised mother that I would go to the pharmacy to refill her prescription, and they close early on Sundays."

Arthur suddenly began coughing violently, and Clara poured him some water. In recent months, he had started a rapid decline into old age: his shoulders becoming hunched, he seemed to be folding in on himself as if he were disappearing. His doctor had detected a heart anomaly.

"Father you do not look well at all. You are so pale," said his daughter.

"Oh, stop fussing. I know what is wrong with me. Dr. Wells sent me to a heart man, and he says there is not much to be done. So, with any luck, I won't be present for the unraveling. It's your problem now, Theo."

His son felt his face burning with rage. "How can you blame me for our financial disaster? I have never been involved in investments and business ventures. It was you who lost hundreds of thousands in wild railroad schemes. And I was under the impression that we had sufficient funds in the accounts to maintain the house and pay the servants."

"Well, if you had taken an interest in the family business, you would know that in the past year, our accounts have been drained in order to keep up appearances, and after what happened this week, we are paupers."

"Papa, how is that possible? You must be mistaken," cried Clara.

"I spoke with our banker and our accountant on Friday. I had most of our money in copper and metal stocks. Do you know what that means, Theo?"

He looked at his father blankly.

"It means that we have lost everything. Charles Barney was trying to corner the copper market and had a scheme using the Knickerbocker Trust. Well, we lost all our metal stocks and whatever money we had in the Knickerbocker, which has gone under.

It is of small comfort to me that the bastard Barney shot himself in the stomach. Apparently, it took him hours to die."

"Poor Lily and her girls," said Clara thinking of Barney's wife and young daughters.

"I don't give a damn about Lily and the girls," shouted Arthur. "Thanks to Barney we have nothing. We have only Bernadine's allowance to feed ourselves. Thank God she comes into her money in January."

All eyes turned to Bernadine. She held her tongue, but her mind was reeling.

Arthur cleared his throat. "I am sorry, old girl, but we will need to use every last penny of your allowance for the household expenses. I had my banker at City Bank set up the account in my name. I must admit that I resented your parents' decision to delay your inheritance for all these years, but now I am grateful. In January, we shall be set up again, and we will be able to regain our former manner of living. I would venture to say that after I am gone, with your money the entire family will enjoy all the luxuries in life."

"You have no idea," said Theo. "I have information regarding the value of Bernadine's inheritance as it stands as of last month. I have reliable sources that show a large increase in the amount that Mr. Jones left his beloved daughter. There are now approximately two million dollars in bonds, stocks, and cash in the account. And the real estate in Houston has increased tenfold. Our girl is quite the heiress."

Bernadine, boiling with anger, asked, "How did you come by this information? You do not have access to my accounts."

Theo leaned over and whispered, "I will tell you later."

Later that night Bernadine knocked on Theo's bedroom door. He did not respond, but she found the door unlocked, turned the knob and entered. She found him dressing to go out, already drinking out of a small flask that he often carried in his jacket pocket.

She steeled her nerves and confronted him. "Where are you going? It's Sunday night and surely most of your haunts are closed."

"Why do you suddenly care where I go?" he asked with a sneer. "I have an appointment with a few friends at the club. There is to be a card game, although I doubt that anyone has the cash on hand to bet tonight."

"Go where you wish and do what you want. I could care less. But right now, you are going to listen to me." She clenched her jaw, trying to control her anger and fight back tears of rage. "I have put up with this farce, this hypocrisy, for far too long. I have lost my freedom and my self-respect. Before I lose my mind and my soul, I am going to cut all ties with this family. I plan to file for divorce, no matter what the cost, and Martha will live with me.

"You have lost your mind if you think that I will allow you to leave now, just when I need your money."

Holding her head high and squaring her shoulders, she looked straight into his eyes, without fear. "How will you stop me? I have my money, and I will use it to hire the best team of lawyers."

"You don't have the money, yet! He scoffed. "Not until January. For the moment, what little money you do have is in the family account. So, there is nothing you can do."

Bernadine fumed and the words poured out with intensity that surprised Theo.

"In two months, I will have my money, and you cannot touch it. Mr. Simpson has seen to that, notwithstanding your spy."

"Yes, a little stenographer that I discovered was all too willing to keep me informed for a small fee and a trip to New York."

"Well, good for you. I hope that you enjoyed her! My money is safe in a Houston bank. I have endured all these years. I can survive for two more months. But in January…."

She felt a stinging blow to her cheek. Theo had not touched her in years, yet somehow now, he felt free to strike her. She fell back onto a leather chair. Her face throbbed, and her eyes were blinded by tears. "Theo, you are slipping," she hissed. "That is bound to leave a mark. And now I will not hesitate to tell anyone how it got there." With that, she stormed out of the room without looking back.

Theo fell onto the bed and covered his eyes with his arm. He had to think. He could not let her go: the money, all that money.

Later that evening Theo descended from a cab at the corner of 73rd and Broadway, looking up at the immense seventeen-story façade decorated with nooks, scrolls, and stone satyrs that covered the Ansonia Hotel. A world unto itself, the Ansonia contained a top-rated restaurant, a billiards room, a barbershop, and of course the famous Turkish bath in the basement. He had often thought that it would make a wonderful home if he were to find himself a bachelor or even better, a widower. He walked through the elaborately decorated lobby and chuckled as he passed the lobby fountain with its live seals. He had been friendly with William Stokes, who financed the building of the hotel. He slightly envied the forty-three-year-old society swell with his nineteen-year-old Cuban wife. He had seen them together at a small dinner party. He wondered how Stokes managed to keep her in line. Although considered quite the oddball, people found him amusing. He loved animals of all kinds, to the point where he actually set up a small farm on the roof of the Ansonia. Apparently, there were grazing cows, along with goats and approximately five hundred chicken. The chicken were so prolific that Stokes had the building management deliver free eggs to the tenants every morning.

His mood changed as he entered the Ansonia dining room where he was meeting his friend Percy Cooke. Percy belonged to a small group of friends who accompanied him on his frequent visits to brothels and even the rare night at an opium den. Theo envied him because he had managed to stay single, thus keeping his enormous family wealth for his own pleasures.

Theo spotted his friend seated at a corner table, perusing the menu while smoking a cigar. In polite society, one would call him a stocky man, but in truth he was morbidly overweight. He rose and proffered his plump hand.

"How are you, old man?" he said. "Quite a good offering tonight. I waited to order, but I am famished."

"What looks good?" asked Theo.

"I'm not going to bother with soup. I'm starting with the Cape Cod Little Necks and going straight to the Canvas-back duck. And, of course, the Lobster Newburg is a must. It is one of their specialties."

"I'll have the same, except for the Lobster Newburg. I don't think my stomach can take it tonight."

"What's wrong? Trouble at home?"

Theo scowled. "Is it that obvious? Yes, trouble at home. Let's change the subject. I want to enjoy myself. What do you say to steam in the Turkish bath after dinner?"

"Fine idea," said Percy. "That way I can melt off some of the meal."

Being a Sunday night, the Turkish bath was empty, and the two men spread out on the tiled benches. Both men wore only the towels supplied by the drowsy attendant, who seemed surprised that any clients should appear after ten o'clock. The depraved lives both men led left imprints upon their physiques. The large towel that he wore barely covered Percy's corpulence. He had porcine features and large bags under his small eyes. Theo's once sculpted body contained no fat, but where there had once been muscle, only loose, wrinkled skin remained.

Wiping droplets of sweat from his forehead, Theo sulked. "I don't know how much longer I can keep up this good-boy act in public. Last night I went to Bessie Wortham's place. She has some new girls, very young, twelve or thirteen. She promised me a twelve-year-old virgin. But she is asking a fortune, two hundred dollars. I am dying to have her, but unfortunately, we were wiped out by the Knickerbocker Trust debacle. Wouldn't want to treat me, old boy, would you? We could share the girl, if that appeals to you."

"I don't mind," said Percy wiping his baldpate with his towel. "You don't mind having a fat chap like me around?"

"No, not in the least. You know me. I love to watch. You can take her first, if you like. It would only be fair since you are paying."

"All right," said Percy. "You arrange it since you are in so good with Bessie."

"Yes, good ol' Bessie," said Theo. "I don't know how much longer she will be in charge of things. She has been running that house for twenty years. But apparently, there is a turf war going on. A young Jewish whore named Rachel, who has lately taken to calling herself Madame Sophie, is positioning herself to take the reins. Bessie tried to put Fat Alice in charge, but it was a no-go. Apparently, Alice is a slave to liquor and the opium pipe. Can't even run her own life, never mind a brothel. So, this Rachel maneuvered her way into a position of power. Did I mention that she is a beauty, a mass of dark curls with dark skin and amber-colored eyes? There is something to be said for these Jewish women. I spent an evening with her a few years ago. She did what I asked, and you know I ask a lot. I even fancied myself in love with her for a time, but she would have none of it. I must say that she has established quite an impressive client list. Most men would pick her over any of the younger girls."

"I would very much enjoy being added to her list," said Percy.

"Shall we go there tomorrow night?" asked Theo. I will call ahead and see if Rachel is available and willing. And while we are there, I will talk to Bessie about the young girl. Are you sure that you are in?"

"You bet," said Percy trying to tie a towel around his huge paunch.

The Dodd's butler opened the door of the large brownstone on 80th and Madison. Bernadine tried to hide her face by wearing an unstylish hat with a veil. She intentionally timed her visit in the middle of the day, knowing that Mae would be in school and Ned at work.

The butler showed them into a lovely parlor, where Flora was sitting at a gorgeous Art Nouveau desk with exotic wood, inlaid with designs of blooming magnolias. She had visited her friend many times before in the new brownstone and appreciated the style and comfort of the home. Flora sifted through a pile of invitations with of an expression of consternation on her face.

"You look busy, said Bernadine. "I didn't know that you were giving a party.

"Yes, I am, and with very little notice, I might add. Ned thought it would be nice to have a gathering of about thirty members of the firm and their wives. I am also inviting members of the Morgan family, including Anne. It is to honor Mr. Morgan for his Herculean efforts to save the financial stability of the nation. Most people are completely unaware of what he did, putting up his own money and convincing Roosevelt to go along with a scheme that allowed several firms to merge in order to pool their resources and bail out the banks. So even though the public loves to pillory J.P. Morgan, we will be celebrating Mr. Morgan next Saturday night."

Bernadine walked over to a wall of French doors that looked over a small garden.

Taking off her coat and slowly removing her hat and veil, she turned around and faced her friend, waiting for her reactions.

Flora gasped. "What in the world happened to your face? My goodness! Your cheek is swollen to twice its normal size. What did that monster do to you?"

Bernadine collapsed onto the sofa. "He has gone too far. I really believe that he has lost his reason."

"But he has never struck you before," said Flora examining her friends face, she called to her maid to bring some ice. "He must realize that you would never accept to stay with him after this."

The maid handed a cloth bag filled with ice to Bernadine, which she placed on her cheek. "Actually, that is what set him off. I told him that I decided to file for divorce. That was after Arthur informed the family that they had lost everything in the Knickerbocker crisis. In fact, they had lost most of their money before, but now they are completely destitute. That is except for my allowance, and my inheritance, which I will receive in January. They have taken all the money from my allowance account and placed in their bank account. I don't know how they managed that, but I was incensed. Then Arthur, the old fool, said he would take over the management of all my money when I come into it and they would again live as they have lived in their glory days.

There before my eyes, the conspiracy of my marriage to Theo bore its fruit. As soon as I was alone with Theo, I told him that I was leaving and taking my child and my money with me."

"Finally!" cried Flora. "I am so glad."

"Yes, that is when he struck me. I locked myself in my room. Now, I have come to ask if Ned could refer me to a good attorney."

"Certainly, I will ask him tonight."

Blushing with embarrassment, Bernadine asked, "Do you think that you could lend me a few hundred dollars? I plan to move out as soon as I can make arrangements, and I have no access to my money."

Flora had just started writing out a check, when the doorbell rang and the butler handed her a message from Clara Van Wies. Arthur was dead and she needed Bernadine to help with the arrangements. They couldn't find Theo and she desperately needed her help.

Bernadine looked defeated. "It looks like I am going to have to postpone my departure, at least for a while."

Two weeks after the funeral, still in a state of panic, Clara found herself responsible for running the house. Agnes had not been out of her room since they returned from the cemetery. Taking dangerously high doses of Laudanum, she refused to see anyone but Theo and that was only because he supplied her with the drug. Clara tried to talk to him about the lack of funds to run the house. She informed the maid and the cook that she would not be able to pay them until January. The butler gave his notice on the day of the funeral. His loyalty to his old master could not be questioned, but he had grown to dislike the rest of the family. The maid, Tess, had agreed to stay on since she had no place to go. The cook, Mrs. Schmidt, said that she would remain until she found another position.

Bernadine had spoken with Mademoiselle Monique and told her that she was to receive her inheritance in a few weeks. She and Monique had a warm and open relationship, and she knew that she could depend on her loyalty. Knowing that they would soon be leaving the Van Wies' home, the young woman could not be more relieved. She adored five-year-old Martha, who could now speak to her in fluent French. Bernadine credited her with supplying the warmth and stability that allowed Martha to develop into a happy child all while living in a cold and dysfunctional family. Monique often responded to Bernadine's compliments by insisting Martha's happy nature was the result of having such a wonderful mother.

Theo opened the front door to escape the chaos unfolding in the house, when Clara tried to stop him. "Please, Theo you have to speak to Bernadine. Is there no way she can get her lawyer to send a check from her account in Houston? Our situation is dire and I cannot manage things anymore. Why the grocer is refusing to make next week's delivery unless we pay something on our account."

He looked at his sister with disgust. "So, you are now beginning to realize the seriousness of our situation. You have glided through life for thirty years, never dealing with reality. You have always had your dresses, your balls, and a comfortable home. With all my faults, at least I was aware of our precarious position. I have made the sacrifice and married a woman whom I abhorred."

"What are you complaining about, Theo?" she cried. "Bernadine is beautiful and rich. In a few weeks, when she has her money, things can go back to normal. We can hire a new cook and butler, and I must say we can find better."

"Again, I must point out how detached you are from reality. Two weeks ago, Bernadine informed me that she is going to seek a divorce. Since she will have all the money, she will have the best legal minds to press her case."

"Divorce," said Clara in a whisper. "You can't be serious. And you have known about this for two weeks?" She stopped suddenly, looking at her brother in horror. "That horrible swelling on Bernadine's face the day that father died, that was you! She said that she had fallen down in the street and hit her head. But it was you! No wonder she is leaving you. But what are we going to do now?"

His voice devoid of any sign of emotion, Theo spoke coldly and calmly to his sister. "You are to mind your own business and let me deal with my wife: for she will remain my wife until her dying day. Now call the grocer and tell him that he is to make the delivery and that he will be paid."

Later that day Theo met a young thug named Al who worked at Bessie's.

They sat in a dark bar in the Tenderloin section of town. He knew Al had some very shady connections and had once boasted about being a member of the Five Points Gang.

Al supplied the muscle at the brothel and would eject unruly men, and women who threatened the peace of the establishment. Several of the girls had told Theo that Al had been attached to a young prostitute, named Katie, whom he wanted to keep for himself. A feisty and independent Irish girl, she balked at the idea of being controlled by any one man. She didn't mind giving her body to any number of customers during the course of a night at Bessie's. But no man could tell Bessie what to do in her free time. She was willing to do almost anything a man wanted for twenty dollars, but she bristled at Al's attempts to dictate to her what she could or could not do. Several months ago, she turned up dead, poisoned. No one could prove it, but everyone knew that Al had killed the poor girl. With this in mind, Theo sought him out that afternoon.

"What can I do for you, Mr. Van Wies?" Al growled, his breath sour as he drank from a half-empty whiskey bottle.

"Well, Al, my friend, I thought that we might help each other out."

"No how would we do that, my friend?" Al answered in a jocular, but sarcastic tone. "You being from a high society family and all, I wouldn't think that you would even want to be seen during the day with the likes of me."

"Look, Al, I know that you have means, well, access, to certain substances and that you know how to use them. If you can supply me with such a substance, I would be willing to pay you handsomely. But in order for me to obtain a vast amount of money, a certain person must be…," he hesitated, "eliminated."

Al had been staring at him, eyes half closed until he grasped his meaning. He abruptly sat up straight, a large nasty smile transformed his face. He came closer to Theo his foul breath was nauseating.

"What do you need, Mister? Just come out with it," he whispered in a harsh and menacing tone.

"Do you think that you can get your hands on some strychnine?" said Theo nervously. "I have heard of a case, a famous lady from California, poisoned several years ago and apparently no one was able to prove anything."

"Sure, old man. I can get some easily. I know a few lads who specialize in drugs and poisons and they know how to keep their mouths shut, as do I. But it will cost you."

"How much do you want?"

"I'll be needing two hundred dollars. And I will need it today, that is, if you want the stuff tonight."

Theo hesitated. Then he remembered his conversation with Percy. Two hundred dollars is what Bessie wanted for the night with the young virgin. He could get the money from Percy and say that he would arrange things for the following week. He looked at Al and asked if he could meet him back at the bar in three hours.

"Easy as pie. I'll just walk down to the Bowery and get things started, but see that you have the money when I get back."

Theo nodded, walked out of the bar and hailed a cab. He knew that Percy would be lunching at the club, as he did every day.

He walked into the club and waited until Percy's luncheon group had dispersed and he saw him sitting in the lounge smoking a cigar.

"Theo, this is a surprise."

"Look, Percy," he said trying to hide his nerves and sound nonchalant. "I don't have much time. Do you still want the girl?"

"Girl?" said Percy looking perplexed.

"You know the virgin that we were talking about at Bessie's."

"Oh yes, sure I do."

"Well, listen. There is someone else interested. Bessie told me last night. So, if we want her, we have to act fast. I need to give her the two hundred dollars, today.

Can you get your hands on it?"

"Get my hands on it? Who do you think you are talking to? I have a couple of thousand in my desk at home."

"Let's go get it now. I will take care of paying Bessie and set everything up for next Friday, if that suits you."

Returning home around five o'clock, Theo found only the cook and the maid.

"Tess, where is everyone," he asked impatiently.

"I wouldn't know," she responded in rude tone.

He had noticed her insolence that she did not perform her duties with any effort or regularity; dust covered the furniture and floor; she rarely changed the bedclothes.

He went into the kitchen and noticed that the cook had not started dinner.

"Mrs. Schmidt, what is the meaning of this? It's five o'clock, and you haven't even started preparing dinner."

"Sir, I was told that nobody was eating in tonight. Miss Clara has an engagement, and Mrs. Van Wies is dining with her friend, Mrs.

Dodd, and has taken Martha with her. I was about to make some broth for your mother."

"And what about me? No one asked me!" He feigned anger, but was actually relieved to find the house empty.

"I could make you a little something if you wish, sir," she replied in a surly manner.

"Oh, never mind. Just tell the girl to make up the rooms for the evening and remind her to put fresh water in the pitchers in all the rooms. She sometimes forgets."

He looked in on his mother to find her awake but very groggy. Then he went into the parlor, sat on a comfortable armchair, closed his eyes and dozed.

Meanwhile, Tess walked from room to room turning down beds and fluffing pillows. Theo woke up to the loud noise of her heavy footsteps going up and down the stairs. He could sense her irritation with having to fill the pitchers and carry them upstairs.

He walked out into the hallway and approached her. "Did you fill Mrs. Van Wies' pitcher?"

"Yes, sir. She is not expected until later, so I don't see what the rush is," she said rudely.

"Watch your tone, young lady. You can be replaced you know."

Tess snorted and gave him a smug look. "Yes, I believe that is true. If you will excuse me, sir, I have to go down for the third pitcher. They are very heavy and I can only bring two up at a time."

"Go on then, girl!" he barked.

After Tess had brought up the pitchers of water and finished arranging the bedrooms, Theo went into Bernadine's room. He walked over to her night table. Bernadine kept her room simple and disliked the clutter of knickknacks on furniture. She had a few pictures of her parents on the bureau and a picture of Martha on the night table, along with a small lamp, a glass and of course, the pitcher. All the pitchers in the bedrooms upstairs were identical. Agnes had bought them at a sale. She saw no reason to spend extravagantly for items that visitors would never see.

He slipped his hand into his pant pocket and slid out a small blue bottle. The label read bicarbonate, a precaution taken by Al to disguise the true contents, strychnine.

Theo examined the bottle for a few seconds and then carefully removed the stopper. He didn't know exactly how much to put in. Al had said that a few drops would do the trick, if the trick involved "knocking someone off."

Taking no chances, Theo poured a substantial amount of the poison into the pitcher and swirled it around for a minute. He placed it back in its usual place on the table and quickly exited the room. Having decided that it would be wise to spend the evening out, he quickly grabbed his coat and closed the front door behind him. It occurred to him that he should let himself be seen this evening in order to create an alibi in the event suspicion would fall on him, so he went to his club. He expected an investigation into his wife's death, and perhaps he had not thought out every aspect of the crime. He could only think of his burning hatred for Bernadine and his need for her money.

As he sat at the club, he fantasized about the death that she would endure. He had read articles that told of convulsions and spasms, rigidity of the jaw, and finally death from asphyxiation caused by paralysis. It was said to be a horrible death. And though he had read that it could take the victim several hours to succumb, he felt confident that he had put enough poison in the pitcher that she would die in minutes rather than hours. He also felt reasonably certain that if she were to cry out, her cries would go unheard. He had given his mother a rather large dose of her Laudanum before leaving the house. The nanny and Martha were in the nursery on the top floor at the opposite end of the house. He did not worry about Clara, who would arrive home much later after attending a dinner and ball. As he drank a glass of fine scotch, little by little, he regained his confidence that the plan would work. His mood lightened, and he invited a few friends over to join him for a drink. He remained at the club until two o'clock in the morning and asked a friend to drive him home, feeling certain that would help him shore up his alibi. He walked past Bernadine's room, but decided not to look in. It would be much more dramatic if she were discovered by the maid or even better by Clara. He dropped into his bed and fell asleep without undressing.

The following morning, he slept late. Upon waking he had almost forgotten that he had poisoned his wife, and the fact that he had not be awaken earlier by screams puzzled him. He realized that something had gone wrong.

He put on his robe and opened his door, hearing not hysterics and crying, but only Martha's sweet laughter. He peeked out and could not make sense of what he saw: Bernadine and Nanny went twirling down the hall with Martha, gay as could be.

The color drained from his face, and he felt his body turn cold with shock. What had gone wrong?

It had never occurred to him that she would not drink the water. She must have come home and gone to sleep without even touching the pitcher. He knew that sometimes she brushed her teeth with

Martha in the nursery. Perhaps that was why she didn't touch her water. His emotions vacillated between fury and frustration. He had failed. He closed his door before Martha could see him and retreated to his bed. He would have to either try again or perhaps think of a new plan.

When he finally dressed and went downstairs it was early afternoon, and Bernadine and Martha had gone out with Nanny. Clara stood in the entry, putting on her coat.

"Where have you been, Theo? I am at my limit. Bernadine has not said a word to me about divorce, but I can tell that she is planning something."

Looking at his sister, he had nothing to say. She shook her head and walked out the front door. He returned to his room for the rest of the afternoon, nursing a headache.

When he went downstairs later, the cook asked if Shepard's pie would be acceptable for dinner. He looked at her blankly. Meanwhile the maid ran up and down the stairs, making a racket. She hurried to make his room, without taking the time to sweep or dust. But she did make a point of bringing down the pitchers to fill them with fresh water.

Tess gathered the three pitchers, from Clara's room, Theo's room, and Bernadine's room and put them on the hall table. Two were half-full, but the third pitcher had not been touched. She took the pitchers that needed refilling downstairs to the kitchen where she could find cold water in the icebox. Seeing that the third pitcher was full, she left it on the table. When she brought the two pitchers of fresh water up, she put one in Bernadine's room and the other in Clara's room. The third pitcher, with its lukewarm water, she placed in Theo's room.

Theo spent the remainder of the day and the evening in a Mott Street opium den. After he roused from his stupor, he returned home around midnight. Stumbling up the stairs, he muttered like a madman, cursing his parents for leaving him in this untenable situation and deriding Clara for being a worthless waste of flesh. He sat on his bed, his mouth and throat felt parched, most likely from smoking opium all day. He poured a generous amount of water from the pitcher on the night table and drank an entire glass. Barely managing to remove his shoes and socks, he fell into his bed. He closed his eyes to block out the sensation of the room spinning. For a moment he was alarmed by a onset of nausea, but he told himself that this happened if he overindulged with opium. But, suddenly, his breath became uneven and his muscles began to cramp. Within a few minutes, he realized that he was in trouble. His body contorted, his hands clenched and then he felt his feet cramping and turning inward. He tried to cry out, but he was too short of breath. Terrified, he realized what was happening. These were the very symptoms of strychnine poisoning that Al had described.

When he tried to get out of bed, his twisted feet could not support his weight and he fell violently onto the floor. Panic set in as his jaw clenched, and unspeakable spasms shook his body. This state lasted for what seemed to him hours, but in reality, was actually minutes. He blacked out briefly, and when he regained consciousness, his breath was extremely labored. From that point on, his condition deteriorated rapidly. Again, his jaw clenched and he found it impossible to fill his lungs with air. He said to himself, 'By, God, this *is* a terrible death.' He thought of Bernadine and cursed her good fortune of escaping the fate that he now suffered. The thought that she would be free filled him with bile and resentment. Theo felt no remorse for the harm he had done to Bernadine and others. Fear of death did not enter his mind. He left his life as he had passed through it, full of rage and scorn toward the world.

DORE

JANUARY 1908

Dore waited in the reception area outside of the executive office where she and Ira had been summoned for a brief interview with Robert Ogden and Rodman Wanamaker.

Rodman had just returned home from living in Paris for several years. As the wealthy son of the founder of the chain of department store, he had a reputation for living lavishly. The employees in the executive offices were eager to see if his expensive personal tastes would translate into more extravagance in the management of the store. So far, they had not been disappointed. Ogden continued to manage the store's advertising, while Rodman brought Parisian fashion and culture to New York. Rodman greeted Ira and Dore warmly when they entered his private office.

"I want to congratulate you, Mr. Frankel, on your promotion of the fashion show," said Wanamaker. "As you know, it is very important to me. I want to expose American women to the elegance and sophistication that I learned to appreciate in Paris. Ogden has told me of your hard work."

"He has done a bang-up job of getting the word out. Aside from making up some tremendous ads for newspapers and magazines, Ira has gotten the word out to the ladies at their clubs," said Ogden.

"Actually, that was Miss Abramowitz's doing," said Ira. "She is acquainted with several ladies of the beau monde here in New York. She had some of her friends spread the word at the Colony Club. She told me Anne Morgan is coming to the show and perhaps Alva Belmont will make an appearance."

"Well, we thank you, Miss Abramowitz," said Rodman Wanamaker with a slight bow.

"It was an honor and a pleasure to invite my friends. I can tell you than they are extremely excited and eager to see the changes that Parisian designers have made to the style and line of their gowns this season," Dore said, blushing slightly.

"I notice that you heeded my directive in reference to the illustrations in the ads, Frankel. I was pleased to see an end to the old fashion plates in favor of color lithographs. The ads are much more authentic," commented Ogden.

"Thank you, Mr. Ogden," said Ira. I cannot take credit for organizing the fashion show. That is again all Miss Abramowitz's work. She has a keen eye for fashion and a flare for the aesthetic. You should know that she went to Parsons."

"I am aware," said Ogden. "I would not have given just anybody the responsibility of organizing the show. We will have to consider a raise in salary for Miss Abramowitz."

"Yes, I agree," said Rodman, lighting a cigar. "I want to compliment you on your design of the set and the choice of mannequins. It's just the thing. I couldn't have done it better myself. I would say one could imagine himself in the *Les Galeries Lafayette*."

Dore smiled, grateful for Mr. Wanamaker's approval and for once to be complimented by the somewhat-hard-to-please Mr. Ogden.

After leaving the executive office, Ira and Dore headed toward the employee lounge. Dore poured herself a cup of tea. "Can I get you something?

"No thanks," said Ira. "How is the new apartment?"

As Assistant Direct of Advertising, working under Ira, she now made good money. She had recently moved out of the apartment that she had been sharing with Josephine O'Neil. She enjoyed her new independence.

She smiled sweetly at Ira. She had always hoped that he might show some interest, but in his own discreet way, he made it clear that they would never be more than very good friends. In fact, looking back over the past few years, she realized that Ira never had a steady girl. He was friendly and kind to the female employees at the store and he had some lady friends from school and his neighborhood. On the other hand, she recalled seeing him with one or two attractive men at restaurants that she had begun to frequent in Greenwich Village. Yes, very attractive men indeed.

Dore sighed. "I just love it. It's just the thing for me. I think that every working girl should live in a hotel apartment. The location is ideal, Central Park West. It's a fashionable address anyway, even though it's not The Dakota."

Ira laughed. "Does your family approve of you living alone, and in a hotel?"

"My family!" she scoffed. "As much as I love my parents, they long ago gave up any authority over my comings and goings. There are many young ladies living in the hotel. Some are from out of town and are in the city for extended visits. There are quite a few mother–daughter duos living there, some are widows and some are divorcees. They live in the larger accommodations with kitchenettes and dining rooms. I have no need of either, since I do not entertain and I do not cook."

"You don't cook? I haven't known many Jewish girls who can't cook. What do you do for nourishment?"

"Well, that's the beauty of hotel apartments. There is a restaurant that serves breakfast, lunch, and dinner. I have made arrangements to have my dinner there, since I eat breakfast and lunch at the store. They have made a special price for me. There is also laundry and maid service. It is so convenient. Do you realize that I haven't washed a floor since I left my parents' home when I was sixteen? When I was married to Meyer, his mother would not let me help. I think that she was afraid that I would break something."

Ira looked at his watch. "I think we had better head down to the hall to see how things are shaping up for the show. I know that you will want to check out every dress and make sure that the models are properly made up and coiffed."

Flora and Mae Dodd walked across the Bridge of Progress over 9th Street, connecting the old A.T. Steward Department Store with the newer structure built by John Wanamaker in 1902. Mae brooded because her mother had insisted that she attend a fashion show. Flora knew very well that she had no interest in the latest Parisian fashion. Even though she replenished her daughter's wardrobe every fall and spring, Mae chose the same plain shirtwaist and black or brown skirt to wear on weekends. At Spence she wore the required uniform, which consisted of plain navy skirts and a school jacket. However, in a few months, she would be a college girl, and she would not let her mother dictate what she wore, no more than she would let her father dictate what she would study.

They entered the grand hall, gorgeously decorated with flowers and rich tapestries. The décor suggested the court of Napoleon and Josephine and the scene of their coronation, painted by Jean-Louis David. The theme had been advertised in the invitation as a "Fashion Fete de Paris." They had waited outside for Bernadine, so when Flora and Mae entered the hall, few chairs remained. One hundred of New York's wealthiest and most fashionable ladies had received invitations to the fashion show. Mae fidgeted and made no effort to conjure up enthusiasm for the show. But she beamed when she saw Bernadine waving to them from a table with two available chairs.

"Mae, do sit down!" said Flora. "It is time that you started to take interest in things other than your books. Oh, look, Bernadine. Aren't those frames colossal?" She pointed to a series of tremendous black velvet frames placed at strategic intervals throughout the hall. Inside each frame a live mannequin modeling a French design stood immobile as a portrait.

"Yes, it is dazzling," said Bernadine. "I am proud of Dore. She is responsible for almost everything, from choosing the gowns and models to writing and reading the script that will accompany the show."

"Dore is a good friend of yours, isn't she?" asked Mae shyly.

"Yes, dear, we are very close. Each of us helps the other to learn about the world from her particular point of view."

"I think that is nice. I only see the world that Mother and Father want me to see."

Flora wanted to ignore her daughter's comment, but felt obliged to correct Mae's behavior.

"Young lady, you are now beyond impertinence. Please sit down and watch the show and keep your opinions to yourself, unless you see a dress that you like."

Mae choked back tears. Bernadine could see that her mother's disapprobation cut deep.

A few minutes passed and Dore began her narration. "Ladies, here we have a beautiful gown from the House of Worth. You will notice the new cut, on the bias. See how it molds to the body's natural form. The S-curve has completely disappeared and with it the need for the discomfort of a constricting corset. This particular gown was one of three that caused such a to-do at the races in Paris a few months ago."

Bernadine whispered to Flora," I can't tell you how grateful I am for this new revolution in fashion. I plan to visit the lingerie department before I even order the dresses. I hear that the new undergarments are not only comfortable, but they are gorgeous."

One of the mannequins came to life and stepped out of the large frame. Greeted by a child, dressed as a page, she began to walk gracefully among the ladies who applauded and murmured their approval of the gown. All the while, a violin quartet played softly. Dore continued her narration until all the models stepped from their frames and walked among clients.

As the show came to a close, a crowd of women rushed toward sales girls waiting with their order pads.

Flora turned to Bernadine. "I must order a few gowns. This season is going to be so busy, particularly with formal dinners. Are you coming Bernadine?"

"No, I think I will stay here with Mae, if you don't mind," she said.

"That would be lovely, thank you," said Flora as she looked around to find a sales girl to wait on her. At that moment, Dore approached and offered to find a girl who was competent, as well as a large fitting room where her friend would be comfortable."

"Dore, how kind of you. I know that you are busy and must have a million things to do," she said.

"Not at all, Flora. My work is done here. I am no longer in sales. But before you go, I would like to know how you enjoyed the show."

"Marvelous," said Flora. "I have never seen anything so innovative. You have set a new standard."

Bernadine offered her praise. "It was marvelous. Even in the Parisian department stores, they have nothing like it. I particularly enjoyed your idea of arranging *tableaux vivants* in those large frames. Was that your idea?"

Dore blushed with pride. "Yes, it was. I had to fight for it. They thought I was crazy, and it took a lot of convincing."

One of the older sales girls approached when Dore summoned her. She invited Flora to accompany her to a private fitting room.

She turned to her daughter and spoke sternly. "Mae, you are to stay with Bernadine. I imagine that she will want to look at some more of the gowns and perhaps some lingerie. I don't want to hear from her that you were impatient or that you complained."

Mae forced a smile. “Of course not, Mother. I will be as quiet as a mouse.”

As Flora walked off with the sales girl, Dore turned to Bernadine. “Would you like to see any dresses or lingerie?”

“Actually, I would love some tea. I will come back another day to try on some dresses.”

“I think that you are wise,” said Dore. “It will be mobbed today, and won’t receive the attention you deserve. But just be sure that you wait a few days before you return. Monday and Tuesday, we will be repeating the show for the general public. And though I am not sure how many women will be buying; I am certain that they will be trying the dresses on. The dressing rooms will be packed.”

Dore led Bernadine and Mae to small tearoom. “This is actually reserved for women supervisors and executives. I thought that it would be more peaceful here, and we might be able to talk”

“How nice,” said Bernadine. “I have been wanting to catch up with you. How are you doing?”

“Oh me?” said Dore. “I am always happy when I am busy. But I am more interested in you. How have you been since …,” she hesitated, not wanting to discuss Theo’s death in front of Mae.

Bernadine understood and avoided the topic of her late husband. “I have been living at The Dakota. It’s nothing as grand as Flora’s old apartment, but it’s large enough for me and Martha.”

Dore laughed, “So we are neighbors. I am living at the Buckley Hotel near Central Park. It’s not what one would call elegant or chic, but it’s modern, clean, and practical.”

“We are now both independent women with nobody to tell us how to lead our lives,” said Bernadine. She looked at Mae and noticed that she was listening intently to their conversation. "Now, Mae, that is not to say that a young girl doesn't have to listen to her parents."

Mae bristled. "I am not a girl. I'm going on sixteen, and in a few months, I will be attending Barnard. I know that I must respect my parents, but I do have my own opinions."

Dore interrupted. "Mae, I know that we don't know each other very well, but I think that I understand how you feel. You see when I was younger, actually about your age, I loved to read and was eager to learn about everything. My parents forced me to leave school and go to work."

"And I never went to school, but was tutored in my home," said Bernadine. "Some of my friends went to college, but my father wouldn't allow it."

Mae felt embarrassed, but defended herself. "I think that is very unfair. But you must understand that this is the twentieth century, and I am a modern woman. Things are different. I have plans to study science, particularly engineering and physics. I wanted to go to Stanford University because it is the only school that allows women into its engineering courses. But my parents won't allow me to go so far from home. They say that I am too young."

"I think that perhaps they are right," said Dore. "Maybe they will change their minds when you are a bit older. You could always transfer to Stanford."

"It's just that I am so bored, and I want to get on with it. My life is like living on a merry-go-round. Day after day I see the same people in the same school and homes. They girls are only interested in boys and cotillions. I long to travel and meet people who live different kinds of lives."

Dore smiled. It was as if she were talking to a younger version of herself.

"I know exactly how you feel. But try to look at things from a different perspective. I came from a different land, where people lived a very different kind of life. You probably don't know that I was born in Russia and came here when I was a child. But I remember what our life was like there. We never knew when and where the next pogrom would erupt. Most Jews had little hope of advanced education, and Jewish girls had none. There are many places in the world like Russia, so while you make your plans to see the world, do not forget to put them on your itinerary. It would be a good thing to remember that you were lucky to be born in this country, and even if you came from a poor family, you would have a chance to improve your circumstances."

Mae looked at Dore strangely, fascinated by her strong will. She had never met anyone quite like her.

"You know, Miss, I think you make a very good argument," she said.

"Thank you, Mae, but please call me Dore. You know, I just had a thought. It is possible to see foreign lands and strange sights right here in New York."

"Really, where would that be?" Mae said with a skeptical look.

"On Coney Island there is a place called Luna Park. There you can visit different countries, as well as mystical lands. There is a German town and an Egyptian village, each with its own native population."

Dore turned to Bernadine. "Why don't we make a day of it? Perhaps you could bring Martha."

"I think it might be a little overwhelming for her. She is only five. But I would like to come. Do you think Flora would like to join us?"

Mae laughed. "I don't see Mother going to Coney Island, Bernadine. I don't know if she would let me go. But if I told her that you would be there, she might agree."

"I will talk to her, Mae. I think we should wait until the weather is fine, perhaps in May," said Bernadine.

"I finish school at the end of May, and I will need to study for my exams. Shall we say the first week of June?"

"That sounds fine," said Dore. "Would you both mind if I invite my sister Leah to come along? She works in a factory and rarely has the opportunity to go on excursions. I think that she would benefit from meeting a young woman like you, Mae. And it will give you a chance to meet someone who is outside your everyday circle of friends."

Mae jumped up from her chair, nearly spilling her tea. "Do you think we could really go? Please, Bernadine, you must convince Mother to allow me to go."

Bernadine smiled. "I will do my very best."

DORE, MAE, AND LEAH

LUNA PARK, JUNE 1908

On the first Saturday in June, Dore and Leah waited for Mae on the dock to board the ferry for Coney Island. The chauffer drove up and Mae opened the door and scanned the crowd. Suddenly, she came face to face with Dore.

"Oh, I am so glad to see you. I am not used to such masses of people, and I was afraid that I might not find you," said Mae as she noticed a pretty girl with an olive complexion and a voluptuous figure standing next to Dore.

"I have been keeping an eye out for you," said Dore, as she put her arm around Mae to guide her toward the entrance to the ferryboat. "We had better get in line; the boat is filling up fast, and we don't want to have to wait for the next one. I haven't heard from Bernadine, so I expect something must have come up and she won't be joining us."

"Oh yes," said Mae, slightly embarrassed. "I am to tell you. She called Mother this morning. Martha woke up sick with spots all over her face and chest. She thinks it's chickenpox."

"Oh, poor girl," said Dore. "I remember having them when I was a child. I am sorry, I haven't introduced you to Leah."

Mae shook Leah's hand. Even though the two girls had similar coloring, that is where the resemblance between the two young girls ended. Mae, dressed in a simple yellow shirtwaist, wore white shoes with no heels. A sweet-looking girl with dark hair and blue eyes, her long, lean body showed no trace of womanhood. She had an oval-shaped face; some might say that it was a tad too long, with a strong chin that gave her a stubborn air. Her straight, dark hair cascaded down her shoulders and back.

Leah wore a clingy dress that showed off a curvaceous figure with a small waist and ample bosom. Like many other young women of her class, she had made her best effort to present herself as a paragon of fashion chic. She had arranged her dark curly hair in a bouffant-style coiffure and topped it with a stylish straw hat that was a mass of blue ribbons and white lace. She looked the picture of the confident working girl, with an extra measure of sensuality.

"I suppose this your first time to go on a Coney Island excursion?" Leah asked Mae as she brushed aside a thick curl that had escaped from under her hat.

"Yes," said Mae. "I have been to Paris several times and once to London, but never to Coney Island. I can't tell you how happy I am to see a part of New York that is so close and yet I have never been allowed to see. Have you been to Luna Park, Leah?"

"No, never. I have been to Coney Island several times, but never to Luna Park."

Dore knit her brow. "When did you go to Coney Island and with whom?"

"I come sometimes with some of the girls from the factory. We save up our money for months and then we have a day of fun. What's wrong with that?"

"Well, it all depends on how you behave yourselves. What do you do when you come?" asked Dore.

"Once we went bathing in the ocean. I borrowed a suit from one of my friends."

Dore cringed. "I hope at least you were decent."

"Unfortunately, I was. My friend Daisy lent me her mother's suit. It was hideous."

"What else do you do?" Mae interrupted.

"We go to the dance halls. They are much larger than the one I go to in the city. And you get the chance to meet new people. There are boys who come from all over Manhattan, and they are always willing to pay the entry fee and for refreshments."

Dore raised her eyebrow and stared at Leah. "Leah, you have no business letting boys pay for you. If you take money from men, you risk being labeled a 'charity girl!'"

Mae could not stop herself from asking. "What is that, Dore?"

"A charity girl is someone who has men pay for favors. Then everyone assumes that she is giving him something in return. It sometimes leads to very undesirable consequences."

Leah blustered, speaking in an icy tone. "Listen, you don't have the right to tell me what to do!"

Mae averted her eyes, embarrassed by the exchange.

Trying to lighten the mood, Leah changed the subject. "Mae, I am not much older than you. But when I was your age, I already knew all the dances, the Turkey Trot and the Spieling. I may not be book-smart, but I work hard and I know how to have fun. I sure could teach you a thing or two."

When Leah raised her voice, Mae noticed that a young man at the railing of the boat had been watching them. Obviously listening to their conversation, he smiled. She saw that Leah had flashed him a brazenly flirtatious smile. A handsome young man, he appeared to be about eighteen or nineteen years of age. He had thick auburn hair and expressive blue eyes. He had pleasing features, an aquiline nose and a strong, yet not overtly protruding jawline. One might consider his large mouth to be his only defect, but when he smiled, he revealed perfect white teeth, and the effect stunned her. He wore a light jacket that hung loosely on his tall, slim frame. Mae took in the aspect of the good-looking young man and suddenly realized that she was staring. She quickly averted her eyes, but it was too late. He had noticed her. Smiling broadly, he tipped his derby and winked.

At that moment Dore happened to be looking in his direction and turned to Leah.

"Do you now that young man?"

Leah looked in his direction and waved. "Yes, I know him. His name is Declan Malone."

"Exactly how do you know him?" Dore asked sternly.

"We met at a dance hall. He is a marvelous dancer."

Mae could not help herself, and the question just burst out. "Leah, is he your beau?"

Glancing over at the young man with a smile, Leah feigned shock. "My beau? I am not permitted to have a beau. Isaac would skin me alive."

Dore interrupted. "Don't exaggerate. I'm sure Isaac has other things on his mind these days, such as making a living."

"Well, if you must know," Leah said turning to Mae. "I suppose he is one of them. And the way he looks today, I am going to say that he is definitely my favorite. He is a looker, isn't he?"

Mae turned away because she could feel herself blushing. "I guess he is attractive. I don't have a frame of reference for men his age. As a matter of fact, I don't have much to do with boys because I attend an all-girls school."

Leah fussed with her hair, as she glanced over at Declan. "Well, that's a damn shame."

Dore was riled. "Watch your language, my girl. I don't tolerate that kind of talk from the girls in the store, and I will not permit it from you."

At that moment the boat docked and they disembarked and ran to catch the trolley. A few minutes later they arrived at their destination. The entrance to Luna Park loomed. A large white sing exclaimed *LUNA PARK THE HEART OF CONEY ISLAND.* One then passed under a colorful archway framed by two columns. Mae gasped at the beautiful sight that greeted her. An apparition of towers, minarets, and beautiful domes left her speechless. All the lines of the buildings and attractions seemed to curve and swirl. She took in the huge slides and an open-aired circus.

Dore smiled when she saw Mae's excitement. "Well, does this fit the bill?

This is definitely a change from the Upper East Side. What would you like to do first?"

She handed each girl a guide containing a list of the attractions and a small map. "How about you, Leah? What strikes your fancy?"

Mae looked at the guide. "Here is a ride called *Trip to the Moon.* Oh, I see it over there," she said pointing. "I bet it's fun. Look at the little spaceships with their wings flapping like birds."

Leah gave a little jump and clapped her hands. "Yes, let's do that first. But after I want to see Fire and Flames. One of my friends saw it, and she said it was astonishing. They actually set a building on fire and then the fire engines and firemen come and put out the flames. People are rescued either by ladders or jumping out of windows into nets."

Dore gave a sarcastic laugh. "You don't have to pay to see a tenement fire. Just go to the Bowery, and you can see it for free. Only the outcome is not always a happy one."

"Anyway, I want to see it," insisted Leah. "And then I want to go on the Ferris wheel."

"It's fine with me. Today, we'll do whatever you girls like. But I would like to see the Dragon's Gorge. It says in the guide that one is carried from the North Pole to Havana Harbor, and on the way, you visit the Rocky Mountains. You also get a tour of the bottom of the sea. The attraction also includes a ride in a gondola in Venice. That is all for the price of one ticket!"

Mae, filled with wonder for the attractions of Luna Park, also appreciated seeing it with Dore and Leah. For once, she immersed herself in the experience fully, without worrying about her parents' approval. She allowed herself to laugh loudly and scream when the Ferris wheel carried her high into the air. Yet, she found her mind wandering back to Declan's blue eyes and brilliant smile. For the first time, she felt a strong attraction to a young man, for he was a man of nineteen. The very fact that he might be present at Luna Park and that the possibility existed that she might see him again made her heart beat faster. She found herself looking in mirrors and windows and she did not like what she saw. She considered how she might arrange her long, straight hair into a bouffant style like Leah's. She found herself looking at Leah's full voluptuous figure enviously.

Dore and the two girls spent the better part of the day seeing the various attractions and going on rides, not stopping for lunch. They snacked on hot dogs and ice cream. At four o'clock, Dore suggested to Mae that she might want to visit the various foreign villages that were on display.

"There is an Eskimo Village and a Delhi marketplace with three hundred natives brought over from India," she said.

"How fascinating! Do we have time to see both?" Mae asked hopefully.

"Yes, if we don't dawdle," said Dore. "We could spend an hour at each, and then I would like to have some dinner before we go home."

"Leah groaned. "I don't want to see any Eskimos or Indians. I want to go see some of the sideshows. Did you know that they have babies in incubators on display? How about if we meet up later?"

Dore hesitated. "I don't know. I think we better stay together."

Leah became agitated. Crossing her arms and pursing her lips, she looked at Dore defiantly. "Well, I might as well just come out and say it. I am meeting Declan, and if you are looking for me, I will be at the dance hall later. Otherwise, you and Mae can make your way back home without me."

"I see that I have no say in the matter," said Dore.

"No, as I told you, I am a working girl, and I don't need your permission. Don't worry. I have enough to pay my entrance to the dance hall. I wouldn't want anyone to think that my morals are not what they should be."

"All right," said Dore. "But I will not allow you to go home alone or with that boy. We will meet at the trolley and go home together. I expect you to be there at seven-thirty."

"Okay, Okay!" Leah frowned. "But if I lose track of time, you know where to find me."

Stunned by Leah's rebellious tone and even more surprised by Dore's relenting and allowing her to have her way, Mae remained silent. It would never occur to her to speak to her mother in such a manner. She also felt a sudden stab of jealousy, even though she knew she had no right to be jealous. Although she had only glimpsed Declan from a distance, she couldn't deny that it upset her to think of Leah spending the day with him.

She turned to Dore and asked. "Do you think it's a good idea to let her go off like that? I mean it seems to me that it's not proper. I had better not mention it to Mother."

Dore smiled to hide her concern and tried not to appear vexed. "Well, Leah is an independent girl, and she has a mind of her own. You know I am more than a sister to her, and I more or less raised her when she was very young. Her mother was working away from her home, so my family took her in. I know that she is behaving like many of her friends in the factory do. They work long hours and want to have a bit of fun on their day off. What worries me is this young man, Declan. I don't know him and well, I don't trust him. You see he is not one of us. If he were a Jewish boy, I would know how to approach him and what to expect. But an Irish boy, and a good-looking one at that, I don't know what he is capable of."

Mae seemed confused. Of course, Dore probably had a right to be suspicious of a young man who pursued her younger sister. But she didn't understand what being Irish had to do with anything. Admittedly she didn't know any Irish boys or girls for that matter since none attended Spence. She realized that her parents had no Irish friends in their circle. "What is wrong with being Irish?" she asked Dore.

"Oh, nothing at all. I didn't mean to give you that idea. I lived with a charming Irish girl for a year. They are fine, hardworking people. But they are known to be fun-loving and a little bit too fond of the drink, not that one should generalize. I would just prefer that Leah find a nice Jewish boy, for he might be more likely to respect her and not take advantage."

Mae gave Dore a quizzical look. "Would you ever keep company with a man who wasn't Jewish?"

Surprised by the boldness of the unexpected question, Dore didn't respond immediately. "Mae," she said. "I don't know the answer to that question. I haven't had the best luck with Jewish men, so perhaps I might be willing to be courted by a gentile. The important thing to me is that a man respects me. And I want someone who is hard-working and intelligent."

They had arrived in front of the Delhi market. They both managed to forget about Declan and men in general.

Dore looked at her watch, which read seven-fifteen. The sky darkened, and the lights had just been turned on in Luna Park. Each attraction, including the Ferris wheel and roller coaster, was covered in strings of tiny light bulbs. The shape of the domes and minarets also appeared delineated by the lights. All this distracted Dore for a moment. But she again looked at her watch and said. "Mae, we have to hurry. I told Leah to meet us at the trolley at seven-thirty. If we are late, I am sure that she will use it as an excuse to allow her young man to take her home. I can't have that."

When they arrived at the trolley stop, they did not see Leah. But Dore had a pretty good idea where she might be. She took Mae's hand, and they ran to a large dance hall adjacent to the park. It was crowded with people, mostly young with a few middle-aged couples.

"When I find her, I'll have a few choice words for her and her young man. Come along, Mae. Please don't tell your Mother or even Bernadine that I took you into a dance hall."

"You have my promise," Mae said, secretly excited with the prospect of entering a dance hall for the first time.

Dore held Mae by the hand after they entered the giant hall. Her anger and frustration got the better of her, since it seemed impossible to find one couple among the hundreds of dancers. They walked around the perimeter of the dance floor trying to glimpse Leah and her beau. "I don't know if we can possibly find them in this crowd," said Dore.

Mae spoke up in order to be heard over the music. "Why don't we look at the top of the couples' heads and see if we can find a dark bouffant next to a redhead?"

Dore laughed. "That's a very logical way of going about it. You are a bright little thing."

Dore took out her handkerchief to wipe the perspiration from her face. Suddenly, she spied a tall man with auburn hair. Then she saw the couple dancing. It was Leah and Declan doing some kind of impossible dance. She had heard of modern dances, the Turkey Trot and the Cakewalk. But she did not recognize the dance that the crowd was doing at that moment. Then she heard the orchestra leader sing *Doing the Grizzly Bear.* And in fact, the couples would do a kind of two-step, then stop and raise their arms, pretending to be giant bears. It was simply ridiculous. After a few minutes, the music stopped, and she ran over to where she had last seen Leah.

"So, there you are! Have you lost track of time?"

Leah was flushed, and some of her hair had come loose and a mass of curls fell over her shoulders. "Oh, is it seven-thirty already?"

"No, it's eight o'clock. Did you think that I would allow you to go home without me?" She turned to say a word of reprimand to Declan, when she saw that he had taken Mae's arm and swept her onto the dance floor.

The band now played a slower song, a modern waltz, and the couples glided across the floor, performing the more sedate Castle Walk. Irene and Vernon Castle who owned the most celebrated dancing school in New York had introduced the dance, mainly in cotillion classes. Mae, for the first time, grateful for these obligatory classes, allowed herself to be guided across the floor by Declan, happy to feel his arm around her waist. Many of the younger dancers sat this dance out, so they had plenty of space to move across the floor. Declan led her to a more isolated part of the hall.

Mae's emotions vacillated between terror and ecstasy. She did not have the courage to look into his eyes, but glanced up to take in his face.

"You don't mind, do you?" he asked.

Mae didn't quite know how to respond. "I, I … well Dore is very angry. Did you know that Leah was supposed to meet us at the trolley at seven-thirty?"

Smiling broadly, Declan took on an air of innocence. "I certainly did not. If I had known I would have accompanied her myself. I am sure that Leah's sister must have a very low opinion of me. I know that she would prefer that Leah stick to her own kind. Being that I am Irish and not Jewish like you …."

Mae interrupted him. "Oh, I am not Jewish. My name is Mae Dodd, and we are Episcopalian."

"Oh, I beg your pardon. I thought that you might be a relation. Your dark hair and lovely tanned skin had me fooled. But now that I look into your beautiful blue eyes, I realize that was an incorrect assumption."

"Well, you see my mother is a friend of Dore's and allowed me to accompany her to Coney Island today. I never seem to be able to get past Madison and 80th, and I couldn't pass up the opportunity."

She was out of breath, and Declan suggested that they sit in some chairs on the far side of the hall.

"Let's just sit and talk for a few minutes. It isn't every day that I have a chance to speak with a girl from the Upper East Side. I imagine that you are in a private school."

"Actually, I graduated early from Spence. I just finished my exams."

"Well, how did you do?" he asked smiling.

"If you really want to know, I was the top of my class."

He seemed surprised. "Top of your class, huh? And you look so young. What are you fourteen?"

Mae bristled. "I am fifteen, and I will be turning sixteen in December."

Declan shrugged his shoulders. "It seems a waste for a girl to be so smart. I have known women who are accomplished. But they usually marry, and all the education goes to waste. I suppose that you are now going on your great tour of the continent to see the cathedrals and the art museums."

Mae could feel the heat rise in her face. "I have no plans to marry or travel. I have seen my share of cathedrals, and I have even met some famous artists. But I am going to continue my education."

"Art school?" scoffed Declan.

Not wanting her annoyance get the better of herself, Mae controlled her tone.

"Not at all. I am enrolling at Barnard College in September. It wasn't my first choice.

I was accepted at Stanford University to study math and physics. But my parents wouldn't allow me to go. Too far away, they said. But I know that someday I will get there. My plan is to be an engineer."

Declan's eyes widened, and he turned his head to the side as if he could not believe what he had heard. "Is what you say true, or are you mocking me?"

Mae laughed. "Now, why would I mock you? I don't even know you."

"It's just that it is so unusual, you know, for a girl to be interested in science in general, but engineering is pretty specific. When did you decide on this vocation?"

Mae thought about it for a few seconds. "I have been interested in science since I was quite young. Engineering is a new passion. I am interested in all things mechanical, bridges for example. I can spend hours looking at the Brooklyn Bridge.

Declan stared at her. "Well, it's not just that it is unusual, but it is also a coincidence. You see it is my goal to be an engineer, not mechanical though. There is a new field for engineers dealing in physics and electricity. I have a job, as an electrician's assistant to pay my way through college. It's slow going, working at night and going to school during the day. I don't get much time to sleep or dance."

"How fascinating!" Mae said. But at that very instant Leah came bounding up and put her hands on her hips.

"What on earth is going on here? Declan, I was looking everywhere for you. I am afraid that I have to leave now." She shot an icy look at Mae. "And you, Missy, playing the innocent and then sneaking off and dancing with my beau."

"Come on girls," said Dore as she joined them. "We need to go. But first, I would like to meet your friend, Leah."

"Of course," said Leah. "Dore, this is Declan Malone; Declan, this is Dore who will tell you, if you have the patience to listen, that she has raised me, educated me, and tried to civilize me."

Declan laughed. "It is a pleasure to meet you Miss…?"

"Dore Abramowitz, and it is a pleasure to meet you, Mr. Malone. Now I am sorry, but we have to run."

After the ferry docked at the tip of Manhattan, Dore found Karl, the chauffer waiting patiently waiting outside. Mae climbed into the back of the large Grey Arrow automobile. She often tried to sit in the front seat to try to learn how to drive a car, but Karl would not allow it.

However, this particular night, she settled into the backseat to be quietly alone with her thoughts. She looked out at the lights of the city, and a cool breeze blew her dark hair across her face. Closing her eyes, Mae saw Declan's face, his beautiful blue eyes mocking her ever so gently. The memory of his sensuous smile produced an unusual physical response in her: her hands and arms tingled and a sensation of lightness spread through her body. Aside from the physical attraction that she felt, he was the first young man who ever took interest in what she had to say. He didn't seem to mind that she was not a graceful dancer or that she wasn't beautiful and alluring like Leah. He had the same interests as her, physics and engineering. All this passed through Mae's mind on the ride home, but as they approached her brownstone on Madison, the hope of pursuing any relationship with Declan, a poor Irish electrician, faded quickly. Not only would her parents never accept him, she had little hope of stealing him away from someone like Leah.

BERNADINE

NOVEMBER 1908

Little less than a year ago Bernadine had at last gained her independence from the Van Wies family. In fact, she had survived them all, save Clara. Agnes had died, not long after her son, from a suspected overdose of Laudanum. This was a common phenomenon among women brought up during the Victorian era, and people were not generally shocked or scandalized upon learning that someone died in this manner.

So poor Clara set adrift with no support but a small income she received from the sale of the Van Wies' home, which turned out to be highly mortgaged. Clara, ignorant of financial matters, did not fully appreciate her situation until her lawyer sat her down and spelled it out. He suggested that she live modestly on the money that she received upon the sale of the house. Taking his advice, she moved into a comfortable and reputable apartment hotel.

Recently, Bernadine had received surprising news. Bea, who never let a piece of good gossip go to waste, told her that she had learned that Clara had married. A middle-aged bachelor wooed her in a matter of weeks. Bea met the couple as they dined at Delmonico's and described the man as stout, bald, and generally unattractive. She said that she didn't know how the man had met Clara, but suspected that it was more or less arranged by woman known for fixing up matches for ladies who found themselves in desperate situations. Although Bea couldn't remember the gentleman's name, she recalled vividly that he came from a small town in Ohio and made a good living in some kind of trade. Bernadine wondered why such a man would propose to Clara, and so quickly. Bea laughed, and told her that the matchmaker had convinced him that his future bride not only belonged to New York High Society but also descended from the original Dutch settlers that founded the city. Since the gentleman made no further inquiries as to the reputation of the Van Wies family, he felt satisfied that he was making a good match and that his new wife would elevate his social standing in his small town in Ohio, wherever it may be.

Bernadine lived comfortably and serenely in her apartment at The Dakota with Martha and Mademoiselle Monique. However, recently she decided that the moment had come that she might reinvent herself to a greater extent. She decided to transform the apartment and hired a decorator known for her skill of mixing modern furnishings with more traditional-style apartments. Olivia August, who had changed her name and her accent to present herself as more British upper crust than her true origin, had exquisite taste. Bernadine asked her to find pieces of craftsman furniture to place alongside Art Nouveau *objets d'art.*

In the corner of the large parlor, she found a spot for her blue-green peacock screen. She had managed to salvage it from her patents' house, and it had been in storage for the past eight years. She kept it to serve as a reminder of her past foolishness and as a warning to never again allow herself to become a victim.

Now she made her own decisions on how to raise Martha and how to spend her money and her time. Concerning her money, she had few worries. Mr. Simpson in Houston continued to oversee her investments that showed considerable profit, mostly due to the rise in value of her real estate holdings. As to her time, except for outings with her daughter and occasional social obligations, she spent the greater part of it working with Lillian Wald at the Henry Street Settlement House.

She had recently started going into the slums on home visits, helping overwhelmed mothers, and looking out for the health and welfare of their children. Some of the things she saw rattled her sensibilities. But she now recognized that this poverty existed in New York, alongside the Opera House and Delmonico's. She could no longer ignore it and felt strongly that she must make people of her class aware of its prevalence.

The last week in November, Mary Harriman Rumsey hosted a dinner party to promote her organization, The Junior League. Mary, who came from the wealthy Harriman family, had formed the organization as a young woman attending Barnard College. Her husband, Charles Rumsey, was a sculptor and a polo player. Many of Mary's friends said that he helped to soften her hard edges. She had the reputation of being a bit too serious, and Charles always managed to lighten the mood at their parties.

Normally, Mary invited only women to her luncheons and meetings, mostly debutants and an increasing number of young married women. But tonight, the husbands and some single men had been included. Mary had been talking with Anne Morgan when she saw

Ned and Flora arriving with Bernadine Van Wies. The Dodds had wanted to invite a single gentleman, an associate at Ned's law firm, but Bernadine had declined. She gently told them that she did not need to be on the arm of a gentleman at each social event she attended. Bernadine noticed there were indeed a number of unaccompanied young women. Tonight's dinner invitation described the event as a series of short lectures delivered by experts in the various branches of social work. Dinner would be informal, and discussion would take place at table. Bernadine picked up a list of the speakers and the topics, pleased that it included social, health, and educational challenges in the slums. The discussions covered the hardships endured by factory girls and the beginning of unrest in the garment industry. Bernadine planned to relay all that she heard here to Dore the next time they met.

Looking around the Rumsey's living room, Flora couldn't help but comment.

"It's very tastefully decorated, apart from Charles's sculpture. Don't you agree, Bernadine?"

Bernadine nodded in agreement, but suddenly let out an audible gasp and her body momentarily tensed. She recovered quickly, but Flora followed her gaze across the room and it fell upon Eliot Havemeyer, standing with his arm around the waist of an attractive woman. Flora grabbed Bernadine's hand and tried to calm her.

"Are you all right? I didn't know that Eliot was going to be here and I have no idea who that lady is."

"I'm fine," she whispered. "I haven't seen Eliot in years. It's just so unexpected."

After all these years, there he stood with a charming woman. She appeared to be older than him, in her mid-thirties. Trying to avoid his detection, Bernadine turned her head and spoke briefly with one of Ned's associates. But she could feel the heat of Eliot's stare. There was no denying that the magnetism between them was still strong.

He caught her eye and walked over with his lady on his arm.

"Bernadine, what a pleasant surprise. It has been such a long time," he said awkwardly.

Bernadine trembled and tried to control her nerves and appear as cordial as possible. "Why Eliot, how nice it is to see you. I didn't know that you were interested in the Settlement Movement or in charity works."

Eliot tripped over his words. "Well, not, not I. It's my wife who has shown a desire to help out the less fortunate people in our city. Oh, forgive me. This is Caroline, formerly Caroline Wilson of Buffalo. She did me the honor of becoming my wife last year."

Bernadine took her hand. "It's a pleasure to meet you, Mrs. Havemeyer."

Caroline forced a stiff smile. Could it be that she was aware of their former relationship?

"Oh, please do call me Caroline. It's nice to meet you."

Bernadine noticed a distinct edge to her cold tone. She wondered how a passionate and caring man such as Eliot could fall in love with such an inimical woman.

Caroline droned on. "I am so interested in charity work. I admit that I never did a thing in Buffalo, but I never noticed a need for it. People there lead pleasant lives. But as I am still not settled in my new life here, I thought it would be an opportunity to meet ladies of quality. I hope to make many new friends, while helping out the poor. I do have a lot to learn and that is why I insisted that Eliot come with me tonight."

"You certainly have come to the right person to guide you," said Bernadine, immediately doubting that Caroline's true motivation was to help the poor, but rather to make advantageous social connections within her own class. "Mary has been organizing young women to do settlement work since she went to Barnard. I have been working at the Henry Street Settlement House for a few years. But I have only recently started making neighborhood visits."

Caroline's enthusiasm dampened. Furrowing her brow, she took Eliot's arm and leaned into him. "You mean that you actually go into the neighborhoods where these people live?"

Suppressing a smirk, Bernadine attempted a polite answer to the absurd question.

"Why yes, my dear. We go into the neighborhoods and into the homes. It is our job to offer moral support, particularly to women who are in untenable situations. We educate them on various health and social issues. For example, I recently helped a woman who had just given birth to a stillborn child. She needed tenderness as well as information on how to find a midwife or a doctor. She delivered that baby at home with the help of her twelve-year-old daughter. It was her tenth pregnancy. She has six school-aged children, none of whom were attending school. All but the youngest were working in some capacity, either in sweatshops or scrounging for rags in the street. I told her that this was not helping them and they must go to school. I took them all to a local public school and registered them."

Caroline turned pale. She stiffened and spoke in a very cold tone. "Well, I must say that I do have a lot to learn. I will probably request administrative work or perhaps I could help with publicity, making posters to raise awareness."

Eliot changed the subject. "How is your daughter, Bernadine?"

"She is doing well. I have put her is school, a public progressive school run by some professors from Columbia. As she is only six, she attends kindergarten and she is blossoming."

Bernadine could see that Caroline's face clouded when Eliot asked about her child. She wondered if she knew about their relationship, but quickly brushed off the notion. They had hidden their relationship well. Even Theo never knew the true identity of her lover. And it all happened years ago, while Caroline lived in Buffalo.

Mary asked the guests to take their seats as the lectures began. Later, sitting at the table, Bernadine could feel Eliot's eyes on her. Immediately following the meal, she told Flora that she didn't feel well.

"Do you think that we could slip out early?" she asked Flora.

"Of course, Charles is waiting outside with the car. In any case, Ned wanted to leave early because he has a big case tomorrow. I hope it's nothing serious. Do you think we should call a doctor to meet you at home?" asked Flora.

"No, it's just an awful headache. Charles should drop you off first since your house is closer and then he could drive me to The Dakota."

She saw Eliot at the other end of the room trying to get her attention. Instead, she turned her head and went to gather her coat.

Two days later at ten-thirty on a cold, but sunny November morning, Bernadine emerged from the front door of The Dakota to find Eliot standing on the sidewalk.

Irritated and yet elated, she said, "Eliot, what is the meaning of this? Did I give you the slightest encouragement the other night or any hint that I wished to see you?"

"No, and I am sorry." He spoke so pitifully, that her anger dissipated. "But I had to see you. There is so much that was left unsaid between us. It was you who left me no choice, no hope. I would have risked everything to be with you. I never stopped loving you, never."

People began to stare at them, and Bernadine dreaded creating a scene in front of the employees and neighbors.

"We really can't discuss this here in the middle of the sidewalk!"

"I know. Please, can we go someplace where we can be alone and talk?"

She tried her best to look and sound annoyed, even exasperated, Bernadine huffed, "I have an appointment and I have errands to run."

"Let's just walk a bit in the park," he begged. "Please, I won't take up too much of your time. I just want to know more about my daughter. I think that even though I have never met her, I do have the right to ask about her."

"I don't know if it would be wise for either of us to go down that road," said Bernadine discreetly, walking toward the park and away from the prying eyes of the doorman. "Martha doesn't know the truth, of course, for she is very young. To her Theo was her father, albeit a horrible and distant one. It would be very confusing to introduce her to you at this point. I mean, what would you be to her, a long-lost uncle?"

They had entered a deserted area of the park, and he reached for her hand.

"Well, you wouldn't have to say anything right away. Perhaps we could arrange a chance meeting, and you could introduce me as an old friend?"

"No, it's absurd!" she protested. "Why do you want to get involved now? You have a new wife, and I am sure that she would not understand your sudden interest in my child and me. Why, I am sure that you are planning on having children with her and she would not appreciate having your attention diverted from your own family."

A shadow crossed Eliot's face and he took a deep breath. "We will not be having a family."

"Don't be silly," said Bernadine. "I can see that Caroline is older than you, but she can't be more than thirty-five. She can still have children."

"No, you see, she cannot. She was married before and was unable to have children with her first husband. She miscarried twice. She consulted several physicians, top men in their specialty, and the diagnosis was always the same. The condition makes it impossible for her to carry a pregnancy to term."

"I am sorry for her," said Bernadine.

"I was sorry for her too. Her first husband, the cad that he is, filed for divorce using the fact that she couldn't have children as grounds. That is why she left Buffalo. She couldn't bear the shame. Her situation was common knowledge, and no man, or at least no acceptable man, would propose marriage, despite her family's great wealth. We met when she moved to New York and was looking for an apartment."

"And did you fall in love with her as you did with me? Did you use empty apartments as we did?" said Bernadine, choking on the words and fighting back tears.

"I did not fall in love with her at all. But I was lonely, and you left me with no hope. She was charming, and she seemed to care deeply for me. I don't know why I married her. As I said, I was very lonely, and as you know, I have needs."

"I understand your loneliness, Eliot. I really do. I have been lonely too."

"But, wait. I need to tell you everything," he pleaded. "To make things worse, she didn't tell me that she couldn't have children until we were on our honeymoon. She deceived me, but I have stood by her, perhaps out of pity."

Conflicted and confused, Bernadine searched for her words. She was genuinely sad for Eliot, but what could she do? Certainly, he was not suggesting that Martha serve as some kind of surrogate child for him.

"I am truly sorry, Eliot. Perhaps you could adopt. I know for a fact that there are many sweet and loving children in the orphanages that I have visited in my charity work"

"I have thought of that and suggested it to Caroline. But she will not hear of adoption. She says that one never knows what one is getting in an adopted child. She is resigned to her fate and refuses to discuss it further."

"Well, she is wrong!" Would you like me to speak to her? Perhaps she would listen to a woman who has had experience with orphans. I am sure that I could make her change her mind."

"Nothing will make her change her mind," he said. "Anyway, I don't think it would be wise to let her know that I have discussed this with you. I can't be sure, but I think that she sensed something between us the other night, and if she knew I told you about her problem, it would probably make her even more suspicious."

Bernadine blushed. "Oh, of course, you are right. Indeed, it would not do for me to speak to her about such a private matter. So, I guess that there is nothing to be done."

Eliot grabbed her shoulders, pulling her close to him. "Yes, there is. You could let me see my daughter, and you could let me see you. I love you. I have never loved anyone but you. I married Caroline because I believed that you had forgotten me. It was you who closed the door on a life that we might have had. I can see that you still care. Please, don't send me away."

He kissed her, and she gently pushed him away. "Eliot, we are in public. Let me go!"

When he released her as suddenly as he had held her, she saw that his eyes were brimming with tears. He turned away, trying to steady himself.

"So, let's finish this conversation in private," he entreated. "Meet me somewhere tomorrow. If you can convince me that you no longer care for me and that you refuse to allow me to know my own daughter, I promise to leave you in peace. I know that you had a dreadful time of it with Theo and his family, but I cannot believe that your suffering has hardened you or made you cruel."

"Fine," she said, losing her resolve. "Come to my apartment on Friday morning at ten o'clock. Martha will be at school, and the nanny has the day off." She handed him her calling card with her telephone number. "Call before you come, and I will be ready."

Eliot smiled, took her hand and looked at her with gratitude. "Thank you, thank you."

Friday morning when she awoke, Bernadine doubted her decision to meet with Eliot alone in her apartment. Was she showing weakness? Where was her compassion for Caroline? She dug down deep in her soul and she could find none. How could that be? Suddenly her mind cleared and she realized that Caroline had deceived the man she loved, and therefore did not deserve her compassion. For once she intended to put her own happiness first. After all, she had a daughter to think of, and Caroline did not. But more importantly, she could no longer deny the fact that she still loved Eliot.

She had to admit that her feelings for him were as deep and passionate as they had ever been, and she found herself reliving their past and fantasizing about him. She conjured up memories of their lovemaking and found her body beginning to respond. The loud ring of the hall telephone roused her from her erotic daydream.

Eliot spoke, his voice full of anticipation. "I am just down the street in a restaurant. I can be there in ten minutes, five if I run."

She couldn't help laughing. "There's no need to run. We will have the apartment to ourselves."

While she was waiting for him to arrive, she began to consider his plea to spend time with his daughter. On the one hand, she could see the benefit for Martha to have a father or perhaps an "uncle" in her life. Having been raised by women, she had never really had a male influence in her young life. That of course excluded the Van Wies men. It reassured her that Theo hadn't had much to do with her, except when he was putting on an act in public. It was quite revealing that Martha had shown little sadness or distress when she learned that Theo had died. More importantly, Eliot was her real father, so he had a right to see her. Bernadine wondered, how he would manage to keep the truth from Caroline if he planned to see his child regularly.

She looked at her reflection in her vanity mirror, examining her face closely. She was almost twenty-eight, and she searched for the tiny lines that many of her friends fretted over. But she could find none. Her bronze complexion was lustrous and smooth. Perhaps her face had lost some of its fullness, but it was no longer fashionable to have a cherub, moon-shaped face. The woman in her mirror had full lips and chiseled prominent cheekbones. She stared into her cornflower blue eyes with the black rings encircling the irises. This always made her think of her mother, who had the same unusual feature. Sometimes she speculated if there was some meaning to these rings. She had read that the circle represented many things, eternity, for example. At that moment the bell rang, her pulse quickened, and her hands and face tingled with excitement. Taking a moment to compose herself before answering the door, Bernadine smoothed her hair and glanced one last time at her reflection in the foyer mirror.

"Eliot, please come in," she said.

As he entered the apartment, he looked around taking in the design and furnishings. "It's quite different from our townhouse, which is crowded with oversized antiques and immense portraits."

His gaze shifted to her face and then his eyes wandered over her beautiful body. She had changed very little, at least outwardly. She appeared more self-possessed and slightly more reserved, but after all that she had been through, that seemed only natural.

She led him into the parlor. "Please sit down and make yourself comfortable.

Would you like some tea, or perhaps coffee?"

"No, thank you. We have so much to talk about, and I don't want to waste a minute."

"Well, as I said, we have plenty of time. No one is in the house. I asked the cook and the maid to do the marketing, so they won't be back for hours."

Suddenly they both understood that they had been talking around the truth. They both wanted the same thing. Without a word, they embraced, and she could feel the all too familiar ache to feel his naked body next to her. He could hardly contain his fervor as he awkwardly tried to unfasten the buttons and clasps of her dress. She laughed and grabbed his hands.

"Eliot, there is no need for such haste. I cannot deny what I feel for you or my desire. But let's go to my bedroom where we can be comfortable and make love on a real bed. It will be novelty for us, don't you think? She laughed and he could not contain himself. He gathered her up in his arms.

"Which way, my love?"

At first their lovemaking was volatile, almost violent. It had been years since she had felt the touch of a man. He let his body follow her lead as she guided his hands and mouth and set the rhythm. Later, he slowed the pace, making the pleasure last, reveling in each sensation. Not a word was said, but Bernadine and Eliot did not need to speak.

He looked concerned when she began sobbing, her shoulders shaking. "Please don't tell me that you think we made a mistake, Bernadine. I couldn't endure it."

"No darling, these are tears of joy and regret. Joy for what we have just done and regret for all the years we wasted apart."

The house was quiet, and they spent the remainder of the morning in each other's arms. No obstacles were discussed and no plans were made.

A few weeks later on a cloudy afternoon, Bernadine walked through the front door of the Colony Club, the first social club for upper-class women in New York City. It had recently opened, initiated by Anne Morgan and designed by Stanford White. A young woman intercepted her at the reception area to ask if she was a member.

"No, I am applying for membership. That is why I am here for tea. I have an appointment with Miss Morgan and Mrs. Dodd. I am Bernadine Van Wies."

"Oh, pardon me, Mrs. Van Wies, I was told to expect you. Please go into the restaurant where they are serving tea today. It's straight ahead through the French doors."

She removed her winter coat, her hat, and her gloves and handed these to the woman in a huff, annoyed because she did not want to keep Flora and Anne waiting. As she entered the restaurant, she was struck by the color of the walls and the furnishings. She thought that whoever had decorated the club obviously had exquisite taste. If one were to assign a theme to the décor, it could only be eighteenth-century French, but with a contemporary touch. The pastel colors transported her back to her stay in France during her honeymoon, and reminded her of the home of the Bloch family.

She saw Flora and Anne seated at a table with two women. One, extremely elegant, dressed with impeccable style. The other in contrast, appeared almost masculine in her dress and demeanor. As she approached the table, she almost ran into Mary Rumsey who appeared to be in a rush to leave.

"Oh hello, Bernadine. I wish I could stay, but I am meeting Charles at his exhibition and it would be unpardonable to be late."

"I understand for I am late myself," she said with an embarrassed laugh.

Trying not to appear to be rushed, she approached the table where Flora and the other ladies were sitting.

"I do apologize for being late," she said as she took a seat at the table. "I was down on Mott Street for a home visit this morning, then I had to rush home to change."

Flora didn't say a word, but Bernadine could sense her irritation. But she stood and embraced her friend. Anne Morgan smiled and shook her hand.

"Hello Miss Morgan," said Bernadine. "I would like to thank you for considering me for membership in the club."

"Well, it's a pleasure," said Anne. Anyone recommended by Flora Dodd is sure to be an asset to us. Please have a seat. I would like to present Miss Elsie de Wolfe and Miss Elizabeth Marbury."

"It's nice to meet you both," said Bernadine.

"I suppose that you remember that it was Elsie who worked on the interior design of my brownstone," Flora interjected. "And now you see what she can do on a grander scale. She is responsible for the creation of the club's interior design. I'm sure that you will agree that she has created a beautiful and welcoming sanctuary fro the noise and frenetic activity of our city streets."

Elsie smiled modestly. "I cannot take all the credit. Stanford White designed the building and the layout of the rooms. It is a pleasure to meet you, young lady. I am sure that you will easily gain admission to the Colony Club."

Bernadine shook her hand. "I hope so. To be frank, I owe my welcome into New York Society to my former husband's family name and their long lineage back to Dutch settlers. I am just a girl from Galveston. And now I am the only surviving member of the Van Wies family living in the city. My sister-in-law recently married and relocated to Ohio."

Elsie smiled and replied with a tinge of sarcasm, "I do not believe that the old family names mean that much these days. On the other hand, old family money still holds great influence."

"Well, my money, Miss de Wolfe, comes from Texas cotton and real estate. I think it is not a great secret that the Van Wies' name was about all they retained from their ancestors."

Elsie's friend laughed. "I do admire your candor."

"Oh, I am sorry," interrupted Flora. This is Elizabeth Marbury, a dear friend of Elsie's. She is a talented theatrical producer and a literary agent."

Elizabeth rose and shook Bernadine's hand. "I think that you will be formidable member of the Colony Club Mrs. Van Wies. We need some new blood, particularly if its provenance is Texas." She looked at Elsie. "Come on, old girl. We have to meet the accountant, an unpleasant task. But you have to go over the figures for all this fine furniture."

Anne motioned for Bernadine to take a chair closer to her. She remembered meeting Miss Morgan on several occasions, the first being at her wedding to Theo, although only for a few seconds on the reception line. She had seen her at the fashion show at Wanamaker's briefly. But she had never had the opportunity to have a conversation with her. Flora had been Anne's friend for years, since childhood apparently. Yet it struck her how different the two women appeared to be. She knew that Anne was interested in settlement work, of course, not to the same extent that she was. Anne would never make home visits or spend hours educating working girls on how to improve their lives.

But Bernadine had heard of her commitment to many of the causes and her willingness to provide financial support to many organizations. She particularly advocated for women's causes. Knowing that J.P. Morgan was one of the wealthiest men in the country and had the reputation of being unscrupulous in his business dealings, Bernadine thought it remarkable that his daughter even considered the plight of the poor. She admired Anne for seeing beyond the horizon of her sheltered and limited life on Madison Avenue and for rising above her carefully crafted education most likely provided by governesses and tutors. The thought occurred to her that she had more in common with Anne Morgan than Flora did.

Flora had no desire to see the harsh realities of life. In fact, she had changed a great deal in recent years, dating back to the birth of her son. It seems that the woman who had once had the temerity to travel to Chicago six weeks before her wedding had become complacent. She had somehow regressed to take up the role of the perfect Victorian wife and mother, which was absurd because it had never been in her nature to be governed by the rules and sensibilities of her social set.

Ned set the pace and path of their lives. Flora followed all his instructions involving the education of their children, the running of the household, and the social obligations that were expected of the wife of an important lawyer and advisor to J.P. Morgan. Sometimes Bernadine sensed that Ned intimidated Flora, but then at other times she thought that she must be mistaken. He had a mild nature and treated Flora and all women respectfully. It was true that he could be stubborn and overly strict, especially where it concerned Mae. Whatever the case, she felt Flora drifting away and she longed for the close relationship that they had in the past.

Anne was speaking with Flora about some potential members for the Colony Club, when she turned to Bernadine. "Would you mind telling me a little about your visit on Mott Street? I have heard horrid things about the conditions in the tenements, and it may surprise you to know that I have given the situation of the poor much thought, especially where it concerns women and girls."

Bernadine was pleased to hear of Anne's interest in the plight of struggling women and responded with enthusiasm. "Today was particularly trying. A mother had discovered that a man of forty had abducted her thirteen-year-old daughter. An aunt and several of the neighbors intimated that she had actually gone willingly. Apparently, the man in question offered to set her up in an apartment and buy her a new wardrobe. I could not ascertain the truth of the matter, but I did contact the neighborhood police."

"Well, I do hope that they found the girl. Did they charge the man with kidnapping?" asked Anne.

"Not at all," sighed Bernadine. "The policeman told me that this sort of thing was all too common and that there was little to nothing that could be done. In fact, he had the effrontery to tell me that the girl was probably better off. I asked for his name and badge number and I told him that I would report him for his insolence."

Flora interrupted, speaking hostilely. "Do you not see the problem? I do not understand either of you. How do you expect to help these people? Even though she is poor, the mother should have instilled some morals in her daughter. And what hope is there of changing a venal older man? No amount of settlement work will accomplish that. Furthermore, what more confirmation do you need to the complete lack of morality of these people than the nonchalant statement made by the representative of the law, the neighborhood police officer? Of course, I do hope that the mother recovers her daughter unharmed."

"Flora, although I have no direct experience with these situations, I believe in the human spirit and the will to strive for a better life. I believe in hope," said Anne.

Bernadine did not recognize her old friend. She searched for the right words to reach her. "Flora, you and I know of a case where a young woman has overcome poverty and ignorance. We know Dore. Dore, who came to New York from Russia as a poor child, speaking no English and starting her new life working in sweatshops and living in squalor."

"Well, Dore is an exception," said Flora. "She is bright and focused on her work."

"Yes, and there are many others, who, given an opportunity, could succeed. I have spoken to Dore about the working conditions of these girls. It is a life of thankless drudgery with cruel and lecherous supervisors. It is no wonder that they go wild during the few hours of freedom they have one day a week."

Anne's interested piqued. "If what you say is true, it seems to me that there is a solution; it lies in the improvement of the girls' working conditions. Perhaps women in our privileged situations should engage with these girls who have to work to survive. I will go see Lillian Wald at her settlement house. I could pledge more money. But I was thinking that it might be enlightening for me to meet this friend, what was her name, Dore? Do you think that you could arrange that, Bernadine?"

"I certainly can. I know that she can explain things much better than I can."

"Then I leave it in your hands. I must fly. I have dinner arrangements to make for my father and some of his associates. Goodbye, Flora. It was a pleasure speaking with you Bernadine."

Later, as they retrieved their coats from the cloakroom, Flora turned to Bernadine.

"I would like you to stop by my house for an hour. I have to talk to you about something very important."

"I would love to, but I have so much to do," said Bernadine.

"Really? You have time before Martha comes home from school and you have already done your social work for the day. I can't imagine what is so pressing that we can't spend some time together catching up."

Bernadine flushed and searched desperately for an excuse. "Well, I have some things to put in order in the apartment."

"In that case," said Flora "I could come to The Dakota with you. It's been ages since I have been there, and I would like to see if things have changed."

Eliot was to meet her in the apartment in a half hour, and she did not want Flora running into him.

"Dear, could I have a rain check? I am exhausted and a little out of sorts."

"Of course," said Flora. "We can see each other anytime you wish. But don't think for one moment that you are fooling anyone." She guided Bernadine into her waiting car and told her driver to take them to The Dakota. "I won't come up, but we can talk in the car. You see, word has gotten around about you and your *petite aventure* with Eliot Havemeyer and not just in our set. After all you are living in The

Dakota where there is no guarantee of privacy among the residents or the help."

Bernadine couldn't believe what she was hearing. She felt the heat rising to her face. "Everyone knows? But we thought we were being so discreet, always meeting in the morning when nobody was around."

"Obviously you were not careful enough. What are you thinking? He is a married man and you, a young widow with a child."

"We can't help it, Flora. We love each other, and Martha is his child. You have always supported me in the past, and you knew everything from the beginning."

Flora's tone was reproachful, and she held her chin high. "That was a long time ago, and you were suffering so living with Theo. Eliot wasn't married then, and you didn't have a young child. And don't you see how you are hurting Caroline? Really, Bernadine, many of my friends are asking me questions, and I don't know how to respond. The worst of it is that Ned has heard people in his office speak of it, and he has asked me to distance myself from you."

Bernadine could not believe that Flora meant what she had just said.

"Of course, I would never abandon you. But I cannot condone this behavior."

"Eliot is Martha's father," said Bernadine. "I cannot deny him time with her.

He wants to be part of her life. She knows him as Uncle Eliot and has already grown attached to him. And I love him so much. I can't imagine not having him in my life. I would miss our mornings of lovemaking and the idea that there is a man who loves and respects me."

"I cannot tell you what to do, but I warn you that when Caroline finds out, she will be vindictive. I have been told that she can be bitter and that she is cruel to her help. Please don't put me in the difficult position of having to defend you, especially to her.

I will always be your friend, but you see how you are making things difficult for me."

They pulled up to The Dakota, and Bernadine descended from the car. "I will think about what you have said, but I am so happy with him, and I will need time to find a way to break it off."

December in New York could be beautiful in the right neighborhood. Madison Avenue resembled a fairy winter wonderland, with its clean, white snow cascading in drifts up to the beautiful entryways to the stately homes. These homes were all decked with Christmas wreaths and red ribbons.

Bernadine thought about the contrast been the dirty streets of the Bowery, where snow mixed with mud, coal dust, and the ever-present horse manure. She had soiled her shoes as well as the hem of her dress while making an early morning home visit. It was an emergency, and she had not intended on volunteering this particular morning. She had returned home to change before heading to J.P. Morgan's home. Anne had invited her to a late afternoon tea. It was a holiday affair, doubling as a get-together for young women and debutants. Mothers and daughters of New York Society were gathering with no other purpose than to show off their winter wardrobes and to catch up on gossip. She had accepted the invitation because she knew that Mae had agreed to come with Flora. Mae resisted her mother's pleas to attend, but finally relented when she learned that Bernadine would be there.

As Bernadine stepped out of the hansom cab, she ran into Mae and Flora in front of the Morgan residence. She hugged her friend and her daughter, and noticed that Mae was staring at the building that adjoined the home.

"Bernadine look at that building, it is designed like an Italian Palazzo," said Mae. I can't decide if it's beautiful or just too ostentatious.

"That is Mr. Morgan's library," said Bernadine. "It is rather large. I think it takes up half the block, and it is supposed to be exquisite inside. But what is most impressive is his collection, which includes first editions of classic and modern books, art, and antiques."

"Yes," added Flora. "Mr. Morgan travelled the world to accumulate these works.

He is particularly interested in the Near East and has an impressive collection of strange items called cylinder seals from Ancient Egypt. I believe he has over a thousand."

"Do you think that we could have a tour of the library if we ask Miss Morgan?" Mae asked her mother.

"I will talk to Anne about it. I don't see why her father would object. After all I think he is quite proud of his collection."

They walked into the foyer and took off their coats. "How was your first semester at Barnard?" Bernadine asked Mae.

"Oh, it was fine," said Mae somewhat appearing somewhat disheartened. "I was required to finish the entire liberal arts curriculum before starting my science classes. I may be able to transfer to Columbia for the spring term, where I can enroll in math and physics courses. I am waiting to hear their decision. Keep your fingers crossed."

The three women walked into a parlor and suddenly heard loud voices coming from a room in another part of the house. Fortunately, not one guest had arrived, and they were the only ones to witness a strange scene that was playing out in J.P. Morgan's study. Anne came running into the parlor, her face was pale, and she seemed frightened.

"My word!" she said, looking alarmed. "A business associate is arguing with my father, and I am not sure what to do. The other guests will be arriving soon and I cannot have a scene. Father is irate and has told him to leave, but he won't budge. They are arguing over some investment. From what I can understand, and that isn't very much, it has to do with something called a radio wireless system and a building at Wardenclyff. I think that is somewhere on Long Island. I really can't make any sense of it. It is not unusual for Father to lose his temper with business associates, but he is incensed."

"Who is this man?" asked Flora. "Have you seen him before?"

"Yes, on several occasions over the past few years he has met with Father. He is hard to forget, striking and a little strange, tall and lean with dark hair and astonishing blue eyes. He is foreign, from Serbia, a brilliant man, and at times he can be charming. But at the moment he is being obstinate and rude."

Mae quietly and unobtrusively drifted toward the voices and stood quietly outside the study, where the door was slightly ajar. She could hear two men engaged in a heated argument, but she could only see one of them. He was precisely as Miss Morgan had described, tall and dark, mysterious with large, intelligent eyes.

Oddly, she felt that she had seen him before. He waved his hands and pleaded with Mr. Morgan. His speech was heavily accented and bizarre.

"Mr. Morgan, you cannot give up on the project now!" He implored. "Do we have a contract? Yes, but most important is that the tower is near complete. Do you not see what my invention will do for all the world? Men will be able to communicate across thousands of miles. And if you continue to fund my research, it will be possible to provide energy to the whole world's population without expense."

"Well, I don't see how there is any profit in that!" answered the man who was hidden from her sight "Furthermore, I do not believe in your ability to see this project through. Marconi's telegraph system is being used around the world; he has a patent. I don't think that you can possibly compete with him."

Fascinated by the conversation, Mae approached the door to the study so that she might hear more. But she need not have bothered as the tenor of the argument rose, and the men were shouting.

"I beg of you!" said the foreign visitor. "It is not because profit, but of advancing scientific knowledge and helping mankind that I do this research."

"I am not in the business of helping mankind free of charge. Everything has a price. Now if you don't leave, I am going to have to call my men."

The argument escalated and Anne, Flora, and Bernadine hurried down the hallway to the study. Flora, furious to discover her daughter eavesdropping at the door, noticed Mae's transfixed expression. She didn't even perceive her mother's presence. Suddenly, the door opened. Nothing could have prepared Flora for what she saw. A tall, dark man with angular features and large, luminous blue eyes and tan skin stared at her in disbelief.

It was him, but older, his face gaunt and wizened. She felt her legs about to give out, and grabbed her daughter's arm to avoid falling to the floor.

Mae reacted quickly supporting Flora. "Mother, what is it? Are you ill?"

At that moment the two women realized that they were not alone. "Anne, please take the ladies out of here," said Morgan sternly. "You know that I don't want strangers around when I am discussing business."

"But, Father," Anne protested, "you know Flora Dodd very well. She is not a stranger."

At the mention of her name, the visitor looked at Flora in amazement. It was clear that he recognized her, even after all the years that had passed. His face reflected a confusion of emotions ranging from bewilderment to joy. He looked as if he were about to speak, but then realized it would be unwise and he looked away. His gaze fell upon the pretty young woman, who looked back at him with what appeared to be his own eyes.

Realizing what was happening, Flora tried to gather her wits. She took her daughter's hand and pulled her from the doorway. "Come, Mae," she whispered, "we mustn't disturb Mr. Morgan; please do excuse our intrusion sir"

Bernadine and Anne, worried about Flora, who appeared pale and in shock, made her sit down on a sofa outside the study.

Mae, also worried about her mother, could not help but think about the gentleman speaking with Mr. Morgan. As Anne and Bernadine tried to calm Flora, Mae returned to the study. "I have no desire to intrude, Mr. Morgan, but I heard what this gentleman said, and I just wanted to say that I think it would be a brilliant idea, if only it could be realized."

The great J.P. Morgan turned and scowled, his huge bulbous nose frightened Mae.

"Well, that seems to be the issue. He has spent years and a great deal of my money trying to do just that, but to no avail!" Morgan looked at her, not quite placing her.

"Oh, pardon me. I am Mae Dodd, Ned and Flora Dodd's daughter. My father is one of your attorneys."

The tall, dark gentleman smiled at her with a curious expression. "And pardon me, my dear young lady. My name is Nikola Tesla. It is unusual to meet a person so young that has the vision and intelligence to appreciate my work. Perhaps one day you will have the opportunity to understand what I have tried to accomplish with my experiment."

Mae was beaming with excitement. "I believe that I am on the right path. I plan to study physics and engineering at Columbia University. Did I hear you correctly? Are you really the famous Nikola Tesla? I have read about you, and it is indeed an honor to meet you."

By this time Flora had regained her senses and saw her daughter speaking with the man who had been her lover all those years ago in Chicago. Rattled, she did not know what to do or say. She turned to Anne, desperate to retrieve her daughter and leave. "Anne, please go tell my daughter that she is being impudent and rude. She has not been brought up to interrupt business discussions and give her unsolicited opinions."

Anne noticed that Flora's breathing was irregular and that her face appeared pallid. "Can I get a doctor?" she said.

"No. Please just tell my daughter that we are going home."

Mae came out with Anne. "What is wrong, Mother? I just wanted to speak with Mr. Tesla. You know that he is a great scientist and how lucky I am to have met him."

"If you don't realize that your behavior was shameless and rude, then I haven't done my duty as a mother. Come and get your coat. We are leaving!"

"I'll come with you," said Bernadine. "You do not look well. Shall I call Ned?"

"No, please don't. But I would be happy if you would come home with me."

When they arrived at the brownstone, Flora sent Mae to her room and went into the parlor, throwing herself onto the sofa. Bernadine sat next to her and stroked her hair.

"Do you want to tell me what that was all about? You don't have to, but I am pretty sure that I know. You see, I looked into his eyes and then I looked into your daughter's, and well, I knew. If you don't want to talk about it, I understand. But if you need to tell someone, I am your friend and I will never betray your trust."

Flora cried quietly; being able to tell the truth about her affair in Chicago and the resulting pregnancy was a relief. She did trust Bernadine, so she told her everything about the night she made love with Nikola Tesla.

Bernadine listened silently until her friend had told her everything. Then she said gently, "And Ned?"

"Yes, Ned. He knew that Mae was not his, not at first. But when she was born two months early, he suspected. And as Mae grew older, he could see that she did not belong to him. And I know it may seem odd to you, but he never spoke of it. Even though he never made accusations or demanded explanations, he knew the truth. To his credit, he has always been a loving, if strict, father to Mae. Things changed completely when Wren was born. Where he was exacting and stern with Mae, he was indulgent and even-tempered with his Wren. Our son's birth restored my husband's love to me. I felt all the tenderness and regard that Ned had shown me when we were courting before my trip to Chicago and Mae's birth. I gave him a son and that seemed to even our account."

Bernadine listened to Flora with compassion, not judging her, as she had been judged. Then the two women sat in silence for quite some time. The daylight faded and the streetlights were turned on. Bernadine could hardly make out Flora's face in the darkening room.

"Would you like me to turn on a light?"

"No, please don't. My face must be a sight. I should go upstairs and freshen up before Ned comes home. But tell me honestly: What do you think of me now? You must think me the greatest hypocrite that ever crossed your path."

"No," said Bernadine softly. "I think that you are a woman who experienced a moment of great passion and that you have paid for it with your peace of mind. I am glad that you and Ned have worked it out and that you are happy together. You know that I would be the last person to judge you."

Flora said. "I have been so harsh and intolerant with you, and I am truly sorry. I supposed that was because I could not forgive myself; I was incapable of compassion or understanding for you."

"That is not true," Bernadine protested. "You have been a true and constant friend to me. You supported me during my nightmare marriage with Theo and you understood my relationship with Eliot when we were first together in Newport. I don't think it is helpful to mull over the past. But there is something that you must urgently address: Mae. I saw her reaction when she met Mr. Tesla. I cannot be certain, but I sensed a connection. And one thing is undeniable, he recognized her as his daughter. Do you think that he will keep your secret?"

"I don't think that he will say anything. After all, he has no proof and why would he want to stir up a scandal?" said Flora. "But it was striking to see her fascination with him"

"Yes," said Bernadine. "It does seem to shed some light on her interest in science, and physics in particular. She has such intellect and drive. I hope that you can convince Ned to give her the space and freedom to pursue her interests."

Flora sighed. "I see that I must. It is not wise or kind to fight against her nature. I should have nurtured her talents all along. But I didn't want to argue with Ned.

"Well, she is a college girl now, a twentieth-century woman," said Bernadine. "You must make him see that there is no turning back. Mae will lead a life that we can only imagine."

DORE

JANUARY 1909

Ira Frankel sat waiting on a cold January afternoon in front of Café Boulevard, located at the corner of 10th Street and 2nd Avenue. He had invited Dore to attend Emma Goldman's speech on the topic of Gender and American Puritanism. Dore ran up to him, terribly out of breath, and apologizing for being late. She hugged him and kissed his cheek, an unusual display of affection for her. But she had missed her dear friend since he left his position at Wanamaker's to forge a new career in the publishing world.

"I'm glad to see you, old girl. It's been months, and I have missed your bright smile and dimples," he said.

"I have missed you too. You know there is no law that forbids you from coming by my hotel for tea or for dinner."

"I have been extremely busy learning the ropes of publishing advertising. I have to make new contacts and navigate an entirely different industry from the department store world. Come on, we need to go in. The restaurant is full to capacity and I have a friend who is saving seats for us."

As they entered the restaurant, Dore saw a young man waving. They made their way to the other side of the room.

"Dore, this is my friend Hutchins Hapgood," said Ira. "He is one of the most talented journalists in the country."

"It's a pleasure to meet you, Mr. Hapgood," Dore said. "I have read many of your articles."

"Please call me Hutch," said the young man. "Well, I have had some luck. Lincoln Steffens found me and was nice enough to give me a chance."

Ira's new position at the Lincoln Steffen's *New York Daily Commercial Advertiser* was in the advertising department. But as many people considered the paper to be quite radical, Dore imagined that it must be a difficult job to find businesses willing to place their advertisements in the publication.

"Ira is doing a bang-up job for us in advertising. I don't suppose you could talk to them down at Wanamaker's?" He said with a discreet laugh.

"I don't think I dare bring it up," said Dore.

"Well, there are plenty of other businesses. Ira has been brilliant. He sure is a schmoozer. At least that is what he claims," said Hutch.

Dore laughed. "It seems to be a job made to order. It is true. He is the greatest schmoozer on the East Coast."

"So, Dore," said Ira. "Have they offered you my old job yet?"

Dore's face darkened, and she grew sullen. "Well, in fact I am the most qualified for the position. But Mr. Rodman brought in one of his Philadelphia lackeys, a real yes-man named Clark. He has no experience in advertising. I actually think he was the head of shipping office."

"Can't you speak to Rodman?" asked Ira. "It won't be good for business to have a man who doesn't know what he is doing."

"You know I didn't want to do that," she said. "I thought that it would get us off to a bad start. But finally, I had no choice. I was trying to get the fall fashion show together. It was crucial because, as you know, there has been a revolution in the cut of dresses, which affects everything including intimate wear and corsets."

Ira smiled at Hutchins, who was blushing. "Of course, Hutch, you know about the new French Revolution."

Dore was frustrated. "Stop mocking me. The change is quite astonishing and Wanamaker's has ordered hundreds of high-end gowns and day dresses. We must be the first to show them."

She had gone to Mr. Clark and told him that she would make the arrangements for the fashion show and he had looked at her as if she were mad.

"He didn't see any reason to use funds from the advertising budget for a fashion show," she said incredulously. "I had to explain to him that most of the finer department stores had copied Wanamaker's original idea of having fashion shows and that our elite clientele expects us to have them at least twice a year. After all, we have finally convinced the wealthy clients to buy at least part of their wardrobe locally, as opposed to going to Paris."

"Did he see reason in the end?" asked Ira.

"Not in the least," she said. "I had no choice but to speak to Rodman, who gave him a real dressing down."

Suddenly the room grew quiet, people hushed each other, and then there was a huge applause and shouting. A small, plump, and rather homely woman stepped on to the platform and began to speak.

Emma had discussed tonight's topic with Dore on several occasions, so she knew where her friend stood on the laws passed by Mr. Anthony Comstock. He was no longer in his prime, but his influence had not waned and he considered himself to be the moral voice and conscience of the nation. He and other traditionalists warned that young girls had lost their moral bearings by frequenting dance halls and other resorts. He tried to frighten the public with stories of White Slavers. Young girls, who allowed men too many liberties and went out unaccompanied, risked being abducted and held hostage in brothels and opium dens.

Emma Goldman, an advocate of the Free Love Movement, did not agree with him. To the contrary, she contended in her speech that Puritanism was not inherent to the American psyche. She stated that powerful government forces, many initiated by Comstock, imposed Puritanical beliefs on the American public.

Dore found the speech interesting, but she knew all about the girls on the street and the dance halls. After the speech ended, Ira and Hutchins discussed the Free Love Movement. Dore asked how men interpreted the philosophy behind the movement and the details of the various domestic arrangements.

"I'm sure that men see things quite differently from women, particularly women in the middle class or high society," said Hutch. "I don't imagine the movement will ever catch on with people who live on Park or Madison."

"As I am sure that Emma has told you Dore," said Ira. "The Free Love Movement is just a term for people who live together without the benefit of marriage."

Hutchins interrupted. "Not just that, old man. It is a way of life among young and not so young intellectuals, many of whom live in Greenwich Village. It all boils down to the idea that you can love whomever you want, whenever you want. For example, there are couples who cohabitate and may change their partners when their desires lead them in that direction. I believe that Emma was in that situation at one time. She has had many lovers and I know that she was married once, when she was very young. I believe it was an arranged marriage."

Dore blushed, not about all the talk of cohabitating and changing of partners, but because the mention of arranged marriages stabbed at her heart. She asked Ira to tell her more about his job and the magazine that he worked for.

Seeing her embarrassment, Ira began to discuss his work. *The New York Daily Commercial Advertiser*, or as we like to call it, *The New York Daily*, belonged to another publisher before Steffens bought it. He took a stale, dull paper and transformed it by hiring young Ivy League–educated writers: Hutchens here came aboard first. Then of all people, he hired Abraham Cahan."

Dore was astonished. "Abraham Cahan? You mean the man who publishes all the Yiddish journals and novels?"

"Yes, said Ira. "He is covering the immigrant community for the paper and he gives us his point of view and insights."

In fact, Cahan wrote about the qualities and benefits that Jewish immigrants brought to America. He interviewed individuals from a broad spectrum of the Jewish community: the sweatshop worker, the rabbis, entertainers, intellectuals, the successful store-owners, and the street vendors. He drew a comprehensive and objective picture.

Hutchins stood up. "I am sorry to leave you, but I have an interview in an hour and I have to get uptown. It was a pleasure to meet you Dore and I hope to see you again."

Dore shook his hand. Ira proposed that they go to a small Italian restaurant that was a few blocks away, promising that the food was great and that they might run into some of his colleagues, as it was a favorite among journalists and artists because the prices were reasonable.

Sitting at the table in the crowded and smoky restaurant, Dore's senses awoke to a new world, a new awareness, and it reminded her of her first moments on American soil. But instead of arriving in a new land, she felt a shift in her state of mind. Energy that emanated from the young men and women in the restaurant entered her body and mind, transferring their sense of freedom and pure joy of living into her soul. She listened to couples engaged in arguments about politics and literature. The women, for the most part, were not beautiful or even fashionable, but they radiated intelligence and confidence. It occurred to her that she longed to discuss more important issues, things that mattered. She enjoyed her work and felt proud of her success, but suddenly she felt that there must be more to life.

She and Ira had just finished their meal and were drinking a bottle of Chianti, when a young man approached the table.

"I told you that we were sure to run into a colleague," said Ira. "Would you mind if my friend joins us?"

"Not in the least," said Dore as she got a closer look at the handsome man who approached the table.

"Dore, I'd like you to meet Christiaan Roberts, who is also a journalist at *The New York Daily.* Christiaan, this is Dore Abramowitz. We used to work together in advertising at Wanamaker's."

"It's nice to make your acquaintance, Mr. Roberts" she said almost stumbling over her words.

For a brief moment a doubt passed through Dore's mind, given that Ira's romantic interests tended toward men, that he might be one of his lovers. But something in the way this man looked at her, told her otherwise. She was instantly drawn to him.

"It is indeed a pleasure to meet you. Please call me Christiaan," he said.

"Join us for a drink," said Ira. "We have already finished eating."

"Well, that's good, because you have to get going. Hutch told me that you might be here and that Steffens wants to talk to you about a possible new account."

"You can keep Dore company, and the perhaps the two of you can finish the bottle of wine. Actually, I am off. It's not good to keep the boss waiting," Ira said.

Dore was flustered. Her experience with men was limited to her professional relationships with Rodman Wanamaker, Robert Ogden, and her nemesis, her new boss, Mr. Clark. As for romance, she had little luck since her divorce from Meyer. She had not met anyone who tempted her and therefore rarely thought about romance. Yet at that moment, sitting with this beautiful stranger, her body involuntarily reacted. Her heart raced and she felt a physical attraction that was new and exciting.

As the two men said their goodbyes, she took in the physique and features of Christiaan Roberts. Although, not tall, he was well-built, rather sinewy, and lean, as if he had led a physically demanding life. He had delicately sculpted features and a ruddy complexion that was clean-shaven. Only his amber eyes failed to correspond the rest of his physiognomy. Something in those eyes revealed a profound inner life, perhaps a life of adventure or great suffering.

At first Dore searched for her words and for a topic that they might have in common. "I hope that you will not think it rude of me if I were to inquire about your accent," she asked. "Are you by any chance British? I know that you are not Irish for I have many Irish friends and they speak quite differently."

He smiled patiently at her as if he had been asked the question a thousand times.

"I understand your difficulty in placing my accent. There are not many of my kind about. I am from South Africa, or to be more accurate, I am from the Orange Free State. At least I was born there."

Dore looked at him quizzically. "I am afraid that I have never heard of the Orange Free State. They don't teach about it in American schools, at least not in the eighth grade. So, am I to understand that this is a part of South Africa?"

"Well, it was an independent Boer Republic until about five years ago," he said.

"I am sorry, but what is the Boer Republic?" she asked, slightly embarrassed by her lack of knowledge of geography.

"If I explain a little about my country, perhaps that will help you to get to know who I am," he said thoughtfully. It is quite complicated, so would you mind if I ordered another bottle of Chianti?"

"I certainly don't mind. Please do, but I think that I have had enough wine," she said laughing softly.

Well, to begin with, young lady, the Boers are inhabitants of South Africa or rather they make up a significant part of the population. They originally came from Holland, France, and Germany about a hundred years ago. "

He went on to explain how these immigrants had staked out parcels of land to farm. Of course, the British had colonized most of South Africa, but the two populations lived for a good while in peace.

"But eventually things became contentious and complicated. It involved gold and greed, and of course, the natives played a role. Suffice it to say that the British and the Boers entered into what became known as the Boer Wars, which makes it seem that we were the only ones fighting."

"I didn't even know that the British were at war," said Dore.

He shrugged his shoulders and told her that it didn't surprise him that Americans were unaware of what happened half a world away. He explained that the war was all but over by 1902, but it had been a bloody and ruinous affair. It had not made for an idyllic childhood.

"My name, Christiaan Roberts, also tells the story of my youth. My surname is British, as my father originally emigrated from England. My Christian name, Christiaan, spelled with a double "A", is Dutch."

Dore listened as Christiaan recounted his life in South Africa; his mother was Afrikaans and lived on a farm that she inherited from her parents, which his father took over after they married. He grew up speaking Afrikaans and English. Afrikaans, he told her, would sound like Dutch to most Americans.

"I have been told that my English does have a slight Dutch inflection to the American ear," he added.

"In any case, it's a lovely accent," she said. "Was it difficult for you growing up during the war?"

"Not in the beginning," he replied, taking a large sip of wine. "I was too young during most of the war. Unfortunately, my father left us—my mother, my two sisters, and me. He just couldn't face the hatred of the Afrikaans farmers. Lifelong friends turned against him. He tried to get my mother to move the family to Johannesburg, but she refused to leave her parents' land. So, we stayed behind, which was a grave mistake."

"It must have been a struggle, raising her children and working on a farm," said Dore. "I always thought that we had a rough time of it in Russia, but at least I had both my father and mother."

He said that his mother kept things going for about a year and he did what he could to help. But when the British got the upper hand in the war, they burned his family's farm, along with many others. Then they opened the camps.

"Camps?" she asked. "What do you mean by camps?"

Most of the world had never heard about the concentration camps, which they called refugee camps, and claimed they opened to care for displaced Afrikaans civilians. Dore could see that the anguish it caused Christiaan to talk about it, but he continued. His face flushed when he told her how the British forced his family and thousands of others to live in places of death and horror. Apparently, they used these camps as a threat in order to discourage guerilla fighters.

"What did they do to you? Did they beat you?" she asked horrified.

"Oh, much worse," Christiaan said, tears welling up in his eyes. "Tens of thousands of women and children were forced to live in overcrowded, filthy conditions. Many died from disease because of the poor sanitary conditions. Many simply starved.

My sisters both died of measles. My mother held on for a few months, and I lost her to typhoid and a broken heart. I don't know why I was spared. There must be a reason."

For a moment he remained quiet and pensive. Then he shook his head and smiled. "Perhaps I was spared so that I could tell the story of the suffering in the camps. No one speaks of it, not even the survivors. But more than my own personal suffering, I feel compelled to shed light on the despair and hardship of others, wherever I find it. So, I came to New York to be a journalist, for it is in this country where one is free to speak his mind. Perhaps I will write a novel, a novel about my mother and my sisters."

"I would love to read that novel," said Dore. "Although I'm sure it will be heartrending. In the meantime, I will follow you in the *New York Daily.* May I ask what you are writing about now?"

They drank their wine and relaxed into their chairs. Dore felt a sensation of lightness and warmth spread through her body. Unaccustomed to drinking alcohol, except for a little wine on the Sabbath, she nursed her drink, but the feeling just seemed to grow stronger and she felt her face grow warm. She listened to Christiaan as he told her about the investigative piece that he was working on, but found it hard to concentrate as she looked into his eyes, those deeply sad and intelligent eyes.

He shook off his sadness and was suddenly quite animated. "I have been working on an article about the conditions in the garment factories. I have several contacts who are members of various unions, but I am mostly interested in the Women's Trade Union League. The NYWTUL is an organization made up of workers, as well as middle-class and wealthy women. I have interviewed Mary Drier, who is a very religious lady of German background. And of course, I often confer with Ida Rauh, Max Eastman's wife. Max works with Hutch and me on *The Daily.*"

Dore was slightly annoyed with his name-dropping. "You know that it's all very well to speak with the intellectuals and the social workers. But you would be better served by speaking directly with the workers. Honestly, I can tell you much more than those well-intentioned ladies. After all, I worked in a sweatshop when we first arrived in New York, and my father works at The Triangle Shirtwaist Factory, as does my sister Leah. If you like, I can arrange a meeting with her and some of her co-workers."

A blush passed over his pale skin. She felt bad, for she hadn't meant it to sound like a criticism.

"You are entirely correct. I would do better to speak to people who are living and working under the harsh conditions. That is what Jacob Riis did and that is what I will do. I must admit that you puzzle me, Dore," he said staring at her. "Before you mentioned that your family immigrated from Russia, I had you pegged as a middle-class girl from one of those Uptown Jewish families. Ira told me that he had worked with you at Wanamaker's in advertising. I wrongly assumed that you worked for your own fulfillment, not to make your living. I humbly apologize."

Dore laughed loudly. The idea struck her as absurd and comical. "I don't know how to respond. I suppose that I should take it as a compliment. I was raised on the Lower East Side, although I live Uptown now in a hotel apartment."

"Please do take it as a compliment," he said smoothly. "I find you to be a lovely and clever young woman and I think that we should spend more time together, a lot more time."

Dore blushed and fooled with a strand of her blond curls that had come loose from her coiffure. "I think that I would enjoy spending more time with you, Christiaan. Shall we plan an outing one of these Saturdays? I could introduce you to Leah, and you could use the opportunity to interview her."

Christiaan smiled and took her hand. "Please, let's make it soon. We will mix pleasure with business."

DORE, LEAH AND MAE

FEBRUARY 1909

A few weeks later on a snowy afternoon in February, Dore arranged to meet Leah at a restaurant in Union Square, near the Triangle Factory. Because work and spending time with Christiaan kept her so busy, Dore rarely made it up to Harlem to see her parents and Leah. She wanted to ask her sister if she would be willing to speak about the work conditions at the factory in an interview. She did not want to have the conversation in front of her father because of his new situation at work.

Isaac had recently given up his position as a cutter at the Triangle to become an inside contractor. He no longer earned a direct salary from the factory, but received a fee for finding outside contract workers to operate machines at the factory. He also received a percentage of their output and had the responsibility of supervising their work. This set up benefited Isaac, for he made more money, and it helped the owners, Harris and Blanck, because the contract workers could not strike for higher wages. Isaac appreciated his new position of authority.

He naturally owed loyalty to the owners, supporting them as opposed to the workers.

Dore saw Mae walk through the door. After lunch, the two were going to a Suffragette lecture. She thought that Leah would benefit spending time with Mae, who was now a college girl. As the young woman navigated through the crowded room, Dore noted that she appeared older than sixteen. Dressed in in a simple, yet elegant black coat, she wore her hair swept up with an attractive chignon, and just a hint of lip rouge. Dore imagined that she had a new set of stylish friends and she must be emulating their sense of fashion.

"Hello Dore, it seems like ages. I am sorry that we don't have a chance to meet more often," she said as she removed her coat, revealing an elegant linen and lace shirtwaist and a stylish skirt. "I have been so busy with my courses at school. I'm taking an extremely heavy course load. I am adamant about starting physics classes at Columbia next term."

"How nice to see you, Mae. I saw your mother just last week. She comes by the store fairly often, and she has been keeping me informed about your progress. I hope you don't mind having lunch with Leah before the lecture. I need to talk to her about something important and with the two of us being so busy, I have to grab her when I can."

"I am happy to see her," said Mae. "I think a better question might be whether she minds me being here. I got the impression that she didn't like me very much when we were together at Luna Park."

Dore smiled wryly. "In my opinion she objected more to the attention Declan showered on you and the fact that he danced with you. She is quite taken with him, and I believe that she is hoping that she might rope him into marriage."

"I didn't realize that they were so serious," Mae said, trying to sound casual and unaffected by the news. "He told me that he is pursuing a degree in engineering at City College and working nights. I can't imagine that he is in a position to get married."

Before Dore could reply, Leah entered the restaurant, brushing the snow off a rather garish red coat with an imitation fur collar. Under the coat she wore a rather tasteless outfit. Her shirtwaist had a transparent inlay that revealed her flawless dark skin and her skirt, cut on a bias, accentuated her full sensuous hips. In spite of the gaudiness of her attire, the clients in the restaurant reacted to her beauty. Women smirked and sniggered, while the men stared admiringly.

Leah did not even try to hide her displeasure upon seeing Mae. "You didn't tell me she was going to be here. I don't think that your Upper East Side friend is interested in what goes on at the factory or what us working girls have to put up with."

"Oh no, you are quite wrong," said Mae. "First let me say how glad I am to see you again. You look lovely. I am indeed interested in what goes on in the factories. The girls in my college are very concerned about the working and living conditions that other girls our age endure."

Taking out a small compact, Leah fiddled with her hair and surreptitiously looked around the room to see if the male diners were still admiring her. "It's very kind of you and your friends to be concerned about the hardships we face, but I don't see how that will change anything for me. I learned early that if I don't take care of my own self, no one else will."

Dore spoke up, taking exception. "I don't think that's fair. We took care of you and Mama and Papa still do."

Leah responded with embarrassment. “Of course, I am grateful for what you have done. But you’re not living with us anymore, and it has become unbearable. I am not a little girl anymore, and I want to have fun with my friends and go out with men. Your father never stops criticizing and threatening to throw me out.”

“By men, I suppose you mean Declan? asked Dore.

Mae looked up from her tea.

“Yes, Declan and I see each other,” said Leah. “Not as often as I’d like because he is busy working and studying. But I manage an evening or an afternoon several times a month. I have told him that I need to see him more often because I promised that I wouldn’t keep company with other men. I have stopped going to dance halls with my gir!friends, just the occasional show”

Dore furrowed her brow. “Do you think that it is wise to close yourself off to other opportunities? You are a pretty girl and there are sure to be many young men who would like to take you dancing and perhaps marry you.”

Leah hissed. “You mean young Jewish men! I am not interested in them. All those mama’s boys going to schul with their fathers, selling pickles, or working as clerks don’t tempt me in the least. And the greenhorns, why I can’t stand to look at them, with their beards. Even the modern ones, the students, bore me. I want a good-looking man, who can show me a good time. Besides, eventually Declan will be an engineer, and will live very nicely, thank you very much!”

Mae couldn’t hold back and asked timidly. “Oh, so you are engaged?”

“No, Mae, we are not engaged, at least not yet.” Leah snapped. “But just you wait and see. I won’t be long. He is, shall I say, warming up to me. He has been such a good boy when I get him alone in his room. But he won't be able to resist me forever. I am meeting him later this afternoon. I wouldn't waste this outfit on just anyone."

Dore couldn't help but scold her. "Leah, don't talk like that. You just get those ideas right out of your head. Do you want to end up like your mother?" As soon as the words were out of her mouth, she regretted speaking them.

Leah said, "What do you mean by that? You are always making strange remarks about my mother, and I would like to know what you are trying to tell me, or rather what you are hiding from me."

"I don't mean anything really," replied Dore, trying to downplay the comment.

"It's just that she had to raise you on her own after your father died.

I don't want to see you get in trouble and be left with a child to raise."

"Don't worry about me so much. I have the situation in hand. Now suppose you tell me about this interview with your friend."

"He is working on a story for *The New York Daily*, and I suggested that he speak to people who actually work in factories, instead of social workers and political organizers."

"Well, I don't mind. But he will have to buy me lunch or dinner. You said he wanted to speak to several girls, so he'll have to treat them too. I think I'll invite Ivy, Golda, and Maria, so that he'll have an Irish girl, a Jew, and an Italian. Maria is my only Italian friend because so many of them can't speak English and besides she is different. Most of the Italians can't get out of the house in the evenings to go to dance halls, but Maria always manages

BEA AND CAROLINE

MARCH 1909

Bea regretted accepting Flora's invitation to the settlement house charity outing.

She had only agreed to come after receiving an unexpected and puzzling letter from Caroline Havemeyer, asking her to reserve a few minutes to discuss a matter of great urgency.

Bea had very little to do with charity work, especially when it involved being in the company of the poor and their children. Because she had never married, she had become a self-absorbed and bitter woman, preferring to travel to Europe in season to helping the riffraff in the Bowery. She confined her society to other single women, divorcees, and widows for the most part. Of course, she had her old circle, childhood friends, and her former debutant set from years ago. She had recently formed an alliance with Caroline, a new arrival to New York, who had made a fortunate marriage with Eliot Havemeyer. The two women got on well together, being cut from the same cloth of resentment and sullenness and existing in parallel worlds of contempt for just about anyone who did not fit into their conception of refinement and good breeding. And of course, money was paramount.

Bea walked past a group of ragamuffins playing in a large sandbox, turning her head aside to hide her expression of distaste from wealthy settlement workers who had organized the event. She hurried past a concession stand where elegant society women served ice cream to waifs with greedy, grabbing hands. At a clearing, she saw Caroline, standing alone, appearing detached from the general gaiety that surrounded her.

"Caroline, my dear," said Bea. "I was so surprised to learn that you were attending this affair. I wondered what you could be thinking by subjecting me to an afternoon of watching dirty little urchins playing in the mud and eating hot dogs and ice cream. But since you were so insistent…."

"I know that it is a lot to ask of you, but I had a good reason," said Caroline. "This carnival has been organized by Flora Dodd and her friend Bernadine Van Wies, and I have a matter that I want to take up with them."

"Yes, Flora has recently become very involved in settlement work," Bea said with a smirk. "I am sure that it is due to Bernadine's influence. Flora has changed, and we have so little in common these days."

"Let's sit on that bench over there," said Caroline taking Bea's arm. "I have something to discuss with you and I don't want to be overheard."

The two women sat on a bench under a grouping of oak trees. "Bea," said Caroline hesitantly, "how well do you know Bernadine?"

She shrugged her large shoulders. "Oh, not well. I know her through Flora. When she first came to New York, I saw a lot of her because Flora had taken her under her wing. But that was years ago. We hardly run in the same circle now."

Caroline pursed her lips, deep in thought. "Are you still close to Flora? I mean do you see her regularly?"

"I wouldn't say regularly, but we have maintained our little circle of friends, Lizzie and a few of the other girls. Mostly we meet to play bridge or at luncheons. Tell me, what is this sudden interest in Flora and Bernadine? They hardly seem your type."

"Oh, I quite agree. We are very different. I especially dislike Bernadine, a girl from some backwards town in Texas. But unfortunately, there is one thing that we do have in common."

Bea laughed sarcastically. "Now what would that be?"

Caroline's face reddened, and Bea noticed her clenched jaw. Taking a moment to compose herself, she tried to control the pitch of her voice. "What we have in common is my husband! She has been carrying on with him for months."

Bea feigned surprise and disapproval, for she had heard rumors about the couple's adventure in Newport years ago. "Are you quite certain?" she asked. I find this hard to believe, because frankly, I usually know what is going on in New York Society, and I haven't heard a whisper." Bea was an adroit liar and was quite capable of keeping a straight face.

"Would I make an accusation if I weren't certain," said Caroline acerbically. "Why I can hardly bring myself to utter the words, but there it is."

"But how do you know?" said Bea, fishing for details.

"Eliot has been aloof and cold toward me since November. I considered the timing and put it together. He ran into her at the Rumsey dinner party. I assume that you were not there, not your crowd. Anyway, he introduced us, and she droned on about her charity work with all the boring details. I tried my best to listen. Well, his coolness toward me seems to date back to that evening."

Bea interrupted. "Are you sure that you are not imagining his indifference? You haven't been married that long. Perhaps it is his character to be aloof."

"No, I am not imagining it," said Caroline, losing patience. "He has definitely changed and to put it as delicately as possible, his physical passion for me has subsided almost completely. He rarely comes to my bedroom and if he does, he does so grudgingly."

Bea didn't know how to respond, having absolutely no experience in marital relations and passion. "Oh, that is odd," was all that she could manage.

"Quite. I have told you that I was married before, so I know something of the physical passion between husband and wife. And at the beginning of our marriage, Eliot was quite attentive in these matters."

Bea continued to play the game. "But how do you know for sure that he has been seeing Bernadine? It could be anyone."

Caroline sighed, frustrated by Bea's naiveté. "I had him followed for several weeks. I know of a discreet agency, and I engaged a man to see where he went during the day. It was not an easy task because Eliot is in real estate and that involves visiting many apartments and homes. But eventually, the agent reported that he visited The Dakota inordinately often and at odd times, quite frequently at nine o'clock in the morning. Of course, my man could not enter the building because they are very stringent with their rules. However, he eventually paid off one of the building maids to follow Eliot to see which apartment he was visiting. I am sure that you can guess where he went."

Again, Bea played innocent. "Caroline, perhaps he has business in the building.

He might be showing an apartment."

"Really, Bea!" said Caroline. "Are you serious? The girl was paid to keep an eye out for his visits and she claimed that they were frequent and long. She said that he would stay for hours and would reappear disheveled and smiling when he left"

Bea gave her best impression of disbelief and disgust. "And you think that Flora is aware of these morning trysts? Really, I must come to her defense. We have known each other since we were children. I do recall her having a short-lived wild streak. I believe it was right before her marriage during our trip to Chicago. But she has never stepped over the line into impropriety."

"It is not my desire to discredit or embarrass Flora," objected Caroline. "My intention is to press her to talk to Bernadine and dissuade her from carrying on with my husband. I just would like you to talk to Flora and to inform her that I will not tolerate this situation, and to convince her to make Bernadine see the necessity of ending this affair. If not, there will be consequences."

Bea's expression vacillated between disdain and pleasure. She liked nothing better than a big scandal, particularly if it touched people she didn't like, and she did not like Bernadine. "What kind of consequences? What is your plan, and how can I help?"

"Let's see if a vague threat can stop them from seeing each other," said Caroline.

"If not, I know that you will help me by spreading the word among people who might be likely to condemn such behavior. My goal is to close all of society's doors to the woman who is breaking up my marriage."

"I don't know that you can be confident in turning Flora against Bernadine," said Bea. She had noticed that recently the two friends had grown closer than ever before. But she decided to play along to see just how far Caroline was prepared to go with her plan.

"Are you quite sure?" asked Caroline.

"Well, just look around you," said Bea raising her hand and pointing to the crowd of tenement women and children enjoying the event that Flora had organized with Bernadine. "Even as recently as a year ago, I doubt that Flora would have been involved in this kind of carnival. Bernadine influence over her is stronger than ever before."

Caroline took in the scene and shook her head. "I don't think that I can stay a moment longer. What I ask of you is to set up a meeting for me with Flora. I mean to discuss the situation with her and ask her directly if she will try to intervene on my behalf with her friend. She must try to make Bernadine see that what she is doing is cruel and immoral."

"I will ask her to meet with you, of course. But shall I tell her what you have revealed to me concerning the details of the affair?"

"Yes, I fear that you must, if you can bring yourself to speak of such things to her."

Bea tried to hide a smile of satisfaction, for nothing would please her more than to condemn Bernadine's behavior. She had always been jealous of their relationship, and perhaps now she could win back Flora's approval and friendship by opening her eyes to the truth.

"I will get her alone and speak to her before I leave and make arrangements for her to meet with you," said Bea.

Caroline squared her shoulders and held her head in a haughty manner. "I cannot thank you enough. And just know that you are doing a great service to not only me but also Flora, for I feel that she will be grateful to know Bernadine's true nature."

FLORA AND BERNADINE

APRIL 1909

The two women sat on wicker chairs, watching their children launching their toy boats from the edge of a pond in Central Park. A stranger might find it hard to believe that their age differed by only a few months. Wren, almost two inches taller than Martha, had limber, yet solid body. His windblown chestnut hair persistently fell over his eye, and he pushed it back with his free hand.

Martha appeared older than her six years, not because of any particular physical maturity, but rather because of her bearing and self-assured air. She had a sweet face with delicate features, blond hair like her father and her mother's sky-blue eyes. One would not call her thin, but her willowy and graceful gait evoked the image of a young colt.

Bernadine and Flora watched the children from a distance, leaving them in the care of Mademoiselle Monique. Flora looked at her friend and saw the picture of serenity. Her upturned face absorbed the sun and the light breeze of the mild April day, her half-closed eyelids fluttered occasionally and her beautiful black lashes touched her tanned cheeks. Flora wondered if Bernadine's was thinking of Eliot.

As it happens at that moment Bernadine was reliving one of her morning visits with her lover. The memory filled her body with excitement and her spirit with tranquility. It occurred to her that she never imagined that she would be leading a purposeful and fulfilling life

Flora didn't want to disrupt the serenity of the moment and dreaded broaching the unpleasant topic, the gossip that was circulating about Bernadine and Eliot.

"Aren't they precious together?" she sighed watching as Wren helped Martha retrieve her little boat that had gotten away from her.

"Yes, they are. And I can't say exactly what it is, but there is something so special about their friendship. Even though they don't spend much time together, it is as if they cherish every moment. In a way, I can see our reflection in them."

Flora beamed. "What a lovely observation. I hope that they will be lifelong friends. A true friendship should be something inviolate and sacred."

"I believe that is true," said Bernadine. "That is what our friendship is to me, sacred."

This made it even more difficult for Flora to continue. But she felt that she had no choice. "I am glad that you feel that way, because I have to talk to you about something, well, something rather unpleasant."

"I am sure that I can guess what is on your mind. It's Eliot and Me. You have not mentioned it in quite a while, so I thought that you had gotten over your misgivings."

Flora smiled and spoke in a kind tone. "In fact, I had more or less accepted the idea that nothing could dissuade you from seeing him and making him part of your life, as well as Martha's. And I want you to understand that I do not judge you, for you have the right to some happiness. If anyone deserves it, you do. But I just want you to be aware of the talk that is going around."

"So, I imagine that Caroline is spreading her bile. Eliot told me that she had him followed and confronted him about our meetings."

"Yes," said Flora. "Bea told me of Caroline's accusations, and she took great pleasure in telling me. I never understood why she takes such delight in scandal."

"I am sorry that you had to put up with her spiteful performance."

"But wait," she said. "I haven't told you the worse. Caroline had the audacity to show up at the Colony Club, insisting that I speak with her about you and Eliot. Bea had tried to arrange a meeting before, but I adamantly refused. So, they took it upon themselves to ambush me in the parlor at the club. I didn't want to make a scene, so we went out to the garden where I was forced to listen to Caroline's tirade of grievances against you, the upshot being that she is prepared to make your life miserable and create a scandal, if you continue the affair. I'm just concerned that you might be hurt, and of course, I worry about Martha."

"You might be surprised to see who is going to be hurt," Bernadine shot back.

"Eliot and I realize that people know about us, and we are prepared for the consequences. These are the very same icons of morality that welcomed Theo and his money-grubbing family into their homes. Hypocrites!"

Flora was astonished, yet delighted by Bernadine's defiance. But she was cautious. "I know that you say you are willing to take the consequences. But my one fear is that Caroline might discover that Martha is Eliot's child. With that knowledge, I am sure that she would do her best to hurt not only you and Eliot but also your child."

"I don't see how she would ever find out. Aside from you and Eliot, nobody knows. Of course, Alva Belmont might suspect. But if she did know, she wouldn't lower herself to repeat it to anyone, much less to Caroline."

"Well, you know that you can trust me. So, what is to be done about Caroline?"

"What about Caroline?" said Bernadine laughing contemptuously. "Eliot is going to divorce her and believe me he has grounds."

"Forgive me, but if anyone has grounds, it is she." Flora was perplexed. "After all, Eliot has been deceiving her"

"You might think that is the case, but you don't know the truth about this woman."

Bernadine told Flora the details about Caroline's first marriage in Buffalo and the husband who had divorced her on grounds of fraud.

"You mean he divorced her because she cannot have children?" asked Flora. "I didn't know one could do that."

"Oh, I think he might have had other grounds. But it did become public knowledge during the trial. The fellow didn't come off looking very honorable, but I think that Caroline bore the greater humiliation. Everyone in Buffalo knew that she would never be able to have children."

"And the humiliation was so great that she felt that she needed to leave?" asked Flora.

"From what Eliot could gather from an old college friend, she was not greatly appreciated by the Buffalo Society even before her marriage. She probably realized that finding another husband would not be easy. All she had to offer was her family money, and surely she didn't want to marry a fortune hunter."

"So, she moved to New York, where she made a fresh start and found a handsome and lonely man, who was ignorant of her history," said Flora.

"Handsome, naïve, trusting, and yes lonely. I am responsible for his situation. If I had only been brave enough to defy Theo all those years ago."

"I don't see how you could have taken any course, besides what's done is done."

Flora stood up to get a good look at the Martha and Wren. They were looking at two small children who were riding in a little cart being pulled by a goat." Smiling, Flora turned to Bernadine. "I'm sure that Wren is going to want a turn in that cart."

"I'll just go tell Mademoiselle Monique that she should get them in line for a turn, and I'll give her some money," said Bernadine. But when I return, I need to tell you how the situation stands."

When she returned Bernadine explained to Flora how Caroline had made love with Eliot after only three weeks of courting. He felt more or less obligated at that point to propose and they married within three months of their first meeting. From the beginning of their short engagement, he spoke to her of his desire to have children.

"She never told him the truth about her inability to bear children, that is not until a week after the wedding," said Bernadine. "He was devastated, but agreed that they could adopt children."

"Well, that would seem to be a solution. After all, Eliot has Martha, even though he must never admit it."

"One would think that she would be happy to adopt, not only so that she may have the love of a child but also to keep the love of her husband," said Bernadine. "But she adamantly refuses to even consider it. She is heard-hearted. And she is also foolish."

"Foolish?" asked Flora, not understanding Bernadine's meaning.

"Foolish, because Eliot feels that her outright refusal to adopt, along with her original dishonesty about being unable to have her own children, gives him solid grounds for divorce. He has consulted with a lawyer, who believes he might have a case."

Flora was dubious. "I don't know if that will work. She might play the victim and paint you as a conniving home-wrecker."

"I am not so sure," said Bernadine. "Given her personal history, I believe that she might prefer a quiet divorce. Let's be honest. She cannot go back to Buffalo. She moved here to start with a clean slate. If there is a court case and the truth comes out, it would not be advantageous for her. I imagine that it would not be hard for her to find another husband in New York City if all the facts of the case never come to light. Eliot is going to try to reason with her and convince her to make a quick and private settlement."

"Eliot is going to try to reason with her!" said Flora, suddenly realizing that she had raised her voice. "Are you at all confident that she has a rational character?"

"Well, one can only hope," said Bernadine. "She has her faults, but she is not stupid. Maybe we will be lucky and another man will catch her eye."

Flora stood up as Wren came running up, laughing at Martha who cried when she was not allowed to take another ride in the goat cart. She chided her son and told him that he should be kind to his little friend. Wren turned to Martha and put his arm around her shoulder, promising that they would return soon and he would save up his money so that she might have two rides.

MAE

SEPTEMBER 1909

Mae was not alone in her passion for science for she had met two girls in her classes at Barnard who shared the same interests in physics. Adeline Howell, a tall athletic girl from the Midwest, was in her biology class. Adeline had piercing blue eyes and freckles and wore her curly blond hair unfashionably short. She planned to study medicine and then to specialize in surgery.

Unlike Adeline, Andrea Shapiro was a New York girl. She came from a wealthy Jewish family and had been brought up on the West Side in one of the brownstones built by the moneyed scions of finance. Her father, a very successful stockbroker, was liberal-minded and encouraged his daughter to pursue an education. Whereas her older brothers worked in finance, Andrea had always been fascinated by inventions of all kinds, and had great curiosity of how these worked. She did not necessarily see herself working in any particular field. She wanted to study physics because she found the branch of science fascinating.

The three girls met at the door of the large amphitheater. Peeking in, they were distressed to see that almost every seat was occupied except for a few empty seats in the very last row way at the top of the room. They tried to be discreet, but it was futile. The men began snickering and some even whistled softly. Mae flushed with embarrassment, Adeline bristled, but Andrea appeared to enjoy the attention and smiled coyly at several of the more attractive young men.

When the professor entered the amphitheater, he admonished the men for their rude behavior and gave a slight bow to the three girls, welcoming them to class. He suggested that in the future, the men should leave three empty seats in the front row.

After class, several of the male students crowded the girls, offering them help and tutoring if they found the concepts of physics too difficult.

"How considerate of you, boys," Andrea responded, flirting, but with a slight sarcastic tone. "But how could we possibly choose among so many bright and handsome men?"

Adeline glared. "Do you boys really think that we need you to guide us through a course in physics? Do you have any idea how difficult it is for women to be admitted to this class? The three of us have been ranked top of our class in Barnard in all the science disciplines. Really, you are pathetic!"

The men walked away defeated, except for one who asked Andrea to meet him for coffee.

The following Saturday the three girls met in front of Millbank Hall at Barnard and walked together to the subway to head downtown to hear a lecture on innovations in engineering and physics. The lecturer, a brilliant undergrad student from Yale named John Hammond, Jr., was the son of a wealthy industrialist.

Mae and her friends arrived early hoping to find seats close to the stage, at Andrea's insistence, because she had heard that the twenty-year-old Hammond was attractive and single.

Mae laughed. "I don't know how a girl with a one-track mind has room for all the scientific knowledge that you have learned."

"Don't you worry about me," said Andrea laughing. "I manage to lead a full life.

Science is just one of my interests; men are another."

Adeline interrupted acerbically, "I don't see why you waste your time. I am perfectly content without a man in my life, someone to order me around and tell me that I shouldn't study medicine and who would lock me up in a house with five or six children to care for."

The room suddenly became quiet when Jack Hammond walked out onto the stage. He was indeed a good-looking young man. He spoke at length on his work involving radio waves and his experiments with what he called remote controls, which he used to guide the small boats from a distance. Then suddenly Mae was surprised to hear him mention the name of Nikola Tesla, the intriguing man that she had met at the home of Mr. Morgan.

"I have asked my father to arrange a meeting with Mr. Tesla," he said, 'the Serbian high priest of telautomatics'. Happily, we are to speak while I am in New York before I return to Yale."

Mae wished that she could speak to the young Mr. Hammond about Mr. Tesla and find out more about the details of their proposed discussion. She felt that providence had led her to attend the lecture. Her curiosity about electricity intensified, and she longed to know more about Hammond's experiments, but he rushed off stage and left the hall the minute his speech ended.

She turned to Andrea. “Do you think we could speak to Mr. Hammond?”

“I sincerely doubt he would waste his time on us,” she said with irony. “He is extremely knowledgeable, but he is not interested in teaching. My information is that he is obsessed with obtaining patents in order to make money. He is the copy of his father.”

Perhaps you are right,” Mae sighed. “I suppose he is more like Mr. Morgan than Mr. Tesla in that respect. It is disappointing.”

Quite unexpectedly Mae felt a hand on her arm. Looking up, she saw the handsome face of Declan Malone.

“Hello, Miss Dodd,” he said, flashing an alluring smile. “Do you remember me? I was your dancing partner at Luna Park.”

“Of course, I do!” she responded. “It has been quite a while, and I am sad to say that I have not had the time or opportunity to improve my dancing.”

He took her arm to guide her from the crowded lecture hall. “I haven't had much time for dancing either, much to the chagrin and annoyance of Leah. Between working and going to school, I have neglected the finer aspects of life. But how have you been? Have you pursued your interest in physics?”

“Why yes I have,” she answered, turning to Adeline and Andrea. “May I present my friends and fellow students? Adeline Howell, Andrea Shapiro, this is Declan Malone. He is an engineering student at New York University.”

Declan tipped his hat and bowed slightly. “Nice to make your acquaintance, ladies,” he said, offering a discreet wink of the eye to Andrea who was smiling coyly.

"How rare to meet three such lovely girls at a lecture on electricity on a Saturday afternoon."

Mae felt a stab of jealousy when she noticed Andrea boldly flirting with Declan.

She had tried to put him out of her thoughts because she knew that Leah was in love with him, but she could not deny her feelings now that she was in his presence.

"Hey, why don't we go to The Village," Andrea said abruptly. "A friend of mine told me about a swell tearoom called The Mad Hatter, or if you want something a little more substantial, there is the basement café in The Brevoort Hotel. Apparently, Emma Goldman dines there quite often."

"Unfortunately, my mother is expecting me for dinner," said Mae. "It's a gathering of her closest friends. As a matter of fact, I believe you know one of the ladies, Declan. Do you recall Dore? But perhaps you would like to accompany Andrea?"

"First of all, I recall Dore very well," he said. "How could I forget her disapproval of me that evening at Luna Park? And unfortunately, I cannot take time for dinner for I am off to work. But I would be glad to escort you home, Mae, if you would allow me. I don't like the idea of you riding the subway alone."

Mae could feel Andrea's icy stare, while Adeline seemed pleased with the turn of events.

"I would love to go with you Andrea," said Adeline "if you are treating."

Declan and Mae walked toward the Astor Place entrance to the subway. Standing in front of the faience plaque with beavers, which represented the origin of the Astor family's wealth in the eighteenth century, she thought about the gulf between herself and the handsome young Irishman who stood next to her. And yet they had so much in common—their love of science and learning and the desire to do something important. She wondered if Declan was in love with Leah and if he planned to make a life with her. Suddenly the possibility of the two actually marrying made her heart race. She felt dizzy and she began to tremble, losing her balance, she tripped and grabbed for the stairway railing. Seeing her predicament, Declan placed his arm around her and held her close.

"Are you all right, my girl?"

Recovering as quickly as she could, Mae responded. "Oh, yes, I am fine. It's just that my coat is too heavy and I felt too warm."

He lifted up her chin gently with his hand and looked into her eyes to be sure that she was fine. He did not anticipate that looking into her large blue eyes would elicit feelings of tenderness toward this girl. It was not the sensuality and desire that he felt when he was with Leah, but something else that he did not understand. Here was a young woman of wealth and social standing, who was also intelligent and ambitious, and yet she was timid and humble.

After accompanying her to the door of her brownstone, Declan walked back to the subway trying to pin down his feelings and what, if anything, he should do about them.

DORE

SEPTEMBER 1909

On a fine and sunny day in late September, people from all strata of society packed the streets from the Battery to Riverside Park. The American public had come from up and down the East Coast and even from as far as the Midwest to attend the Henry Hudson Festival. Almost the entire New York City population attended. A crowd of over a million souls lined the Hudson River to witness the opening of the celebration that honored Henry Hudson and Robert Fulton. Women wore their finest dresses and sported large and extravagant hats; men wore stiff collars and their finest suits with the latest style of pants with a slim leg. Street vendors sold popcorn, sarsaparilla, and a new creation known as the ice-cream cone.

A parade of ships sailed up the Hudson, including gunboats from Britain and Germany, firing their guns in salute. Balloons, known as Montgolfier to the French, filled the sky, and Wilbur Wright flew his new invention over the city skyline. A tangle of ten-thousand automobiles created terrible congestion along the river.

Dore had arranged to meet Christiaan and his friend Hutch, as well as Ira and his latest love interest, a man named Teddy. Knowing that the restaurants and cafes would be packed, she had made a reservation at Murray's, a popular eatery off of Broadway. Even though she arrived early, at five o'clock, she found the restaurant crammed full. Christiaan and Hutch arrived at five-thirty.

"Sorry, that we are so late, old girl," said Hutch. "It took almost forty minutes to walk five blocks. It's madness out there."

Christiaan took the chair next to her and gave her a light kiss on the cheek.

"Oh, don't think twice about it," she said. "It is unbelievable, isn't it?"

Hutch called over a waiter. "I am dying of thirst. Can I offer you to some refreshment?"

"I have had an entire pot of tea while I was waiting, but you to go ahead and order," she said.

Hutch ordered a pitcher of beer and some pretzels.

"When are Ira and his friend supposed to arrive?" asked Christiaan.

"They are coming around six, so I think we should wait to order dinner, if you don't mind," said Dore.

"That is fine. Dore, do you mind if Hutch and I talk a little business? We have an interview that we need to finish for publication and we need to review our notes."

"Not at all, but I don't know if I can refrain from making a comment or two."

"Comments are always welcome," said Hutch.

"I am sure that you will be interested in the case," Christiaan said. "We interviewed Fania Cohn and Pauline Newman, two friends of Clara Lemlich."

Dore's eyes widened. "Oh, I know Clara. She used to live on our block when we first came to New York. She worked briefly for my father when he was a sweater, but she was such a talent that she soon found a better-paying job as a draper at Leiserson's Shirtwaist Factory. I remember that she loved to read and we would often meet at the public library."

Christiaan looked at Dore with a jaunty smile. "I guess we will have to reference you in our article."

Dore laughed. "Don't be silly. I just happened to know her back then. Why, I haven't seen her in years."

Hutch took out some notes and reviewed the questions and answers from the interview. "September tenth was the date, right Christiaan? Around what time?"

Christiaan nodded. "Right, it was a Friday evening as she was leaving a picket line at a factory off Fifth Avenue, just north of Washington Square. It wasn't late according to Fania," he continued, consulting his notes. "She was headed downtown to the library to pick up some books. Pauline had been with her on the picket line."

"Is that when it happened?" Dore interrupted, realizing that they were talking about the terrible beating of Clara Lemlich. "You are actually going to publish an article about the attack? Well, I am glad that somebody is finally going to shed some light on the incident."

"It's true that most of the papers don't care about the suffering of one immigrant girl, but we believe that such a horrific act of violence perpetrated against a young woman must be covered," said Hutch, as he shuffled his papers, his face grew red with anger. He pounded his fist on the table, causing the diners at the neighboring table to look up with startled expressions. "Of course, the fact that she is quickly becoming a leader in the garment union movement adds significance to the story. I believe that this incident will change the course of garment workers' walkouts, and it might even lead to a general strike."

"So, what happened?" asked Dore, eager to know the details. "Who attacked her?"

"It was Charley Rose," said Hutch, and a thug named William Lustig, a back-room Bowery prizefighter, apparently helped. Charley did time for burglary and is a brute."

"It appears that the police officers at the picket line watched as the gangsters followed Clara when she left," said Christiaan. "They have standing orders not to interfere with the strikebreakers or the thugs that harass the girls. I have been researching so-called detective agencies that supply the muscle to the shop owners and managers. These pious businessmen are more than willing to rough up men, women, and young girls in order to, as they say, protect their property."

"So, the police actually let them beat a defenseless girl?" asked Dore, thinking about Clara Lemlich, the sweet, delicate girl who she had admired when she was young. This is beyond the pale! And they were never arrested?"

"No," said Hutch. "The police ignored the entire incident. The men caught up with her not far from the picket line on a deserted street and beat her savagely. The whole affair took only a few minutes, but they managed to leave her bleeding on the sidewalk with several broken ribs."

"But Clara, slip of a girl that she may be, is not one to be easily intimidated," said Christiaan. "Within days she was back at the picket lines in the Garment District. Her wounds only enflamed the strikers and inspired her comrades to stand strong against the bosses and the hired thugs."

Dore felt a pang of jealousy as she listened to Christiaan praise Clara. Even though she knew that it was absurd, she felt that she did not measure up to Clara's courage and determination. For the first time, she understood the depth of her feeling for him. It was true that they were not lovers and he had made no promises, but suddenly she realized that she was deeply in love with him.

Hutched looked around for a waiter, but they all scurried about, taking orders and carrying overflowing trays of food. "If you will excuse me," he said. "I will go to the bar and order another pitcher of beer."

At that moment, Dore was surprised to see Ira entering the restaurant alone.

"Christiaan,' she said discretely, " why don't you both go to the bar and have a drink. I would like to have a few words with Ira alone, if you don't mind."

The men excused themselves and headed for the bar, as Ira looked around the restaurant trying to find Dore. She stood up and waved to him and smiled briefly.

"Ira, sit down. You look so distraught. First of all, where is Teddy? I was so looking forward to meeting him."

Ira dropped down into one chair and kicked another violently, making a racket.

Again, the people at the neighboring table looked up with expressions of displeasure.

"Teddy is with his wife and daughter," said Ira. "I guess I should have been honest with you, but I was so sure of him. He told me that they were separated and that he had asked for a divorce. He really had me convinced. That's what I get for falling in love with a married man and an Episcopalian to boot. It's almost a cliché. Isn't it?"

She reached over and squeezed his hand. "I must admit that I have never truly understood your penchant for men. You may laugh, but at one time I thought that you and I could make a go of it. I can see that you are genuinely in love with this man and that you are heart-broken. But, Ira, he is not worthy of you. It may be true that you found physical pleasure in his arms, but that is not enough to make a life together. If he has a wife and child, then he made his choice long ago to live a conventional life. Must I point out the painful and obvious truth that he will never leave that life to live with you?"

Dore had never seen Ira cry, and she didn't know how to react.

"I know that now," he said wiping tears from his cheeks. "But for a few weeks I really thought that he loved me. What a fool I have been to believe that he would ever leave his wife. It was absurd to think it possible. I mean he works for her father's sporting goods company, one of the largest in the state. And he is set to take the reins when her father retires. I guess that I always knew that he would not abandon his family and the money for a homosexual and a Jew."

"I think that it is best not to dwell on it," she said. "I am sure that one day you will find a man who will be true to you and to himself. Never give up on love. I am glad that I haven't."

"No, you haven't. How long have you been seeing Christiaan? More importantly, how serious are you two? He is very discreet, and I don't want to put him on the spot by discussing it at work."

"It's true that he is very guarded and doesn't show his emotions. We share that characteristic. We have spent a lot of time together, going to concerts, poetry readings, and even political meetings."

Ira laughed. "I hope he hasn't been hoodwinked by the anarchists."

"Not in the least," she said. "He is not in with the anarchists or even the socialists. He calls himself a progressive, cut from the cloth of Jacob Riis and President Roosevelt."

"Yes," said Ira, raising his eyebrows. "I know how much he admires Roosevelt.

But how much does he admire you? More importantly what are your feelings for him?"

"It's difficult to find the words to explain how I feel. It is something that I have never experienced in my life. You see I have never known romantic love. You know my history. I have studied and worked to improve myself, but I have never received a word of praise or encouragement from my father. I have rarely been praised by men, with the exception of you, and an occasional "well done" from Rodman Wanamaker. All my support has come from my female friends. And now at last I have met a man who cares for me and respects me. He is interested in my opinions, and most importantly, he is not using me to further his own career or flatter his ego."

"But what do you feel for him?" Ira insisted. "Do you love him? If you don't want to tell me, I don't mind. But I just want you to know that he is a good man, at least from what I know of him. He is dedicated to his work. And if it makes you feel more secure, he is not known as a skirt-chaser."

Dore smiled and her beautiful complexion reddened. "I am very happy to hear that, particularly today."

"Really? Why today in particular?"

"Becausc, Ira, it is a day of joy and celebration, and I feel as though I am floating on a cloud of delight. And because I propose to ask him to accompany me back to my apartment to spend the evening and perhaps the entire night."

"Finally," he said, a smile curling the edge of his mouth. "You deserve to be with a man who can show you what it means to feel pleasure. I have always felt that life has been inordinately unfair to you, particularly as it pertains to men. You could not have picked a more suitable partner, and you must promise to keep me apprised of developments."

After dinner Ira asked if anyone would like to see the fireworks that were planned for after-dark. Hutch said that he had some work to do and, Christiaan declined.

"Well, I think I'll go to Riverside Park and join the festivities," Ira said, winking discreetly at Dore.

Once they were alone, she looked directly into Christiaan's eyes and asked boldly.

"Would you like to see where I live?" They decided to walk instead of taking the subway. The crowd thinned out, and she felt that she could breathe more easily. The sun had set hours ago and the electric streetlights had been turned on. The fireworks were not scheduled to begin for another hour, but they would most likely be able to see them from her window.

Christiaan seemed uncomfortable walking through the lobby, as if he were a schoolboy afraid to be caught in a girls' dormitory. When they stepped off the elevator on her floor he exhaled, as if relieved that the corridor was empty.

"You don't have to worry," she said with a soft laugh. "There are no rules forbidding men above the first floor. You do realize that this is an apartment hotel and all the residents, men and women, are free to have guests at any time?"

"It's not that," he said. His fair skin reddened. "It's just that, well, I am wondering if you are sure about inviting me to your room at this hour?"

"Christiaan, if you are asking me if I have decided that we should be lovers, the answer is a definite yes. Don't you think that we have waited long enough?"

"I sure do. But I didn't want to rush you. From what you told me; you had a difficult time of it with your first marriage. I thought that I should be sure how I felt about you before asking you to take this step."

"And how exactly do you feel about me, Christiaan?" she asked as she took her key out of her purse, opened the door, and turned on the light. He gently enfolded her into his arms and kissed her first softly, then more passionately.

"My girl, I am in love with you. I think that I have been since the moment we met."

Unexpectedly she began to cry, first quietly and then she sobbed irrepressibly. She threw herself onto a chair and covered her face with her hands, trying to control the wave of emotion that she had managed to dam up over the years.

"My goodness, this is not the reaction that I expected. I can only be honest about my feelings and you did ask." He approached her, trying to comfort her.

"No, it's not that. I mean it's not you," she said trying her best to regain her composure. Drying her tears with a handkerchief, she took his hand and kissed it.

"You see, I am almost twenty-three years old, and I have been married and divorced, and this is the first time that a man has told me that he loved me. More importantly, it is the first time that I can say that I am in love."

Christiaan was surprised. "All I can say is that American men must be blind and stupid. But I am all the more fortunate, for you have no other ties and are free to love me."

Dore stood up and kissed him gently. "Would you like something to drink? I don't have any wine, but could offer you tea or coffee."

"No," he said. "I am not thirsty. Do you think that we might go to your bedroom?"

She was not afraid, a little nervous perhaps. She had imagined this scene a hundred times, but now that it was playing out, she did not have a clever response. She took his hand and led him to her bedroom and quickly began to undress, as did he.

Their lovemaking was hurried and ardent. After, they slowed down and began to kiss and explore each other. It was the first time that Dore had reached climax and she wanted to experience it again, only more slowly.

After Christiaan held her in his arms. "It's almost as if you have never been with a man. I know that you were married, yet you make me think that this was your first time."

"Well, in my mind," she said, "it was."

He was quiet for a while and he looked at her with an expectant expression as he spoke slowly and deliberately. "I don't know how to put this. I would like it if we could live together. I cannot offer marriage, not yet. It may be possible someday when I am more financially secure. But I want you to be with me every night, and I want you to be in my bed every morning when we awake."

She was taken off guard and searched for her words. "There is nothing that would make me happier, but I cannot forget my family or my position at the store. It would be a shock to my parents, especially since you are not Jewish. To be honest, I would be willing to face my father's anger, but only if it were a question of marriage."

"I am sorry, Dore. I am in no position to take a wife, or have a family," he said.

"I understand. You have made that clear. I am not in a hurry to get married, and I want to go on seeing you. But I cannot live with you. If my superiors at Wanamaker's should hear of it, they would be scandalized. I would surely lose my position. You mustn't think that everyone is as liberal-minded as the people at your paper."

"Would they have to know?" he asked naïvely.

"It's too big of risk," she said. "I love you, but you must understand that I cannot jeopardize my career. I have worked too hard. But please tell me that my refusal to live with you doesn't change how you feel about me."

"It does not and never will. In a way, I love you more for it," he said.

DORE AND LEAH

OCTOBER 1909

The women sat at their machines on the eighth floor of the Triangle Shirtwaist Factory, each looking at her neighbor with nervous expectation. Who would be the first to stand? The silence was pervasive. Suddenly a young girl stood up with a defiant expression. In unison all the women, who made up the workforce of the factory, got to their feet, pushed their benches under the long rows of tables and proceeded to the hallway to retrieve their coats and hats. The walkout had begun, and one brave woman had put things in motion with a few words spoken the night before.

The venue at Cooper Union Hall was filled to capacity with union men and women from various trades, including garment workers, in addition to the various proponents of socialism and even a group of anarchists. Speakers from various political and social alliances and agencies spoke on behalf of their supporters. It seemed that everyone had an opinion, but the concerns for the improvements of working conditions for the girls in the factories received little attention. When a group of women tried to bring up the idea of a general strike, more vociferous groups shouted them down, saying that now was the time for strategies that addressed the political trajectory of society on grander scale. Samuel Gompers rose to address the women in a rather patronizing tone, asking them why would they want to risk losing their jobs and take the food out of their children's mouths.

When he had finished speaking, a lone woman of slight build and delicate features stood up. She spoke in a steady, clear voice and her message was brief. "I have heard enough. Tomorrow, I call for a general strike."

The room erupted in applause and shouts of approval. Twenty-three-year-old Clara Lemlich had turned the tide, overriding the most powerful men in the labor movement. The strike was on.

A week later Leah stood outside the Triangle Shirtwaist Factory, which occupied the eighth, ninth, and tenth floors of the Asch Building at the corner of Greene Street and Washington Place. She had been among the many girls who walked out to protest the owners, Max Blanck and Isaac Harris, who refused to meet the workers' demands. The Women of the Garment Union were the force behind the strike, asking for shorter work hours, higher pay, and better conditions. The owners were amenable to these demands within reason. But the strikers had one condition to which management refused to concede—a closed shop. Blanck and Harris would allow union members to work in their factory, but they insisted that nonunion workers be employed as well. This was a point on which nobody would budge.

It was quitting time when the strikebreakers were leaving the factory, and the strikers gathered at the exit to try to persuade them to join with them in the fight against the bosses. The girls, who had taken the place of the workers, were mostly young Italians, who didn't speak English. They were meek and pliable, many sent to work by their fathers to bring in extra money. Leah and her comrades pleaded with them to join the strike, but they were surrounded by policemen who shielded them from the strikers.

As Leah shouted insults at the police, she heard some of the girls scream and saw that her friend Ida had a bloodied nose. Unexpectedly, a group of garish prostitutes appeared, shouting and taunting them and clutched at their signs. Then the streetwalkers began to swear and kick, tearing at the girls' clothes and hair. Leah screamed when she felt sharp nails digging into her neck and turned to face her assailant, a lewd and unkempt whore. Suddenly, she saw a woman grab the assailant by the hair and slap her face.

"Let go of her, Betty. Tell the other girls that'll do and to back off." The attacker immediately walked off, scowling and swearing. The older woman, who was attractive and well dressed for someone of her profession, quickly turned away as if she were trying to disappear into the crowd.

A strong feeling of recognition hit Leah like a blow. She quickly pursued the woman, running down the street, grabbing her arm, and pulling her close so that she could see her face.

"Mother!" she shouted. "It is you."

The woman liberated her arm and tried to get away. "I'm sure that you are mistaken, dearie. I am nobody's mother."

"Yes, you are!" shouted Leah. "I remember you. Is this why you left me, to become a whore? Chicago, my ass!"

Rachel Sefarti turned and ran down Greene Street, tears streaming down her heavily made-up face.

It struck Leah that deep in her soul she always knew that her mother had not gone to Chicago. But she imagined that she had found a wealthy man who took her as a mistress. Of course, introducing a child into that scenario would not have been convenient. The reality that her mother was a prostitute hit her hard.

Dore walked up the steps from the subway onto the streets of Harlem. She noticed that the apartment buildings were wider and well maintained. She was pleased that her family lived in better conditions than they had on the Lower East Side. She had not planned to see her parents that Sunday, but Leah had contacted her to come by so that they could talk over an urgent matter.

As soon as Leah opened the door, Dore knew that something was seriously wrong. She was irate, her face tearstained and her voice trembling with anger. Rebekah was crying as Isaac was putting on his coat.

"I will not stand here and listen to his," he barked. "After all that we have done for you, that you should speak to us this way."

Dore looked at her father. He seemed to have aged quickly in past few months.

"What is wrong, Papa?"

"You talk to Leah. I am leaving, and I think when I come back that she should not be here anymore." With that he slammed the door.

"I should tell you what is going on?" she said sarcastically. "More like you all should have let me in on the big secret. My mother, who you said is working in Chicago, was outside The Triangle on Friday. She was directing a group of her whores to attack the strikers. I heard her shouting orders, so I know the girls worked for her."

Dore looked worried. "Did you confront her?"

"You bet I did," said Leah. "But she ran away. So, I decided to go down to the Bowery and ask around. They told me to go ask at a certain house in the Tenderloin District. I found her house and I treated one of the girls to lunch to pump her for details.

Apparently, it is not just any brothel, but one of those that caters to swells, bankers, and the men from Tammany Hall. Seems that 'Madam Sophie' as she likes to be called, runs a classy joint and welcomes the upper crust to mix with her ladies."

Dore didn't know how to respond. She turned to Rebekah for help.

"Leah, it is true," said Rebekah. "We knew what your mother was doing, although we didn't know that she was so successful. I am sorry that we hid the truth. We wanted to protect you and spare you any pain."

"I understand that you didn't want to tell me when I was young," said Leah a bit more calmly. "But I am grown up now and I deserve to know the truth."

Dore intervened. "Well, now you know. But instead of being angry, I would think that you would be a little grateful to us. After all we cared for you and protected you. It's true that we lied, but we did so out of kindness. As for Rachel, she didn't want to take you with her when she left, she couldn't. But she has always cared for you in her way, and she even came by several times to see how you were."

Leah was quiet and had a calculating expression. "Seems to me that she must have put aside quite a bit of money. Maybe I should go down there and see her. After all, she owes me. I am her daughter."

Rebekah let out a short cry.

Dore stood up and clenched her fists. "Don't you dare do that!" she said. "If you do, I will never speak to you again."

"I didn't say that I would really go see her. But what is she going to do with all that money?"

"I suppose she is investing it in a bigger establishment," said Dore. "And then, of course, there are the bribes and protection money. All I know is that she has never offered to pay a cent for your room and board. If she had, perhaps you wouldn't have had to work in sweatshops or at The Triangle."

"Well, it's unfair," said Leah. "She better not bring her girls back to the picket line or I'll tell her what's what!"

BERNADINE AND FLORA

DECEMBER 1909

Flora had noticed that Anne Morgan and Elisabeth Marbury had become extremely close and intimate. It came as quite a surprise, for although she knew that these romantic relationships existed between many women, she had never thought of Anne as having such penchants. She could see that Anne was smitten by the much older woman, but she found the whole thing rather odd, in view of the fact that Elisabeth and Elsie de Wolfe were currently living together at Irving House.

The upshot was that Anne emerged from her cocoon and the confines of Madison Avenue. She began to dabble in social issues and took a new interest in the plight of the working women and in particular the garment union strikers.

So, it was arranged that on December 15th, a committee of members of the Colony Club invited the strikers and their leaders to a luncheon. Over one hundred club members attended the event, which was held in the club's gymnasium, where the well-heeled society ladies listened to the complaints of the poor, mostly immigrant garment workers.

Flora was waiting for Dora and Leah at the club cloakroom. She particularly awaited with interest meeting Leah, for Mae had brought up her name on more than one occasion. Knowing that she was like a sister to Dore, she had high expectations and assumed that she would resemble her in demeanor and dignity.

Bernadine entered the club with Dore and an attractive, but rather overly painted, young woman. Flora's eyes widened as she tried not to stare. There was no resemblance between this girl and Dore; where Dore was businesslike and soft-spoken, her sister tended toward the dramatic. Bernadine read her thoughts by her expression.

"You do realize, Flora, that there is no blood connection between Leah and Dore?"

Trying not to appear judgmental, Flora managed a sweet smile. "Yes, I know that she was taken in by Dore's family. It's just that I had imagined that Dore's sophistication and education might have influenced Leah. She is very common."

Bernadine sighed. "Well, prepare yourself. The girls that are coming here today are much more common than Leah. But that is the point, isn't it? We have invited them to listen to their grievances, not to discuss the latest novels and concerts. The point is to understand why they are striking and if there may be a way to support them."

At the luncheon, various girls stood up and expressed their discontent. Many could barely speak English. A thin Italian girl stood up shyly. "I work at the Triangle Shirtwaist factory," she said in haltingly. "I live very far from there, and I have to walk because I cannot pay for the trolley. So, when I come in five minutes late, they send me home and I lose a day."

A lively Irish girl with sparkling blue eyes stood up defiantly. "We are made to work eight days a week." Several of the society ladies tried to stifle their laughter. "You don't believe me? We work from seven in the morning till late at night, and on Saturdays. So that makes more than seven days. You ladies should just try it," she said crossing her arms, sitting down in a huff.

Clara Lemlich spoke to the clubwomen, eloquently describing the terrible working conditions at a few shops that she mentioned by name. "I challenge you, my dear ladies, to go and visit these factories. Go and see how we suffer daily to make the shirtwaists and hats that your maids and cooks wear on their days off."

There was a murmuring of surprise in the room when Elsie took off her elegant hat and passed it around to the wealthy women, asking that they contribute so that the working women would have enough money to sustain themselves and their families through the long strike that lay ahead. Anne smiled and said that she would triple whatever the club members raised for the cause. Flora wondered if Anne might have been competing with Elsie in order to impress Elisabeth, who promised to speak with her wealthy theater connections to raise funds.

Support for the striking garment workers became a common cause for the wealthy women of New York Society. Mae had gone with a group of college girls from Barnard and Vassar to visit a tenement. Some of the students decided to move in with the poor immigrant families in order to fully appreciate what their daily lives were like. Unfortunately, when Mae asked her father if she might live for a few days in an East Side tenement, he told her that she was being absurd and that if she was so adamant about her studies, she should spend her time in class or in the library.

New York Society was astounded to learn that Alva Belmont had spent an entire night in the Jefferson Market Courthouse. She sat stoically on a hard-wooden bench in the last row of the courtroom, as hour after hour, common criminals passed before the judge. At eleven o'clock the first strikers were paraded before the judge, accused of trumped-up charges. The prosecutor charged one young woman with shouting "scab" at a strikebreaker. Alva politely asked her neighbor to clarify what was meant by the term. At three in the morning, four young women were dragged in. They had no money for bail, so Alva Belmont, saying that she had brought no money with her, offered her Fifth Avenue home as security. She had brought the deeds to several other properties, if that would also be required.

Leaving the courthouse at dawn, she complained bitterly about the judge.

She told a reporter, "There will be a different order of things when we have women judges on the bench."

Just when the tide seemed to be turning thanks to the involvement of wealthy, progressive women, the movement suddenly weakened. The women of the Colony Club, who had been stirred to help the strikers, became the objects of criticism and scorn. The radical members of the WTUL claimed that the running of the strike did not belong in the hands of Madison Avenue heiresses.

Carnegie Hall was packed with strikers on the evening of January 2nd. But the tone contrasted greatly with that of the meeting at the Colony Club. The fissure between New York Society activists and the labor movement appeared the moment that a banner bearing the words

Socialist Women's Committee unfurled. Several fiery speeches delivered by well-known agitators made the wealthy women in attendance very uncomfortable. Morris Hillquit, a leader of the city's Socialist movement took to the podium and spoke of establishing union-only shops and castigated the cruel factory owners. He went as far as to criticize the exploitation of the poor by the great industrialists. This hit too close to home for the daughter of J.P. Morgan.

Anne spoke with Flora the following day. "I am sorry that I can no longer support the strikers. It is unfortunate that they have aligned themselves with socialists and anarchists. These are fanatics, and I fear that in the end they will do more harm than good to these struggling young women."

Flora had to agree. "It is true that these men are aiming for something that most of the garment workers do not want. The girls at the club were asking for better conditions and shorter hours, not a revolution."

The Garment Union strike ended quietly in January. The owners of the Triangle Shirtwaist Factory did not give in to a closed shop, but they did make concessions: shorter hours and higher wages. They felt that their working conditions more than met the standards of a safe environment.

DORE AND LEAH

APRIL 1910

Things were quiet at the Triangle Shirtwaist Factory; the strike was over and the slow season had begun. The owners had engaged a construction crew to make improvements to the ninth floor of the Asch Building. A city inspector had ordered the owners to install adequate restroom facilities and other amenities.

Christiaan Roberts stood at the corner of Washington Place and Greene Street, waiting to meet Dore and Leah. Almost a year had passed since he had first attempted to set up an interview with Max Blanck and Isaac Harris, the owners of the factory. Unfortunately, the long strike had delayed the meeting with the owners, who had more pressing problems to solve. But now the men appeared eager to be interviewed for they were enthusiastic to show the public that they had addressed the city inspector's required modifications and met the strikers' demands. Blanck realized that an article, published in a progressive paper such as Steffens' *New York Daily*, would go a long way to improve the Triangle's tarnished image.

Christiaan was earning a reputation as an aggressive, yet even-handed journalist.

Working for Steffens opened doors to important political figures, enabling him to include an array of opinions in his writing. He had covered the garment strike, showing sympathy for the workers, all while trying to see the realities from the owners' point of view. He hoped that this interview might convince his editors that he should have his own column that would deal with social issues in the city.

While ascending to the ninth floor where they were to meet the owners, Dore introduced Leah to Christiaan. "Leah, this is Mr. Roberts, who will be conducting the interview. We are very good friends and I know that he can be trusted to write an unbiased article."

"Good afternoon, Mr. Roberts." She smiled slyly. "Dore has spoken about you many times. I always assumed that you were her beau, but maybe I am mistaken."

Dore blushed and shot a severe sideway glance at her. "Leah, why do you go out of your way to embarrass me?"

Christiaan responded with an affable smile. "Dore, you may as well be honest with the girl. I am sure she means no disrespect."

Dore crossed her arms and looked at Leah. "Oh, unfortunately, this young lady is often disrespectful." Then she softened and smiled. "But I can't help but love her anyway."

Leah lifted her chin and smiled at the good-looking young man. "I am glad that she has found a nice gentleman such as yourself." Then she gave Dore a hug. "I am sincerely happy for you, Dore."

"Thank you, Leah," he said. "Please feel free to call me Christiaan. I want to thank you for helping to arrange this interview."

"My pleasure, I am sure," said Leah. "But I think you really have to thank Dore's father and Mr. Braverman. They spoke with Mr. Blanck."

The elevator jerked to an abrupt halt on the ninth floor, jarring the passengers. Leah took the opportunity to take hold of Christiaan's arm and leaned her shapely body into his.

Christiaan slid the door open, and the three came face to face with Simon Braverman. Dore bristled, standing erect, her spine stiffened. She had not expected to see her former father-in-law, even though she knew that he had negotiated the particulars of the interview.

"Hello Simon," she said icily.

"Why, Dore, I was not expecting to see you," he said, doing his best to hide his displeasure. "I did not realize that you had any connection with Mr. Roberts."

She decided to ignore this remark. "Where are Mr. Blanck and Mr. Harris?" she asked.

"They will be down in a moment," he said. "They wanted me to show you onto the factory floor." He looked at her up and down and then said disparagingly, "So you don't even ask about Meyer? We are so proud of him. He is on staff at Mount Sinai, and he has just opened his private practice."

Dore tried to maintain her composure, but felt the heat rise to her face and heard a buzzing in her ears. Not wanting to give Simon the satisfaction of seeing her anger, she breathed deeply and responded briefly, "So, good for him."

At that moment they heard the elevator doors open, and the two owners stepped out. Max Blanck, a large blustery man, was the dealmaker and salesman of the duo. Proffering his large fleshy hand to

Christiaan, he emanated goodwill and ease. In contrast, Isaac Harris was a slight, dark man. He was reserved, giving an impression of timidity. He had married into Max's family, and there were rumors that he had abandoned his first wife and children to enter into the marriage. Both men had emigrated from Russian at the end of the past century, arriving with nothing, to start new lives as many of their current employees had done. They had started out in the tenement sweatshops. By the turn of the century with the advent of the shirtwaist, which was popularized by the portraits of young women by Charles Dana Gibson, the partners concentrated their efforts on the mass production of the garment that made them wealthy beyond their wildest dreams. Now they had several factories, the Triangle being the largest. During the strike, they had opened a factory in New Jersey, where they imported strikebreakers who went unnoticed by the New York union workers.

Max brusquely dismissed Dore and Leah. "I thank you ladies for directing Mr. Roberts to the interview. Mr. Braverman will take you down.

A few minutes later, Isaac Harris made his excuses, mentioning that he had a meeting with a group of buyers within the hour. So, Christiaan conducted the interview with Max Blanck alone on the ninth floor of the almost deserted factory. After a minute of awkward silence, Christiaan gathered his wits and started to ask one of his prepared questions. But he was brusquely interrupted by the owner.

"Young man, let me point out the fact that despite the complaints that were so widely publicized by the press during the strike, our workers, particularly the young ladies, feel fortunate to be working at the Triangle. You must put things in perspective, for if you compare this room to the hot basements of laundries or the squalor of the sweatshops, the contrast is quite striking."

Christiaan looked at the large windows, which admitted abundant sunlight into the room. The factory, often called a loft, had high ceilings giving the room a feeling of spaciousness. But the impression dissipated once he looked at the long sewing tables that covered every inch of floor space. Opening his writing pad, Christiaan began taking notes. He turned to Blanck, who was looking over his establishment with great pride.

"Mr. Blanck, I was told that the inspectors from the City Labor Department have drawn up a list of required improvements."

"Yes, this is true, and Mr. Harris and I have complied with required modifications. If you would be so kind as to accompany me, I will show you the changes that we have implemented."

They walked further onto the factory floor, where the owner pointed to the new floorboards. However, despite the shiny new floor, rows of sewing tables ran from north to south and jutted up to four long tables at the rear of the room. So, it was evident that the girls would have great difficulty navigating this complicated floor plan if they needed to leave in a hurry. Christiaan made a note of the danger of this L-shaped arrangement in case of an emergency.

"Don't your employees find the arrangement of their working space rather crowded?" he asked Mr. Blanck.

"Why not at all," the owner said. "They are quite content to be close to their friends and gossip as they work. Again, notice the abundance of light and good air." He led Christiaan off the main floor toward the front of the loft. "Come along. I want to show you the new facilities that we have just added for the ladies."

In the front of the large room, adjacent to the freight elevator that conveyed the workers to and from the factory floor, was a newly constructed dressing room where the ladies could hang their coats and their fashionable hats and behind were toilet facilities and washstands.

"We have seen to the comfort of our ladies," Max boasted, puffed up with self-satisfaction. "Our employees are delighted with these changes, and I assure you that we do not foresee a strike in our future."

Listening to the owner's haughty tone, Christiaan understood that he would have to pose more challenging questions. Yet he feared that Blanck would end the interview if he probed too deeply. Nevertheless, he forged ahead. "Is it true that all the girls are required to line up in front the freight elevator at the end of their shift in order to have their bags searched?"

"Yes, this is true. Regrettably there are dishonest girls who try to filch bits of lace and even finished shirtwaists. You can certainly understand our position. We would quickly lose our profit margin if we were to allow this kind of theft."

"But Mr. Blanck," he asked cautiously, "don't the women find this, how shall I put it, humiliating?"

"I don't believe so. This goes on in all the factories and most employees, if they are honest, have no qualms about it."

Max Blanck appeared to be losing his patience with this upstart journalist with the odd accent. He pressed the button to call the elevator. He spoke with an annoyed tone, mixed with frustration. "Mr. Roberts, my partner and I have been through a very difficult time with the strike. We have made concessions and many improvements and quite frankly, we are fed up with being portrayed as villains. I thank you for your interest and your time."

The elevator arrived, and an elderly man approached and opened the door "The janitor will see you out. Good day."

Christiaan exited from the Greene Street door. He was surprised to see Dore and Leah waiting. The late April afternoon had grown chilly, and the women had both pulled up their coat collars to keep warm.

"I apologize, ladies. I did not realize that you would be waiting. The interview went longer than I expected, even though it ended abruptly when I asked an inconvenient question."

Leah was bursting to hear what the boss had said. "Oh really, what did you ask the old codger?"

"I merely asked him if it were true that they examine your bags when you leave for the day."

Leah laughed, smiling widely and showing her beautiful white teeth. "Well, everyone knows that. They also check us when we leave for lunch. They are afraid that we are going to pinch some lace or buttons. I have done it in the past. But then I figured out it was smarter to hide items in my garter. They wouldn't dare to check us there."

Christiaan admired the girl's pluck. "So, it really doesn't bother you?"

"We are used to it. But what really makes us fume is the time that we waste standing in line. Already we work until seven, but then we can spend more than half an hour waiting to get out. Many of the girls have beaux who complain about having to wait for them in the street, especially in the winter."

Christiaan was about ask another question, when she interrupted him. "What is really vexing is that there is no way to sneak out even if you tried. They lock all the doors except the Greene Street exit."

Christiaan started. “Do you mean to say that there is only one exit for the entire factory floor?”

“Yes, that is what I am saying. Don’t you doubt it. Us girls have all tried the Washington Place door. It is always locked.”

Dore, who had been uncharacteristically quiet up to this point, blurted out. “Why that is dangerous! Suppose there were to be a fire? How would the employees manage to get out?”

Leah smirked. “I am sure they have thought of that, but do you think they care?”

ALBERT LASKER

NEW YORK, MAY 1910

"Bernadine, it is such a pleasure to hear your voice," said Albert Lasker. "I got your telephone number from Ken Simpson when I was in Houston last month."

"Albert," said Bernadine standing on her toes to speak into the mouthpiece of her recently installed telephone, "where on earth are you?"

"My dear girl, I am here in New York. I am stopping at the Waldorf Astoria. There is some very important business that I must attend to, and I will be in town for a few weeks."

"Oh, how wonderful. Is your wife travelling with you?" she asked, slightly embarrassed because she could not recall her name.

"Goodness no." Albert seemed surprised by the question. "Flora is at home with the little ones, and we are expecting another in a few months. She is in no condition to traipse around the country with me."

"It is a shame, for I would love to meet her. But I am thrilled to hear about your growing family."

"Thank you. She has brought much joy into my life, and much more than that, she keeps me on an even keel. These days I just can't stay still for more than five minutes. But that's enough about old Albert. How are you, my girl, and when can I see you?"

"When you like," said Bernadine. "I can come and meet you for tea or lunch. The Waldorf is very accommodating to unaccompanied ladies. So, I won't mind waiting if you are detained by business. Shall we say lunch tomorrow at one-thirty in the Empire Room?"

Bernadine strolled through the arcades of Peacock Alley, brushing the Sienna marble columns with her gloved hand. She had always admired the lovely blending of colors on the walls, salmon-pink with cream colors and pale greens. She made her way to the Empire Room, the Waldorf's restaurant, considered to offer the finest dining in New York, surpassing even Delmonico's.

For a brief moment her mind flashed back to the nightmare that played out on her wedding night in the bridal suite several floors above the lobby where she now stood. But she remained strangely calm and detached, almost as if the horrible assault had happened to someone else. Yes, she thought, it was someone else.

Suddenly her mood lifted as she saw Albert waiting for her at the entrance to the restaurant. She almost missed him for he had greatly changed. He had filled out both in his body and face. This was no longer the teenage boy from her youth in Galveston, but a mature and somewhat serious-looking man. It was immediately apparent that he had prospered. He wore this prosperity like a badge of honor. He smiled when he saw her, and she was relieved to find that the soul of the young man, her dear friend, still existed in the wealthy businessman.

Albert grinned as he took her hand in his, clasping it tightly, He almost hugged her, but he saw the other guests staring and pulled back. "If we were in Texas, I would give you a big old bear hug, but I don't want to shock the ladies."

"Oh, I don't care about them," she said. "I have grown a thick skin in the past few years. But I want to know more about you. How is Chicago?"

"Chicago has treated me well. Every day I thank my father who had the idea that I should go into advertising. But I had to start at the bottom as an office boy. But now I am a partner in Lord and Thomas Advertising."

They were ushered to their table, located in a discreet corner of the dining room.

"So, as you said you are here on business. May I ask about the details?" she asked.

He smiled, trying not to appear too self-satisfied. "I am here to open a new branch office. In fact, in a few months, we will be opening in Los Angeles, San Francisco, and London."

"London?" Bernadine was surprised and pleased. "I had no idea that your agency was doing so well."

"Yes, it's been just marvelous." He leaned over. "Can you keep a secret?"

She drew closer and nodded.

"I am currently in talks to buy out my partners. In a few months, I will be the sole owner and president of Lord and Thomas."

She was thrilled for her friend. "Albert, I always knew that you would do something wonderful. Are you happy with the work?"

"Happy cannot begin to describe how I feel," he said. "There are days when I am elated. I feel as though I could conquer the world. In a way, I am changing the way that the American public looks at consumer products and that means the way that they perceive their world."

His eyes were gleaming when he spoke and he had a faraway look. For a moment a wave of concern washed over Bernadine. Could a person be too exultant? But she brushed the thought aside and listened to his accomplishments and future plans.

"I am working on something now that is crucial. It is so fascinating that if you look at things from a different perspective, it can change a disaster into an opportunity.

We are promoting a new product, and it all came about because of the orange crisis in California."

She furrowed her brow in confusion. "Orange crisis? I am unaware…."

He interrupted her. "Fact is they had a bumper crop and could not sell what they had grown. They had started destroying the oranges because there was a glut in the market. And then I had an idea. Came to me like a bolt of lightning. Why not take the surplus of oranges and make juice? People drink tomato juice, don't they? I am going to market and advertise orange juice, foremost as a breakfast drink."

"I know many people who have fresh squeezed orange juice at breakfast, Albert."

"Yes, but this will not be fresh squeezed," he said dramatically. "It will be pasteurized like milk and put into containers and sold at the grocery store. The company is to be named Sunkist, and we are to be their sole advertising agency."

After luncheon as they walked arm in arm through the arcades towards the Fifth Avenue exit, Bernadine made an unexpected request.

"I hope you will not think it presumptuous of me if I were to ask for a favor."

"Of course not, anything for my oldest friend. How may I be of service?"

"You see Albert, I have a friend who is in advertising. She is an assistant to the Director of Advertising at Wanamaker's and has been for a number of years. She is very talented, but Rodman's lackey will not promote her because, of course, she is a woman.

Well, I was wondering if you would perhaps meet with her. If you are to open an agency in New York, she would be a great asset. Her taste is sublime, and she is quite artistic. She studied at Parsons. In fact, she told me that she is currently taking some courses in photography and advertising."

Albert smiled broadly. "This is an excellent notion. I will be needing competent staff and perhaps she may even know of some other talented young people, willing to start at the bottom, of course, who might want to build careers in advertising."

"Then I will arrange a meeting," she said, pleased with herself for championing Dore. "Just let me know when it would be convenient. It has been so nice, Albert." Ignoring the stares of the businessmen, she gave him a gentle hug."

Flora sat in her dressing table on a Friday evening trying to put the finishing touches on her hair and makeup. She and Ned were already late to a dinner party, but in her present state, she was not sure if she would be able to attend. She felt the anger rising, first constricting her throat so that she could hardly speak and then filling her head with a dull throbbing pain. Ned had become impossible. She asked herself: *What happened to the understanding man who had courted her all those years ago?*

He had become short-tempered when she disagreed with any of his demands, and he turned sullen when she expressed opinions that did not meet with his approval. She always did her best to please him, especially in matters that touched on his professional life. But she felt that his latest request was quite the limit.

"I don't know why you find it objectionable!" he bellowed, throwing his briefcase violently onto the bed. "One would think that you would be tickled pink to be chosen. It is quite the compliment to be selected to pose for a *tableau vivant* photographed by Maurice Viaud. And of course, Mamie knows that we will be summering in Newport until the end of August. There is no way to gracefully decline."

She struggled to keep a civil tone. "It's just that I do not like being on display. You know that I am not of a nature to show off in front of a crowd. And a *tableau vivant* is just that, a gaggle of society ladies in déshabillé for no purpose other than to attract the admiration of men and the envy of women.

Ned softened his tone a bit. "Then think of it as something that you are doing for me. I am trying to sign on Stuyvesant Fish as new clients for the firm. You needn't think that you are above this sort of thing. Frick's daughter Helen is going to pose. She is only sixteen. If she can do it, then you can make an effort not to be so timid."

Realizing that there was no way out of it, Flora agreed to participate, but on the condition that Bernadine might be invited to pose as well.

"I suppose they would welcome her. After all she is a great beauty," he said as pensively stroked his chin. "But there is the problem of her relationship with Havemeyer."

"Oh, Ned, you exaggerate. Of course, we know about it, but it is not commonly known. They have kept it a great secret. Besides Caroline has not gone through with her threat to expose them. I think that she is weighing her options. You need not worry on that account."

"Very well, I will make inquiries. You speak to Alva. I am sure that she will put in a word with Mamie."

"Very well, then I will pose," she said with a sigh. "Do you know what the theme of the *tableau* is to be?

"Oh, it will be a typical "Mamie" extravaganza. The theme is a grouping of Roman goddesses in a harvest scene."

A strong wind gusted down Broadway as Flora and Dore walked toward the Flatiron Building. Albert Lasker had chosen to open his office in the striking tower because it had been designed by Daniel Burnham, a Chicago architect who he knew well. Dore had always loved this building and the way its unusual sharp angle design dominated the wedge of land at the crossing of Broadway and Fifth Avenue.

The two women chatted as they walked, arms looped around each other's waist.

Suddenly, a blast of air came blustering up 23rd Street, causing Bernadine's skirt to fly up and reveal her ankles. This was a common spectacle in front of the building and not a few voyeuristic swells loitered in the general area in hopes of seeing a pretty leg. One man whistled and while Bernadine's face quickly reddened, Dore turned to the young man and gave him a sarcastic smile. She was wearing the new-style Rainy Daisy skirt that was cut short, six inches above floor-length, so her ankles were already on display.

"Bernadine, if you blush at an appreciative whistle over a display of a bit of ankle, how are you ever going to manage posing for the *tableau vivant?*

"Oh, I will be fine," she said. "Honestly, I was surprised when Mamie asked me to participate for, we are not particularly close. But later Flora came to see me and admitted that it was she who insisted that I be included."

Dore raised an eyebrow. "But why is she being so insistent?"

"You must realize that although Flora grew up in the bosom of Old New York Society. She has grown wary of being the center of attention, particularly in recent years." Bernadine was quiet for a moment, reflecting as if to pin down a fleeting thought.

"I fear that she and Ned are having difficulties in their marriage. She has been tight-lipped, but I have seen the signs. Anyway, I think she wants me there for moral support."

Dore did not feel comfortable discussing Flora's private affairs, so she changed the subject. "Flora asked me to help make up your Roman goddess attire, as well as hers," said Dore. "I have inquired about what the other ladies are wearing and although they believe that their costumes are a closely guarded secret, I have my spies. Each one is trying to outdo the other. I have already ordered yards of white gauze and silk for you, Juno, queen of the gods. I have an idea for an elegant, yet provocative drapery with a few decorative touches."

They walked into the lobby of the Flatiron and ascended to the nineteenth floor.

When the exited the elevator, they faced a wall built of mahogany with stained-glass inserts framing the entrance. A large brass sign bore the name Lord and Thomas.

A stylish receptionist, dressed in a smart suit made of dark flannel, ushered them into a large office, comfortably furnished with leather Chesterfields and stylish Art Deco–style armchairs. Behind an enormous desk, overflowing with papers and cardboard posters, sat Albert Lasker.

Looking up and smiling, he rose quickly and approached his visitors. "Good morning, ladies. Welcome to Lord and Thomas."

"Albert," said Bernadine in a formal tone. "I would like to introduce Dore Abramowitz." Then looking at Dore she said, "Dore, this is Mr. Albert Lasker."

Brimming with confidence. Dore answered, approaching Albert and shaking his hand, "It is a great pleasure to meet you, Mr. Lasker. Your advertising methods were widely discussed at Parsons. I admit that I have used some of your approaches in my work at Wanamaker's."

"I am happy to hear it. It certainly makes a man proud to know that his techniques are being taught in an esteemed institution like Parsons. Won't you ladies have a seat?" He continued. "Miss Abramowitz, I won't beat around the bush. Bernadine has recommended you for a position with our firm in this New York office, and I never question her judgment."

Bernadine blushed at the comment, thinking back to the night of the announcement of her engagement to Theo. She recalled Albert's sudden departure from the party. This was the first time that she had caught him in a lie, for he undoubtedly had questioned her choice of husband.

"I did however, take the precaution of having my assistant inquire about your work at Wanamaker's," he said. "He was very discreet and did not speak with anyone presently employed in the store's publicity department. I believe my man spoke with a Mr. Ira Frankel, who is now doing all the publicity for Lincoln Steffens and Ida Tarbell at the *Commercial Advertiser*, or rather *The Globe*, as it is now called.

Dore smiled for she had anticipated that Mr. Lasker would contact someone from the store and had worried about the consequences of the inquiry. She was relieved because there were no guarantees that she would be offered a position.

"He could not have been more complimentary, although he seemed to think that he was responsible in some way for your professional advancement. Claims he gave you a push just when you needed it."

Dore wanted to laugh, for it sounded so much like Ira.

"It is true, undeniably true, Sir. For I am a Russian immigrant from the tenements of the East Side, and Ira was my mentor."

Grinning widely, Albert clapped his hands together. "Well even better. It always gives me pleasure to give employment to someone of my race."

She looked at him quizzically.

"What? Bernadine didn't tell you that I am a Jew? Born in Germany, raised in Galveston."

"No, she did not mention it, Mr. Lasker."

Bernadine interrupted. "Albert, you know that religion never entered my mind when we were growing up." She turned to Dore. "You see we just all mixed on the island. Why several of the finest families in our society were Jewish, including my best friend, who is a Kempner."

"I see that it still matters among some people in this city," said Albert. "But that is all changing and very quickly: money, and more importantly, commerce matter. And commerce is going to be swayed by advertising. And that is where we come in, right Miss Abramowitz?"

"I certainly hope so," she said tentatively.

"Not a question of hope. You just give your notice to Rodman Wanamaker and show up here in, let's say, two weeks. I believe that is customary."

Dore stood and shook his hand. But she hesitated at the office door.

"Oh," said Albert. "I suppose you want to know the salary. It is our custom to start low, but to rise quickly. You will start as an account manager, $75 a week. It's up to you where you go from there."

BERNADINE

JUNE 1910

Eliot crossed the courtyard of The Dakota heading toward the entrance, when he met Martha and Mademoiselle Monique leaving the building. Martha was turning into a sweet girl and had shot up several inches in the past year. She resembled her mother more and more, but she had her father's smile and blond curls. She ran up and gave him a hug.

"Mommy is inside. Mademoiselle and I are on our way to the museum to meet Aunt Flora and Wren. I hope you will be here when we return."

"I don't think so, my dear. I have some business appointments that I must rush off to."

Martha frowned. "Men are always so busy. You must learn to enjoy life, Uncle Eliot," she said sternly. "Very well, goodbye then."

Bernadine opened the door and they walked into the parlor. She looked pale and was still in her robe, which was unusual for this time of day.

"Are you alright, my love? He said. "You look exhausted."

"I am well," she said. "I'm just tired from lack of sleep. And to quite blunt, we need to discuss our future.

Eliot avoided her glance for a moment and then took her in his arms, kissing her tenderly.

"Caroline and I hardly speak, but when we do, she is vicious. She is threatening to take action if you and I continue to see each other."

Bernadine scoffed. "What action can she take? We both know that she does not want a divorce. If it were up to her, she would never let you go."

"Well, she said that she will expose our affair and that she will sue you for alienation of affection."

"That is absurd," Bernadine laughed. "She would only be setting herself up for ridicule. I don't think that anyone would care about her claims. She has very few friends, except for Bea and a few bitter old maids and unhappily married women."

Eliot rubbed the back of his neck as he considered his options. "Still, she could do considerable damage to your reputation and to my business. The real estate business is built on trust and human relationships. I have spoken to an attorney, who specializes in divorce, and he has suggested a strategy that will pretty much force her to acquiesce."

Bernadine stretched out on a velvet sofa. "Really, what does he advise? I cannot imagine any way of avoiding scandal. Caroline is just spoiling for a public row."

"No, my dear, he really has a well-thought-out course of action. Unfortunately, it means that we must not see each other for a while."

Bernadine flushed and abruptly sat up, clasping his arm. "No, Eliot, how can you even suggest that!"

"Let me explain. The attorney said that she must not be able to use our relationship to her advantage if there are to be divorce proceedings. He has advised me to let it be known to family and friends that I want to adopt a child, a newborn. Then when she protests, which we know she will, I am to speak very publicly about my frustration and disappointment. The more that she resists the adoption, the more likely it is that people will begin to talk. You see it's a question of perception. This will be important when we go in front of a judge."

Bernadine's face grew even paler and tears welled up in her eyes. "Eliot, I couldn't bear it, not seeing you and knowing you were living a charade."

He seized her hand and kissed it. "I am sorry. I know that this is cruel. But if we want to be together in the long run, this is the best course. It won't be easy for me either. I must play at living in a happy marriage for months, when I can hardly endure being in the presence of my wife."

Bernadine brushed a strand of dark her from her face and dried her tears with the back of her hand. "My darling, exactly how many months do you have to go along with this ruse?"

"The lawyer said six months. For if Caroline was to make a pretense to her friends that she was trying to conceive a child, it would be evident that she was a fraud."

Bernadine smiled sadly. "Exactly my love, in six months it will also be evident that you are going to be a father. Rather, I should say five months, for I have had confirmation that I am six weeks pregnant."

Ecstatic, Eliot kissed her. "This time I will not deny my child, and furthermore, I want Martha to know that I am her father."

"But Eliot, how will we tell her?" Bernadine fretted. "And think of your family. What will they think? I am sure that they will never accept me once the truth comes out."

He gently lifted her chin and looked into her eyes. "All that I know is that we have suffered for far too long and that I have loved you from the first time I saw you in Newport. For God's sake, we are living in the twentieth century. Divorce is not uncommon, even among our set. Why, look at Alva, who once forced her daughter into a loveless arranged marriage. She evolved and divorced a Vanderbilt in order to marry Oliver. Don't forget that she is our champion."

Bernadine's demeanor changed, as Eliot's words drew back a curtain on the travesty of a marriage that she submitted to for so many years. At that instant, the world was tossed on its head. Nothing mattered any longer, nothing but her love for Eliot and Martha, and for the child that she was now carrying. She was silent for several minutes, and Eliot was concerned about how she might react. But he was relieved when she smiled brightly and a look of determination appeared on her face. She kissed him and then took his hands and put them on her belly.

"We are going to be a family, and I have a plan," she said.

BERNADINE AND FLORA

NEWPORT, RHODE ISLAND,
AUGUST 1910

As the end of the season in Newport approached, many people stayed on for the September Horse Show. The spectacle and the pageantry of the seaside town never disappointed. A vibrant blue sky with fleecy piles of cumulus clouds complimented the golden sands of Bailey's beach, and the blinding white marble of the cottages offered a sense of classic simplicity, even though there was a tinge of artifice in the pervasive blue hydrangeas found on almost every property.

The Dodd family spent the last week of their summer at Rosecliff with Tessie Oelrichs, an heiress in her own right and the widow of the millionaire Herman Oelrichs

Her handsome and eligible son, Herman, would be staying for the last two weeks in August before returning to Columbia Law School.

Bessie and Harry Lehr were also guests at Rosecliff, which pleased Flora. She had been friends with Bessie for years and knew that she could share any problem, and it would never be repeated. She trusted her as much as Bernadine. Flora had not been back to Newport since Wren's birth, and the Oelrichs mansion had not been completed at that time. She marveled at Stanford White's work that evoked the architectural design of the Grand Trianon of Versailles.

Flora, Bernadine, and Bessie Lehr strolled around the grounds as Tessie saw to their rooms. Known to be a stickler for detail and quite the perfectionist, Tessie reviewed her guests' accommodations for the third time.

"Rose, please make sure that the two large guestrooms are spotless and that the Dodd's luggage is placed in the larger room. Mrs. Van Wies is to have the other large suite. Then make sure that the adjoining doors are locked. Also, please remind the staff that they are to use only the service stairs."

"Yes, mam," said the stout Irish housekeeper. She had been working for Mrs. Oelrichs for almost eight years and knew her mistress's demanding nature well. She always met her expectations.

"Put the children in the smaller rooms toward the back of the house so that their parents may have some peace in the mornings. I think we can put Mae next to Bernadine's girl. Oh, what is her name again?"

"It's Martha, mam," Rose said, always one step ahead of her employer.

"Oh, yes, of course, Martha. Lovely girl. Yes, Mae and Martha next to each other. Now I don't think that we should put the boy, um...."

"Wren, mam," said Rose.

"Yes, Wren. Now there is a Dodd, without a doubt. I don't want him too close to Herman. I am afraid that he will be up early, and Herman may be keeping late hours since he is on holiday. He will want to sleep in, and the Dodd boy will be bounding around making all kinds of noise."

"And the Lehrs, Mrs. Olerichs?" asked Rose, slowly raising an eyebrow. "I assume that they will want separate rooms?"

"Yes, Rose," said Mrs. Olerichs. "I am afraid that they will have to settle for two of the smaller rooms in the front. Let's do keep Mr. Lehr away from the children. You know how eccentric Mr. Lehr can be. I don't want the young ones to have any unpleasant surprises."

Down in the garden, Bernadine was almost blinded by the shining whiteness of the terracotta tiles. The French baroque revival style brought back pleasant memories of Paris.

"Flora, I am so happy that we are all together in this beautiful home," she said and then turned to Bessie. "Bessie, I hope that this stay will afford us with an opportunity to get to know each other."

Bessie smiled and looked at Bernadine thoughtfully. "I have wanted to make your acquaintance for a long time, but fate never seems to have pushed us together. For you see, we do have so very much in common."

Flora reddened and appeared worried. "Bernadine, I must make a confession. Bessie is a dear friend and, well I confided in her. We are quite open about our personal lives, and I am afraid that I told her about your life with Theo. Are you furious?"

Bernadine was taken aback, but when she saw how Bessie looked at her with tenderness and concern, she felt an instant connection, and her anger dissipated.

"Actually, I am not. I have every right to be, but I am not. After all Theo is dead, so I have nothing to fear. But I do wonder why Bessie would be interested in my horror stories."

Bessie laughed and said acerbically. "That is a question easily answered. Because I have my own farce of a marriage, and I think that we may have quite a lot in common."

Flora shot a meaningful glance at Bessie. "I think that you can tell her the truth. For one thing, I know that she will not be shocked."

The three women walked past a rose garden and stood facing the sea.

"When Flora confided in me regarding the events of your wedding night, I was astounded by the similarities with my own experience with Harry."

Bernadine's blue eyes widened, and she put her hand to her mouth. "Did he hurt you? I mean to say, did he handle you violently?"

Bessie looked down sadly. "No, he didn't handle me at all. My wedding night was different from yours in one respect. You see Harry told me bluntly that he did not, never had, and never would love me."

"Why, those are almost the exact words that Theo used," Bernadine said, in amazement.

"But wait. Then he said that he had no desire to touch me and that we would live separate, but pleasant lives."

"You see," intervened Flora. "Harry never laid a hand on Bessie, either in anger or in passion. We all know how charming he can be to the ladies. Just ask Mrs. Astor.

But as charming as he can be, he has no interest in a physical relationship with any woman."

"Oh, I see," said Bernadine. The situation was clear, and she felt sorry for Bessie. "How awful it must be. Do you still love him?"

Laughing, Bessie said. "No, I tolerate him. I wanted to divorce, but while my mother was alive, I didn't dare. Now, I am not sure. I have a son from my first marriage, so there is no rush for I don't want more children. If one day I find someone else, someone with whom I might want to share my life, I may seek divorce. For the time being, I stay with him. You do understand that he has no money of his own? That first night he admitted that he married me only for my money."

Bernadine was stunned. She looked at Flora. "I can see why you spoke about to her about me." She looked at Bessie with sad smile. "My marriage to Theo was arranged for his family's financial well-being. I knew it. But before we married, Theo showed such tenderness toward me. I thought he loved me, so I didn't mind about the money."

"I am sorry to hear about what you went through," said Bessie. "But you are well out of it. I hope that you find happiness with another man."

Bernadine looked at Flora. "So, I see my friend has not told you everything."

"Everything?" asked Bessie.

"Well I have no qualms about sharing my happy news with you. Since we have shared a parallel misery in our marriages, it may give you hope to know that I have found love again. I have been in love with another man for many years. As a matter of fact, we first became lovers here at Newport. Unfortunately, at that time I was not able to divorce Theo. As fate would have it, I gave birth to my lover's child, although she is known to the world as Martha Van Wies."

"But now you are free to marry him, are you not?" asked Bessie.

"Unfortunately, later we parted for many years, and he remarried. He is miserable and he told me that he never loved her. He wants to leave her and be with me. Actually, it has become not only desirable. It is imperative. You see I am pregnant with his child."

Flora gasped and hugged her friend. "I had no idea! Why haven't you told me?"

"I was worried that you would talk me out of coming to Newport and taking part in the *tableau vivant*, Flora."

"I may well have tried," she said. "Dore showed me your costume. It will be evident to everyone. How far along are you?"

"I am going on five months and that is exactly why I want to wear that particular costume, so everyone will see."

"I don't quite understand," said Bessie.

"To put it simply, I am going to make a scene. It will be a scene within a scene, so to speak. For once in my life, I am going to show the world that I am not ashamed of being in love with Eliot."

Bessie was ebullient. "Bravo! I admire your courage."

Flora felt a chill crawl up and down her spine. Was her friend looking for a disaster? Then she selfishly thought of herself. How would Ned react to this scene within a scene?

"Bernadine," she said harshly. "You cannot go through with this. Just imagine the scandal."

"I am sorry, Flora. I have made my decision. I know that this may cause some friction between you and Ned, but it really has nothing to do with him."

After lunch, Ned and Flora sat on a terrace overlooking a large stretch of immaculately mowed lawn. Mae was giving the children some instruction in archery. She had won the grand prize in the Newport competition a week ago. Flora smiled as she watched her show Martha how to hold the bow and position her body. All the while Herman Oelrichs watched attentively and seemed quite captivated by Mae.

"Now that's a sight for sore eyes," said Ned. Herman is a fine young man, and he will graduate from Columbia Law this year. Just the thing to distract our girl from all that physics and math nonsense."

Flora looked at Herman and then at Mae, who seemed oblivious to his presence. "I wouldn't get your hopes up, Ned. She hasn't spoken two words to him. And I am not sure, but I believe Tessie mentioned a young lady from Philadelphia and an impending engagement."

Ned's features hardened, and Flora felt his irritation. He was becoming more and more mercurial by the week, and she wondered if he might be having problems at the firm.

"You seem to be missing the point," he said. "Tessie's son is not the only eligible young man in Newport this summer. I had hoped that Mae would find at least one prospective husband. I secretly wished that someone would catch her eye and that I might cancel your trip to Europe in September. You know it gives me no pleasure to send you both away. But yesterday I bought your passage and booked at the Ritz and Cap d'Antibes."

Trying to hide her exasperation, Flora turned and pretended to study a bed of yellow roses that were in full bloom. "How long do you want us to trot around the continent?" she said, choking back her anger.

"I should not like to be without your company for too long my dear. I thought you could stay until the end of October." He was quiet for a moment and then he addressed his wife firmly. "I have considered the matter very seriously my dear, and I think that Mae would benefit enormously from a year at that school in Montreux."

At the mention of the Swiss finishing school, Flora stood up and ran toward the house, trying to hide her panic and her anger. When

Mae saw her mother's distress , she approached her father. "What is it, Papa? Why is Mother crying?"

Ned was flushed with anger. He abhorred public airing of family disagreements.

"Hush, Mae. We will discuss the matter when we return to New York. I don't want your mother upset. Tomorrow when she poses for the *tableau vivant* at Crossways, I cannot have her photographed with her eyes puffy from crying."

Walking past his daughter, he approached Herman Oelrichs. Taking his hand, he smiled pleasantly and introduced himself. "Hello, young man. We have not had the pleasure, although I knew your father in a business capacity. I hear that you are taking up the law. You could not have chosen a more noble profession."

Herman smiled amiably. "Yes, sir. That is exactly how I feel. I am thinking seriously about corporate law, and I would be grateful for any advice from you, given that you have worked so closely with Mr. Morgan."

"I would be happy to talk things over with you. Why don't we meet for a drink at the Yacht Club? Wait, I have an idea. I just bought a new automobile, a Maxwell four cylinder with leather seats. I was lucky to get it. Morgan is a partner with Maxwell and he put in a word. How about we take it for a spin and then have our drink?

A grin spread over Herman's handsome face. "It would be an honor, sir."

"Fine. Shall we meet at the garage in about an hour? Perhaps you might want to leave your hat. I have been trying to see how fast I can get her to go, so you might be in for quite a ride."

When she reached the top of the stairs, Mae could hear her mother crying softly in her room. She opened the door to find Flora stretched out on a chaise longue with her arm flung across her tear-stained face.

"Mama, what's wrong?" she said bending down and taking her mother's hand. I have never seen Papa so angry. I heard him say Montreux. So, it's definite. I am to go to finishing school?"

Flora sat up, controlling her breath in order to stop the sobs. "Nothing has been decided as long as I have anything to say about it. Let me try and reason with him."

"Couldn't I try and talk to him?" asked Mae. "After all, I have already agreed to put my studies on hold and go to Europe with you. It will mean missing an entire semester, but if it will keep the peace…."

"No," said Flora, despairingly. "I don't think that he would hear a word you say. He doesn't listen to anyone these days. Mae, your father wants to see you married. I know that you are young and finding a husband doesn't seem to be a priority for you, but there is nothing wrong in taking an interest in young men. Why, look at Herman Oelrichs, for instance. He is handsome and has a promising future, not to mention a large fortune.

I saw the way that he was looking at you. Yet you gave him no encouragement at all."

Mae blushed. "Mama, he is very nice, but I feel nothing for him."

"Dear, these things take time. Give him a chance. I would never want you to marry a man that you didn't love or at least respect, but neither do I want to see you become an old maid."

"I want to marry someday," she said as she stood and headed for the door. "As you said, it just isn't a priority"

In fact, she had closed off her heart and mind to the possibilities of love. She had deep feelings for Declan, but she knew he would never measure up to her father's expectations. Herman Oelrichs, handsome and charming as he was, could never evoke the feelings that she had for Declan. So, what was the point of even trying to find a replacement?

TABLEAU VIVANT

CROSSWAYS, NEWPORT, RHODE ISLAND

Even though Mamie Fish had offered her mansion as the venue for the event, Alva Belmont took on the role of the principal organizer of the details of the *tableau vivant.* Maurice Viaud had arrived earlier in the morning to set up his lights. Fortunately, he planned to take the photograph indoors, for the weather was anything but fine. Menacing dark clouds rushed across the sky, with squalls visible out at sea.

The servants and decorators applied the finishing touches to the scene, a mythical forest set up in Mamie's enormous drawing room. Large branches had been gathered from various trees in the garden and squash and pumpkins were transported from Canada. Alva and Mamie debated heatedly regarding the placement of the apples in the scene. Tessie Oelrichs saw to other details, such as where the various goddesses would stand. She consulted with Monsieur Viaud regarding the lighting and how it would best compliment the ladies who were posing.

"Monsieur Viaud, you have superior subject matter for your photograph," said Tessie. "I cannot take all the credit, for Mrs. Belmont and Mrs. Fish had the final word in choosing the models for the *tableau.*

Well, I leave the important decisions regarding your art to you, but please do not hesitate to ask if you need anything at all."

All three of the older women had made the decisions regarding the choice of models for the *tableau vivant*, but Alva assigned the roles. Tessie and Mamie had opposed many of Alva's casting decisions. They found the roles incongruous with the personalities of the ladies chosen. But one could hardly win an argument with Alva these days, as she had become tenacious since the death of her dear Oliver. Her newest crusade, women's rights and in particular the right to vote, consumed her. She attended suffragette meetings in the spring. Bessie Lehr had expressed surprise about her involvement in the *tableau*, given that it could be interpreted as objectifying the participants. She also told Flora that she didn't understand Alva's decisions on the ladies' roles. However, the conversation with Bernadine added some clarity to Alva's choices, particularly as they pertained to Caroline Havemeyer's role.

That Caroline was taking part in the *tableau* came as surprise to many of the guests. After all, as an outsider, and one who was not universally liked, New York had not welcomed her with open arms. Yes, she was wealthy and her husband's family was on solid footing with most of the important families. But most people questioned Alva's insistence in including her and even more so her assigning her the role of Diana the Huntress. Bessie, who was well acquainted with Roman mythology, knew that this particular goddess had no children. She asked Flora if perhaps it had been an unintentional gaffe on Alva's part. Flora smiled and declined to answer.

At first Flora didn't understand the choice of Bernadine to pose as Juno, queen of the gods, but now she appreciated the apt decision. Juno, aside from being the queen of the gods, the wife of Jupiter, also represented fertility and childbirth and held the role of arbiter of marital disputes.

Flora also thought it appropriate that Bessie had been assigned the role of Minerva, goddess of war and wisdom. Considering her friend's strength and astuteness in dealing with Harry Lehr and her ability to rise above the shame and ridicule of her marriage to the man known as King Lehr, she fit the role perfectly.

Tessie Oelrichs came out of the drawing room and gathered all the models together. "Ladies, Monsieur Viaud has finished preparing the lights and his camera and the décor is complete. I ask you to go upstairs and dress so that we may begin. Shall we say one hour?"

Flora and Bernadine shared the dressing room adjacent to Mamie's bedroom. Two maids helped them prepare. The beautiful costumes needed some last-minute pinning, so two maids tended to any problems. They also helped the models with accessories and hairpieces.

Flora portrayed Venus, the Goddess of Love and Beauty. Dore had chosen the fabrics and the cut for her costume, as she had done for Bernadine.

Bessie and Helen Frick dressed in a guest bedroom. Helen, a timid young woman, did not resemble her ruthless steel magnate father in the least. She had spent most of her young life in Pittsburgh and had no close friends in New York.

"Mrs. Lehr," said Helen. "Would you help me arrange the floral wreath in my hair? The maid cannot seem to get it right."

"Of course, my dear," she said. "I am glad that my costume is relatively uncomplicated. Just let the girl finish pinning the shoulder strap and I will help you. I need the strap to be secure. I have to hold a spear in one hand and balance a stuffed owl on the other arm. I will not have a free hand should something come loose."

"I hope that you don't mind if I confide in you Mrs. Lehr. I am worried that I will not fit in. It was my father who pushed me into posing. I really find this whole thing rather embarrassing."

"Helen, please call me Bessie," she said, smiling kindly. "I was once painfully shy like you. We came to New York from Baltimore. So, I understand your feelings.

But you are a beautiful and sweet girl. And let me tell you that I suspect that people's attention will be fixed elsewhere today, so you needn't fret."

She helped the young girl affix the wreath of wildflowers to her auburn hair.

"Oh, I see that you are the Goddess Flora. What a perfect choice, youth representing the Goddess of Spring."

As the goddesses took their places in the scene, the other guests wondered into the drawing room from various parlors. Ladies left behind their bridge hands on the card tables, and gentlemen left their cigars still smoldering in ashtrays. Alva told the onlookers that they must keep their distance until the models took their places and removed their cloaks. At that moment, the curtain would be opened and the scene revealed. Then, Monsieur Viaud would immortalize the goddesses on film.

Behind the curtain, the ladies took their places. Bessie, dressed as Minerva stood erect and proud in front of a backlight, the effect showing the contours of her voluptuous form. In her right hand she held her gilded spear, while a decorator quickly secured a taxidermy owl to her left wrist. Helen Frick standing quietly next to a column wrapped with lilies, nervously touched the clasp of her cloak. Flora approached her and asked if she might have a peek at her costume.

"Of course," she said as she undid the clasp of the girl's cloak, revealing a pale pink silk dress with a high waist. The overall effect was of a tender and gentle young goddess.

Bessie smiled. "Why, you look lovely, my dear. You have absolutely no reason to worry, for I dare say that you would eclipse many of our New York debutantes."

Caroline took her place in front of a grouping of branches. A light, meant to mimic moonlight, cast a milky illumination on Diana the Huntress. Symbolically, it highlighted the fact that she was a virgin.

Bessie chided Caroline, "Do take off your cloak, Caroline. I am just dying to see your costume."

Caroline obliged, revealing a short, white, draped garment, exposing her legs and knees.

"Why, Caroline," said Flora. "I had no idea that you had such lovely legs. Aren't you fortunate that they are so plump and well-formed?"

Caroline glared at Flora. Astonished, because she had not spoken to the woman since the meeting at the Colony Club. Flora obviously represented the goddess Venus, wearing a golden robe with embroidered stars. Her long blond curls flowed down her back, and a brilliant diadem crowned her head.

Bernadine took her place next to Flora. Even Flora's golden beauty paled next to Bernadine's dark, exotic splendor. She was directed to lie on a bed of gilded leaves at the center of the scene, ruling over all the goddesses and mortals. Behind her, the decorator had placed a chariot and a stuffed peacock, her beloved and sacred bird.

Before reclining on the bed of leaves, she took off her cloak, revealing a beautiful gauzy, sheer white dress. The silk and gauze fabrics were cut in a manner that left little to the imagination. The plunging décolletage barely covered Bernadine's breasts, and her rounded belly made it clear that she was at least five months pregnant.

Caroline gasped audibly, and the other models could not help but stare. At first, no one reacted. But suddenly, Caroline seemed to lose her senses and lunged at Bernadine.

"Whore!" she hissed. "You must be mad to show the world that you are carrying a child when you are unmarried. Are you trying to shame yourself or are you seeking some twisted revenge on me?" Realizing that only a thin curtain separated her from the elite of New York, she tried to lower her voice. But it was too late.

Bernadine stood and defiantly faced Caroline. "Why? Isn't this what you wanted, for me to be exposed as your husband's mistress? Well now they will know."

The next moment the curtain opened. The goddesses had all assumed their poses for a few moments while Monsieur Viaud snapped his photographs. But rather quickly, a general murmur seemed to spread across the audience. Many women whispered, covering their mouths with their hands. The men smiled appreciatively at the scene of beautiful women, particularly the lovely Madonna at the center. But no one seemed to pity Caroline, even though quite a few suspected that Eliot Havemeyer was the father of "Juno's" baby. In the end, the *tableau vivant* was a great success.

When the photographing was completed, Eliot walked up to the scene, passing by Caroline and held out his hand to Bernadine to help her rise. Then, without hesitation, he embraced her and led her out of the room.

They passed by Mae and Ned as they left the room. Mae blushed with embarrassment and confusion, but she gently touched Bernadine's arm as she passed. Ned blinked his eyes rapidly and then directed his furious gaze at his wife.

Most of the models had left the scene, but Flora remained, immobile and numb. Ned walked up and grabbed her arm roughly. "Go put on your cloak. We are leaving."

Flora trembled, "But, Ned, what about the luncheon?"

Trying to control his fury, he spoke in a low voice, "I don't give a damn about the luncheon. How can you expect me to face Alva and all her friends? You have humiliated me in front of my colleagues and my clients. Why, for God's sake, do you realize that Frick is here?" He made a feeble attempt to thank Mamie and then asked Tessie if she or her son would see Mae back to Rosecliff.

Mae looked at her mother. She had never heard her father speak in such a manner. "Mama, please stay," she said. "I am afraid for you.

Flora had put her cloak on over her costume, leaving her clothes upstairs. Ned whisked his wife away as he shouted to the servants to have his car brought around.

The ocean squalls had moved inland, and the rain was coming down hard and steady. Flora gathered her cloak tightly around her face and body. Ned drove quickly out of the circular driveway onto Ocean Avenue. Screaming above the fray of the pouring rain, he berated his wife.

"I have given you a home and my name, while you have done nothing but deceive me since the very beginning of our marriage. I was willing to overlook your betrayal during our engagement and I accepted Mae as my daughter."

Flora looked at Ned and tried to reply, but he cut her off.

"Don't deny it! She is not mine. I admit that I was not certain at first. But seeing how she grew up to be so headstrong, so defiant, I understood. Nevertheless, I took the high road and I thought that when Wren came along that we could get things back to the way they were. But you continue to interfere in my decisions regarding the raising of the children. And now this! Everyone knows that Bernadine is your dearest friend and now they know what kind of woman she is. You will be put in the same category."

"But, Ned, she loves Eliot. And besides, I didnt know that she was pregnant and could hardly imagine what she was planning to do today."

As the rain came down even harder, Ned pressed down on the accelerator. Flora looked at the speedometer. They were going at the unheard speed of sixty miles an hour. "Ned, for God's sake. Slow down!"

He did not hear her. "I don't know what I will do with you. I would be well within my rights to file for divorce, but that would do more harm than good to my professional reputation." The roads were slick, and the car began to swerve precariously close to the cliff that stood above the ocean. "But one thing is definite. Mae will go to Switzerland and you will stay in Europe for at least six months. I will make arrangements for Wren to go to a boarding school. Perhaps with everyone out of the house, I can have some peace of ....

At that instant, one of wheels began to wobble, and the car spun around and went off the road, falling toward the ocean below.

BERNADINE AND MAE

SEPTEMBER 1910

Two weeks after the funeral of Ned and Flora Dodd, Mae stepped out of her family's automobile and walked through the courtyard of The Dakota. Ever since he parents' death in the horrendous accident, she had avoided riding in the vehicle. But she decided that she needed to overcome her irrational fear. When she exited the elevator, Bernadine greeted her at the door of the apartment.

"I hope you don't mind, Mae, but Eliot is here," she said. "He wanted to offer his condolences and to see if he could be of any help. Please come in." Mae walked into the apartment and looked around for Martha. "Martha is in school. She is devastated. You know how she adored your mother, and she doesn't know what she should say to Wren."

Mae tried to control her emotions, but could hardly stifle her sobbing. She had been at the Oelrichs' cottage when a policeman delivered the awful news of her parents' death. She had done her best to hide her grief for the sake of Wren. But now, being with Bernadine, she allowed her sorrow to pour out. For all her bravado as a modern woman, she remained a vulnerable and loving daughter, who was now alone in the world.

Eliot walked into the parlor. He stood immobile and averted his eyes, not wanting to embarrass Mae. After a few minutes, he approached the two women. "Mae, please let me tell you how dreadfully sorry I am about the loss of your parents. I cannot imagine the pain that you are feeling and if there is anything at all that I can do, please do not hesitate to call on me."

Bernadine motioned to Mae, bidding her to sit on the sofa. She put her arm around her and gave her a handkerchief. Mae brushed up against her swollen belly, and her thoughts went back to the shocking scene that had unfolded during the *tableau vivant.*

"I suppose you are wondering about my condition and what I plan to do," Bernadine said earnestly. "I want you to know the truth because Bea has already started spreading her venom. Your mother knew about Eliot and me for years. But she did not know about this," she said, hugging her abdomen. "Well, actually I told her the day before the accident, though she had no idea what I was planning to do at Crossways."

Mae felt distressed at the very mention of that day in Newport. Yet she wanted to know the truth about what had happened that day. "Bernadine, why did you create such a shameful scene? You must have realized how people would react. Didn't you think about Martha and my mother, who was always so loyal to you?"

"I will have to live with that decision for the rest of my life. I had no choice. Eliot's wife was determined to thwart any attempt of divorce. However, after such a public humiliation, she had to react. She has filed for divorce and plans to move back to Buffalo."

Mae looked at Eliot. In a way she felt sorry for him because he had put up with an unpleasant and cold wife. She wondered at his courage to flout all the conventions of New York Society. He didn't even seem to worry about his good family name, or even his business.

Almost as if he had read her thoughts, Eliot spoke, "Bernadine has agreed that I should tell you the entire truth about our relationship. This may come as a shock, but Martha is my daughter. We have kept it hidden all these years, at Bernadine's insistence. I can no longer deny that she is mine."

"Does she know?" asked Mae, her brows lifted in surprise.

"Yes," said Bernadine. "We told her a few days ago. She was overjoyed, for she loves Eliot and has almost no memory of Theo."

"I plan to start adoption proceedings as soon as my divorce is final," said Eliot. "Caroline knows this, and therefore, she is rushing her lawyers so that she can leave the city."

"You see, Mae, we no longer care what people say or think about us," said Bernadine.

"I am happy for you both," Mae sighed. "I only wish that my mother could be here to see you together, a family at last. Although we will never know what led to the accident, I felt that my mother was in danger when she left Crossways that day. My father was so angry. I tried to stop them from leaving."

Bernadine's face softened, as she tried to console Mae. "I know that you will never get over the loss of your parents. But I feel that you should know the truth about your how your mother loved you and fought for you. She stood up to your father on the most important issues. She gave in on the little things, but when it came to you and Wren, she would not relent. The fact that you were able to finish Barnard, well, you owe that to her."

"I knew that they argued," said Mae, "but I never realized that it was about me."

"Yes," said Bernadine. "About you and Wren. She fought quietly, but persistently."

Tears ran down Mae's cheek. "This has been so hard on Wren. I don't know what I shall do. I must be a mother to him, when I feel like a child right now. You see, when they read the will, I discovered that there is no family besides me. I have been made his guardian. Of course, since I am not yet twenty-one, the lawyers will be executors concerning all financial matters. But I will be responsible for raising him, so my dream of attending engineering school has come to an end."

Bernadine gave Eliot a meaningful look and then turned to Mae. "We have a proposition regarding Wren. We want you to consider it seriously and take your time making a decision."

LEAH

DECEMBER 31, 1910

Esther and Gilda met Leah in front of their apartment building on 78th Street near the East River. Bursting with excitement and anticipation, she gave each girl a warm embrace.

"I can't thank you both enough for letting me have your apartment tonight. I have been trying to find a way to be alone with Declan for ages."

"So, he agreed to spend the night with you?" asked Gilda with a sarcastic tone.

"Yes, I told him that I am making dinner. After all, it's New Year's Eve. He can hardly come with an excuse. No one is working tonight."

"I know," said Esther. "But you have been talking about this fellow for years. I don't understand what his problem is. Perhaps he doesn't like girls, if you know what I mean."

"That's ridiculous!" Leah snapped. "You should see how he makes love to me. He has the appetite, all right. He has shown me in many ways. But he is careful not to go too far because he claims that he is only thinking of me. He doesn't want to get me in trouble."

"Well, he sounds reasonable to me," said Gilda.

"Oh, Gilda, I don't want him to be reasonable," said Leah with exasperation in her voice. "I want him to marry me. And there is only one way to make that happen."

Esther smirked. "Really? First of all, how can you be sure that even if you persuade him to do as you want that you will manage to become pregnant?"

"I have figured out the timing. I know my cycle and I have no doubt that the timing is right. I just need enough time and some privacy to encourage him."

"Are you sure that he will do right by you?" asked Gilda. "What if he drops you? What will you do then?"

"Don't worry, Gilda. He is the honorable type. He would never abandon me if I told him that I was pregnant."

Gilda handed her the key. "We'll be out all night. Good luck."

Leah had arranged to meet Declan at a neighborhood pub later that evening.

He was seated at a table near the bar when she walked in. She deliberately arrived late, so that he might have a few drinks before she set her plan in motion. A few men whistled appreciatively as she walked by wearing a red velvet dress with an Empire-style high waist, which complimented her buxom figure. She had made the dress herself, creating a black lace overlay. Instead of sleeves, she opted for thin black lace straps and purchased long black gloves. She spent over an hour on her coiffure, placing several feathers in her mass of dark curls.

"You look lovely, Leah," he said in a husky voice.

"Thank you, darling. I must say it is a miracle. I have been cooking all afternoon." She noticed that he slurred his words, which encouraged her. She asked if they might leave after just one drink.

Actually, she had asked a neighbor to prepare a roast chicken and potatoes. She had a friend that worked in a fancy bakery supply her with some *petit fours.* Then she bought several bottles of cheap red wine. She hoped that Isaac and Rebekah would not see that she had borrowed their good Sabbath wine glasses.

She struggled to guide Declan up the stairs to the third floor. When they entered the apartment, she lit a gas lamp and some candles that she had placed on the table in the room that served as a parlor and dining room.

"Declan, would you please open this bottle?" she said handing him a bottle of red wine. "I will serve dinner."

Declan picked at his food, but drank copious amounts of wine. Leah pushed back her chair and walked to the kitchen to bring in the *petit fours.* Bending over, she placed the plate on the table. He pulled her too him, kissing her neck and breasts.

"Come with me, my love," she said breathlessly. "Come see how I have arranged the bedroom." Taking his hand, she led him to the bed, which was covered with a green velvet bedspread with gold fringe. She had put candles on the dresser and had even found a rather risqué poster, which she placed on the wall facing the bed.

Normally, Declan would caress her and allow her to grope him until he reached climax. Tonight, however, he was not in control of his actions, and he followed her lead.

She undressed quickly and stretched out next to him, doing her best to arouse him. The first round of lovemaking was disappointingly brief, so she caressed him more vigorously and they made love again; this time it lasted long enough for her to finally experience orgasm.

Several days later, Leah waited for Declan outside the Engineering building at New York University. She knew that he had only a few minutes between his last class and the time that he reported to his job. His reaction the morning after they made love disappointed her. He appeared confused, not realizing where he was or how he had gotten there. When she kissed him, he drew away as if he had committed a terrible crime. It seemed to her that he couldn't get away fast enough. He got up, dressed quickly and sheepishly asked her forgiveness if he had taken advantage of her. Those were his last words as he rushed to the door and left.

She decided to wait a few days before confronting him and asking him to explain his cold reaction. As he walked down the stairs outside the school with a group of friends, she made a point of waving so that he could not pretend that he didn't see her. His friends noticed her.

"Who is that good-looking girl waving at you Declan?" asked one of his fellow students.

Caught off guard and embarrassed, Declan responded casually. "Just a childhood friend from the old neighborhood. Excuse me, gentlemen." He ran down the stairs and took her arm. "What on earth are you doing here? I would think that you would be at work."

"I haven't heard from you since New Year's Eve, and I was afraid that you were angry," she said with a quivering voice. "I couldn't believe that you left me there lying alone that morning. You may not remember, but you told me that you love me," she lied. "You have always said that you would never take advantage of me. So, given what we did, it must mean that your feelings have deepened and that you are in love with me."

His fair skin reddened, and he found it difficult to meet her gaze. "Leah, I can't discuss this on the street. Don't you see my classmates staring at us? I don't know what to tell you. I have very little memory of that night. But given the state of things, I mean, our waking up in bed together, I realize that I let things get out of hand. For that I am sincerely sorry."

"Sorry!" she shouted. "What do you mean by that? There was no hesitation or regret in the way you made love to me. Are you ashamed of what we did?"

He answered in a low and gentle voice. "Leah, I am only ashamed of myself. I had too much wine, and I know how that can affect me. I should have controlled myself. I also know how you feel about me, and I had no right to exploit your feelings."

"So, are you saying that you don't love me? I always thought that you didn't want to make love because you wanted to wait until you were employed and were in a position to marry and have children."

"Children! My God, Leah, I won't be in a position to have children for many years. I owe money for tuition, and I can hardly keep my head above water."

Now she wept loudly, and people began to look at them. Declan took her arm and guided her across the street to a small park where they sat on a bench. Looking up at him with a wounded expression, she unexpectedly rallied and became calm and thoughtful.

"What if I could help, I mean with your expenses?"

He smiled, calling on all his patience. "How could you possibly help me with my expenses? Are they giving you some wonderful promotion at the Triangle?"

"You just leave it up to me," she said. "I know someone who has a great deal of money and who is obliged to me."

"I don't know what to say. I must be honest with you, Leah. I am not in love with you. I don't think that you would want me on those terms, would you?"

"That is for me to decide," she said defiantly.

DORE AND CHRISTIAAN

JANUARY 1911

The snowdrifts piled up along the streets of Manhattan and the elevated had stopped operating, yet Christiaan managed to make his way uptown to spend the day with Dore. She ordered dinner from the restaurant downstairs since the pantry in her tiny kitchenette contained nothing but coffee, tea, and bread.

Christiaan sipped his coffee after finishing off a slice of cherry pie. He had a serious expression on his handsome face and his voice quavered as he spoke. He reached across the table and took her hand. "You may find it surprising to hear me admit this, but sometimes I am very lonely. I find myself imagining you waiting for me when I come home or waking up next to me in the morning."

Although she suspected that his feelings for her had grown stronger, she found the admission unexpected, but not unwelcome. For a few seconds, she entertained the fantasy that he was working up to a proposal of marriage. But her hopes were dashed by the very next words that he uttered.

"I was thinking that you might reconsider my idea that we live together. We could share expenses." He looked at her with a sheepish, charming smile.

"Live together? Not in this hotel!" she said. "They look the other way when men come upstairs to visit. But they draw the line at cohabitation for unmarried couples. I haven't changed my feelings about your idea. I find that kind of arrangement, how shall I put it, noncommittal."

"Dore," he protested. "You know that I am committed to you. I love you. Isn't that enough? I am not interested in other women. I want to live with you, but if it is marriage that you are looking for, I am not your man."

Not wanting to sound needy or inflexible, she tried to make him understand her feelings. "You see me as an accomplished professional woman, but I come from a very conservative home. It's true that I enjoy my freedom, probably more than the average woman, for I have worked hard and suffered for it. Yet I find myself wanting more out of life. You might find it absurd, but I feel time slipping away. I am not a young girl, but a woman of twenty-four. I want a husband and a home. And every day, I feel a longing to hold a child of my own in my arms."

"You are still young, my girl. You have time enough to have children." He appeared visibly shaken by her desire to have children. "The idea of having a family, the responsibility, frightens me. I don't know if I can explain why I feel this way, but I believe it has its genesis from my time in the concentration camp. I saw my mother and my sisters die and I, being a young boy, was powerless to help them. I don't think that I could bear to have children because I would always have a deep-seated fear of losing them or seeing them suffer."

Dore was taken aback. She had never seen Christiaan afraid or hesitant. "My love, loss is part of life. But so is joy. There is always a chance that a child might die. I have seen it all too often in the Bowery and in Russia when I was a child. Think about it. You survived the concentration camp and came to New York, while I survived the pogroms in Russia and came here too. We met. We fell in love. To me, it is *beshert.*"

"It is what?" he asked.

"*Beshert,* destined to be. We were meant to meet and to love each other. And while I would never try to force you to marry me, neither will I live with you in some kind of modern Free Love arrangement. We are not Emma Goldman and Sasha Berkman. I will not sacrifice my future and my desire to have a family, even for a man that I love. You will have to decide. And if you cannot take this step, I shall have to make my way alone."

Suddenly he turned away, his blue eyes rimmed with tears. When he spoke, his voice cracked. "Dore, please don't say that you will leave me. I need time. You must give me time. I will not make a promise now that I cannot fulfill. But I love you too much to lose you."

Despite her resolve, his strong display of emotion moved her. Taking him in her arms, she tried to comfort him. Her pity quickly turned into passion, and the next moment they were in her bed. She was not certain, but she thought she felt a new openness, vulnerability, in their lovemaking, which was more fervent than ever before. His groans of pleasure were laced with laments and pleas for her to stay with him.

After, she begged him to leave. "Please, Christiaan, I must be alone. I am so confused and I think that we need a few weeks apart to sort things out."

He left the apartment looking despondent. She took this to be an encouraging sign.

Later after her bath, sipping a cup of tea, she thought about the news that she had withheld. She felt that if she told him that she had been offered a promotion and that it involved a move to Chicago, it would sound like an ultimatum. Nevertheless, it was a decision that she would have to make, and soon. Mr. Lasker had been in touch with the New York office of Lord and Thomas and the head of the branch had praised her highly. He believed she possessed untapped talent and that a year or two working directly under Mr. Lasker would be of great benefit to the young lady and to the agency. And so last week, a contract had been proffered for the position of Assistant Director of Fashion Advertising in the Chicago office. She asked her superior if she could have some time to consider the matter since it meant moving across the country. Lasker gave her three weeks to decide. She had made many difficult decisions in her life, some wise and some foolish. This would be the most difficult and consequential choice that she would ever face. How could she leave a man like Christiaan, a man so intelligent and so kind? Would she ever find a man so attuned to her physical desires? She agonized over the decision every waking hour. He claimed he needed time to commit, the one luxury that she did not have. Two weeks remained before the door closed on the opportunity of a lifetime. In ten days, she would ask him for his decision. Then she would make hers.

The snow had been cleared from the streets and Dore decided to take a walk during her lunch hour. She wandered the side streets off Broadway and then found herself in front of New York University. Contemplating her future, as she did during her every free moment, she abruptly bumped into a tall man. Looking up she saw the smiling eyes and broad smile of Declan Malone.

"Miss Abramowitz, what an unexpected pleasure," he said.

"Why, hello, Declan. How are you? I am surprised that you remember me."

"I remember you well, just as I remember our day at Luna Park, even though I was an uninvited guest," he said.

"Not at all. Except for keeping Leah so late at the dance hall, I found your presence very welcome. Leah speaks of you often and she seems to be quite taken with you. She told me that you are continuing your engineering studies, all while working nights. I know what that is like. I attended night school while working at Wanamaker's."

He smiled proudly. "Hard work never hurt anyone. In a year and a half, I will have my degree. Then I hope to find a position with an engineering firm. With all the electrical installations and power plant construction planned for the city, I should have my pick of jobs."

Dore smiled. "I am pleased to hear that things are going well for you. I imagine that you have not seen my friend Mae Dodd since Luna Park, but I am afraid she has had some bad news." She noticed that he appeared a bit shaken by her statement. "She lost her parents in a tragic automobile accident in August."

"No, I had no idea. I haven't seen her since last spring. We would sometimes run into each other at academic conferences. But with my busy schedule, I haven't had time to attend any recently. I guess that I missed it in the papers. How horrible! Tell me, how is she?"

Dore immediately regretted telling him. She did not expect such an intense reaction. "My friend Bernadine helps her out with her brother Wren and there are bankers and lawyers to handle finances. I believe that she is back at Barnard, finishing her last semester."

She wondered for a fleeting moment if he might care for Mae. It seemed improbable, given that, as he said, they saw each other only rarely. However, the very idea that Declan might care for someone else compelled her to ask about his intentions toward Leah.

"Declan," she said, trying to be as tactful as she could. "May I speak frankly with you about Leah?"

His pale skin reddened. "Of course, you may."

"You know that she is like a sister to me. I care what happens to her. But I wonder, what are your feelings for her? Do you love her? I dare to ask you because she loves you and she hopes to marry you."

Declan cleared his throat and averted his eyes. "Dore, let me be honest with you.

I'm not a cad and I don't go make a habit of using young woman and then dropping them. I have been with Leah for a long time. She is a lively and pretty girl and we have always had fun together. But recently she has made herself available, I mean, well, frankly, a young man has needs. To be truthful, I am not in love with her, and I am in no position to marry anyone."

"Thank you for being so honest and for not biting my head off for the audacity of asking such questions. But I will trouble you once more with a request, which you may find impertinent."

"I would be happy to oblige if it is at all possible," he said, gallantly.

She spoke hesitantly, searching for her words. "I would ask you to consider breaking things off with Leah. Lord knows that it will not be easy. But you would be doing her a great kindness, even if she does not see it that way."

Declan's face took on a serious aspect. "I have wanted to end our relationship for a long time. I even tried to keep my distance from her, hoping that she would take the hint and perhaps find someone else. But she has become more and more demanding. It is unfair to continue seeing her if she is hoping for marriage."

Relieved, Dore sighed. "Thank you so much Declan. This takes a great burden off my mind."

"I will speak with Leah soon." He remained quiet and pensive for a moment. "Do you suppose that it could wait until after my midterm exams at the end of February? I really have very little time to study and I cannot afford any distractions."

"Of course, since I imagine that you will not be seeing her until after you have finished your exams."

Dore wondered if he would take the time to see Mae in the interim. She did not feel that it was her place to ask, but she suspected that he would soon head uptown to present his condolences.

LEAH AND RACHEL

FEBRUARY 1911

It came as a surprise to Leah that her mother's apartment was only ten blocks away from her own apartment that she continued to share with Isaac and Rebekah. Located on one of the more elegant blocks of Lenox Avenue and 110th, she found it contrasted greatly with the buildings in the neighborhoods only blocks away. She checked the address on the façade of the ten-story building, climbed the front stairs and pushed the door open. It surprised her that the building had a spacious elevator. She pressed the button, ascended to the seventh floor and knocked on the door to 7C.

Leah had not seen her mother in over two years and she found her greatly changed. She noticed a shock of white in her lustrous black hair, pulled back in a tight knot, giving her a severe look. Although her flawless bronze complexion had not one wrinkle to be seen, her once voluptuous figure now tended toward plumpness. But to most people, Rachel would still be considered attractive, and Leah wondered if she still worked in her former trade.

Feeling awkward, not knowing whether she should embrace her mother or shake her hand, Leah gave her a quick peck on the cheek. This seemed to please Rachel, who smiled and responded with a hug.

"Leah, I can't believe my eyes. You have grown into a beauty," she said as she led her daughter into a comfortable parlor, and they sat on a somewhat over-ornate sofa.

"Well, I suppose I come by it naturally. You look wonderful too. I must say, quite an improvement from the way you looked outside the Triangle two years ago."

Rachel lowered her eyes. "I am sorry for that fiasco. But you must understand that it was business. And I want you to know that after that day, I never engaged in that kind of activity again."

"I am glad to hear it," said Leah smiling with satisfaction.

For a moment they sat in an uncomfortable silence. Finally, Rachel stood, picked up a teapot and poured out two cups. "I was surprised to get your letter, Leah. You are a clever girl. How did you find out the name of my hotel?"

"It wasn't hard. But I would like to know if it was an unpleasant surprise."

Rachel appeared abashed. "Why should it be unpleasant for mother to hear from her daughter, especially after so many years?"

"Well for one thing, during your long absence from my life, you have not supported me morally or financially." Turning her head and taking in the apartment and its furnishings, she added. "I can see that now you have so much to offer."

"I had my reason for staying out of your life, Leah," said Rachel. "You know how I make my living. It was shame that kept me away."

Leah laughed coarsely. "I don't mind you sheltering me from the source of your money, but you might have shared your good fortune with me."

"I did want to," she lied. "But Isaac and Rebekah forbade me from contacting you. And later I invested my earnings, and I did not have much cash to spare."

"I see that you are doing well now. You must have some cash on hand at present."

"Oh, if you are speaking about the apartment, I am renting. I do have some cash, but most of my money is tied up in a recent investment."

This revelation incensed Leah and she quickly lost her patience. "Mother, I will speak plainly. I need money, and I need it now. I find myself in a sticky situation." She placed her hands on her belly and looked directly into Rachel's eyes. "Do you understand?"

"Why of course I do," she said. "We can easily deal with this problem, and it won't cost very much. It is somewhat of an occupational hazard for my girls, and I have contacts to take care of these matters."

Leah pushed herself up from the sofa, standing over Rachel, her arms crossed.

Speaking tersely all while trying to remain calm, she set her mother straight. "You do not understand me. I am going to have this baby, and I need money, a great deal of money, in order to convince the father to marry me."

"Why is that necessary?" asked Rachel. "A beautiful girl like you shouldn't have to pay off a lover. What's wrong with him? Does he drink? Oh God, please don't tell me he takes opium?"

"Don't be absurd. Now I understand what kind of world you live in. No matter what floor your fancy new apartment is on, you are still a woman of the street."

Rachel felt as if she had been slapped. Although offended, she realized that she probably deserved the reproach from her daughter. For the first time, she fully appreciated the damage that she had inflicted in abandoning her child and she decided to try to make amends. "How much money do you need to convince him to marry you?" she asked.

"I can't state a definite figure," she said. "He is a student and he works nights to pay his tuition. He doesn't know about the baby yet. When I tell him, I want to offer him enough money to pay for school and to set us up in a nice apartment."

"I see," said Rachel. "I would like to help you. I do owe you that much. But the investment I have is somewhat complicated and it will take time to withdraw some of my funds."

Hopeful, but tentative, Leah asked, "How much time? I would like to let him know about the baby as soon as possible. I have to tell him before I begin to show."

"I could probably get it by the second week of March. I will send word to you at the Triangle and then you can come by and pick up a check."

"And what would be the amount on the check?" she asked eagerly.

Rachel narrowed her eyes, as she performed her calculations. "My total investment in the proposed new hotel is ten thousand dollars. I could give you seven thousand. It will mean a smaller profit for me, but I have many irons in the fire. Would that be sufficient?"

"It sure would!" said Leah, hardly believing her luck.

DECLAN AND MAE

MARCH 5, 1911

Standing outside Milbank Hall, Declan hesitated. It was his third trip to the Barnard campus in Morningside Heights. On the previous visits, he had simply walked the grounds looking for Mae, but now he decided to go inside the building and ask at the desk if they might give her a message. As he advanced toward the steps, he caught sight of her speaking with an older gentleman. He waited until the man had walked off and approached her. She smiled and waved when she spotted him.

"Declan, what a surprise. It has been ages. What brings you Uptown?" she said as she shook his hand.

"Mae, I have come to see you because I ran into Dore a few weeks ago and she told me about your parents. I am sorry that I didn't come sooner, but I had no idea. I am so sorry for what happened. How are you holding up?"

She could feel her pulse racing as he spoke, and her throat constricted at the tone of concern in his voice. At first, she found it difficult to respond and she struggled to find her words. "I am doing the best I can. I was numb for weeks after the accident. It was so horrible, so violent. Everyone was in shock. Yet somehow, I had a presentiment that something was going to happen. My parents had been arguing for months. It's difficult to describe. I felt that things were sliding away and our lives were spinning out of control, much like what happened on the road in Newport."

"I wish that I had been there for you," he said forlornly. "I am generally useless in this kind of situation, but I would have done my best to comfort you."

"How could you have known? It's not as if you run in the same circles as me. But I am happy that you are here now," she said, softly. "I am free for the rest of the day. Do you have time for a walk? It's a fine day, isn't it?"

He breathed in deeply and straightened, lifting his face to the blue cloudless sky.

"I have plenty of time. I just finished my midterms, so I have a few days' break from class. Let's go over to Central Park."

They sat down on a bench and Declan took her hand. Mae tried to gage her emotions, and realized that she could not treat this as she would a physics equation or a chemistry experiment. It was question of delving deep into her soul and accepting what she found.

Declan looked into her eyes, took her hand and touched it to his lips. Mae, I have tried for so long to put you out of my mind. I think I fell for you that first day at Luna Park when we danced the Castle Walk. But I told myself that a poor Irish lad such as myself had not business trying to court a girl from Madison Avenue, there being too many obstacles—money, class, and family connections.

Not knowing how to respond, she squeezed his hand. She took her time to gather her thoughts and to clear her throat that was constricted with emotion.

"You see I have been busy building a life. All the while, in the back of my mind you were there. I studied hard, working nights to pay for tuition. I was sure that you could only love an educated man, a man with a profession. So, I stayed away and worked to narrow the gulf that separated us. But when I heard about your parents, I knew that I had to see you. I have no idea if you care for me, Mae. I just know that I have never felt this way about any other girl."

No longer stopping to ponder or analyze her feelings, Mae threw her arms around his neck and kissed him, right there in Central Park. "There you go Declan Malone, my first kiss. You don't think that I would do that with somebody that I didn't care for deeply."

Tears filled his eyes and he turned away in embarrassment.

They stood and went in search of a private spot off the main path. Taking her face in his large hands, he lifted her chin and kissed her tenderly.

"Mae," he said, hesitantly. "Do you think that someday you might consider marrying me?"

"Well one thing I know," she said emphatically. "I will never marry anyone but you."

"And can you wait for me? I mean can you wait until I get my degree?"

"I can wait for you, if you can wait for me," she said. "I am considering taking a graduate degree."

"Oh no, please don't make me wait until you get your doctorate."

"No, my love. I could never wait that long," She said laughing.

DECLAN AND LEAH

SATURDAY, MARCH 19, 1911

On a Saturday evening at six o'clock, Declan left the electrician workshop to go home to clean up before meeting Mae in Greenwich Village for dinner. He had not expected to see Leah standing on the sidewalk waiting for him.

"Leah, what are you doing here?" he asked, rather abruptly. "We have no plans for this evening. I have…."

She cut him off angrily. "You need to hear what I have say, whether we have plans or not. Dore keeps warning me off you and tells me it's for my own good. I am tired of everyone telling me what I should do. I know how I feel and given time; I know you will feel the same way."

He opened his mouth to protest, and she quickly put two fingers to his lips to silence him. She guided him from the crowded sidewalk to a quiet side street. "Listen to me, darling. You are going to be a father."

His face transformed by panic, he appeared visibly appalled and incredulous. "That is absurd! Are you talking about New Year's Eve? I don't even remember what really happened," he grumbled.

"Well, I remember all too clearly and it was lovely. I look forward to many more nights like that after we are married. I know that you will not abandon me now. You are not capable of that."

"I don't know what I am capable of right now," he said angrily. "But you know that I can't afford to have a wife and a child. It would mean giving up everything, my studies, my career...."

"Your dreams of marrying a wealthy Uptown Society girl," she taunted. "Never mind all of that. You won't have to give up on your degree. I have arranged everything. In a few days, I will have enough money to pay your tuition and to buy a sweet little apartment for us. You can quit your night job and finish school all the more quickly. Just think of the evenings you will be able to spend with me and our child."

He froze, unable to speak, not wanting to believe what he was hearing.

"Leah, let me ask you something. Was this something that you planned? I mean did you intend to become pregnant that night we spent together?" He said slowly, finding it difficult to utter the words.

"Desperate measures, my love." she said contemptuously. "I had a hunch that your Irish heart was beginning to wander. I really had no choice and believe it or not you did enjoy yourself. If you don't believe me, I have the proof right here," she said, as she took his hands and placed them on her stomach. He appeared stunned when he felt her protruding belly. "You see. This is our wee babe. You know that it's true and that you cannot abandon us. I could never love you if I didn't believe that you were an honorable man."

At that instant, he felt like slapping her. But he directed his anger inwardly, berating himself for his weakness. He swore that he would never take another drink. For all the years that he had resisted the temptation to make love to her, it only took a few beers and a bottle of wine to weaken his resolve and ruin his life. He felt his future slipping away.

He turned to her, trying his best to keep his composure. "You know me well, Leah. I could never abandon my own child. But do tell me something. Where do you plan to get this large amount of money to pay for my college and an apartment?"

"I don't see why I should keep it a secret," she said defiantly. "My mother is giving it to me. We had a lovely visit and she was so happy to see me that she offered to help us. And she is thrilled that she is going to be a grandmother," she lied.

Declan didn't know how to react to this revelation. He had never met Leah's mother. He seemed to remember that she had abandoned her when she was a child.

He suddenly remembered that Mae was waiting for him in The Village.

"I have an engagement tonight, Leah. Could we meet tomorrow and discuss things?"

Leah's face darkened and she fiercely shook her head. "I will not have you meeting her! No tonight!"

"But I can't…."

"Not tonight," she insisted. "We have wedding plans to make. She will hear the news soon enough."

Early the next morning, Dore awakened to a loud insistent knock at her door. Putting on her robe, she hurried to open it.

Leah stood in the hall and then rudely brushed past her. "Get dressed, Dore. I need your help. We are going to Madison Avenue to speak to that pathetic little snob."

Rubbing her eyes, Dore then looked at her incredulously. "What? Who are you talking about?"

"Mae, of course. She needs to know that Declan is going to marry me and that we are having a child. The thing is that I can't do it alone. I need you there for support. Besides, you know the exact address."

It took a few seconds for Dore to process what she had just heard. "What did you just say? You are pregnant, since when?"

"Since New Year's Eve," she said boldly. "I have told Declan and he is willing to do right by me and this baby. So, you see, she has no business chasing after him, and we have to let her know what is what."

"Why should I have to witness the poor girl having her heart broken? I have grown to care for her too much to see her hurt."

Leah's anger flared. "Because I need your support. We are family, aren't we? More than she is anyway."

"Yes, we are family and for that reason, I have to tell you that you are a little fool. You are letting yourself in for a lifetime of misery with a man who doesn't love you and who probably loves someone else. I will come with you, but only so that I might soften the blow."

"That's wonderful," said Leah, sarcastically. "Taking her side already!"

"Stop already," said Dore. "Let me get dressed. It's much too early to go waking people up. Let's have a cup of coffee and maybe some breakfast downstairs and then we can catch a cab and go over to Madison around ten."

"No!" shouted Leah. "We need to tell her before Declan goes to her. I want her to hear it from me."

Dore remained quiet and thoughtful for a moment and then turned to Leah and spoke in a low, serious tone. "My girl, I think that you are handling this all wrong. If you confront Mae and she runs to Declan in tears, you might hurt your own cause. Think about it. You might sabotage all your plans."

Leah looked confused, but listened carefully.

"Declan loves her and it would hurt him to see her suffer. Did you ever consider that you might be pushing him into her arms with this plan of yours? I think the truth would be much more tolerable coming from me. You should not be involved. I will tell her in a compassionate and calm manner. That way, she is less likely to go running to Declan in tears. Don't you agree?"

The corner of Leah's mouth twitched slightly and she nodded her head. "Yes, I see what you mean. But, please, do hurry. I don't want Declan to go to her. In fact, you should tell her that she must not see him. Seeing that I am pregnant with his child, she can have no claim on him now."

"Don't worry. I hardly think that Declan would be knocking on her door at this hour. I will handle it. Now let me get dressed so I can get started."

THE TRIANGLE SHIRTWAIST FIRE

MARCH 25, 1911

If Saturday hadn't been payday, Leah would have skipped her final day of work.

But she considered it to be a matter of principle to collect her last pay envelope. After all she had put in the work. Besides she could not resist showing off her new clothes and her engagement ring to the girls in the factory. There were also several friends who she wanted to invite to the wedding, which would take place the following Saturday.

As she took the elevator up to the ninth floor, her mind buzzed with the flurry of activity of the past week. She had met Rachel at her bank. The official-looking banker, who helped her open an account, intimidated her. Having never been in a bank before, Leah found it daunting dealing with the bulk of paperwork and the quantity of signatures required to transfer her newly found fortune into their keeping. Before agreeing to go the bank, she argued with her mother, saying that she preferred to keep the money in a safe place in her new apartment. But Rachel assured her that it would be much more secure in the bank.

Still refusing to accept her mother's advice, she complained, "But can I get it whenever I want? They won't hold it back, will they? I have many expenses, what with the wedding, the apartment, and Declan's tuition."

"Of course, you can take out as much as you want, whenever you want. It's your money," Rachel shot back. "But take my advice and don't spend it too fast. You never know what life may throw at you. I had no idea that your father would be killed by a streetcar and that I would be left with a young child to raise. And you don't know what Declan might get up to, even if he has agreed to marry you. Did you ever consider that once he finishes school that he might abandon you and the child?"

"Not likely," said Leah. "He is not the type. If I had suspected that he was, I would never have gone through with my plan," she said smugly, patting her rounded belly. "I'm not worried."

With only a week remaining until her wedding, she stepped off the elevator, glowing with happiness and satisfaction. She went into the cloakroom to hang up her coat and hat. When she walked out onto the floor, a flock of girls rushed over to congratulate her and comment on her beautiful new dress. Leah chose that moment to hold out her left hand, showing off her new engagement ring.

"Oy, what a ring!" exclaimed Natalie Lefkowitz. "It must have cost an arm and a leg."

"So, when did he give it to you?" asked Gussie Segal. "You weren't wearing it yesterday."

"We went out after work yesterday and bought it," said Leah. "My mother knows a man who sells jewelry to gentlemen who frequent her hotel. Do you see that little stone, the one in the middle?"

Gussie squinted. "Ya, it's small, but I can see it."

"Well, that's a real diamond," Leah said proudly. "The rest is paste, but that one is real"

The girls moved on to their long table, which was the last in a row of eight, and sat at their machines. They had always sat next to each other in the long line of machines and had become close over the years.

"Nattie, you're coming next Saturday? I am counting on you," said Leah.

"Of course. Would I miss it? I've never been to a civil ceremony wedding. I hope the reception isn't going to be civil," she said, laughing.

"What are you thinking?" joked Gussie. "Half the guests will be Irish. We are in for a fine time."

"I can't make any promises," said Leah. "I don't know his family very well. His father is dead, but I did meet his mother. What a sourpuss!"

"Does he have any good-looking brothers?" asked Nattie. "I wouldn't mind a dance and a bit of kissing, if they look like him."

"He told me there are two older brothers. One is back in Ireland and the other is out West. So sorry to disappoint you girls."

At that moment Samuel Bernstein, the factory manager, walked by. The girls fell silent, but Leah gave him a sweet smile. He treated the workers fairly and never let his hands wander like some of the other supervisors on the floor. After lunch, she planned to tell him that today would be her last day at the Triangle.

After treating her friends to lunch at an inexpensive restaurant in Union Square, Leah returned to the factory. She went in search of Mr.

Bernstein. Since he wasn't on her floor, she made a quick trip to the tenth floor and approached a bookkeeper named Mary Alter.

"Have you seen Mr. Bernstein?" she asked rather haughtily.

Mary didn't bother to look up. "Not here. Isn't he on the eighth floor?"

"I wouldn't know," said Leah with a sharp edge to her voice. "I work on the ninth. I want to give my notice."

Mary was hard at work typing some invoices and didn't have time to waste talking to a factory worker. "He'll be on the floor soon. Just tell him when you see him."

Leah turned and walked off in a huff. She found the bookkeeper's tone insulting.

She thought. *She thinks she's so important just because she works in the office. She is a nobody. I am going to be an engineer's wife and live in a big house one day.*

She walked toward the elevator and bumped into a little girl, running wildly through the office. She was about to give her a piece of her mind, when she heard a man call out, "Watch yourself, Mildred. Realizing that the man was Mr. Blanck and the girl was his daughter, she dashed for the elevator and returned to the ninth floor. She was in a foul mood when she returned to her machine.

"What's wrong?" asked Nattie.

"Oh, I just can't wait to tell Bernstein that I am quitting. If we weren't getting our pay envelope today, I would walk out of this place right now."

"Come on, my girl," said Gussie. "You can stand it for a few more hours."

So, Leah put in her last few hours of work at the Triangle, sewing on her last lace collars. By 4:30, she had had enough. She noticed Mr. Bernstein walking onto the floor and she stood up at her table to get his attention.

He smiled pleasantly as he approached. The news of her marriage had already spread, so he knew why she wanted to see him.

"I hear congratulations are in order," he said in a friendly tone.

"Yes, indeed, Mr. Bernstein. I would like to give my notice. I was just going to freshen up in the washroom and get my things, if you don't mind. The groom and I are meeting to make some arrangements after work."

"Of course, my dear. But don't leave before five. I won't be giving out the pay envelope until the end of the day, as usual."

"That's fine," she said. "I just want a little head start."

It was 4:35 when Leah entered the lady's washroom. She fixed her hair, applied some rouge, and then put on her hat and coat. But when she tried to exit the lady's cloakroom at 4:45, she was met by mayhem. Ten or more girls pushed her back while screaming "fire!" The harder she endeavored to get out, the greater the force of the crowd shoved her backward. There was faint hint of smoke, which quickly became stronger and denser. Leah managed to break free from the throng blocking her way, only to run into a wall of fire. It was a horrendous sight of flames exploding and spreading across the floor. She tried in vain to make her way through the mass of terrified girls, but she could not move. The fire descended from the air as if it were a living creature, burning the young women alive, their hair, their clothes, and their limbs. Leah closed her eyes to the horror, as she struggled to fill her lungs with oxygen, but found only smoke. As her world went black, her last thoughts were of the beautiful wedding dress that she would never wear and the child in her womb that she would never hold.

MAE

MARCH 27, 1911

When Mae heard about Leah's pregnancy and impending marriage, she didn't know what to think, even though Dore swore to her that Leah had most likely ensnared Declan. For the first time in her life, Mae experienced the sharp edge of sheer hatred toward another human being.

But after the Triangle fire and hearing about Leah's death, her emotions were in turmoil. She wondered how she could have despised the poor girl. After all, she should have understood her strong feelings for Declan, when she knew what it was like to love him. She also realized that while she had every advantage in life, Leah had very few, only her beauty and her cunning. When she thought about things in that light, it was easier to understand why she had gone to such extremes to force him into marriage.

Two days after the fire, Dore asked Mae to meet her for lunch at a restaurant near her office in the Flatiron Building. Dore appeared shaken, her beautiful complexion ashen and her eyes swollen from crying.

Unable to swallow a morsel of food, she looked at Mae and began to speak slowly, struggling to maintain her composure. "I wanted to let you know that we identified Leah's body yesterday. It was a horrible scene, all those poor girls lined up in their wooden coffins on Charities Pier. There were so many mothers and fathers and husbands. The saddest were the sweethearts."

Mae appeared flustered and asked shyly, "Was Declan with you?"

"No, we haven't heard from him," said Dore sadly. "But we sent word to his mother, so he knows that she is gone."

Mae decided it would be best to make no further comments about Declan.

"Was it awful, Dore, I mean identifying her body?" She asked somberly. Perhaps it was a gruesome subject, but she felt that Dore wanted to talk.

"It was dreadful," said Dore. "It was almost impossible to recognize most of the dead. They were so badly burnt. Many had injuries from hitting the ground after they jumped from the building to the street below. I was told that many chose a quick death rather than the agony of the flames and the smoke."

Despondent, Dore choked back her tears and made a great effort to continue. "We identified Leah because of her ring. You see, the night before the fire, Rachel had helped her buy an engagement ring from a jewelry dealer. We all met in my parents' apartment. It was awkward, but in a strange way it was like old times, all of us together. How were we to know that it would be the last time?"

"How sad for her mother, after finally reconciling with Leah, only to lose her so suddenly," Mae said.

"Yes, she was heartbroken, which frankly surprised me. I always imagined that her heart was cold and impervious," Dore said. "After claiming the body, we all went back to my parents' place, where they are sitting Shiva. Do you know what that means?"

"Yes," said Mae. "I have quite a few Jewish friends at Barnard and they once explained the tradition to me. Do you think that I should go and offer my condolences, even though we have never met?"

"I think that would be a kind gesture. If you would like, I can go with you."

"Thank you, Dore, that would make it less awkward for me."

As the two women finished drinking their coffee, Mae decided that some happy news might lift Dore's spirits. "I don't know if you have heard about Eliot and Bernadine."

Dore shook her head. "I have been so busy with work and now this tragedy. I haven't spoken to Bernadine in months."

"Well, she had a baby girl, who she named Flora," she said, tears welling up in her eyes. "It was so kind of her to make such a tribute to my mother. Anyway, they were married last month when Eliot's divorce was finalized."

"I'm so happy how things worked out for them. Bernadine is a courageous woman. I will go and see her after the funeral when things calm down."

"Oh, they are not in town," said Mae. "Actually, they were married in France, and they are spending a few months there with little Flora. Of course, Martha is in school, so she could not go with them. Wren and I go over once a week to see her. Mademoiselle Monique is with her, as always."

"Speaking of Wren," asked Dore. "How is he holding up? It must have been difficult for him, dealing with the loss of your parents."

"He is doing as well as can be expected. Sometimes I can hear him crying in his room at night. But I don't go in because it would embarrass him."

"I don't know how you manage, caring for Wren and going to school, not to mention dealing with your own grief."

"It's hard, really hard. I don't know how to be a mother. There are so many decisions to make, school for Wren and finances. My lawyer thinks that it might not be worth the expense and effort keeping the brownstone, given that it's just the two of us. After all, it's not likely that we are going to entertain very much."

"And how is school going?" asked Dore.

"I have very little time to study for my upcoming exams. Fortunately, I will graduate from Barnard in less than two months. I have abandoned all my plans for graduate school, at least for the moment."

"How about you? You haven't mentioned your beau. How is Christiaan?" Mae asked smiling slyly.

Dore smiled and the color returned to her cheeks. "Christiaan is doing quite well. We both are as a matter of fact."

DORE AND CHRISTIAAN

JUNE 1911

In a small wooded grove, chairs had been set up outside a small Craftsman style house. Dore and Christiaan had opted for the beauty and tranquility of the Adirondacks for their wedding. They had discovered beauty of the mountains when Christiaan travelled there in order to write articles about the Craftsman art communities for his paper. Dore fell in love with the natural setting as well as the creative and friendly people who lived in the area. The venue also avoided the issue of the religious differences between the couple. She knew that her father would like her to be married by a rabbi in a synagogue, but it would be absurd for Christiaan to be married in such a ceremony. So, they would say their vows to each other in front of a judge, a good friend of Hutchin Hapgood's, who was known for his liberal views and elegant manner.

Many of the Dore's friends from her days at Wanamaker's had made the trip up for the wedding. Ira Frankel showed up with a rather homely, but intellectual-looking man, not exactly the type Dore would have expected. Of course, Mae had come up with Wren.

Mae watched Dore's mother helping her husband Isaac to his seat. He was thin and frail. Mae could see that they were proud of their daughter's success and thrilled that she had at last found happiness in her personal life. She heard Rebekah boasting about her son-in-law, the brilliant journalist.

She glanced across the aisle at Bernadine and Eliot seated with their children.

Even though they had loved each other for ten years, they looked like newlyweds. Martha Van Wies had taken the name of her real father and was now known as Martha Havemeyer. Little Flora Havemeyer slept quietly in Bernadine's arms through the entire ceremony.

Afterward at the casual reception held in the beautiful Craftsman house, Mae spoke with Dore and Christiaan and he introduced her to his circle of friends: writers, journalists, and several artists who belonged to the Ashcan School now so popular in Greenwich Village. She was thrilled to meet Christiaan's boss, Lincoln Stepphens who had driven up for the wedding.

Later Bernadine asked her to come outside so that she and Eliot could speak to her privately. They wished to make a proposal. At first, they seemed hesitant and somewhat nervous, but they relaxed when they saw that Mae was receptive to their idea.

"What I propose," said Bernadine, "is that Wren come and live with us. That way you can continue your studies, and even go to Stanford."

Mae at first remained silent, not knowing how to respond to such an offer. "You are both so generous and it certainly would make it easier for me to go back to school. I am grateful, but I fear it is too much to ask of you."

Bernadine looked at Eliot and then took Mae's hand. "We have something else to tell you and it may affect your decision. Yet, you need to know what our plans are for the future. You see, we have decided to leave New York and start life anew in Texas. I miss the rhythm of life and the sincerity of the people. I still have many friends from my youth in Galveston. Of course, we will be living in Houston. It is a growing city and there are many great opportunities in real estate. I actually own quite a bit myself and Eliot's experience will be a great asset. So, if you were to let us take Wren, we would be taking him far."

Mae leaned against a tree to steady herself. She did not know if she would be doing the right thing for Wren. It would allow her to go back to school and even move to California. "Bernadine, I don't know. Wren is my brother and the only family that I have left. If we do this, he might think that I am abandoning him."

"Let me be clear," said Bernadine. "We are not talking about adopting him. He will always be Lawrence Dodd, the son of Ned and Flora Dodd and your brother. And you shall come and see him often, anytime you like and stay for as long as you like."

At that moment, Wren and Martha ran out of the house and began to chase each other, running among the trees, and knocking over chairs. Mae could see how much they cared for each other. She thought of her mother who loved Bernadine like a sister, and she realized that she would have wanted her to accept the offer.

MAE

DECEMBER 1914

Mae celebrated her twenty-first birthday at Dore and Christiaan Robert's small, but lovely home in Park Slope in Brooklyn. A boisterous, blue-eyed toddler ran about, tugging on ladies' skirts and men's pant legs. Everyone could see that the little boy was rarely scolded because his mother was so ecstatic to have a son of her own. Christiaan seemed to be the picture of contentment and Mae thought he must be a doting father.

Mae thanked Dore for inviting her former Barnard classmates. Dr. Adeline Howell and her companion Sara came up from Philadelphia. Andrea Shapiro brought along her fiancé, the son of a wealthy Jewish banker, who worked as a broker on Wall Street, a choice that Mae would have never predicted.

Unfortunately, Bernadine and Eliot could not make the trip from Houston due to social and business commitments. However, Wren and Martha arrived several days before the party and had been staying with Dore and her family. Although she made the trip to Texas at least twice a year to see her brother, it surprised her that he had shot up several inches since the last time she had seen him about eight months ago. At thirteen, the two youngsters were no longer children, but stood on the verge of adolescence. Martha already appeared to be developing into a great beauty like her mother, with the same astonishing blue eyes, with distinct dark rings around the iris. Wren, tall and lanky, constantly brushed his straight, light brown hair out of his eyes. Suddenly Mae felt a wave of crushing sadness, wishing her mother could be with her on this day.

The first week in January, Mae occupied a luxurious private compartment in a train headed west to Palo Alto, California. She had finished her graduate studies at Stanford, but she still needed to write her dissertation in order to receive her doctorate in physics and engineering. She had not yet made a final decision as to whether she wanted to teach, pursue a career in research, or work for an engineering firm. She felt conflicted, wondering that working in academia might not be the best use of her talents, except perhaps in providing encouragement for other women to study physics.

As the daylight faded, she turned on a lamp in the compartment and tried to read.

But her thoughts drifted and the words on the page blurred. She thought about Declan and the last time she saw him. It was about a year after Leah's death. She had been surprised that he contacted her, but she decided to meet him in Washington Square. It would have been unkind and cowardly to deny him an opportunity to talk about what had happened between them.

They had met right before Christmas on a cold, bright morning. He had asked if she wanted to go to a café or restaurant, but she declined, saying she found the weather fine, even if a little cold. At first, they discussed their studies and career plans. He had finished his undergraduate studies and was working as a research assistant while pursuing his doctorate at New York University. Then the conversation became awkward and painful.

"Mae, I want you to know that I never meant to hurt or betray you," he said sadly.

"I know. Dore told me what happened between you and Leah. I don't blame you and I don't blame her either. But at the time, I didn't know what to feel, and then when she died, I…."

"I know," he said. "I was numb for months. I didn't want to see anyone. I felt guilty about how I treated Leah and I know it might sound strange, but I was mourning the death of my unborn child."

"It does not sound strange," said Mae. "That is why I refused to see you. I could not bring myself to face you, not when you were dealing with such a loss. Then the more time that went by, the more I felt that we needed to go our separate ways."

"So, you were able to forget what we said to each other that day in Central Park?

I envy you. I took me a long time. I still care about you and if things were different…."

"Declan," she said hopelessly. "I did think that I loved you, but I was so young. I bear you no ill will, but I see no future for us, especially since we are living on opposite sides of the country."

Tears filled his blue eyes. "I know that what you say is true, but perhaps someday, I mean when we have both finished our studies, maybe we can find a way to be together."

Mae steeled herself and lied. "No Declan, I have been seeing a young man at Stanford, another graduate student. It is quite serious and I expect a proposal very soon. I am sorry, but I don't want to give you any false hope."

She could see that he was deeply hurt, yet she had no choice but to lie. She had sensed herself weakening and she needed to end the conversation before she gave in to her feelings. She stood and shook his hand, saying that she wished that he would always remember her as a dear friend. As she walked away, she too had tears in her eyes.

After she had dinner in the dining car, she returned to her compartment. She looked out the window at the lights of small towns that appeared briefly in the dark. Her thoughts wandered and she thought about the world that was changing around her. She thought about the anarchist on Lexington Avenue who blew himself up while building a bomb meant to murder John Rockefeller. She thought about the assassination of the Archduke Ferdinand and his wife. Europe was at war. Just before she left New York, five thousand men and women gathered in Union Square to march for peace and to insist that the United States stay out of the war. *We will have to see if the powers that be take heed.* She thought.

Then she thought about the loss of great men, for Jacob Riis and George Westinghouse died this year, as did Isaac Abramowitz, a hardworking immigrant from Russia.

Mae Dodd would go on to become one of the first women to earn a doctorate in physics and engineering in the United States. Later she would open her own firm, specializing in electrical engineering. Dodd Engineering installed the infrastructure that illuminated the great city of New York and other cities around the United States.